LEGACY

OF

CHAOS

Also From Larissa Ione

~ DEMONICA/LORDS OF DELIVERANCE SERIES ~
Pleasure Unbound (Book 1)
Desire Unchained (Book 2)
Passion Unleashed (Book 3)
Ecstasy Unveiled (Book 4)
Eternity Embraced ebook (Book 4.5) (NOVELLA)
Sin Undone August (Book 5)
Eternal Rider (Book 6)
Supernatural Anthology (Book 6.5) (NOVELLA)
Immortal Rider (Book 7)
Lethal Rider (Book 8)
Rogue Rider (Book 9)
Reaver (Book 10)
Azagoth (Book 11)
Revenant (Book 12)
Hades (Book 13)
Base Instincts (Book 13.5)
Z (Book 14)
Razr (Book 15)
Hawkyn (Book 16)
Her Guardian Angel (Book 17)
Dining With Angels (Book 17.5)
Cipher (Book 18)
Reaper (Book 19)
Bond of Destiny (Book 20)
Bond of Passion (Book 21)

~ MOONBOUND CLAN VAMPIRES SERIES ~
Bound By Night (book 1)
Chained By Night (book 2)
Blood Red Kiss Anthology (book 2.5)

~CONTEMPORARY/WOMEN'S FICTION ~
Snowbound
The Escape Club

LEGACY

OF

CHAOS

NEW YORK TIMES BESTSELLING AUTHOR

LARISSA IONE

Legacy of Chaos
A Demonica Birthright Novel, Book 2
By Larissa Ione

Copyright 2024 Larissa Ione
ISBN: 978-1-963135-09-1

Published by Blue Box Press, an imprint of Evil Eye Concepts, Incorporated

Author's Acknowledgements

As always, there are people who are absolutely vital to the creation of my books. In the case of Legacy of Chaos, I want to give extra special thanks to Liz Berry and Jillian Stein, who went above and beyond, reading it in its roughest stages to provide valuable input. I love you, ladies! Go team!

All the huge thanks to Kim Guidroz and Chelle Olson for their incredible help behind the scenes, and to Hang Le for the most stunning covers *ever*.

Grace Wenk, I adore you, and I'm so happy you're part of the team now!

M.J. Rose, thank you again for your support and faith in me. It means so much.

And thank you, Steve Berry, for your hospitality, generosity, and stories—fiction *and* nonfiction!

I have been so blessed with good friends and a supportive publishing team, and my gratitude is endless. THANK YOU!

Dedication

I want to say that this book is special, but the truth is that all books are. We put our hearts and souls, blood and tears, into each one.

But…some of them just resonate a little more. They might come easier (*Passion Unleashed, Rogue Rider, Reaper*), or they might tear us apart (*Reaver* nearly killed me.) Whatever it is, some books rise just a bit above others, and for me, *Legacy of Chaos* is one of those.

Stryke's book takes up a lot of space in my heart, and I think it's because I understand him so well. His genius, his quirks, and his emotions are all familiar to me because they are borrowed from real people in my life.

Humans are complex. No two people are wired the same, and every individual will process the same event differently. What is traumatic for one person is shrug-worthy for another. Don't believe me? Toss a snake into a crowd and see what happens. For every person who faints, screams, or runs away, there will be someone like me, who will be all, "Ooh, a snake! Cool!"

(Also, please don't toss a snake into a crowd.)

We're shaped by our environments, our experiences, and our genetics, making each of us unique, often in ways others can't comprehend.

So, this book is dedicated to everyone who has ever felt judged. Or felt different. Who feels like no one understands them. Maybe you taste colors or see music. Maybe you learn better at your own pace than when you're forced to learn with the herd. Maybe you're more comfortable inside your own head than you are with other people.

Be unique. Be yourself. Be kind.

Celebrate what makes you different.

This book is for you, my unique friends. I love you all.

Glossary

Aegis, The — Society of human warriors dedicated to protecting the world from evil.

Decipula — A marble-sized trap designed to capture and contain the souls of dead demons until Sheoul-gra can be rebuilt.

Dermoire — Located on every Seminus demon's right arm from his hand to his throat, a dermoire consists of glyphs that reveal the bearer's paternal history. Each individual's personal glyph develops at the top of the *dermoire*, on the throat.

Fallen Angel — Believed to be evil by most humans, fallen angels can be grouped into two categories: True Fallen and Unfallen. Unfallen angels have been cast from Heaven and are earthbound, living a life in which they are neither truly good nor truly evil. In this state, they can, rarely, earn their way back into Heaven. Or they can choose to enter Sheoul, the demon realm, in order to complete their fall and become True Fallens, taking their places as demons at Satan's side.

Harrowgate — Vertical portals, invisible to humans, which demons use to travel between locations on Earth and Sheoul. Very few beings own, or can summon, their own personal Harrowgates

Ligorial — Binding thread for angels. Restricts the use of their powers. Worn loose but will physically bind an angel at the whim of the Ligorial's user.

Memitim — Angels assigned to protect humans called Primori. Once earthbound until they completed their duties and ascended to Heaven, all Memitim now belong to their own Order and may reside in Heaven or on Earth

Primori — Humans and demons whose lives are fated to affect the world in some crucial way. Their status is kept hidden from most, even in Heaven.

Radiant — The most powerful class of Heavenly angel in

existence, save Metatron. Unlike other angels, Radiants can wield unlimited power in all realms and can travel freely through Sheoul, with very few exceptions. The designation is awarded to only one angel at a time. Two can never exist simultaneously, and they cannot be destroyed except by God, Satan, or the Heavenly Council of Orders. The fallen angel equivalent is called a Shadow Angel. See: Shadow Angel.

ReSpawned — Demons whose souls were returned to their former bodies and released from Sheoul-gra when Azagoth destroyed the realm. The freshly respawned demons were sent into Azagoth's war with the fallen angel, Moloch. Millions were killed, their souls free to wreak havoc, but those who didn't die became known as ReSpawned.

S'genesis — Final maturation cycle for Seminus demons. Occurs at one hundred years of age. A post-*s'genesis* male is capable of procreation and possesses the ability to shapeshift into the male of any demon species.

Sheoul — Demon realm. Located deep in the bowels of the Earth, accessible only by Harrowgates.

Sheoul-gra — Until its destruction, it was a holding tank for the souls of evil humans and demons. A purgatory that existed independently of Sheoul, it was overseen by Azagoth, also known as the Grim Reaper. It is currently under reconstruction.

Ter'taceo — Demons who can pass as humans either because their species is naturally human in appearance or because they can shapeshift into human form.

Quanimus — The part of the soul that can connect with the energy around it, including from other dimensions. According to some, everyone—including humans and animals—possesses a *quanimus*, but not everyone can access it. The access point for all magical and supernatural abilities, it is an organ unseen but capable of great power, similar to the heart, except that it circulates spiritual energy instead of blood.

Ufelskala — A scoring system for demons based on their degree of evil. All supernatural creatures and evil humans can be categorized into five Tiers, with the Fifth Tier comprised of the worst of the wicked.

Demonica Family Tree

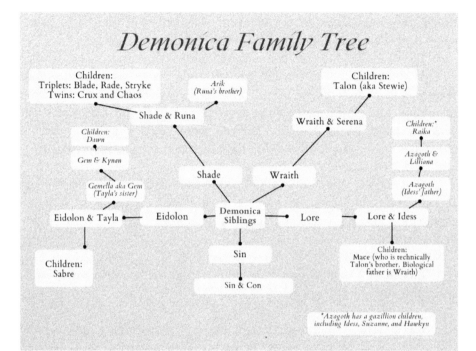

Demonica Family Tree

Children:
Triplets: Blade, Rade, Stryke
Twins: Crux and Chaos

Arik
(Runa's brother)

Children:
Talon (aka Stewie)

Shade & Runa

Wraith & Serena

Children:
Dawn

*Children:**
Raika

Gem & Kynan

Azagoth &
Lilliana

Shade

Wraith

Gemella aka Gem
(Tayla's sister)

Azagoth
(Idess' father)

Eidolon & Tayla

Eidolon

Demonica
Siblings

Lore

Lore & Idess

Sin

Children:
Sabre

Children:
Mace (who is technically
Talon's brother. Biological
father is Wraith)

Sin & Con

Azagoth has a gazillion children,
including Idess, Suzanne, and Hawkyn

Four Horsemen Family Tree

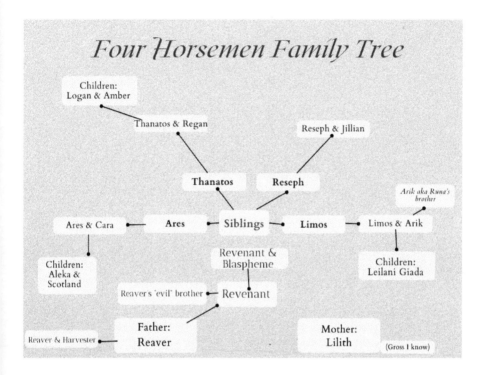

Four Horsemen Family Tree

Children:
Logan & Amber

Thanatos & Regan

Reseph & Jillian

Thanatos

Reseph

Arik aka Runa's brother

Ares & Cara

Ares

Siblings

Limos

Limos & Arik

Children:
Aleka &
Scotland

Revenant &
Blaspheme

Children:
Leilani Giada

Reaver's 'evil' brother

Revenant

Father:
Reaver

Reaver & Harvester

Mother:
Lilith

(Gross I know)

Reader Note

This is a work of fantasy, set in a world in which demons are out in the open, so you should expect the usual death, destruction, and evil beings. But it also deals with real issues that affect us mere mortals, like PTSD, loss of a loved one, depression, and suicide.

If you are struggling with PTSD, please know you aren't alone. The National Mental Health Hotline is there to help at 866-903-3787.

If you or someone you know is in crisis, help is available via voice, text, and chat options by dialing 988 for the Suicide and Crisis Prevention Lifeline, or dial 1-800-273-8255 for the National Suicide Prevention Hotline.

Prologue

"Let's go to the merry-go-round, Stryke! C'mon! Hurry!"

Stryke groaned down at his little brother, tugging on his hand. "There's no hurry. The thing runs every three minutes, and there's no one in line because it sucks."

The little shit bit him. Right there in the webbing between his thumb and forefinger.

"Ouch. Dammit, Chaos!" He shook his hand out as his seven-year-old twin brothers, Crux and Chaos, darted ahead toward the carousel, their new white sneakers pounding the hot pavement, making the soles light up with every step.

Unbelievable. They were in a theme park filled with loopy rollercoasters, splashy log rides, and speedy race cars, and the little weirdos wanted to ride something they could find at a big city mall. For the third time in an hour.

"Dude, he's a handful." Logan, son of the Horseman known as Death, shook his head. At eighteen, just four years younger than Stryke, he was the spitting image of his father: tall, blond, and with a stare that made people move out of his way. "How'd you draw the short straw to be their babysitter today?"

The cute blonde popcorn stand girl gave Stryke another seductive smile as they walked by. She'd been flirting with him the entire time he'd been stuck in the lame-ass kids' section of the theme park, and each smile was more suggestive than the last one. When he bought popcorn for his brothers, she'd brushed her hip against him in blatant invitation. He would have blamed her advances on his lust demon pheromones—and sure, he was probably putting them out there in pulsing clouds—but she'd had her eye on him even before he got close enough to affect her.

And he'd definitely had his eyes on her.

"Blade took them to the San Diego Aquarium last week," Stryke said after they'd passed Popcorn Princess. "Rade took them to a movie before that. Apparently, it's my turn to help out during summer break. My parents don't seem to give a shit that I'm in the middle of working on my doctoral thesis."

"Yeah, yeah, we all know you're working on your second doctorate," Logan drawled. "How can we forget the boy genius who makes the rest of us look bad?"

Stryke rolled his eyes hard enough to hurt. These guys would never know what it was like for him. His brain was in a constant state of manic sensory input and calculations, focusing on a million things at once. If he couldn't spill some of it out by working on something, his head felt like it would explode. He needed to either organize everything by learning more or release it by creating things like doctoral theses or rocket engines.

Funny, NASA was happy to accept—or, more accurately, *steal*—his designs, but actually hiring him, a demon, turned out to be a hyperdrive too far.

Also, at twenty-two, he was hardly a boy. He'd gone through his first maturation phase a year ago. Still, in a way, he wished the painful ordeal had never happened. Before the change that had made him sexually mature and insatiable, he'd been able to direct one hundred percent of his concentration into education, research, and science.

Now, far too much of his brain power got diverted into finding sexual partners so he didn't die. Thankfully, his uncle Eidolon had developed a drug for their kind that allowed them to go up to twenty-four hours without sex as long as they kept up with their injections at six-hour intervals. And from the way his dick was pointing at the popcorn girl, it was clear he needed another dose.

"I'm gonna go find Sabre and Blade," Logan said. "We're gonna ride the Ice Tornado. See ya."

"Yeah, have fun," Stryke said absently, digging through his pocket for his injector pen. Shit. It must have fallen out on a ride. Maybe Blade or Sabre had one on them. He'd grab one from them after Crux and Chaos got off the carousel.

The twins queued at the end of the line, but the ride hadn't stopped yet. Stryke glanced back at the popcorn girl, who was hanging a *Be Back in Ten Minutes* sign.

Perfect timing. He might not have to bug his cousin or brother for an injector pen and be subjected to relentless mockery, after all.

He caught Popcorn Princess as she stepped out from behind the cart.

"Hi," she said. Her glossy red lips turned into a mischievous smile that made him wonder how they'd feel wrapped around his cock. Depending on the viscosity of her gloss, the friction of her lips on the skin of his shaft could create intense sensations. She gestured at his arm. "Love your sleeve. Do all those symbols mean something to you?"

Given that every glyph from the fingertips of his right hand all the way up the right side of his throat was a history of his paternity, yeah.

"You could say that."

She traced her finger over the swirls of his ten-times-great-grandfather's personal symbol. "Must have taken a long time to finish it." Shivers of arousal shot straight to his groin.

Seeing as how he'd been born with the *dermoire*, no, it hadn't taken any time at all. But the very top symbol, a plain, boring square, hadn't appeared until he was twenty-one, so he felt justified in saying, "Took years."

"Hmm." She batted her eyelashes at him. "I was hoping you'd come over."

He was hoping he'd *come*. "Yeah? What time do you get off work?"

She glanced at her Blain Industries comms unit. First generation. Stryke had just gotten the second gen. Had some cool upgrades, but he could have done them better. He *would* do them better. Someday, he would put Blain Industries out of business. He even had his future company named.

StryTech.

"Not for another four hours," she said. "But I've got ten minutes and a secret spot. You got any juice?"

Juice. Drugs. Stryke wasn't into that shit. His mind was already in a constant spin. "No, but I have a condom."

Not that he needed one. He wouldn't be fertile until his second maturation phase, which wouldn't happen for another eighty years or so. But he couldn't exactly say that, not to a human. At least, he assumed she was human.

She probably assumed he was human too.

"S'okay." She started down a winding path off the main pedestrian area, her tight ass swinging under her short, white skirt. "I got some J."

He glanced back at the carousel, which had stopped and was unloading. He should have four to five minutes before Crux and Chaos were done with the ride. Perfect.

They passed a sign that said *No Entry*. A small building designed like a tropical hut and disguised to blend in with the landscaping loomed ahead. He assumed they were going inside, but Popcorn Girl gave him a flirty look and a "shh" finger against her plump lips before slipping into the brush.

They eased up behind the hut in a little alcove littered with a few candy wrappers and cigarette butts.

"I'm Micha, by the way," she said as she pulled a wadded bit of plastic from behind a tree.

"Stryke." He waved away her offer of one of the liquid-filled ampules in the baggie. "And you don't need that shit. You'll like what I'm going to give you way more."

Reaching out, she dragged her finger from his sternum to the button on his jeans. "Oh, yeah?"

"Yeah."

Done flirting, he tore the baggie from her hand and tossed it to the ground. Flirting was an instinctive skill for most Seminus demons, but Stryke somehow lacked that gene. He wrapped his arm around her waist and tugged her to him, his other hand dipping under her skirt. Her cheap panties didn't stand a chance against his probing fingers, and she gasped as he slipped a couple inside her slippery core.

"I don't usually do this," she breathed, hiking one leg up against his hip.

"I'm sure you don't." He hoped he didn't sound sarcastic because he definitely wasn't judging her. And then he realized he didn't give a crap. He'd never see her again.

Except that he liked how willing she was to fuck a complete stranger. Maybe he should get her number afterward and get a sex-only relationship going. No small talk, kissing, or dinner dates. Just pleasure and a *see ya later*. His cousin, Mace, had about a dozen of those, but Stryke doubted Mace was truly as utilitarian about it as he claimed to be. His cousin liked to flirt. He liked to impress the females. And he loved to be adored.

Stryke couldn't care less about any of it. Sex with a female was a biological necessity for him, as important as breathing and eating. But that didn't mean he had to turn every lunch or fuck into a seven-course meal. Who had time for that shit?

"You got a boyfriend?" he asked as he unbuttoned his jeans and backed her up against a tree.

"Not really."

Again, he didn't care. But it seemed like a normal question to ask when making small talk.

He guided his cock to her entrance and sank inside her with a groan. He didn't like the build-up to sex, the courtship and then the foreplay, but once he was balls deep inside a hot female, it was bliss. A few precious seconds for his mind to stop thinking and recharge.

He started pumping, letting his body take over for his brain. He didn't have time to work her up and get her to come before he did, but he had that covered. His semen would trigger a series of powerful orgasms that would rock her world for up to half an hour.

She would be late getting back to her popcorn stand, and she wouldn't care at all.

His orgasm ramped up quickly, a searing bliss that built in his balls and blew up his shaft in wave after wave of ecstasy.

"Ah…yes…" He threw back his head and focused on the tension escaping his body and the sounds of the female's climax.

Around them, the park noises grew louder, intruding on Stryke's precious few moments of mental silence.

So much screaming.

Some ride must be scaring the shit out of people.

Weird. They were in kiddie land. Why would there be so many screams?

The human was still coming, contracting around his cock and pumping her hips against his. But all around, the gut-wrenching sounds of terror echoed off buildings. Through the gaps in the trees, he caught brief glimpses of people—adults dragging children and strollers, running from the direction of the carousel.

The carousel.

He tore away from the female, leaving her propped against the tree, moaning through multiple orgasms. Heart racing, Stryke scrambled up the path, tripping over tree roots and his feet as he simultaneously ran and buttoned up. He burst onto the main drag, colliding with a man cradling his mangled arm to his chest, his face dripping red. Ahead, the popcorn stand lay on its side, one wheel spinning lazily. People weren't running now. They were limping. Crawling. Dragging themselves.

"Crux!" he screamed. "Chaos!"

Then he saw the demons. A half dozen inky, nightmarish motherfuckers with jaws full of razor-sharp teeth, Freddy Kreuger claws, and way too many burning crimson eyes.

Logan, Sabre, and Blade rushed toward the carousel, Logan armed with the sword he could summon at will. With an agile leap and a smooth swing of his blade, he sliced the head clean off one of the demons.

Fuck, yeah!

Stryke shouldered past stumbling, panicked people. There! Crux! His little brother, his tawny hair matted with blood, was scrambling over bodies and dodging a demon's sweeping blows and driving punches.

No! Terror became Stryke's entire world as he calculated the distance to his brother and the odds of the demon's next two blows killing Crux. Motherfucker, he wasn't going to make it.

As Stryke threw himself at the demon, knowing he couldn't get there in time, Blade swooped in like a superhero and hit the thing from behind. He drove his fist into the back of the monster's head, his *dermoire* glowing with power usually meant for healing but now weaponized. The demon snarled, striking out and knocking Blade away.

Close enough now to smell the beast's rancid, smoky odor, Stryke slammed into him, engaging his power and serving up a massive heart attack. The demon screeched as its heart seized—all six fucking chambers of it.

Stryke felt Blade's power join his, causing tears in the bastard's veins and bleeding him out from the inside.

The thing collapsed. Blade instantly went after another demon as Stryke, his body vibrating with adrenaline and fear for his brothers, scooped up Crux.

"Where's Chaos?" he shouted, spinning around in search of the other twin. Chaos!" he screamed. "*Chaos!*"

Clinging to Crux, his feet slipping in puddles of blood, he navigated around overturned strollers and mangled, eviscerated bodies, some missing limbs. Or heads. He searched the carousel, desperately hoping Chaos was hiding behind a hippo or lion. He called Chaos's name over and over, screaming over the sounds of slaughter and pain. The stench of hot blood and bowels filled the air, mingling with the buttery smell of popcorn.

"*Chaos!*"

In his peripheral vision, he saw Logan, Blade, and Sabre taking down demons like machines, but Stryke's focus was on the ride, where a child was hiding behind an elephant, a tiny hand clinging to the carousel animal's ornate tail.

Abruptly, a stab of pain shot through his skull and down his spine as if he'd been impaled by a rod of white-hot iron. Agony filled him, ripping his voice and breath from his throat. And then, as quickly as it had come, the rod of pain was gone, leaving an emptiness inside as if it had taken a core sample of his soul.

The part of his soul that had been connected to Chaos.

He's dead. My brother is dead.

Stryke's gut plummeted to his feet, which became leaden and unsteady. He staggered at the magnitude of his loss.

Crux screamed as his connection to Chaos was severed too.

A hand came down on Stryke's shoulder. "Stryke..."

Shell-shocked, he wheeled around to Sabre, whose tortured expression and haunted eyes made everything even more real. Sabre was a cousin, not a sibling, so he wouldn't have felt Chaos die.

But he'd seen it.

Stryke's brain, which always crackled with energy, went numb. At some point, he must have set Crux down because Sabre knelt and hugged the boy to his chest, shielding his eyes from the massacre around them.

The din of screaming and moaning grew dull as Stryke's sense of hearing became a victim of shock. His balance went next, his legs turning watery as he leaped awkwardly off the ride and stumbled, heart pounding, to Blade.

Blade, who knelt next to a pair of blinking shoes and...*oh, gods.*

"*Please, no. Please, no!*" he screamed inside his head to whoever would listen. "*Take me. Take me instead!*"

Blade, his dark head hanging, his shoulders slumped, turned slowly to Stryke. Tears streamed from his eyes and cut paths through the blood splattered on cheeks gone pale with trauma.

"Where were you?" he rasped. "Where the fuck were you?"

The world spun and went gray. The last thing Stryke saw before he lost consciousness was Blade's scorching, accusatory glare and those brand-new flashing shoes.

Chapter 1

Pride is the master sin of the devil, and the devil is the father of lies
— Edwin Hubbell Chapin

"Mr. Stryke. You're telling me that the greatest minds at every major scientific institution, from the National Institute for Nuclear Physics and CERN to Stanford University and the Chinese Academy of Sciences, are wrong, and *you* are right. Is that what you're saying?"

Stryke stared at the life-sized, holographic image of the vice president for the World Council on Supernatural Governance from where he stood in the middle of his three-thousand-square-foot office, his feet centered on a glowing symbol etched into the marble floor.

"Yes, that is what I'm saying." He took a sip of his coffee. "And most of those minds aren't all that great."

The dozen other holographic bigwigs sitting at the WCSG conference table put their heads together and murmured among themselves, but Ethan Winston Whitmore the fucking Third just kept looking at Stryke like something scraped off a shoe.

"So, you believe you may have solved the world's energy and climate crisis," Whitmore said, his voice dripping with mockery.

"Yes," Stryke repeated for the third time. These guys were as dense as osmium. And much like the platinum metal, they were brittle and hard to work with. "And if I keep having to answer the same question dozens of times, we're going to be here until the damned apocalypse."

Whitmore snorted and turned to his colleagues. "This is preposterous. There's no way an element found in the demon realm of Sheoul can be *tamed* and made into a liquid that will fuel everything gas and oil have powered for centuries—"

"*And* remove some of the carbon dioxide from the atmosphere that was put there by the burning of fossil fuels," Stryke interjected. "Don't forget that."

Whitmore huffed, his agitation and voice ramping up a few levels. "We should convene with every global coalition to ban the research and development of what could clearly be a dangerous element."

This guy was such a douche. "I'm guessing you own a lot of oil and solar stocks." Actually, Stryke didn't have to guess. He knew. He'd researched these guys down to the color of their underwear. He knew what they ate for breakfast, where every cent of their fortunes came from, and who they were fucking instead of their wives.

"That's irrelevant—"

"I'd say it's very relevant."

Whitmore glared daggers. "You should not have been allowed to buy an entire oil drilling operation in the North Sea and then keep regulatory agencies and world governments in the dark about what is happening there."

"You're kidding, right?" Stryke took a leisurely drink of his coffee. When he was done, he strolled over to his desk and took his time placing the mug on a coaster. He loved making powerful people wait. And not just wait. Wait for a *demon*.

"You should be *thanking* me for purchasing the *Sea Storm*," he said as he returned to stand on the glowing glyph that prevented anyone from recording him. "Humans aren't equipped to handle what that oil company drilled into. If StryTech hadn't sealed the breach when we did, the world would be dealing with a lot worse than the handful of orca-sized demons my people hunted down. You can't even begin to comprehend the kind of evil that would have escaped into our oceans. Sentient, soul-eating acid clouds and gigantic, demonic leviathans never before seen. So, you know, you're welcome."

There was still some concern about the instability of the anomaly, but he'd keep that to himself.

"That's enough, Mr. Stryke. But we *will* discuss this later." Whitmore adjusted his glasses and brushed a lock of gray hair off his forehead. "Right now, let's move on to the incident that brings us to the main focus of this meeting."

The incident. When one of StryTech's weapons was used in a violent *incident* between the two biggest rival demon-fighting agencies in the world. During a cooperative interagency effort, a rogue Aegis idiot killed two Demonic Activity Response Team agents. Which then caused an international crisis that worsened when the vengeance demon fiancé of one of the dead agents went full John Wick on every Aegi he could find. The images and live footage had gone super viral, triggering an avalanche of outcry and protests.

Worldwide furor continued to intensify, fueled by the hungry-for-conflict media, as well as warring religious and political factions vying for power. The flames of dissent were spreading like wildfire through an already on-edge, largely anti-demon public. Cries for DART to be defunded for employing demons were met with demands for The Aegis to be held accountable for killing *"innocent demons."*

It was a shitshow the World Council on Supernatural Governance was trying to sort out before the world caught on fire.

The problem was that the WCSG often allowed politics to override smart decisions.

Stryke spent the next hour answering dumb questions and dealing with hostile jerks who hated demons and pretty much everything Stryke did. Yet the WCSG installed StryTech's demon-detection devices in every building. They'd spent millions on the DeTecht devices, as well as his other communications and security products.

The comms unit on his wrist—a StryTech next-gen prototype—pulsed, alerting him to an upcoming meeting. "Are we done here?" He walked behind his desk. "I have things to do."

"We all have things to do, Mr.—"

Stryke severed the link to the virtual meeting, putting an end to Whitmore's nasally, narcissistic drone. The guy was an insufferable asshole.

And Stryke was an expert on those. Took one to know one and all that.

The moment the hologram disappeared, a light flashed on his comms pad, and his assistant's voice, touched with a hint of an Australian accent, rang in his ear. "Mr. Stryke, Kynan Morgan is here to see you. Also, your—"

"Send him in."

Stryke glanced at the clock. He'd hoped to have more time to prepare for this. The WCSG inquiry had gone on longer than it should have. Now, he had just a little over two minutes to catch up on his messages.

There were seven notes from the heads of various departments, two media requests, and one message from his uncle Eidolon, all of which got mentally sorted into a response queue in order of importance.

Last on the list was the visual missive from his uncle Eidolon.

It wasn't that Stryke didn't like the guy. On the contrary, he had mad respect for the doctor. Eidolon was intelligent, rational, and had built a medical empire from nothing. He was pretty much the only family member with whom Stryke felt comfortable.

Eidolon's eyes were never full of blame or disappointment.

But Stryke still didn't feel like dealing with him right now. Didn't feel like being lectured.

"You need to dial back on your use of sexual suppressants. They're not good for you. They interfere with your sleep. Suppressants are meant to be used only occasionally. No more than twice per day unless it's an emergency situation."

Yeah, yeah, whatever. Stryke was intimately aware of the side effects of the suppressant. How could he not be? He'd developed it himself when he decided the formula Eidolon created for their kind wasn't long-term enough. And if using it cost Stryke a few years of his life in missed sleep, so what? His species had a five-hundred-year lifespan. What was a decade or two?

The elevator door slid open, and Kynan stepped out, dressed as usual in dark jeans, combat boots, and a half-tucked blue button-down. Around his battle-scarred neck, dangling from a chain, was a crystal amulet named Heofon that made him immortal and practically immune to violence. He hadn't aged a day since being gifted with the literal piece of Heaven, and no one looking at him would know he was in his sixties and not his late twenties or early thirties.

"Stryke." Kynan strode toward him, every step lighting the embedded symbols in the pearlescent floor. White flashes spread from his footprints, identifying him as someone with angelic lineage. "Thanks for seeing me."

Stryke pushed to his feet and extended his hand as was customary for humans. "When the Director of DART, a human charmed by angels, wants a meeting, I give him a meeting."

Kynan stopped in front of Stryke's desk and clasped his hand. "See, I can't tell if you're being sarcastic or not." His voice, already gravelly from the injury that had turned his neck into a busy network of scar tissue, went even rougher with mild reproach. "Mainly because you rarely agree to meet."

Stryke gestured to his bank of computers and whiteboards. "I'm very busy."

"So you tell everyone."

Stryke snorted. Very few people would call him out like that. It was both irritating and admirable. It was also accurate. He *was* busy. And his cousins, brothers, parents…they were doing fine without him.

"I sent the list of the features we want in the new weapon design," Kynan said, skipping awkward personal small talk. Much appreciated. "Have you had time to look at it?"

"I did. You're asking for a lot." Stryke brought the list up on his pad and flung it into the air between them, making it the size of a large TV screen and suspended as a 3D hologram. "You're asking for a weapon that not only kills demons but also captures their souls. Everything you've described would take some kind of bullet from a firearm. Our agreement with The Aegis for a demon-killing firearm is exclusive."

Kynan's gravelly voice warped even more. "I'm more than familiar with the weapon you created for The Aegis."

Of course, he was. The Smiter had killed two of Kynan's people. Regrettable, certainly, but StryTech had merely created the weapon. How it was used was out of his company's hands. Still, Stryke felt obligated to help Ky out.

"But," Stryke said, "we might be able to develop a different kind of projectile."

"Like what? An arrow? Or a crossbow bolt?" Kynan crossed his thick arms over his chest. "Neither of those are practical, tactical, or easy to conceal. Even the smallest ones are way too obvious, especially in public."

Stryke threw out a 3D sketch of a sleek hybrid weapon he'd drawn last night when his mind had been too busy to let him sleep. "What if I can develop one that's no bulkier than, say, a Colt 1911?"

"You think you can do that?" Kynan analyzed the sketch like a commander studying a battle map. "And still make it powerful enough to kill Ufelskala Five demons?"

"I'm confident my team can size it to your liking. Powerful enough to kill?" Stryke shrugged. "Eh. Depends on the demon. We'll see. But it'll cause injury and collect the demon's soul after it dies. I can have some designs and rudimentary figures drawn up for you."

Kynan zeroed in on a word at the bottom of the screen. "Reaper?"

"That's what I'm calling it. Seemed appropriate, given what it will do. Feel free to rename it."

Sharp gaze focused on the sketch, Kynan appeared to consider that. He'd probably had his little human heart set on a high-octane pistol or a rapid-fire rifle, but StryTech's exclusivity agreement with The Aegis was rock solid for another five years.

Besides, if Stryke could make it work, this weapon would be a game changer, allowing *anyone* to capture a soul. Right now, trapping demonic spirits required an ability to see them and StryTech's proprietary containers.

"No, I like it. The name and design both," Kynan said. "What about my suggestion to work with my people on this?"

That wasn't going to happen. Stryke had built StryTech from the ground up. He'd overseen the construction at every level. He'd personally hired every single employee. It was a well-oiled machine that worked because everyone here had been hand-chosen for their ability to synchronize with the company and its other employees.

Stryke wasn't about to toss a bunch of unknown loose cogs into his machine.

"We don't work with anyone on the outside," he said. "I'm sure you understand."

"That's the thing." Kynan wandered over to a whiteboard covered in equations. "I don't understand." He frowned at the writing. "I don't understand this, either. What is it?"

"Calculations for a floating hydro-reflective disk. Basically, a nearly invisible umbrella."

"No shit?" Kynan glanced back at him. "Why?"

"I hate carrying a bulky umbrella, but I also hate getting wet." Hell, he didn't even like getting into his pool and hot tub. He'd only built them for Masumi. "Wouldn't you love to have a device the size of a penny that you can activate during a rainstorm and suddenly have a shield over your head?"

"Huh. That does sound cool." Kynan swung back around to Stryke. "You know what else would be cool? Letting my people work with yours."

"Why? You don't trust me?"

"Stryke, I've known you since the day you were born. Your parents are some of my best friends, and your brothers work for me. It's not about trust. It's about making sure we know exactly how our weapons work. We want to be able to maintain them and not be beholden to

StryTech every time we need a repair." He glanced out the window at Sydney Harbor, its blue waters glittering in the noon sunlight. "We appreciate all the tech you've developed for us, but it's invasive as hell."

"Invasive?" Stryke gave the other male a flat, questioning look. "Invasive, how?"

"Oh, come on." Kynan pulled a shiny disc from his pocket and held it up. "This is what I'm talking about. The tracking on these Harrowgate coins. You know every time we use one. It's bullshit."

"That was part of our agreement."

"It's still bullshit. We only agreed because you had us over a barrel. We need to be able to get humans through Harrowgates alive. We also bowed to your requirement that all our demon DNA scanners be connected to your servers. We've agreed to many contracts that favor StryTech, just like everyone else has. We've followed your rules and have *never* asked for special treatment for friends and family." He met Stryke's gaze, the cool denim-blue in his intelligent eyes making it clear he was ready to dig his heels in on this. "But I'm playing the friends and family card today. Giving our people input into Reaper's development isn't an unreasonable request."

Stryke had been ready to put his foot down. He could, and he knew it. DART wanted this weapon so badly that if he asked Kynan for his only child as payment, Dawn would show up wrapped in a ribbon.

Well, not really. Kynan would draw the line at pimping out his daughter, but still, Stryke figured there wasn't much the guy wouldn't do to make this deal.

But Kynan had a point. He'd never asked StryTech for more than anyone else had. Allowing this one small thing could help rebuild a measure of the goodwill StryTech had lost when Smiter smote Kynan's people.

Plus, Stryke really did respect the guy, and that wasn't something he said about many people.

"How many are we talking about?" he asked.

Guarded optimism flickered in Ky's eyes. "I can get a three-person team together by the end of the week. A technomancer, an engineer, and an arms expert."

Three was too many. Even two sounded like a lot.

"You can send one. The technomancer. My senior Mancer is out on paternity leave."

There was a heartbeat of hesitation, and Stryke wondered if Kynan would push for one more. Stryke would push back. One was more than enough.

Finally, Ky nodded. "That'll work."

"Great. Let's have our people hash out the details." Stryke sank down in his chair. "Now, were these minor negotiations so important that you demanded an in-person meeting instead of our usual virtual chat?"

Kynan came back toward him. "You know they're not."

Yeah, he did. "You want to know what went down at the WCSG's inquiry."

"My agency's future is at stake," Ky said. "I'd be lying if I said I wasn't stressed out."

No doubt he was. DART and The Aegis had been in a cold war for decades, and just as they were trying to make an effort to work together…well, a lot of people died. And one of StryTech's weapons had been at the center of the incident.

"They mainly wanted to know about Smiter's capabilities. They were more curious about that than anything. But I got the feeling they believe DART's version of events over The Aegis's. How they feel about a DART agent turning into a vengeance demon and killing a dozen people is a mystery."

"Sarcasm?"

"No. Seriously. They gave no indication at all."

Kynan gave Stryke a resigned nod and looked down at the time on his comms device. "I need to go, but thanks for seeing me." They both got to their feet. "One more thing."

Fuck.

Don't say it.

"We're having an office party for your mom's birthday Friday after work. You're invited."

He said it.

"I'll try to make it."

"No, you won't." Kynan spoke as he downloaded the 3D weapon designs into his comms. "But you should. How long has it been since you've seen her? A couple of years? How long since you've seen all your family together? Ten years?"

Twelve.

"Make an effort," Ky said. "Your mom misses you."

Stryke forced a smile to keep from clenching his jaw. "If we're done with the guilt trip portion of our meeting, you can see yourself out."

Kynan nodded and headed for the exit, but as the elevator door opened, he turned back to Stryke, his expression apologetic. "I didn't want to do this, Stryke. He guilted me into it."

"Who guilted you into what?"

A big, dark-haired male dressed from head to toe in black leather exited the elevator, and Stryke's gut plummeted to his feet. "*Dad.*"

Shock collided with anger that Kynan would sneak his father in like this. And what the hell? Why hadn't his assistant warned him?

But Kalis *had* tried, hadn't she? Dammit. He'd cut her off.

Kynan stepped inside the elevator and gave Stryke a fatherly look. The one that said, "*Do the right thing.*"

Yeah, well, in this case, the right thing was avoiding being anywhere near his family. His presence put a damper on everything. Eventually, tension would spark an angry fire that would smolder for years.

No, thank you. Nothing Kynan or his father could say would change his mind.

"I've been trying to get ahold of you for three months," Shade said, stopping halfway between the elevator and Stryke's desk. He glanced around, his dark eyes taking in the floor-to-ceiling windows, the wall of computers, and the expensive, random artwork Stryke had put up for the sole purpose of making people speculate about why he'd chosen it. In truth, he hated all of it. Art was messy and chaotic, and it rarely made sense. "Is there a reason you can't answer a damned techmail?"

Kynan would pay for this.

"Your techmails consisted of details about the party for Mom, but they said nothing about an RSVP. I saw no reason to reply since you didn't ask if I was coming."

"That's because pressuring you has never worked and usually ends in the exact opposite of what your mom or I want. But this is important. DART is presenting her with an award for her contributions and support, and it would mean a lot if you were there."

Stryke swept some pens off his desk into a drawer and slammed it shut. "No one wants me there, Pops."

"This isn't about you or your brothers," his father said. "It's about your mom. *She* wants you there."

"And what do you want?" Stryke regretted the question the second it fell from his lips. It hung in the tense, thick air between them for an agonizingly long time.

Finally, Shade shook his head. "I want our family to heal."

"And you think my attendance at a party can do that?"

"I don't know," he said, tucking his hands into his jacket pockets.

"But it would be a start. And it can't hurt."

"Oh," Stryke muttered as he braced his hip against the desk, "it can definitely hurt."

Shade studied him, his eyes shadowed and so much like what Stryke saw in the mirror every morning. His mouth opened, but he seemed to think better of whatever he wanted to say.

"Go ahead and say it," Stryke said. "I'm a big boy. I can handle it."

There was a heartbeat of hesitation. Another. Then, softly, "We never blamed you for what happened to Chaos, Stryke."

Stryke's throat closed up. Turned out he *couldn't* handle it.

This was why he avoided his family. They always wanted to talk about shit. They wanted to dig up the worst day of Stryke's life, and he had to relive his little brother's death over and over.

The words *heal* and *closure* got bandied about a lot, but how could there ever be healing and closure for something like that?

"You blamed me, Dad," Stryke said softly. "But no more than I blame myself."

"I did not—"

"Bullshit," Stryke snapped, losing the cool composure he'd honed over years of practice and instruction from the Judicia. His uncle Eidolon's mother and adoptive father were Judicia, demons who actively suppressed emotions in pursuit of perfect decision-making, and E had asked them to teach Stryke their ways at a time when Stryke was at his lowest.

Eidolon didn't know it, but he'd probably saved Stryke's life. Or maybe he *did* know. The guy was always a step ahead of everyone else.

Shade's hands fisted at his sides. "I never once said his death was your fault."

"You didn't need to."

The questions that day, and for several days—months—after, had been of the, "*How far away from the twins were you?*" and "*Why didn't you ask someone else to stay with them while you took care of yourself?*" variety. Every single question had been a spear to the heart until he bled out over and over, and nothing was left but a dry husk.

Closing his eyes, Shade took a deep breath. When he opened them again, the sadness in their dark depths sent a fresh stab of guilt through Stryke's core.

"I understand you're in pain," Shade said quietly. "But so are we. Your mother and I didn't just lose Chaos that day. We also lost you."

Stryke's eyes stung with the tears he fought to hold back.

"Please, son—"

"I can't," Stryke said roughly, needing to end this right fucking now. As if on cue, his wrist comms buzzed in an urgent tap. Eidolon again. "I have to get this."

Had his father not been there, he'd have blown off his uncle. But in this shitty scenario, the lesser of two evils was Eidolon.

Shade nodded and turned toward the elevator. "Just think about coming. For your mother."

He disappeared into the lift, and Stryke held his breath until the door slid shut.

Exhaling, Stryke sought the Judicia calmness that quieted his mind and emotions. But it had been a long time since he'd faced his father, let alone talked about Chaos, and finding self-control took longer than he'd have liked. So long, in fact, that his comms buzzed again, this time more forcefully.

Giving in to his uncle's persistence, he threw the holo call onto the floor in front of him. A millisecond later, the tall, dark-haired doctor stood before Stryke in a beam of light.

"Stryke. Finally. You need to come to the hospital."

Stryke froze as he went to take a seat. "Why? Is someone hurt?" He couldn't lose anyone else in his family. He couldn't even contemplate it.

"It's your test results. I need to talk to you."

Relieved that no one was injured or dead, Stryke sank into his chair. "Then talk."

Eidolon hesitated, and a twinge of trepidation went through Stryke. "I really think this should be in person."

"This *is* in person," Stryke said, not budging. "So, what is it?"

"First of all, stop being a jackass. I'm trying to help you." Eidolon glanced at a clipboard in his hand and then looked back up. "Second, you've got to stop taking your suppressant."

Not this again.

"I told you I'm not switching back to yours. It doesn't last long enough."

"That's the thing." Eidolon tossed the clipboard onto his desk. "You can't take mine, either. You can't take any."

"What are you talking about?"

"Your dependence on it is what's causing your symptoms. You came to me because your heart is racing, and you're suffering from dizzy spells. You said you trust me. So, trust me when I tell you that you have to stop. Now. Or tachycardia and vertigo will be the least of your problems."

Eidolon was a great doctor, but he was too conservative and overprotective when it came to his family. He'd also been critical of Stryke's formula from the very beginning. Maybe because Stryke's product outsold Eidolon's in the underworld market ten to one. Twenty-four hours of relief, or up to forty? There was a clear winner, and it had to chafe.

"I'll think about it."

Stryke wouldn't think about it at all.

"Dammit, Stryke. I don't have time for your denial of reality. I'm dealing with an Oni pox outbreak and a virus in the hospital's security software." Eidolon stepped closer, his eyes flashing gold with anger. "Your body is shutting down. I don't know how much more you can take."

"Bottom line it for me, Uncle. I have a busy schedule today."

"Bottom line?" The doctor's deep voice turned grave. "I don't know if it'll be the next injection or the fiftieth, but at some point, the suppressant will kill you."

Chapter 2

Cyan stared at her chalkboard and growled in frustration. None of her calculations were correct. Again.

Son of a bitch.

Viciously, she erased her pretty, blue, yellow, and red formulations to upgrade the comms implants that could translate demonic languages. When there was nothing but a blurry blackboard, she cursed and hurled the eraser to the floor. A rainbow cloud of colored chalk dust poofed into the air and left a coating of pigmented dust on her desk.

She took a deep, calming breath and turned her attention from the board and back to her actual job at DART—one she loved, which allowed her to afford a nice apartment in an upscale Brussels neighborhood. Except, now that her roommate and best friend was dead, Cyan would have to tighten the purse strings.

Which made her want to cry. Not for her new budget since Shan had been in the middle of moving out to go live with her fiancé anyway, but for the loss of her friend.

Blinking against the sting of the tears in her eyes, she grabbed a plastic evidence bag off her freshly sanitized lab table and dumped a comms unit into her palm. According to her boss, Kynan Morgan, the thing was possessed by a demonic spirit. Usually, the souls of dead demons were handled by the Spirit Management division, but not even Logan, who had the extraordinary ability to expel demonic souls from physical bodies to trap them, could force this spirit out of its home.

Kynan hoped Cyan's ability to manipulate electronics would allow her to exorcise the demon ghost.

Cyan charged up her powers, pulling from deep inside her to pierce the bit of tech. Instantly, the circuitry and programming codes popped into her head. From here, she could do almost anything to the comms unit with a tech spell. By simply reimagining the programming, she could turn it into a device that could immobilize a pickpocket or boil the blood inside a rude waitperson. Or she could turn it into a ticking time bomb for the wearer. Just a little tweak in the coding, and she could make it connect with the user's implant chip and cause a life-ending shock.

Not that Cyan had ever done that. But it was sometimes fun to think about.

Today, she wasn't running hypothetical scenarios through her head. She was looking for a literal ghost in the machine.

"Cyanide?"

She jumped at the sound of her boss's voice on the intercom. He always called her by her given name over the comms systems but used her nickname in person. He had some odd quirks.

"Yes, Mr. Morgan?" She powered herself down, and the inner workings of a very expensive communications device faded away.

"I need to see you in my office. Got a minute?"

"Sure thing, boss. I'll be right up."

She hurried out of her lab and took the stairs to DART's main floor, where she returned waves and greetings as she slipped inside the elevator. When the door opened on the second floor, she stepped out into a massive atrium with a spectacular view of the main floor fountain below.

She loved the design, openness, and modern touches of the old building on the outskirts of Brussels' historic center. Kynan had hired her just after the renovations on their global headquarters had been finished.

Nineteen years ago.

Almost two decades with DART, and she still hated the freakishly beautiful broad-leaf plant outside Kynan's office. Watered with blood and fed bits of raw flesh, its crimson and black stalks vibrated as she approached, its lacy leaves rattling whispers that sounded like voices. The thing sensed what those nearby were thinking, serving as an early warning system. If anyone intended to harm Kynan, the plant would screech like a banshee.

Since she wasn't planning to kill her boss, the plant merely said things like "*angry*" and "*sad.*"

What an asshole.

She glared at the stupid bush as she walked past and heard Kynan's voice call out as she reached his open doorway.

"Come on in." He waved her over, and she took a seat across from him. "Thanks for coming."

He said it like she'd had a choice. "No problem. What's this about?"

"A couple of things." He braced his elbows on the surface of his polished oak desk and leaned forward. "First, how are you doing? You didn't take any time off after…"

After Shanea was gunned down in cold blood in this very building.

It had been barely a month since The Aegis murdered Shan, and Cyan still wasn't dealing well. Heck, she wasn't dealing *at all.* She'd buried herself in work, unwilling to return to the apartment they'd shared except for essentials.

Shan had been in the process of moving out, but she hadn't boxed up everything yet, and the reminders lying around their place ripped Cyan open, refreshing the pain every time she saw them.

"I'm fine."

Kynan nodded as if he bought it. "Xoei told me you've been sleeping here for weeks."

"That little snitch." Cyan clenched her fist as if it were wrapped around her lab assistant's neck.

"Cyan," Kynan said gently, "I know how close you and Shan were. And I know how you felt about Draven too. You lost your best friends, and I don't think you're dealing."

"You don't know anything," Cyan snapped. He was right, but she wasn't ready to hear the truth. She was too angry, too hurt, and too stubborn. But Kynan was also her boss, and she shouldn't go off like that. Exhausted and frustrated with herself, she rubbed her eyes with the heels of her hands. "I'm sorry. I just don't want to talk about it."

"I get it," he said. "But DART has people you can talk to if you need to, okay?"

"Thank you." She forced a smile to assure her boss that everything was hunky-dory. "Why else am I here?"

He shoved a packet of papers across the surface of his desk. "These are some design ideas and notes about a weapon StryTech will be working on for us."

The very mention of StryTech put a knot in her gut. She'd be happy to see that place burn to the ground—and its CEO with it.

Although a new weapon would be nice.

Curious, she pulled the papers over and scanned the diagrams and notes. "So, this new weapon…looks like a device that would allow anyone to capture souls."

"Exactly. We wouldn't be limited to only having Logan and a handful of his people doing it. Anyone who popped one of those projectiles into a demon before it died would be able to capture its spirit."

That was fucking awesome. A huge advantage for Team Good. She flipped the page. Blinked in surprise.

"Wait." She held up the packet of papers and peered more closely at a sketch and specs of a microprocessor. "This weapon would also have a guidance system?"

He nodded. "It could be programmed to seek out the demon closest to death."

"Wow. That's innovative. So, again, why am I here?"

Kynan leaned back in his chair and steepled his fingers over his flat abs. "Because I don't want this to be like everything else we get from StryTech."

Ah. "You mean hampered by its rules and accountable to the Almighty Stryke?"

"Exactly. I'm sending you to work on their team."

She inhaled sharply. Managed a hoarse, "What?"

"The weapon will contain ensorcelled microchip electronics," he said. "Your expertise makes you the perfect choice for the assignment."

Oh, hell, no. Kynan was wrong for so many reasons. "I wouldn't be a good fit. Send Xoei."

He pulled the papers back across the desk. "Xoei is talented and smart, but she doesn't have your experience or innate skill with electronics and weapons. I want our best on this, and you're it. I'm sure—"

"I can't," she blurted, not caring that she'd interrupted her boss. "I can't work with Stryke." She swallowed and took a moment to temper her voice, if not her words. "I think I'd want to kill him."

"You and everyone else," he muttered. But Kynan didn't get it. He hadn't worshiped the ground Stryke walked on, only to have his idol prove to be a disappointment at best and an accessory to murder at worst. "You probably won't even see him. And I don't need to tell you how much of a game changer this weapon would be for us," he said, echoing her earlier thoughts.

"And the Smiter was a game changer for The Aegis." She closed her eyes as if doing so would shut out the mental image of Shanea, her body torn apart by The Aegis's new demon-shredding firearm. It didn't, and she reluctantly looked back at her boss. "I'm sorry, Kynan. I can't do it."

He tucked the papers into a folder and stuck them in a desk drawer. "I wish you'd reconsider, but I understand."

"With all due respect, I don't think you do."

Yikes. Instant regret. She shouldn't have said that, especially not in that bitchy tone. Fortunately, Kynan was the most even-tempered human she'd ever known in her thirty-seven years of life, and he merely sat back in his seat, his expression contemplative.

"I'm not going to get into a pissing contest over who's gone through the most shit," he said quietly. "I know Shanea's loss is still raw, and you're grieving. Maybe you should take some time off. Isn't Benjamin Franklin Day coming up? It's a big holiday for your species, right? Go celebrate."

She stiffened. "Is that a suggestion or an order?"

"It's a suggestion, Cyan. Nothing more. I won't force you to work with StryTech's team or take a vacation. But doing one or the other instead of hanging out in your dark lab might be a good idea."

"My lab isn't dark." At his steely don't-fuck-with-me stare, she relented, knowing she'd pushed him about as far as was wise. "Fine" she said. "I'll think about it. Is there anything else?"

He shook his head as if she were a lost cause.

She probably was.

She stood, intent on returning to the lab, but Xoei was probably back from lunch, and Cyan didn't want to deal with her lab assistant's super positive, upbeat energy or questions right now.

Maybe Kynan was right. Perhaps she needed a break.

But taking a break from work meant facing her empty apartment. It meant dealing with her loss.

And, unfortunately, there was no tech spell to make it any easier.

Chapter 3

The suppressant will kill you.

As Stryke stepped into his personal Harrowgate at the back of his office, Eidolon's blunt words rang through his head.

Stryke didn't merely *hear* the words, either. Thanks to his synesthesia, they pulsed in fluorescent orange in his mind, so bright and vivid that he could almost taste them the way he could taste music. Oh, wait…yup, there was just the slightest hint of anise on his tongue.

Apparently, impending death tasted like black licorice.

Figured. He hated licorice.

As if the topic of suppressing sexual urges was a trigger, a sudden wave of arousal made his cock twitch as he pressed the symbol for his house. He glanced at his watch. Yup, it had been exactly four hours since his last injection.

The next one could kill you.

Yeah, yeah, whatever. Eidolon was such an alarmist.

Growling under his breath, Stryke stepped out of the Harrowgate and into a foot of fresh snow. Son of a bitch. He wondered for the millionth time what he'd been thinking when he had the gate installed outside on his deck instead of inside his living room.

Well, he knew what he was thinking. Security. If an inside gate ever malfunctioned or was hacked, demons could potentially pop into his house. But outside on his deck, warning systems, traps, and a couple of lethal countermeasures ensured that no uninvited visitor made it to the bulletproof, fireproof, and magic-proof sliding glass door. Not in one piece, anyway.

They'd never been activated, but as the wealthiest, most powerful, openly demon tech giant, he had a lot of enemies. From religious zealots and demon-haters to jealous rivals and political schemers, his human detractors were constant threats.

Then there were the demons. Since most of his company's products were developed to detect their presence, kill them, or trap their souls, he was generally hated and feared by underworlders.

The only people he didn't worry about were the angels. They allowed him to exist as a useful idiot as long as he toed the demons-are-bad line and created weapons to use against them. An Archangel named Gabriel even checked in on him every couple of years to make sure he hadn't gone evil or some shit.

The suppressant will kill you.

Yeah, yeah, back to that.

The deck door slid open, and he stepped into a blast of warm air. A second stab of arousal went through his groin, but this time, it was accompanied by a jolt of pain. As the door closed behind him, he reached into his pocket for his injector pen.

When his fingers touched the smooth plastic surface, he hesitated.

This, his sixth injection in a row, would halt the sex pangs for approximately three and a half hours. The next one would be effective for three hours. The next, two and a half. And so on, losing about half an hour per dose until they stopped working, and pain and nausea forced him to find relief with a female.

If he didn't, he'd die.

According to his uncle, he was dying right now. Eidolon told him to stop the injections immediately, but that would mean finding release multiple times a day.

He didn't have time for that shit.

Another spear of arousal stabbed him in his cock and balls before some invisible vise grabbed his sac and twisted it so hard he nearly passed out on the hardwood floor. He staggered to the couch and braced himself against it while he caught his breath.

He needed sex.

Or a shot.

Either way, this couldn't wait.

Gradually, the pain eased, leaving a heavy, pulsing need spreading through his pelvis. He eyed the delicate, ornate jade vase on the other side of the room, and his cock swelled, practically pointing at it.

He groaned through another wave of pain. When it retreated, his need had doubled, and his dick felt like it was on fire.

"Masumi," he croaked.

A stream of pearly liquid bubbled from the vase's narrow, phallic mouth and flowed to the floor, where it took the shape of a slinky, bronze-skinned succubus wrapped in a sheer ruby shawl and nothing else.

She shoved her waist-length black hair away from her face, her dark, almond-shaped eyes, tilted up at the corners, wide with surprise.

"I didn't expect your summons so soon. You usually run the full course of injections before seeking my services." Her husky voice conveyed concern as she glided toward him, her curvy hips swaying hypnotically. "You don't look well."

Clenching his jaw, he rode out another round of his genitals being squashed in a clamp. The pain was enough to make his vision go dark for a few heartbeats, and then Masumi's warm body eased up to him, her hands working the fly of his pants.

As a species of demon created to service Seminus demons, she sensed his need as if it were hers. Her very existence relied on sexual exchanges with Sems, so she went eagerly, *hungrily*, to her knees in front of him.

Her warm mouth took him in, and instant, hot pleasure shot through his body.

Followed by dark, twisted self-loathing.

He hated sex. He hated being aroused. He hated everything that made him a lust demon with needs that took priority over everything.

Like his little brother's safety.

Agony ripped into his chest like claws, and he tore away from Masumi. Panting and trembling, he scrounged for the injector pen.

Masumi's hand came down on his wrist as his fingers closed around the device.

"You don't need that." She caught his earlobe with her teeth and nipped him before licking the sting away. "I'm here. Let me ease you."

"I'm fine," he gritted, his body reacting to her breathy words and warm heat even as his mind screamed to get away. "I'm sorry I bothered you." His hand shook so badly that he barely managed to pop the cap off the injector.

"Stryke—"

"Go!"

With an angry, frustrated snarl, he jabbed the needle into his thigh and flopped back against the couch. Relief came quickly as the solution streamed through his veins to all the parts of his body that needed the chemical hit an orgasm would normally provide.

Masumi's curses echoed in his ear as she dematerialized back into her vase. She was pissed, and he couldn't blame her. He wasn't worried about her getting what she needed to survive, though. Her vase's twin, her second home, resided at the compound shared by his brothers Rade and Blade, and his cousins Mace and Sabre. Between the four males, she got a lot of action, and they didn't have to waste time looking for partners several times a day.

Not that all of them considered the pursuit of females wasted time. Mace definitely enjoyed the hunt for sex. According to Masumi, he only summoned her a couple of times a week, and half the time when he did, it was to join him and another female.

Snow swirled against the windows, giving him something besides Masumi to focus on as the meds took effect. He breathed a sigh of relief as his blood shot back up to his brain, and he reached functional status again.

Damn. Those injections were a miracle.

Maybe Eidolon's prognosis was wrong. Perhaps the lab had gotten Stryke's blood mixed up with someone else's.

And maybe he was a fucking idiot in denial.

His uncle wasn't one to screw up. And *something* had caused the symptoms that had forced Stryke to seek medical help. So, yeah, it was certainly possible that the injections were harming him, but his pride had prevented him from conceding the possibility to Eidolon.

Whatever. It was a problem to solve. And Stryke loved to solve problems because he was really, really good at it.

Goal in mind, his thoughts spinning with theories and calculations, he showered, threw on a pair of sweatpants and a T-shirt, and headed to his private laboratory. Before he got there, he stopped in the kitchen to grab a ham sandwich—just bread and meat. Condiments were a waste of time, and food was nothing more than fuel. Taste wasn't a consideration.

The hidden panel in his living room slid open at his approach, revealing a metal staircase. He took the steps two at a time and hit the bottom, landing with a bounce.

He loved it down here. It was a space full of high-tech equipment where he could do anything he wanted without scrutiny or explanation.

Here, he created and destroyed. Invented and tested. Here, he was a god.

He was a god at StryTech, too, but there were no interruptions here, and he didn't have to explain himself to anyone.

Inhaling the comforting scents of sterile cleaners, chemical concoctions, and cedar chips, he walked past whiteboards covered in hastily scrawled equations, a bank of computers, and a rat in an enormous cage.

"Hey, Squeaker." He took a peanut from the bowl next to the cage and tossed it to the sleek albino rodent. "No mazes for you today."

The rat, the last survivor of the batch of twenty rats he'd rescued from StryTech's labs, absconded with the legume into the little cardboard cave he'd made for himself. Squeaker was the only one Stryke had named, and even then, he hadn't done it until the rat was the only one left after the others had died of old age.

But this guy kept on keeping on, aided by one of StryTech's anti-aging test formulas and Stryke's ability to optimize bodily functions.

He sank into one of the computer chairs and brought up the formula for his sex inhibitor. Maybe he could make it safer if he adjusted or tweaked it a little.

"*None of these inhibitors, not even mine, are meant for regular use,*" Eidolon had said before they hung up. "*Orgasms produce chemicals in our bodies that keep us alive. The inhibitors mimic the chemicals but can't completely replicate them. Without regular sex to fill in the gaps, your body will break down.*"

"*Is it reversible?*"

"*Maybe. But we won't know until you stop using them and give your body a chance to heal.*"

"*Can't you heal me?*"

"*Not from this. I can't replicate the chemicals either.*"

Maybe his uncle couldn't replicate them, but Stryke could. He could try, anyway. And there was no reason to think he'd fail. He rarely failed at anything.

You failed your brother.

Yes, he had. And because of that, he'd dedicated himself to protecting others from evil demons. He'd built an empire and had become the richest, most notorious person on the planet. He was as powerful as any president, king, or supreme leader of any country in the human realm.

And all it had cost him was his entire family.

Cyan stood in the middle of her living room, staring at the boxes piled next to the door.

Shanea's boxes.

On one of the shelves, a selfie of Cyan and Shan at an office party looked back at her. Behind them, her fiancé, Draven, photobombed them with a goofy face.

Fresh pain sliced through Cyan's heart. She missed them both so much.

She smiled sadly at another reminder, a holoimage of Cyan, Shanea, and Xoei at brunch at their favorite Parisian restaurant. Next to that, hanging on the wall, was a picture of Cyan and Shan at Disney World.

And next to that…

Cyan went cold. Her inspiration board, a four-foot by four-foot corkboard she'd had since high school, hung there, mocking her with pictures of Stryke and articles about his company, inventions, and success.

She'd idolized him once. She'd felt a connection to his drive and curious mind. She'd wanted to be as notable in her field of work as he was in his. And it didn't hurt that he was one of the most gorgeous males she'd ever seen.

Then, within a matter of months, her parents, Shan, and Draven had all died—victims of Stryke's inventions. And when he was asked to speak publicly about the incident at DART that'd killed three people, including Shan and Draven, he'd basically said that accidents were bound to happen and, overall, the benefits of the weapons outweighed the deaths of a couple of demons.

A couple of demons.

Fuck The Aegis. Fuck StryTech. Fuck everything.

Furious, her eyes burning with unshed tears, she tore down the board and smashed it against the wall. Beat it until the cork shattered and the drywall dented.

Why, why, *why* did Shanea have to die?

Hurling the board's skeletal remains to the floor, she threw herself onto the couch and buried her face in her hands. She wanted to cry, but there was nothing left. So much had gone wrong. Her best friends were dead, her enthusiasm for her job was just as dead, and she'd been a jackass to her boss.

And a *vacation* wouldn't fix any of it.

Someone knocked on the door, and she ignored it for a moment, content to dwell in her pity party. But the knock came again, harder and faster. Both annoyed and grateful for the interruption, she glanced over at the security monitor screen on the wall next to the gas fireplace.

Kynan's daughter stood outside her door, waving at the camera. Weird. She hadn't seen Dawn in months.

"Door," she called out. "Open."

The lock on the door clicked, and Dawn entered.

"Hey." The dark-haired, blue-eyed female was the spitting image of her father, although she'd gotten her mother's slight build and sense of humor. "I'm sorry I didn't comms you first."

Suspicion slithered through Cyan, and she narrowed her eyes at the other female. "Did your dad send you?"

Dawn sauntered inside, her form-fitting black jeans and strategically slashed emerald silk tank top revealing more skin than her father would have liked. "He has no idea I'm here. Why?"

"He wants to send me on an assignment, and I refused. Rudely."

Dawn laughed. "It's good for him to not always get his way."

Maybe, but he hadn't seemed to appreciate it. "I should probably apologize anyway." Cyan gestured to the kitchen, where Shanea's teapot sat on the stove, collecting dust. "Would you like a glass of wine? Or tea?"

Please, don't say tea. She didn't know why she'd even asked. She wasn't sure she could make it without breaking down.

"Nah, I can only stay for a minute." Dawn held out the bag in her hand. "I wanted to bring you this."

"What is it?" Cyan stood to take the sparkly white gift bag.

Dawn hesitated and then quietly said, "It was a gift from Shanea."

Cyan froze, her fingers clenching the handles tightly. "I don't understand."

"It's your maid of honor gift." Dawn smiled sadly. "She asked me to keep it so you wouldn't see it."

Cyan's legs buckled, and she collapsed back onto the sofa. "Damn."

Dawn sank into the chair next to her and placed a comforting hand on Cyan's knee. "How are you doing? Is there anything I can do?"

Sure, there was. "You can destroy The Aegis and StryTech for me," she muttered as she peered into the bag.

Dawn snorted. "I'd love to."

Surprised, Cyan looked up at her friend. "Really? I mean, The Aegis, yeah. Filthy demon-slaying scumbags. But StryTech? Isn't Stryke your cousin?"

"Sabre is my cousin. Stryke is Sabre's cousin, though. I can't stand him. Stryke, not Sabre." She shifted in her seat, settling in a little. "He's always been a pompous jackass. And his demon-detection software has made my life hell. I wanted to work in human hospitals all my life, but because of him, I can't."

As much as Cyan wanted to jump aboard Dawn's Stryke-hating train, she wasn't sure how Stryke was connected to her friend's career limitations. "Why not?"

Dawn idly plucked at a frayed thread on the armrest that used to give Shan fits. "The DeTecht scanners pick up my Soulshredder genetics, and pretty much every hospital on the planet has installed them. Hell, I can hardly go anywhere. Jessica and I tried to go to a movie last weekend, and I couldn't get in because the theater had a demon detector at the front door."

"Oh, damn. That sucks."

Dawn crossed her legs, her jeans whispering softly against the chair. "I've begged Stryke to develop something to disguise my DNA, but he refuses. Says he can't risk that kind of technology getting into the wrong hands. As if I'd let that happen."

"What an asshole." Cyan put the bag on the cushion next to her. "Why does your family put up with him?"

"They don't." Dawn fetched a tube of lip balm from her purse. "He's estranged from everyone."

Cyan knew he wasn't close with his family, but she hadn't known it was *that* bad. "Your dad seems to have a good relationship with him."

Dawn shrugged. "I don't think it's personal, though. It's more of a working relationship. DART benefits from a lot of StryTech inventions."

So did DART's rivals. How could Stryke arm everyone? Weren't there laws governing the arming of both sides of a conflict?

"Working with StryTech is actually the assignment I turned down." Cyan reached over and ran her finger over the gift bag's silky handle. Before Dawn, Shanea had probably been the last person to touch it. "Kynan asked me to work with a team of StryTech people to develop a new weapon that would also capture souls."

"Wow. That sounds like a great opportunity," Dawn said. "Why did you say no?"

"Why?" she asked incredulously. "Stryke's last anti-demon weapon killed Shan."

"I know." Dawn finished with her lip balm and popped the cap back onto the tube. "And now you have a chance to help prevent that from happening again."

"Prevent it? How? This weapon isn't a counter to The Aegis's Smiter."

"No, but any new weapon in DART's arsenal is something The Aegis doesn't have. DART will become even more valuable to the world. Right now, they're under the microscope because of what happened with Draven. DART could even be dissolved. With a powerful new weapon that would allow any agent to capture souls, something The Aegis can't do, DART becomes indispensable."

Most of what Dawn said after Draven's name was lost on Cyan. "Excuse me. '*After what happened with Draven?*'"

Dawn gave her an are-you-kidding look. "Come on, Cyan. He did kill a lot of innocent people."

Cyan nearly choked on her anger. How could Dawn take The Aegis's side?

"He killed them because The Aegis killed his fiancée!" She shoved to her feet, knocking the gift bag over and onto the rug. "It wasn't unprovoked—"

"I know." Dawn's voice was annoyingly calm as she fetched the bag from the floor. She was so much like her father. "Look, Cyan…" She trailed off, shaking her head. "It's nothing."

"What? Tell me."

"It's just…I know I'm only a quarter Soulshredder, but it's enough. I can see your scars. I can see how much pain you're in. But you're taking it out on the wrong people. If you work with StryTech, you'll kill two hellrats with one club. You'll help DART become invaluable and can make Stryke's life miserable. Win-win."

"Doesn't feel like a win," Cyan muttered.

Dawn gestured to the gift bag. "You gonna open it?"

Cyan looked down at the sparkly tissue and ornate bag that so perfectly fit Shanea's personality.

How could she be gone? And so soon after Cyan had lost her parents to a different StryTech device. Granted, her father's death had been an accident caused by a faulty circuit in a StryTech-designed security panel, and her mother had died of grief, but still.

"I can't," she said. "Not yet. It probably sounds weird, but once I see it, I'll never get anything from her again."

Dawn nodded like she understood and started for the door. "I have to go, but I'm sure I'll see you at Runa's birthday get-together. Dad's always looking for excuses to throw office parties."

That was true. Kynan Morgan loved a good celebration at work. He said it helped boost morale and gave everyone a chance to catch up on things happening in other departments. He even invited everyone from all the DART branches. Most couldn't make it because of time zone differences around the world, but it was always cool to catch up with those who could attend.

Dawn gave her a quick hug. "If you need anything, let me know. I'm serious, okay? I'm not just saying that to be nice. Call me."

She promised she would. After Dawn left, Cyan looked over at the pictures of Shan again. She'd deserved so much better than how she'd died. Maybe Dawn was right. Perhaps working on the weapon project would be an opportunity to do something positive for DART and give Shan's death some meaning.

The gift bag felt as heavy as her heart as she placed it on her dining room table. Later. She'd open it later. After DART had taken possession of the weapon, perhaps.

Which meant she needed to make that happen.

She used her mind to turn on her computer because the first step was always research. She wanted to know everything she could about Stryke and his company—beyond what she already knew.

A basic query of Stryke's name turned up an overwhelming number of photos, articles, and magazine cover shots, including the time he'd been *TIME* magazine's Person of the Year.

Boy, that had caused a meltdown among the humans. Calling a demon a *person*? And giving him that kind of notoriety? People had lost their shit, and *TIME* almost didn't recover.

She used her mind to scroll through more of the media frenzy, and there he was as Most Eligible Bachelor from multiple organizations for multiple years. *Underworld News Today* called him, "The perfect combination of human good looks and demon ingenuity."

Admittedly, the guy *was* drop-dead gorgeous. But then, all Seminus demons were. As incubi, they were designed with females in mind, from their effortless athletic builds and model good looks to their skill in bed and sexual pheromones that heightened female arousal.

And Stryke...he was even more striking than most. His angular, tan features could have been carved with a razor blade, and his dark eyes reminded her of black diamonds: hard, cold, and brilliant. She'd always wondered what, if anything, made them soften.

She had a feeling nothing could soften that male.

And things that didn't soften and bend...broke.

Chapter 4

He'd fallen asleep. On the floor of his lab.

Stryke had never just…fallen asleep.

Groggily, he sat up, unable to remember anyth—

Suddenly, stabbing pains pierced every organ, and his cock felt so hard he thought it might crack right down the middle.

Gasping in agony, he rolled onto his hands and knees. Shit. It felt like he was dying. He could practically hear Eidolon saying, "*I told you so.*"

Panting, he reached up and fumbled on the counter for his injector pen. There. *Yes.*

He jabbed himself in the thigh, and as the pain melted away, he collapsed onto the floor again to catch his breath.

His comms vibrated, and he groaned. He was probably super late to a meeting.

Yep, it was Kalis, wondering where he was because she had a million messages, and someone was waiting to see him. Instead, he was lying on his back on the cold concrete floor, recovering from a marathon of calculations, research, and painful sex pangs he'd chased away with a drug that was killing him.

Coffee. He needed coffee. And a shower.

And sex.

He snarled at that last thought. But it was true. The intervals between injections were growing shorter and shorter, and he needed to reset his body with the real thing.

Soon, you won't need the injections at all because you'll be dead.

The thought didn't upset him as much as it probably should.

Cursing, he forced himself to trudge up the stairs to the kitchen, where the automatic coffee pot had brewed his favorite blend. He poured a cup, grabbed Masumi's vase, and headed to the shower.

The shower and sex were both cold and fast, and he felt better afterward, but still dirty.

He wished he wasn't aware of how messed up that was. He also wished there was some sort of cure, some kind of magical mathematical equation that would help unlink his trauma from his sex drive.

There *was* one thing he could try. His brother Rade could take a little walk inside his head and snip things while healing others. His uncle Wraith could do that too. But if there was one thing Stryke hated more than fucking someone, it was someone fucking with his brain.

He got to the office an hour late, and Kalis was waiting for him, her expression a mask of annoyance. The tiny, black horns, usually hidden in her auburn hair, popped out a couple of inches.

"There you are." She gestured to his desk, where a steaming cup of coffee waited for him. "As usual, the messages on your pad are arranged in both order of urgency and by timestamp. And Ms. Cyanide is waiting to see you."

He looked up sharply. "Cyanide? From DART?"

"Yes. Kynan sent her per your agreement."

Interesting. DART's senior technomancer was known throughout the cybersecurity community. A rare Cyberis demon, she was one of the most powerful Mancers in the world and, unlike so many of her kind, didn't use her abilities for evil.

That Stryke knew of, anyway.

Technically, Cyberis demons were banned from the human realm because of the potential of them abusing their powers. Their ability to hack, operate, and reprogram electronic devices with their minds meant they could shut down vehicles in motion. They could drop planes from the sky. Military experts feared they could even control nuclear weapons. They were also capable of getting past DNA scanners undetected by simply deleting their DNA from the software as they walked by, making them even more dangerous.

Stryke employed a Cyberis technomancer himself, but he had also taken precautions against their particular magic. He trusted his people, but he wasn't an idiot. Most demons were scum.

He wondered how Kynan was getting away with Cyanide's employment. Especially now, when the world was calling for more regulations, scrutiny, and oversight into companies and governments that employed underworlders.

He reached for the StryTech-branded coffee mug. "Send her in."

Kalis bowed shallowly and dematerialized.

A few moments later, the office elevator doors opened. A drop-dead gorgeous, silvery-white-haired female stepped out, her long, slender legs encased in dark, wide-leg pants that swung around a pair of black heels. The neckline of her gunmetal top dipped low enough to reveal a hint of cleavage and a chunky silver necklace with a deep amethyst pendant a shade or two lighter than her eyes.

She was stunning. Her race was known for its elfin good looks and gemstone eyes, but damn. She was something special.

He waited to acknowledge her until she'd crossed his office floor, her shoes making the tiles beneath them glow red with every step.

Red for demons, white for angels, blue for vampires, yellow for humans.

"Hello, Cyanide."

Her already cold eyes chilled even more. She wasn't happy to be here, was she?

"It's Cyan." One eyebrow arched as she glanced at the floor. "I see one of my brethren designed a species-detection floor system. Clever." Lifting her head, she swept her short, messy hair out of her face. "But too limited in scope. It only identifies demons, angels, humans, and vampires. You need it to identify half-breeds, shifters, and weres too."

She was right, but the technomancer who'd designed the system couldn't get what Cyan suggested to work. "If you think you can do better, be my guest."

"I'm not here to fix your employee's incompetence."

Incompetence?

She wandered around as if she owned the place, checking out the view, the lab equipment, the computers. Looking everywhere but at him. Finally, she stopped in front of one of his whiteboards.

"Oh, my gods." She moved closer to the board. "Are these really calculations for an invisible umbrella?"

Surprise filtered through him. Most people wouldn't have understood his chicken scratch. "They are."

She nodded thoughtfully. "Do you plan to enchant an object that will project the shield? Or will you use an electronic chip and technomancy to operate it?"

"That'll be for R&D to figure out."

"Of course." She took a step back from the board and cast a final, cursory glance around the office as if committing it to memory. "Now, if you'll just point me to the lab where I'll be working, I'll get caught up with your team."

"First," he said, "I want you to tell me why you're here."

She pivoted sharply on her heels. "Excuse me?"

"You're putting out vibes that could freeze a frost demon. So, why are you here?"

Her chin came up, and her haughty gaze slid right down her perky nose at him. He might as well have been a cockroach in her kitchen.

"I'm here because Kynan asked me to be."

"So, you're prepared to work closely with me?" Hopefully, minus the attitude.

Her mouth fell open, but she caught herself quickly, snapping her jaw shut so tight she had to speak between clamped teeth.

"I'll be working with you?" If he'd thought she'd seemed unhappy before, she looked ready to spit hellfire-tempered nails now. "I assumed I'd mostly be working with a team."

He smiled, enjoying her discomfort. So few things amused him anymore. "I'm *very* hands-on." Let her take that however she wanted. She knew he was a sex demon, after all.

"Thank you for the warning," she said, her voice as biting as an arctic chill. "Now, I'd like to get started, if you don't mind."

"Eager, huh? I like that." Standing, he gestured to the elevator. "I'll show you to the lab where you'll be working." He came around the desk and didn't wait for her to catch up before starting across the considerable expanse of floor. He loved his giant office. It made people feel small. Put them off balance. "You should feel lucky. I never personally give tours of my facility."

"Oh, so people get to enjoy the tours usually."

Damn, she was salty. No longer amused, he swung around to her.

"Why don't you come clean?" he said. "Why are you here, and what's your issue with me? Spit it out. I don't have time for bullshit."

She strode past him like *she* owned the building. He'd never met a Cyberis demon who didn't have arrogance flowing through their veins. Clearly, she was no exception.

"I'm here to ensure this project's success. But you're right, I'm not thrilled." She turned back to him at the elevator. "Your products have caused a lot of pain and suffering."

"Ah."

The elevator doors slid open, and she stepped inside, standing in the middle of the lift while she waited for him.

"*Ah?*" She glared at him as he entered. "What's that supposed to mean?"

The doors closed with a near-silent *whoosh*. "It means that if you don't like me now, things aren't going to get much better." He reached for the control panel to engage the symbol that would take them to the lab level, but before he could touch it, the symbol lit up, and the lift dropped smoothly down the shaft.

Cyan stared dead ahead, all smug and shit, as if using one's mind to operate an elevator instead of your hand was impressive or something.

You're just jealous.

Yeah, probably. But jealous or not, he had a feeling this collaboration would be as disastrous as the personnel exchange DART had done with The Aegis. Kynan would owe him.

Big time.

Cyan had known she wouldn't like Stryke.

But she'd been unprepared for exactly *how much* she didn't like him. The whole thing about never meeting your heroes was one hundred percent true.

He was arrogant, rude, dismissive, and…the most beautiful male she'd ever seen. The bastard.

He wore his clothes, professional and tailored for his athletic build, with casual grace. The top buttons on his burgundy shirt were undone, the sleeves rolled up to reveal his *dermoire*, the dark symbols flexing over ropy muscles. Shrewd black eyes and short, ruffled black hair complemented his tan skin and rugged face.

He might be wearing expensive clothes and look like he'd been born in an office building, but she could picture him in the fighting gear his brother, Blade, wore too.

Dammit, she had to stop picturing him at all. He might be gorgeous, powerful, and brilliant, but so was Satan.

So, yeah, Stryke was awful, but she fell in love with his facility. She'd always wanted to see it, and it did *not* disappoint.

The sprawling campus stretched beyond the luxurious high-rise offices to several ultra-modern outbuildings. Stryke didn't take her to all of them, merely pointed out where they were, what they did, and why she wasn't allowed in any of them. Mostly, it boiled down to need-to-know, and as it turned out, Cyan didn't need to know jack shit.

But Stryke sure knew how to take care of his employees. Throughout the facility, there were cafés, break rooms with showers and cots for naps, and even a daycare for demonlings, and a separate, smaller child care center and school for human children. The hundred-thousand-square-foot Commons Mall boasted several eateries, shops, and even a beauty salon and grocery store.

Apparently, very few humans worked at StryTech, and those who did, lived in specially built, highly secure campus apartments with walking trails and one of two gyms on the StryTech grounds. Sydney was relatively safe for a demon city on a demon continent, but few humans wanted to live outside StryTech walls in a city populated almost entirely by underworlders.

"This is kind of amazing," she murmured as they passed a crystal fountain depicting a battle between an angel and a demon, the story playing out in moving animations on the surface of the water. Across the stone walkway, a sparkly, rainbow-colored food truck called *A Slice of Heaven* served generous helpings of various cakes. Next to that, a black-and-red truck called *The Devil's Food* offered spicy, traditional demon dishes made with Sheoul-grown ingredients.

"It didn't look like this when I bought it." He gestured at Hawking Tower. "I acquired headquarters first, and then I spent four years building the rest."

"I remember," she mused. "You bought the first building when you were twenty-two. You said you got it dirt cheap because, at the time, Australia was practically worthless after being ceded to Sheoul. You named it after Stephen Hawking and then named every new building after famous scientists."

He gave her a surprised look. "How do you know that?"

Heat bloomed in her cheeks, which was ridiculous. It wasn't as if she'd stalked him or anything.

"That article a few years back in *Forbes* magazine. You gave them a tour of the new, expanded campus."

"Ah, that." He ushered her inside the Curie Research Center, one of four laboratory facilities on-site. "I had to show the world that what I built wasn't a human meat processing plant or something. Didn't stop the tabloids and conspiracy nuts from saying it, though."

She barely heard him, too focused on the magnificence of the hyper-secure biology and chemical labs. The security was insane, with layers of safeguards like machines that could detect weapons and evil DNA, and Senchi demons who could sense emotions and thoughts.

Thankfully, she'd stopped imagining throat-punching Stryke a while ago. Still, the Senchi demons watched her with suspicion as Stryke took her through a misty portal in the high-tech center designed to kill all harmful bacteria. When they stepped out, she came to a shocked, dead stop, her mouth gaping in awe.

For so many reasons.

The first? The person who greeted them…wasn't a person. It was a robotic replica of Stryke, its movements and voice so lifelike she felt the urge to kick it in the dick.

"Welcome to StryTech's engineering facility," it said. "Behind the glass wall, you must wear hazmat gear. If you have any questions, don't hesitate to ask someone else."

With that, the AI bot turned around and strode off.

"Wow," she said. "That thing really captured your sparkling personality."

Amusement turned Stryke's expression from serious to almost playful. Like a cat that wasn't ready to catch the mouse yet.

"My people worked hard to capture just the right amount of dismissiveness." He moved on to a laboratory on the far side of the space. "Let's meet your team."

She tried not to marvel at how good his ass looked in those black slacks as she followed him to a small area where two people, both humanoid and male, were programming a 3D printer, which was, of course, the most cutting-edge technology available.

The dark-skinned guy cast a glance over his shoulder at Stryke. "We should have a mockup of the new weapon's basic design in a few minutes."

"Excellent." Stryke gestured to her, his *dermoire* rippling around his forearm. The scientist in her would love to study that thing. See how it worked. The female in her appreciated how it flexed smoothly over hard muscle and veins. Dammit, she shouldn't be admiring *anything* about him. "This is Cyan. She's here to make sure we don't fuck up DART's precious baby. Cyan, this is Dr. Dakarai. He's the team's engineer." He cocked his head at the blond guy who didn't look old enough to legally drink alcohol in many countries. "That's Dracx. He's a metallurgist on temporary loan from Project 6hell. He's helping figure out what materials will work for what we need."

Dr. Dakarai nodded politely. "Given your species," he said to her, "I assume you are a technomancer."

"I am."

The doctor nodded. "I'm a lion shifter, and Dracx over there is a Geomorph."

Wow. She had to keep herself from staring. Geomorphs, demons originally created using elements from both the human and demon realms, could morph into any type of naturally occurring metal, mineral, or stone. They were rare, most not even of pure blood anymore. Over the millennia, they'd bred with humans and either weakened or lost their abilities. They even claimed their souls were now human. Cyan had no idea if that was true or not. But then she didn't really care.

"What's Project 6hell?"

Dr. Dakarai and Dracx exchanged uneasy glances, but Stryke merely eyed her as if deciding what to say.

"It's our newest undertaking," he said. And didn't that just clarify everything? "It's pronounced *shell* but it's spelled with the number six instead of an S. Makes sense if you know what it is." He looked around the room. "Where's Parker?"

"Getting coffee."

He nodded. "Parker McDavid is the team's weapons and designs expert." The comms on his wrist beeped, and he gave it a quick glance. "I have to go." Pausing, he cast Cyan a lingering look, and she swore one corner of his mouth tipped up in an evil smirk for just a fraction of a second. "Cyan will be team leader."

She wasn't sure why the announcement earned the malevolent amusement pouring off Stryke in waves, but whatever. He was a weirdo.

"I hope to see a lot of progress next time we meet," he said, and with that, he took off.

As soon as the door closed, Dracx gave Cyan a look of pure sympathy. "Better you than me."

"Or me," Dr. Dakarai muttered.

Confused, she dragged her gaze away from the framed photos and bios of famous scientists on the walls. Someone had drawn a goatee and devil horns on the picture of Stryke.

"What's so bad about being team leader?" she asked.

"Nothing," Dracx said. "As long as you don't mind daily meetings with the boss. Starting this Friday."

She blinked. "*Daily*? That's ridiculous. Weekly should suffice, if not monthly."

Dracx gave her an *exactly* gesture with his long, spindly fingers. "Now you see the problem. No one wants to give him daily updates."

"He's usually cool with techmails or comms meetings, though," Dr. Dakarai said. "But if he's *really* invested—or irritated—he'll make you meet him in his office."

"And, dude," Dracx said, "he's invested in this. New weapon for DART? Get ready to spend a lot of time with him."

Cyan will be team leader.

Said with an evil smirk. And now she knew why.

The *bastard*.

Chapter 5

Gabriel was not a happy angel.

As an Archangel, he should be riding high at the top of the Heavenly food chain. For most of all existence, Archangels had been in charge. Sure, some of the other Orders had taken the reins, but without exception, they'd failed miserably, and the Archangels always had to swoop in and save the day.

But Archangels weren't in charge anymore, and it didn't look like they'd be saving anything anytime soon. Not even their own hides. Not when they were imprisoned inside their minds.

But Gabriel wasn't as lucky as his brethren, who hung in stasis chambers, their minds locking them in a fantasy existence and unable to fight against reality. No, the Thrones were literally keeping him on a short leash, beaten regularly as he awaited trial for his part in helping destroy Sheoul-gra and changing the course of all mankind.

"Hurry up." Poria, a dark-haired Throne draped in obnoxious jeweled robes, tugged on his chain, nearly knocking him off balance as they mounted the steps to Throne Hall. "Zaphkiel isn't very patient."

"Yeah, well, Zaphkiel is—"

The fucker zapped him with a bolt of glittery lightning so hot it made Gabriel's skin steam.

"I have permission to fry you into next century if you don't behave."

"Take off these restraints," Gabriel growled, "and we'll see who gets fried."

The reminder that Gabriel, an angel of vengeance and death, was a hundred times more powerful than Poria did not sit well, and Gabriel rode another stab of electricity.

Poria had better hope Gabriel's sentence for helping Azagoth destroy Sheoul-gra was a long one because the second he was freed, he was going after the bastard.

Poria paraded Gabriel through the halls, where other Thrones mocked and scorned him. One even spit on him as if it was medieval Europe, and he was being taken to the headsman for a public execution.

Gabriel added all of them to his revenge list for when he was released from whatever punishment they'd give him. Assuming he was found guilty. But he doubted that would happen. He was a senior Archangel, chosen by the Creator himself to serve as one of Heaven's elite warriors. Archangel orders came to them through Metatron, and even the Angelic High Court wouldn't take a soldier of his caliber out of service for long. Not when Armageddon was nigh.

Nine hundred-plus years nigh, which sounded like forever to beings with short lifespans. But a thousand years was a flash in time for angels and many demons. A snap of the fingers. A flap of the wings.

He moved with purpose, spine rigid and expression neutral, but he committed every face to memory as Poria perp-walked him to Zaphkiel's doorway. As they approached, the cloudy, opaque opening vibrated, turning glittery before disappearing. They entered Zaph's office, a remarkably stark and boring white room that sometimes had furniture, other times not. Today, not.

Zaphkiel stood in the center of the featureless white space, controlled by his mind, so he could have chosen to make it a luxurious palace or a wilderness retreat. But nope. The angel's office space was as unimaginative as he was.

Thrones were so. Damned. Boring.

He looked over at the Celestial standing off to the side, his pale lavender wings tucked behind him, his hands clasped in front of his blue military tunic.

"Hey, Hut," Gabriel said. "Been a while."

Hutriel, a senior Virtue and an angel of punishment, appeared bored. Or maybe it was just the perpetual stick he always had up his ass. His nickname, Rod of God, fit him. "Not long enough, scumbag."

"Aw. You haven't changed at all. Still a rod."

"Enough," Zaphkiel barked. "Gabriel. Thank you for coming."

"Of course," Gabriel said. "How could I turn down your invitation? Oh, right. I couldn't. What the fuck do you want?"

"Your Ordeal begins tomorrow."

Well, if that didn't just drop a wedge of ice into his belly. Gabriel was confident he'd get a slap on the wrist. But he'd expected the trial to begin later. Much later.

"Why tomorrow?"

"Because the sooner you're dealt with, the sooner all angels will accept that the Thrones are now in charge."

Ah. So, not all of angeldom was happy with how the Thrones had wrested control from the Archangels.

"Did the public catch wind of the fact that you've imprisoned every Archangel and are harnessing their powers to keep Reaver shackled?"

The expression on Zaph's face said that, no, the general population wasn't aware of that little detail. "Reaver doesn't need to be shackled anymore. He's immobilized with grief."

The reminder made another block of ice drop into Gabriel's stomach, splashing acid all the way to his heart. Reaver, the only Radiant in existence, an angel of extraordinary power, had been rendered comatose after his mate, Harvester, had been driven through an inoperative portal.

"If you hadn't staged a coup and shaken Heaven all the way to its pearly white gates, that wouldn't have happened."

"We didn't force Harvester to enter the Gaiaportal. She made that choice on her own."

"You think she *chose* death?"

"We don't know that she's dead. Just that her mate bond with Reaver was broken."

"And that her blood rained down on the Temple Mount. Doesn't sound survivable to me." Gabriel rolled his shoulders and worked out a kink in his neck. "So, why am I really here? You didn't drag me down here just to tell me the trial starts tomorrow."

Zaphkiel strolled over to one of the white walls. As he approached, the wall turned transparent, revealing a view of the pristine, Heavenly city of Catali below. Sitting on a vast, verdant plateau like a crown of gold, ivory, and gemstones, Catali shone under an azure sky. Glistening bubbles—angelic homes—floated over ivory structures below that contained more homes, offices, and whatever else anyone wanted them for.

And threaded between the structures, rippling streams and frothy waterfalls flowed through tranquil forests made of all the trees found on Earth. It was a reminder to angels that Heaven belonged to humans as well, and angels were obligated to pass through the Heavenly membrane to the Other Side, the First Heavenly plane, where the humans resided. Keep up appearances and all that.

Zaphkiel clasped his hands behind his back and gazed outside. "What do you know about the Gehennaportal?"

Gabriel blinked at the unexpected question. He'd been sure this meeting would be about his trial, not about the Gaiaportal's evil twin.

"I don't know anything. Why don't you ask whoever built it?" he asked, knowing full well who had constructed the thing.

The Throne didn't seem to have caught Gabriel's sarcasm. "Satan is locked up until Armageddon, so that's a non-starter."

"And I still don't understand how I'm supposed to know anything about it."

Zaphkiel swung slowly around to face Gabriel. "Azagoth used the same materials and methods as Satan used for the Gehennaportal to construct Sheoul-gra. Since you were involved in that project, surely you know something about the portal."

No, he didn't. Azagoth hadn't offered up any info, and Gabriel hadn't asked. The fine details of building a holding tank for demon souls hadn't interested him in the least.

"I know Thrones were in charge at the time of both portals' construction. How did you not work out a deal with Satan to give you its blueprints?" No wonder Thrones' reigns were short. They couldn't govern for shit, and most of the biggest disasters in the Earthly realm could be laid at their incompetent feet. "And why not just ask Azagoth what you need to know?"

"Because his realm is sealed off to us, and he doesn't seem inclined to answer our summons."

No, the Grim Reaper had never been eager to respond to Heavenly requests. It was why Gabriel had disguised himself as a lesser, disgruntled angel and communicated—secretly—with Azagoth for thousands of years. At first, it had been to keep an eye on him. But as Azagoth grew more powerful, Heaven had demanded more and more from him, while offering more and more restrictions. Gabriel's self-imposed watcher role had gradually shifted as corruption began to rot the Celestial ranks.

"Why do you need this information, anyway?" Gabriel asked.

Zaphkiel turned away from the window. "It's possible," he began, "that when Harvester went through the Gaiaportal and activated it, she activated its Hell-based counterpart as well. And I'm sure I don't have to tell you how bad that would be."

It would be *very* bad. Out of fear of what Reaver's twin, Revenant, the King of Hell, could do to Heaven, representatives from every Order had agreed to seal him inside Sheoul.

If he discovered that the Gehennaportal was open, he could escape and bring down the wrath of Hell inside Heaven itself.

Gabriel smiled as an opportunity beamed down on him like the Heavenly Father's Grace. "I could talk to Azagoth for you," he offered. "For a price." He winked at Hutriel. "I'll send Azagoth and Lilliana your best wishes while I'm there."

Outrage lit up both angels but for different reasons.

"You aren't in charge here," Zaphkiel snapped. "You will help us because it's the right thing to do."

"Go Team Heaven?" Gabriel laughed. "The Heaven that wants me to endure a sham of an Ordeal because you need someone to blame for Sheoul-gra's destruction? You want to humiliate me because you know I won't be found guilty. I'll be given a slap on the wrist, and the Thrones will look like fools."

There was no proof that Gabriel had helped Azagoth. He had, of course, but he hadn't known about Azagoth's ultimate, destructive goal. Gabriel had only intended to help Azagoth prevent angels from breaching Sheoul-gra and destroying him.

Which, really, was bad enough.

"Will you help or not, Gabriel? We don't need you so badly that we will agree to your blackmail. You'll do it or not. If you help us, it'll delay your Ordeal and might even create some goodwill in the eyes of the court."

Gabriel had already figured that out. He'd hoped to extract more from the Throne, such as making the Ordeal go away, but since it probably wouldn't be that big of a deal…sure, Gabriel would help. He actually *was* on Team Heaven, after all. The players might have changed, but the concept, the very existence of Heaven, would always stay true.

He opened his mouth to tell Zaph as much when a tremor shot up his body, rattling his bones and teeth.

Zaphkiel's eyes shot wide, and he reached out to steady himself against the wall as the building shook. "What the—?"

"Evil," Gabriel whispered. "That was a wave of malevolence. Something big just happened in Sheoul."

"I know," Zaph rasped, his face pale and expression panicked. "But what? What could have caused something so momentous that we felt it in Heaven's very heart?"

A shiver spread across Gabriel's skin. What, indeed.

Chapter 6

Stryke was horny as hell. Which meant he was pissed off and not in the mood for his first meeting with Cyan since she'd arrived on Tuesday. He hadn't even seen her. Well, he'd seen her from afar, walking with her team. And laughing. Like, genuine laughter, not the sarcastic kind she'd thrown his way.

Dr. Dakarai must be real fucking charming. Same with the team's weapons specialist and former SAS soldier, Parker McDavid. The muscle-bound werewolf seemed to hold her attention the most. Because of course.

Snarling, he refocused on the techmailed notes Cyan had sent a few minutes ago, probably hoping they'd suffice instead of a face-to-face meeting.

But no.

He wanted to see her face. He wanted to know what made her tick. What made her...*her.*

And, obviously, he wanted this information for professional reasons, not personal. He made a point to discover what made each of his employees, colleagues, and adversaries tick. He wanted to know their strengths, weaknesses, and damned IQs. If it could give him an advantage, he wanted it, right down to their grocery lists, bathroom schedules, and grade school report cards.

Dressed in black slacks, a lab coat, and a purple blouse unbuttoned just enough to reveal the smallest, tantalizing hint of cleavage, she arrived precisely on time. He liked that. He also liked how she exited the elevator and walked the intentionally uncomfortable distance with a confidence few managed. Even fewer maintained eye contact the entire way, but she locked gazes with him, and every step she took closer in her black high heels made his pulse race faster. She wouldn't be cowed by him, and she was putting him on notice.

Man, that was hot.

Both wildly aroused and annoyed, he shifted slightly to make room in his pants for his growing erection.

He'd need an injection *very* soon.

She stopped inches from his desk, close enough for him to catch a hint of her clean, almost metallic scent that intrigued him but which he couldn't quite place. A combination of copper and silver, maybe.

"I sent you detailed notes," she said. "I fail to see how meeting in person can add anything. If you had questions, you could have messaged back. You're wasting my time and yours with this power trip."

"That's what you think? That I'm on a power trip?"

"Among other things, yes."

"Meeting with my project leaders isn't about power. It's about nuances."

One delicate eyebrow cocked up. "Nuances?"

He gestured to the chair across the desk from him. "Have a seat and tell me why you don't have a design for the weapon's soul trap."

"I told you in the message."

"Tell me again."

A muscle in her jaw twitched as she struggled to stay calm. She didn't like being told what to do.

Nuance.

She didn't sit. "We're having difficulty developing a vessel that will fit inside the weapon's projectile and also have walls sufficiently thick to hold spells complex enough to contain powerful spirits. Structurally and magically, cylinders are far weaker than spheres."

"Why not use a sphere, then?"

"Because the projectile shaft is a narrow tube."

"So? Create a tiny sphere that will fit into the tube."

She shook her head. "We don't think it's possible to shrink a *decipula* down that much."

"I'm confident you'll find a way," he said. "Personally, I'd hand it off to the physics department and let them figure it out." He leaned back in his seat with a smile. "See? This is why we meet in person. Now, you have feedback to take to the team."

"You could have said the same thing in a message."

"But then I'd have missed your expression when I came up with an idea you hadn't thought of." He winked. "Nuance."

Her delicate snort of amusement made her breasts jiggle and his cock twitch in appreciation. He definitely needed that injection. He might even need to make it hurt, a little reminder that the alternative—actual sex—was a mental hit job and never worth the few moments of pleasure.

Never.

"You really are something," she said.

"Something good or something bad?"

"The context should give you a clue."

Snarky. He normally didn't put up with snark, but he was strangely enjoying their back-and-forth. Mainly because her irritation amused him. And she was about to get more irritated.

He threw up the 3D holoprojection of the rough weapon design she'd sent in the message earlier. "Has anyone on the team noticed the flaw in this?"

She scowled. "What flaw?"

He came to his feet and moved around the desk. He parked himself next to her, intentionally breaching her personal space. How would she react? Move away? Stand her ground? Hit him in the face?

He made a mental bet that she'd stand her ground while *thinking* of hitting him in the face. Reaching out, he rotated the projection ninety degrees, noting that Cyan had, indeed, remained stubbornly in place. She'd stiffened slightly, her jaw clenched tightly, but she hadn't moved away.

He pointed to the area near the crossbow's retention spring. "This won't work with the projectile you've designed." He tapped a symbol floating to the right of the projection, and the 3D design for the crossbow bolt appeared. He dragged it to the weapon and aligned the bolt with the barrel. "The bolt is too big at the base. It won't sit fully against the string, which could lead to a catastrophic failure."

Frowning, she leaned in, brushing against his arm with her shoulder. The neckline of her blouse gaped, and he got a stunning view of plump, creamy cleavage. Not that he was looking. It was just that he noticed everything. Like how the delicate vein in her throat pulsed at fifty-six beats per minute. And how her respirations became shallow and quick when he got close. And how her cheeks flushed pink at the possibility that she'd missed the problem he'd pointed out.

"It looks fine to me," she announced, a touch of defensiveness making her voice rise an octave.

"Are you an expert in crossbow anatomy?"

She turned to him, her taupe-colored lips so close to his he could feel the heat coming off them. "No. Are you?"

"I'm an expert in many things."

"Fine," she said tightly. "I'll let Dakarai and Parker know."

He was actually surprised that Parker had missed that detail. Maybe flirting with Cyan had gotten in the way of his competence.

"You'll also need to design a failsafe in the spell so that when the projectile seeks out the most severely wounded enemy, it doesn't zero in on an injured ally."

"Well, obviously," she said with a sniff, but he suspected she hadn't considered that.

"And—"

His desk comms beeped, and his assistant's voice rang out. "Mr. Stryke, your mother is on line two."

Stryke waved his hand in dismissal. "Tell her I'm busy."

"But, sir...this is her third call today."

"And for the third time, I'm busy."

"Yes, sir."

"Wow." Cyan turned away from the hologram. "You're turning your own mother away? For the third time today?"

"Yes, and it's none of your business, so drop it."

"Fair enough." She turned back to the design and then immediately swung back around to him. "No, wait. I know it's none of my business—"

"Exactly."

"—but I lost both of my parents, and I'd give anything to be able to talk to them just one more time. And here you are with a mother who, for some reason, wants to talk to you. You're estranged from your family, one of them is making an overture, and you're turning it down?"

"Yeah. You get all that from the tabloids?" Those things were the bane of his existence. "What do you know about my family?"

"I work with your brothers, Rade and Blade, and I know your mother. They're pretty damned tight. So, why does everyone walk on eggshells at the mere *mention* of your name?"

"Why do you even care?"

"Because I care about them. I was so inspired by—" She broke off in an angry huff. "Your mother's birthday party is tomorrow. You *are* coming, right?"

"Again, none of your business." He shut down the projector. He was done with this subject. Done with *her*. "Time for you to go."

"Finally." She grabbed her black-and-violet bag off the desk and flung it over her shoulder. "This meeting was pointless anyway, seeing as you only made me come up here for *nuances*." She marched to the elevator, pivoted, and shot him the finger. "How's that for nuance?" she called out as the door closed.

"You need to look up the definition of *nuance*," he shouted. That female was infuriating. And intriguing. He hadn't been intrigued in a long time.

He also hadn't been lectured by anyone outside his family in a long time. How dare Cyan insert herself into family issues she knew nothing about?

His comms beeped, and Kalis's voice droned again. "Mr. Stryke, the king of—"

"I don't care." Reaching up, he rubbed his temples. A gentle pounding in his head reminded him that he needed an injection sooner rather than later. "Cancel all appointments and take messages. I'm done for the day."

There was a pause and a sigh before, "Are you going to be working from home, sir?"

He headed toward his private Harrowgate. "Yes. Forward urgent and family messages and calls only." He rethought that. He didn't need a cousin calling to chitchat. Not that any ever did. But he could definitely see someone calling to guilt him into going to his mom's party. "*Emergency* family only."

There was another pause. When Kalis finally replied, she sounded resigned. "Yes, sir."

The injection stopped the burn in Stryke's veins and the streaking pain in his groin, but only for an hour. He should have had more time. He hadn't even finished his quick lunch of a plain ham sandwich and an apple before his head started pounding again, and cramps racked his insides.

He didn't bother with another shot that would probably only last a few minutes. Instead, jaw clenched in pain and balls throbbing like they'd been smashed with a crowbar, he summoned Masumi to his bedroom.

The sex was fast and hard, a hurry-and-get-it-over-with transaction that left him feeling the way sex always did: sweaty, trembling, and nauseous. Usually, he'd be up and in the shower immediately afterward. Or maybe stumbling out the bedroom door into a snowbank or flying down the stairs to his lab, where he'd drown his brain in work.

But right now, as Masumi lay next to him, moaning through orgasm after orgasm, he couldn't summon the energy to go anywhere.

He. Was. Exhausted.

And it wasn't the sex. It was everything. His dad. Kynan. His mom. Cyan. So much was crashing down on him all at once, and while he usually thrived under professional pressure, he had never learned to manage *personal* pressure.

He looked up at the massive, rough-hewn roof trusses and concentrated on slowing his breathing and heart rate, things that had less to do with physical exertion and more to do with his hatred of the sex act itself.

Man, he was such a fucking head case. It was just sex. He should want it. Should love it. But ever since the day Chaos died, sex had been tied inextricably to panic, horror, and heartbreak. Even if he managed to force his thoughts in another direction—literally any direction—his body couldn't make the separation. As orgasm approached, his adrenaline would spike so fiercely that his gut would wrench, and his heart would race. He'd break out in a cold sweat as nausea sucked away every drop of pleasure his climax brought.

Injections were just so much easier. Plus, the shots took seconds to administer. Sex used up way too much of his valuable time.

Masumi shifted next to him, her shoulder brushing his as she rolled onto her side to face him. "What is wrong?" Her drowsy, sultry voice still managed to convey her concern. "You never linger. Not ever." She went up on one elbow and stared at him with pleasure-glazed eyes. "Are you ill?" The natural, throaty drawl inherent to her species made every question sound sensual, no matter if she was angry or afraid. And every question entered the Sem brain like, "*Do you want to fuck?*"

He continued to study the ceiling. "Just tired." Maybe he'd get out the ladder and dust the rafters later.

She nodded. "I wondered why you seemed less grumpy than usual."

"You think I'm grumpy?"

"Oh, please." She fell back onto the pillow. "You know how you are. Play naïve with someone who hasn't been fucking you for almost fifteen years."

She'd also saved his life more than once, but he wouldn't give her any more ammunition. She already knew how much he appreciated her. He'd paid her former master an obscene amount of money to part with her, and after she'd told him how the other Sem treated her, Stryke had killed the guy.

And then took back his money.

Masumi had been beyond grateful. Even more so when he introduced her to his unmated male relatives. As a succubus whose survival depended on frequent sex with Sems, she'd thought she'd hit the fucking jackpot. He'd secured another vase, had it connected to her original one, and left it in the compound he'd given to his brothers and cousins when he moved to his current building.

She'd probably saved all their lives at least once too.

"Come on." She sighed. "Tell me what's eating you." She pinched his thigh. "Because we all know *I'm* not eating you."

No, he could barely tolerate fast, impersonal intercourse. The idea of oral sex, the intimacy involved, had left him cold every time he'd tried it. Didn't stop Masumi from attempting it every once in a while. He was probably the only incubus in the world who didn't want a female's mouth on him. Well, Rade was pretty fucked up too, so Stryke had no idea what his brother's kinks and aversions were.

But now he was curious. Funny how this was the first time he'd even thought about it in thirty-seven years.

"What are my brothers like?" he asked.

She pushed up onto one arm and looked down at him again. "In bed? You want to know what kind of lovers they are? Why?"

"When a question enters my mind, I need answers, or the mystery will take up too much space in my head." He'd bet Mace was a kinky motherfucker.

"You know I can't speak about my carnal activities." Stretching like a sated cat, she gave him an impish smile. "Discretion was woven into my genes."

"Yes, but technically, I am your master, and you have to obey me."

"Hmm." She tapped her chin, looking both thoughtful and mischievous. "This does present a problem." Sitting up, she reached for her black satin robe at the foot of the bed. "I'll tell you this. Blade is considerate and generous. He often brings me gifts. Mostly chocolate. But when he's very worked up"—she gave a delighted little shiver—"he's deliciously demanding."

Not unexpected. Blade had always been the strong and silent type, careful with females and animals. He was slow to anger, but his fury and grudges ran deep, and when he finally erupted, he gave no quarter or mercy. Followed that he'd be the same way with sex.

"And Rade? Who might be even more fucked up than I am?"

She tightened the robe's sash around her slim waist. "He is... intense. And he doesn't talk much."

Again, not a surprise. A world-renowned interrogator for DART, Rade was cold as ice and as personable as a shark. He spoke little but saw everything, and with his ability to flay open the minds of even the most powerful demons, he was one of DART's most valuable—and dangerous—agents.

"What about my cousins?"

Turning, she gazed out the window at the falling snow and smiled fondly. She hated the cold, so that smile was for something—or some*one*—else. "Sabre is creative and has a delicious naughty streak."

Huh. Stryke would have pegged Sabre for vanilla. Eidolon's son was a stand-up guy, but he'd inherited his father's rigid adherence to law and order. Stryke admired the forensic expert, but yeah, vanilla. Except he *was* part Soulshredder demon, which meant things could get very... unpredictable.

"And Mace?"

She laughed and turned back to him. "He is full of life and mischief. That one will not be easily tamed by any female."

Sounded about right. Mace was a mouthy, cocky playboy who lived life on the edge. Whether it was the edge of a cliff, a building, or pressed up against the sharp edge of a blade, that was where his cousin thrived.

Stryke sat up and forced himself to meet Masumi's gaze. The sudden worry in her eyes told him she knew who he was going to ask about next.

"What about me?"

The way she sobered, as if he'd dumped a cold bucket of water over her head, made him regret asking. Why *had* he asked? Why did he care?

"I must go," she said, starting for the door. "I can feel Blade's need."

He lunged, catching her by the wrist before his brain could catch up with his body. He should let her go. He didn't need an answer.

Except he did. Now that he'd asked, he had to know what she was so reluctant to say. "Tell me."

"Is that an order, *Master*?" She batted her eyelashes, giving him a full, seductive dose of drama.

"Don't pull that master shit on me." He released her wrist and swung his feet over the edge of the mattress. "You're free to leave whenever you want."

"You pulled it on me."

He reached for his pants. "I wasn't being serious."

"You are *always* serious. You have no sense of humor."

No sense of humor? Of course, he had a sense of humor. It was just…discerning.

She tugged the robe closed across her breasts with a sniff. "And you hurt me."

"What?" His head snapped back so hard he heard a crack. "I've never—"

"Not physically." She glided closer, every movement sinuous and seductive, and she wasn't even trying. "Emotionally, perhaps. I don't know. I've been watching a lot of *Dr. Phil* reruns." The mattress dipped as she sank onto the bed beside him, close but not touching. "You only come to me when you're on the verge of death. It scares me to see you fighting yourself, and it hurts that you find me so repulsive."

"*Repulsive?*" He stared at her in disbelief. "Is that what you think?"

"Why else would I be your last resort?"

"I—you're not…repulsive."

"Then why are you always so angry?" She shifted to face him, chin held high, accusation flickering in her dark gaze. "Why do you prefer to inject yourself with poison over being with me? Why do you run from me when you're done?"

Swearing under his breath, he shoved his legs into his pants. "I'm not angry."

"He said angrily." She huffed. "Stryke, you're *always* angry. And cold. And…" She seemed to think on it before saying decisively, "Efficient."

Efficient?

Efficient?

What the ever-loving fuckity fuck of fucks?

Now, he was angry.

Reaching over, she took his hand. "I love you, Stryke. But the hate that fills you, if not for me, then for…whoever it is…makes sex with you…difficult."

His rage faded as her words shredded his overinflated ego. What she'd said stung, but he'd asked for the truth. Whether she was right or wrong, it was how she saw him.

And that was one hundred percent on him.

He wanted to slit his own throat right now. He'd been such an asshole to her. He'd come to her only when he was at the very end of his rope, used her, taken from her, and given nothing back. Well, technically, she needed sex as much as he did to survive, but she got more than she needed with his brothers and cousins.

Still, their relationship, while mutual, had, from the day he'd rescued her, been wholly one-sided.

Which pretty much defined his entire life and every relationship in it.

Whoa. He'd had a breakthrough epiphany, hadn't he?

If he was a decent person, he'd listen and learn. He'd give a shit. If he was a total asshole, he'd ignore it all and go kill someone just for fun.

Stryke was both and neither. So, he'd process the information and use it when appropriate.

Right now, it was appropriate to apologize. A huge apology was called for, really, but his pride could only take so much growth at once.

"Masumi." His contrite voice was rough and rusty from disuse. "I'm...sorry. None of my behavior is because of—or aimed at—you."

She smiled graciously, even though he could have tacked on about ten minutes more groveling and still not fully cover the depths of his dipshittery.

"Thank you. Now, I wasn't lying when I said I felt Blade's need. He's been so busy helping plan your mother's party that he forgets to find a partner." She started toward the door. "I heard him tell Rade that you weren't going."

As if it was any of their business what he did or where he went. "So?"

She rolled one shapely shoulder in a sensual shrug. "If I had a mother, I wouldn't miss her birthday party."

She sounded just like Cyan. And Kynan. And his father.

It was just a birthday party. Why did people celebrate them, anyway? Congratulations, you got hatched from an egg or squeezed out of a vagina. Way to go.

"Just because you don't understand something, doesn't make it stupid or unworthy of concern, happiness, or interest. Don't suck the joy out of things people are excited about."

He could hear his mother's gentle scolding as if she was right next to him. She'd said things like that to him at least once a week when he was growing up. Then she'd hug him and tell him that *he* gave her joy and that nothing anyone did would take that away.

Wanna bet, Mom?

Maybe he should go to the party after all. Then they'd all see exactly why his presence was a huge mistake.

And if nothing else, he could at least look forward to the I-told-you-sos.

Chapter 7

Walking along the pathway from DART's Harrowgate, lit by holiday lanterns that made the walled courtyard festive, Stryke tried to quell his nerves. He was rarely nervous and couldn't even remember the last time he'd so much as felt a stirring of anxiety. But right now, as he stood at DART's private side entrance, his gut roiled and twisted, and sweat made his palms clammy.

Fuck this shit. He'd made dictators and demons alike shake in their boots. He could handle an hour of cake, champagne, and hostile stares.

Inhaling deeply, he shoved his unease aside and opened the door.

The cheerful sounds of music, clinking dishes, and laughter drifted down the narrow hallway from the building's main-floor lobby. All office doors were closed, but ahead, a crowd gathered near a buffet table loaded with food and a punch bowl. More people stood at round tables, drinks in hand, smiling and chatting while classic 2030s music played in the background. In the center of the lobby, in front of the fountain, a five-tiered pink-and-silver cake decorated with Runa's name waited to be cut.

As much as he despised parties, he was happy to see such extravagance in honor of his mother.

He stepped out of the hallway, and everyone went so instantly silent he thought a switch had been thrown.

He was used to being stared at. Females gazed at him with lust, and males watched him with envy. The rich and powerful observed him with calculating eyes. Intelligent people regarded him warily. Generally, he ignored it all.

But not this time. This time, he was acutely aware of every eye in the room tracking him. Their stares burned into his skin. Most of these people knew *of* him, but he doubted they understood his history with his family. Those people gawked.

But those who knew…

Shit.

He walked past Rade and Blade without sparing them a glance, but the heat of Blade's dark eyes left scorch marks on the back of Stryke's skull. It was different with Rade, though. His stare caused frostbite.

Stomach churning, Stryke swiped a glass of champagne off a server's tray and downed it in a single gulp, washing away the taste of the current pop song. He freaking hated bell peppers. Why did music always taste like things he hated? Just once, couldn't a song taste like a chocolate truffle? As he went to replace the empty flute with a fresh one, he froze.

Cyan.

She stood near the fountain, laughing with a male in well-worn jeans and a black sports coat.

Parker.

Her plum dress hugged her curves from mid-thigh to her full breasts, then wrapped around her shoulders and throat in delicate straps—straps Parker was probably fantasizing about biting through.

She looked incredible, her short, platinum hair styled in spikes that suited her personality and made her violet eyes seem even bigger. That female was a menace to all things male, and when Parker leaned in to whisper something in her ear, those gemstone eyes flashed with amusement. She'd liked whatever dumb thing he'd probably said.

Not that Stryke gave a flying fuck about the males she hung out with. But, man…she was so unbelievably gorgeous. Stryke slowed, curious about the state of Cyan and Parker's relationship, even though he didn't care. He really didn't.

But then, a few feet away, he caught sight of his mom. He drew in a quick breath, his palms growing damp with nerves and anticipation. Runa was stunning in a black cocktail dress, her caramel hair twisted into a loose braid that hung over her shoulder and partially blocked the *dermoire* that identified her as Shade's mate. She looked like a queen, standing there with his father by her side. Stryke hadn't seen his mother in years, and he suddenly felt like a naughty schoolboy waiting at the headmaster's office for a parent to pick him up.

He'd been there too many times to count. For some reason, his *"smart mouth and arrogance"* got him into a lot of trouble when he was a kid. People got so offended when you pointed out how stupid they were. Facts were pesky things.

Time seemed to stop as she hurried over, her eyes misty and a smile trembling on her lips. He wasn't sure what to do, say, or feel after so much time apart, but his body knew. It craved a mother's comfort, and he instinctively opened his arms to her.

"I can't believe it." She hugged him close, the way she used to do when he was little. "I'm so glad you're here."

His father came up behind her and mouthed, *"Thank you."*

Runa's warmth flowed through him, and he forgot all the turmoil—both around him…and inside him. All at once, he was young again, but a youth whose mom was proud, and he surrendered to the solace only a mother's embrace could deliver. For a precious moment, nothing but the familiar scent of her favorite Chanel perfume and the soft sound of her breathing existed. Peace filled his heart and head. Closing his eyes, he let himself sink into the first moment of serenity he'd known in years.

In the background, people began talking again, and soft laughter floated in the air. There was so much joy here. So much love for the woman who had given him and his brothers life.

But reality came crashing back all too soon. His mom pulled away to look up at him with a tender smile. She rested her warm palm on his cheek, her eyes locked on his.

"I love you so much," she said softly. "You don't know how much this means to me. I'd have a birthday party every day if it meant I could see you more often."

He didn't know how to respond, so he just pulled a wrapped box from his jacket pocket and handed it to her. "I brought you a gift."

"Weird." Blade's deep voice came from behind him. "I didn't see a celebrity news story about you traipsing through Harrod's or some ritzy shop in Paris."

Stryke's jaw went tight at Blade's not-so-subtle implication that Stryke hadn't picked out the gift himself. He had picked it out. He'd just sent Leilani Giada to get it. The daughter of the Horseman known as Famine, Leilani had charm *and* badass fighting skills, perfect for picking up merch from angels willing to bend the rules.

"Blade, why don't you f—?" Stryke forced himself to shut up. If they'd been anywhere but their mother's birthday party, Stryke would've happily finished that sentence. Sensing trouble, Shade stepped between them, his big body separating Stryke and Blade without a word.

Runa tugged at the ribbon and then carefully unwrapped the package. When she lifted the top of the little box, she gasped. "Stryke. Is this...is it what I think it is?"

"If you think it's a golden pearl from the Heavenly Sea of Tranquility, then yes." He plucked the ultrafine but unbreakable gold chain from its bed of spun silk and held the necklace up so he could fasten it around her neck.

Grinning, she lifted her braid and turned around. "It's stunning."

"It'll protect you from psychic attacks and repel fallen angels." He fastened the clasp, and she spun back to him, beaming.

"I love it." Her fingers skimmed over the cool metal links and the gleaming surface of the pearl. "Should I even ask how you got it?"

Powerful beings owed him a lot of favors. "You probably shouldn't."

Behind him, he heard Blade's quiet snort. Once again, Stryke held himself in check.

Still stroking the necklace, his mother smiled up at him. "I saw on the news that you donated a billion dollars' worth of playground equipment to elementary schools around the world. That was very generous."

"Kids need to play." And they needed to be safe, so all the equipment was enchanted to repel evil. Unfortunately, many schools had refused his gift, afraid it was some sort of deception. Some went so far as to decline his monetary donations as well, citing fears of using funds from a demon.

A slew of newcomers made their way into the room, and gasps rose up as one of the world's most famous pop stars, Grace Obert, crossed the floor, flanked by an entourage of at least a dozen.

Kynan sidled up to Runa. "Shade told me Grace was your favorite artist," he said to her. "We handled a demon ex-boyfriend problem for her, and she wanted to pay me back. So, I called in a favor."

"Lots of favors being called in, just for you," Shade said to her, his gaze so full of affection that Stryke felt a pang of...something deep in his chest.

"I can't believe it," Runa breathed. "This is all so amazing."

Stryke backed away, melting into the background as Grace approached. He'd met the human female at a couple of fund-raising and award galas and had turned down her advances more than once. He didn't want to take any attention away from his mother.

So, as a crowd gathered around, he made his escape, glad to have any and all focus centered elsewhere. He beelined for the exit, but a voice stopped him in his tracks.

"Stryke?"

Stryke's little brother, Crux, called out his name as he exited the restroom, his big eyes, the same pale champagne color as their mother's, as round as saucers.

"You're here!" Crux ran at him like a yearling colt—all long, gangly limbs—and engulfed him in a hug as tight as their mother's had been. "You came!"

He pulled back, grinning from ear to ear. The kid was nearly as tall as Stryke, but hadn't transitioned yet, so he was bony and thin. And as innocent as the day he and Chaos were born.

"Yeah, I came," Stryke said on a ragged breath. "I'm surprised to see you here, though. I didn't think most people at DART knew about you."

"We're telling everyone I'm Kynan's nephew."

That made sense. Plus, Crux's long sleeves and turtleneck kept most of his *dermoire* hidden so no one would know he was a pre-transition Seminus demon. His birth during a time when no demons were being born would cause too much attention and suspicion.

"So," Crux said, "does this mean you're back? We'll see you more? You should come to the house! We can have dinner. Rade is a really good cook. He took lessons from Suzanne! You know, the star of *An Angel in the Kitchen*? Have you had his chili? He says it'll make you piss fire and like it." He shrugged as if confused. "I'm not sure about the fire part, but I do like it."

Fuck. This was what he'd been afraid of. "Crux, I'm just here to see Mom. This doesn't change anything."

But wait, Rade had taken *cooking* lessons? From one of the Grim Reaper's daughters?

"Yes, it does," Crux insisted. "You'll see. If we all just try to get along—"

"No," Stryke said roughly, his voice so clogged with emotion he barely got the word out. Seeing Crux, knowing that Chaos would have looked the same...pain shredded his insides and turned the glass of champagne into acid that threatened to come back up. "No." He tempered his voice. "Not right now. I have a lot of work to do. I'm very busy at StryTech—"

"That's always your excuse," Crux blurted, a rare show of anger that put red blotches on his pale cheeks. "And it's bullshit."

Yeah, it was. But the truth wasn't an option. How was he supposed to tell Crux—or anyone—that he couldn't face the damage he'd caused? That the best way to make up for the past was through his company. He'd built StryTech to right his wrongs and help prevent other families from going through what his had.

Oh, and also to assuage his guilt.

Not that it worked. But at least it kept his mind busy instead of it spinning out of control.

"Crux, I'm sorry." *I'm so sorry I've been a shitty brother.* "How about I send you one of our brand-new drones?"

Crux's thin shoulders rolled in a half-hearted shrug. "Sure. That'd be okay, I guess."

"Great." He gestured down the hall, eager to see his brother perk up. "You should check out who just got here. I think you're all about to get a private concert."

"Really?" Crux craned his neck to peek behind Stryke. "Who is it?"

"Grace Obert."

"No way!" Crux practically bounced on his toes. "I gotta go see. You'll be here later?"

Stryke gave a noncommittal smile. "If you hurry, you can get Grace's autograph before she starts."

"That would be awesome!"

Crux took off like a puppy whose owner had just come home. Stryke's knees nearly gave out. He had to get some air. Needed to get away from all the…emotion.

He started down the hallway he'd used to come in and, wouldn't you know it, he nearly crashed into Logan, who was exiting the break room with a bowl of chips.

"Oh, hey, Stryke." Logan gestured toward the party. "Glad you made it."

"Sure, you are."

Logan punched him in the shoulder hard enough to hurt. "Don't be a dick. I just started liking you again. Well, liking you for the first time."

"I don't need you to like me."

Logan cursed under his breath and inhaled deeply as if trying to keep his temper in check. "I never got a chance to properly thank you for everything you did for Cujo and Eva." His voice was gruff with the effort it took to be nice. He reminded Stryke of a kid forced to apologize to another after a fight.

The air between them crackled as they stood there. After so many years of an antagonistic relationship with Logan, Stryke wasn't sure how to process anything else. Especially when he was out of his element and so off balance after seeing his parents and Crux.

Finally, he managed a shallow nod. "Happy to help. Now, if you'll excuse me, I have to go."

He practically ran to the exit and plowed through the door.

The air was cool and fresh, and he gulped in frantic lungfuls as he stumbled outside and braced himself on the railing that separated the patio area from the Harrowgate built into the tall stone wall.

Shit, he needed to go. He couldn't deal with this. He could leave and then send a message that he'd had to attend to some kind of emergency. Everyone would believe that.

Yeah, that sounded like a plan.

He eyed the shimmering curtain that defined the arched entrance to the Harrowgate. It was only a few yards away. He just needed a minute for his heart to stop convulsing and his stomach to stop heaving as if he'd been running from a demon.

Which struck him as absurdly funny because he *was* running from a demon.

He was running from himself.

Cyan loved a good party, and this one beat them all as far as birthday bashes went. Grace Obert? Wow. The global superstar had won every major music award multiple times and had branched out to acting as well. And here she was performing a private concert.

Very cool.

A server passed with a loaded tray of frothy, sparkly pink drinks piled high with whipped cream—apparently, one of Runa's favorite frou-frou cocktails. Cyan waved him off, preferring less sweet, Barbie-puked-in-a-glass types of beverages. She liked her alcohol the way she liked her men.

Strong, hard, and no-nonsense.

Males like Rade and Kynan.

And Stryke.

Ugh, no. He might be her type in theory, but she didn't like him.

A vampire who had hit on her earlier scowled as he walked past, and no, she didn't like him, either. They'd been having a nice time, chatting about his job as a phlebotomist at Underworld General, and then he'd had to go and ruin it by asking if she wanted to experience his blood-letting skills. With his teeth. In her femoral artery. As if she'd allow a complete stranger to pierce a vital artery with anything, let alone fangs.

Idiot. She'd been so glad when Parker saved her from further conversation with the jackass.

She watched the vamp disappear around the corner with a human DART agent who worked in finance, so it looked like he was going to get a little suck and fuck after all.

As for Stryke…she had no idea where he'd gone. She'd noticed his arrival, how devastatingly hot he was in a fitted black suit, black shirt, and a blood-red tie. Every female who recognized him had probably creamed themselves as he strode toward his parents, his long, smooth strides effortlessly eating up the floor.

He'd been as hard to read as his brother Rade. Blade, on the other hand, reminded her of a simmering pot of hot water.

"Cyan."

She turned to her boss, looking as handsome as ever in a pair of slacks and an untucked blue dress shirt that matched his eyes. "Kynan."

"I'm glad you came." He gestured to the waiting area, a small alcove just off the lobby. "Got a minute? We haven't had a chance to talk about how things are going at StryTech."

She nodded as they stepped a little outside the clamor of voices and music. "Stryke is an ass, but his team is competent. We've already designed a microchip we think can hold the type of guidance weave I would need to inject into it."

"Excellent," Kynan said, his raspy, battle-damaged voice sounding impressed. "Good work. That'll speed up the expected timeline."

"*If* it actually works," she said. Nothing ever came together effortlessly, which was why, when she prepared time estimates for any project, she added a twenty-percent cushion. "We still have a long way to go. Right now, we don't know if we can design a weapon that'll hold multiple projectiles. If we can figure it out, we're still probably looking at several years of research and development."

Years of working at StryTech.

Kynan clapped her on the shoulder. "If anyone can do it, it's you."

She appreciated the vote of confidence, but until the Reaper was thoroughly tested, she wouldn't get too excited about it.

"We'll see."

"Always the cynical one." Dropping his hand back to his side, he nodded at Blade as the demon walked past, headed toward the Harrowgate yard exit like he was on a mission.

"Keep me up to date," Kynan said. "And let me know if we can help from this end."

"I will."

Kynan took off in the direction of his wife, Gem, who was laughing at a table with her sister, Tayla, and the newest addition to DART, Logan's fiancée, Eva. It had taken Cyan time to warm up to the ex-Aegi, but the human had grown on her. Cyan liked her straightforward personality and reserved but friendly nature.

Cyan contemplated getting a drink and joining them, but her species had naturally hyper-sensitive hearing, and the noise was getting to her. In truth, she longed for the quiet solitude of her workspace.

She supposed she should visit the lab…to make sure everything was in order, of course.

Glad for a made-up excuse to escape the party for a while, she started for the comfort of her lab. Oh, how she'd missed it—

What the—?

She halted in front of a window, stopped in her tracks by the sight of Stryke—head bowed, chest heaving, his big body casting a tall shadow on the courtyard flagstones next to the Harrowgate.

Gods, she despised him. And yet, as he stood there alone, fists clenched, there was a vulnerability about him that was completely unexpected. He seemed…sad. No, it was more than that. Something else. But she couldn't put her finger on it.

Not that it mattered. She didn't care.

But she did feel like a bit of a creeper, standing there staring at him while he clearly wanted to be alone.

Then, the door to the courtyard burst open, and he was no longer alone.

But by the expression on Blade's face, that definitely wasn't a good thing.

Chapter 8

"I hope like hell you aren't running away like a damned coward."

Unbelievable. Figured that just as Stryke got his shit together and was on his way out, his brother would fuck everything up.

Cursing, Stryke swung around. "Fuck off, Blade."

Man, it felt good to say that. For years, his conversations with Blade had been brief, tense, and just polite enough to keep from starting shit.

It was time to start shit.

"You *are* running, aren't you?" Blade said, his black Italian leather dress boots hitting the concrete pavers like muffled gunshots. "Asshole. I even defended you the other day when Rade accused you of running away when we needed you the most. I argued. Said we *pushed* you away." His snort of disgust made an angry puff of vapor in the cool night air. "But he was right. Here you are, doing what you do best."

Stryke forced himself to stay calm, even though anger flowed through his veins like blood. Furious gold flecks simmered in Blade's dark eyes, and Stryke wondered if his eyes reflected the same. He hoped not. Blade got even more pissed when he couldn't bait Stryke.

"What I do best," Stryke said evenly, "is develop weapons for people like you to fight demons." He met Blade in the center of the courtyard and bared his teeth. "So, back the fuck off, brother."

Blade tensed, the tendons in his neck practically pulsing with aggression. "You'd like that, wouldn't you? You'd like it if I got out of your face so you didn't have to look into a mirror and see the pain you've caused."

The truth of that hit too close to home, and Stryke growled as he got in his brother's grill and proved him wrong. They went nose-to-nose and chest-to-chest, with years of hurt filling every gap in the remaining space between them.

But the thing was, Blade wasn't wrong. All the pain his family had gone through *could* be traced back to Stryke. As pissed off as he was, he knew he deserved every drop of Blade's animosity.

Self-awareness was a hell of a thing. And damned inconvenient.

"What do you want, Blade?" Stryke asked, his voice rumbling and low with the effort it took to keep from decking his brother.

"I want you to acknowledge what you've done, and I want you to fix it."

Fix it? Had Blade hit his head? "I can't *fix it*, Blade. No one can. Chaos is dead."

"No shit!" Blade yelled. "Fucking hell, Stryke." Blade clapped his hands on his head and wheeled around, his body coiled with rage and frustration. "I'm not talking about Chaos!" He pivoted back around, his hands fisting at his sides. "I want you to fix what you did to our family. What you've done to Mom and Dad. And Crux."

What Blade demanded was impossible. Sure, their mom and dad would probably like to see him more, but his presence would also bring back memories and misery. He couldn't put his family through that.

I can't put myself through that.

It was another ugly truth he wasn't ready to analyze. He didn't have the time nor the desire to open wounds and drain the poison. That would mean apologies and groveling and exploring his feelings. Fuck that. Venomous anger was a far less messy coping mechanism.

"I did what I had to do," Stryke said. "And how am I supposed to *fix it* when any attempt to make peace ends with you being an asshole? I made an effort tonight, but I knew you wouldn't make it easy. I'm not the problem here. *You're* the one who hunted *me* down to rip me one." He took a beat, gathering all the fury and pain that had been taking up storage space in his brain. It felt good to let the rage erupt to the surface in a volcanic blast of relief. "You think I wanted to deal with that tonight? You think I *ever* want to hear about how I fucked up this family, let alone every. Single. Time I see you? You think I need you blaming me for what happened to Chaos—?"

He hadn't seen the blow coming. One moment, he was laying into his brother, and the next, he was tasting blood and hearing bells.

"You don't get to say his name." Blade popped another punch square in Stryke's nose, and blood spurted onto his lips and chin. "Not until you stop hiding."

Self-loathing wrenched through him because, yeah, he was hiding. He was avoiding and deflecting and trying to protect his family from the pain the very sight of him caused. He couldn't be both the cause and the cure for the tension in the family. How could the pain caused by his presence be cured by being there *more?*

The self-loathing expanded, redirecting Stryke's anger at Blade onto himself, where it belonged. So, instead of breaking Blade's jaw, he let his brother take out all his pain and fury on him.

A heavy right cross would have been so satisfying, though.

Stryke absorbed the next jab in the face. And the next. And when a particularly hard uppercut knocked him back against the wall and turned his vision double, he stood there, waiting for another. As many as it took for Blade to feel better and for Stryke to feel nothing.

Because feeling nothing was better than drowning in self-hatred.

Blood and sweat flowed down his face and neck in stinging rivulets that made wispy trails in the chilly night. Blow after blow, his vision grew fuzzier, maybe from the blood in his eyes, maybe from swelling, or maybe from a concussion. Whatever.

Finally, the hits stopped coming. The pain, however, remained.

"You done?" he rasped. "Or are you sending me to be with Chaos?"

He couldn't tell if Blade was unsteady or if he was. And then Blade lunged at him. Stryke braced himself for a hit, but none came.

The piercing beep of a nearby service truck in reverse competed with their ragged breathing as they stared at each other. One beep, two…Stryke counted six before Blade spun away and stormed toward the building. The door slamming closed was perfectly timed with the last truck beep.

Stryke's legs gave out, and he stumbled against the stone wall before sliding to the ground. Throwing his head back, he rested his arms on his knees, closed his eyes, and regretted everything about this day. This night.

This entire hellforsaken life.

Holy shit.

Cyan clapped her hand over her mouth, covering her stunned gasp.

She'd known Stryke was at odds with his brothers, but she didn't know why, and she hadn't thought it was *that* bad. But even through the glare of the party lights on the window and the shadows sprawling across the yard, the pain and anger pulsing between the two males had been blinding.

And that was *before* Blade gave Stryke a boxing ring facial.

Why hadn't Stryke fought back?

He was hardly a coward. He went toe-to-toe with world leaders, demons, and angels regularly. And he hadn't shrunk away from Blade. If anything, he'd met his brother's blows with defiance. At first. But as the beating continued, his defiance became acceptance.

She also had questions about her reaction to the altercation.

She'd enjoyed the first punch. She might have even pumped her fist and muttered, "*Yes!*" Someone finally had the balls to take the guy down a peg.

The second punch had even made her happy. Maybe not as much as the first one, but really, Stryke deserved it. Arrogant ass.

Then…she'd seen his eyes. She'd expected anger, a spark of fury to ignite a good, old-fashioned brawl between bros. The kind that would eventually get broken up by a family member. There was a scene like that in every movie about brothers.

And rage had been there. But alongside it, Stryke's eyes were filled with what she could only describe as despair.

Blade hit him again.

Blood spewed from Stryke's nose as his head snapped back. Her breath caught, strangling a "*no!*" before it escaped her lips.

Music blared from the party, a song with a beat that perfectly matched the timing of Blade's fist into Stryke's face. One punch, a downward power strike, knocked Stryke off balance, his body swaying as he tried to re-square his stance.

Blade yelled something, but music drowned out his voice. She could only read Stryke's expression as the words hit him harder than Blade's fists. This wasn't a fight. It was a beating.

Blade popped Stryke with a sharp uppercut. Stryke, already swaying on his feet, lost his balance and slammed backward into the wall, blood streaming from his nose and mouth.

Like a predator moving in for the kill, Blade rained blows down on his brother with relentless fury.

I've got to stop this.

The thought had barely formed when, finally, Blade took an unsteady step back. Chest heaving, he swayed on his feet, his shoulders hunched, blood dripping from his fist.

Stryke looked up, his head wobbling, a crooked, pained smile on his split, swollen lips. He said something that made Blade surge forward, fist high, poised to strike a devastating blow.

"No!"

As if Blade had heard her through the window, he stilled. Seconds passed, marked only by her pulse pounding in her ears. Finally, Blade stepped back and dropped his fist to his side. She thought she caught a brief glimpse of remorse in Blade's expression before he shook his head, pivoted on his heel, and strode inside the building.

In the courtyard, Stryke slowly slid down the wall until his butt hit a paver. His arms seemed to weigh a ton as he flung them loosely across his knees and threw his head back, eyes closed. He didn't appear to be aware that blood still streamed down his chin, disappearing under his black collar and staining his silk tie.

Well, he deserved it.

She turned away from the window but halted after two steps.

Dammit. She couldn't leave him like that. And she doubted he'd appreciate it if she told Kynan or one of his parents to check on him. He definitely didn't need some rando finding him, taking pics, and publishing them on social media or selling them to the tabloids.

Just five minutes ago, she might have been the one taking the pics and selling them. But at some point during that epic beatdown, she'd stopped enjoying the punishment he deserved for his role in her parents' and Shanea's deaths.

Maybe she should at least see if he wanted a Band-Aid.

Calling herself seven kinds of *fleeshim*—idiot in her species' language—she slipped out into crisp night air that carried the savory aromas of a nearby restaurant and the faint hint of blood.

Stryke's head rocked forward. He blinked. Cursed. "Cyan." He dropped his head back against the wall. "What do you want?"

"I *want* to be inside at the party, but I saw what happened and felt obligated to see if you needed anything. Glass of water? Bandage? A doctor? You look like you could use some stitches. And facial reconstruction surgery."

Because, yikes. She was pretty sure that left cheekbone shouldn't be where it was, and if he didn't have half a dozen orbital fractures, she'd eat a petri dish teeming with e. Coli.

"I need to be left alone." His words were mushy, spoken between lacerated, swollen lips, but he somehow still managed to sound like an ungrateful asshole.

"Gladly." She spun around, grinding her heel into the stone. "Have a nice evening."

She started for the door, her shoes clacking loudly in the quiet night. What a jerk.

"Wait."

Fuck that. Feeling like a *fleeshim* for trying to help, she picked up her pace.

"Cyan."

Nope. She was almost to the door. He could sit there and rot.

"Please." His tone was sharp and frustrated, and if not for the underlying note of sincerity, she'd have kept going.

Through the window, she saw people clapping and dancing to one of Grace Obert's songs. Looked like fun. She could be in there, drinking champagne, maybe dancing with Parker, or, more likely, sipping bubbly in the familiar comfort of her lab by herself.

Or she could be out in the cold with a giant jackass.

Sighing, certain she was making a mistake, she swung back around to him. "What?"

He looked in her direction, but she wasn't sure how well he could track her. His left eye had swollen to the size of a plum, so he was probably blind in that one. The other eye had fared better, but the nasty gash on his brow kept a steady stream of blood flowing into it. He attempted to wipe his face with his sleeve but mostly just smeared the blood around.

"Would you...?" He inhaled slowly, and she couldn't tell whether he was pained by having to ask her for something or by bone fractures. The way he wrapped one arm around his chest said his ribs hurt as badly as his face. "Would you help me get home? I can't see very well."

Damn him. The thin thread of vulnerability in his voice cut through her annoyance. She glanced through the window again, once more weighing her options.

Finally, she shrugged. "You're lucky I don't like champagne that much." She gestured to the party inside. "Is there anyone you want me to deliver goodbye messages to?"

His bitter laugh startled her. "No."

He shoved to his feet in a smooth surge, but not without a pained grimace, and one hand braced on the stone wall. She hurried over before he fell on his ass.

"Come on," she said, taking his arm. "It's this way."

The Harrowgate's glittering opening dissolved into a dark entry-way as they approached. She ushered him inside. Once the door closed, the pitch-black walls lit up with two symbols, one representing Sheoul and the other the human realm. She tapped the human-realm symbol, and a giant world map spread in glowing lines on all the walls. She was just reaching to tap on the continent of Australia when Stryke's hand clamped down on her wrist.

"We're going to Canada, not StryTech. You'll need to use the keypad."

Well, that was unexpected. She pressed her fingertip to the map of Canada and then tapped the symbol to the right of the glowing country. Instantly, dozens of symbols popped up next to the map.

"The code is in Sheoulic. Numbers *inje, vilam, olshek*. You'll need my thumb."

She shot him a surprised glance. "So, someone with the code could chop off your thumb and get access to...wherever we're going?"

"A pulse in the thumb is required."

"Good thinking."

She brought up the Sheoulic language box, entered the code, then took his hand and guided his thumb to the indicated glowing circle. She also took note of the coding in the system—a complex, secure language she'd never seen but figured she could break if she tried hard enough.

Instantly, the gate opened onto the deck of a house nestled in snowy trees as far as she could see into the darkness.

"Wow," she said as she guided him out, his hand still in hers. "I thought you lived at the top of StryTech tower. Where are we?"

"My cabin. The penthouse suite at the top of StryTech is all for show, parties, and interviews."

A blast of icy air made her shiver as they made their way across the deck toward the sliding glass door. "Why am I not surprised?"

"What's that supposed to mean?"

She stepped carefully onto the icy planks. "Supervillains always have secret lairs."

He let out a sound somewhere between a cough and a laugh. "You see me as a villain?"

"You think that's funny?"

"I do." He waved his hand blindly in front of an electronic pad until he finally got it right, and the device beeped and unlocked the door. "But I might have a concussion."

She paused before crossing the threshold. "Maybe I should go back and get Eidolon. I saw him at the party—"

"Absolutely not," he said, slurring the words. "I heal quickly. Just get me to the couch."

"Please."

"What?"

She shook her head in dismay. "How did a polite, sweet woman like Runa raise you? Is it so difficult to say, 'Please get me to the couch?'"

"Please get me to the couch."

She tugged him inside. "I'll accept that because I'm cold, but the sarcasm was a little over the top."

He might have smiled at that, but it was hard to tell because of all the swelling and bruises. But he was right about healing quickly. By the time they crossed the entryway's hardwood floor and made it to the living room throw rug, his gait was steadier, and he was standing straighter. Once they got to the sofa, he sank down with a hiss and a wince, then reclined on the buttery, toffee-colored leather with a contented sigh.

She gave the place a cursory glance, noting the rustic cabin decor but very modern conveniences, like the enormous kitchen with professional appliances that didn't look like they'd ever been used.

"I'll get a washcloth and some ice," she said. "Stay here."

"You don't have to do that. Go back to the party."

"It's no problem." She headed for the kitchen, her feet sinking into the plush ivory rug. How did he keep it so clean? "I'll just be a moment."

"I said, go back to the party."

Gods, he sounded so much like her ex sometimes. Defensive,

angry, broody. There was a reason she'd dumped the technomancer from DART's Paris office, and she'd learned her lesson. She'd put up with Jeth's shit because she'd been stupid enough to love him.

But she didn't love Stryke. So, fuck him.

She wheeled back around. "What the hell is wrong with you?"

She expected him to be angry and fly off the handle like Jeth had if she pressed an issue instead of backing down or walking away. So, her jaw nearly fell open when he chuckled darkly.

"What's wrong with me? I'm a closed-off, self-absorbed asshole who pushes everyone away."

That was unexpectedly candid. "So, you don't deny that you're a jerk?"

He shrugged. "It's no secret, Cyan. People tell me. I hear it from Masumi all the time."

Masumi? She'd heard Blade and Mace mention the name before. She'd assumed Masumi was a shared girlfriend or something. You never knew when it came to incubi.

"Is she your counselor? Shrink?"

"No." He paused. Shrugged again. "Maybe. Sometimes."

Well, that cleared things up. "So, if you know you're a jerk, why don't you just, you know, stop being one?"

He sat up, winced, and flopped back again. "You're confusing knowing I'm a jerk with caring that I'm a jerk."

She stared, unable to believe what she was hearing. "How can you be as smart as you are and not understand that being nice to people gets you more?"

"Really?" he asked, returning her stare. "And what more do I need? I have more money than God, and I'm not sure it's possible to acquire more power than I already have."

His honesty both impressed and infuriated her. "So, you feel justified mistreating people just because you don't need anything?"

"How do I mistreat anyone? My employees are happy. They might not like me, but they respect me. They're paid well and get better benefits than anyone in the human world."

"Okay, maybe *mistreat* was the wrong word. How about rude? Cold? Dismissive?"

"It works for me, Cyan. Why does everyone feel the need to be liked? I don't care. Does that make me a sociopath? I've been called one, but I think that label fits Rade better." He paused. "Can demons really be called sociopaths? If sociopathy is a feature of our kind and not a disorder?" He tapped his comms. A holoscreen popped up, and his fingers flew over the controls.

"What are you doing?"

"Notes," he said absently. "I'm taking notes."

"Right. Of course, you are." Gods, he was weird. And she had a pretty high tolerance for eccentricity. He ignored her, so engrossed in what he was doing that she no longer existed to him. That champagne sounded good again. "Well, if everything's okay, I'm just going to…"

She started to turn away, but a crash spun her back around in time to see Stryke hit the floor. Face pale, teeth clenched in agony, he writhed on the rug, his arms wrapped around his abdomen.

"Stryke!" She scrambled over and kneeled next to him. "What is it?"

His hand clamped down on her arm, his damp palm burning her skin. "Need," he gasped. "Came on…too…fast."

Need? What did he need? Her head felt fuzzy as tingling heat radiated out from where he touched her. Streaks of pleasure seemed to race from their point of contact through her nervous system. Her muscles loosened, and her breasts tightened. Lower, her sex pulsed, and her panties grew damp. What the ever-loving hell was going on?

Arousal pumped through her, and the same thing must have been happening to Stryke because his gaze had gone liquid gold, drawing her into its swirling, hypnotic depths.

"What…what is happening?" she whispered as she lowered her face to his, her body stretching against his hard form.

"Need…" He arched against her, driving the hard bulge between his legs into her belly. "Injection." He wrenched away from her. "Bedroom…bathroom. Counter. Hurry."

She blinked, dazed until he snapped at her again.

"Hurry!"

Snapping out of it, she kicked off her shoes and hurried into the kitchen. There was a half bath just off it, a door to a dark stairwell, and a sliding door that opened to a glass-enclosed dome with a luxurious pool. She only took a second to gaze at the snow surrounding it like a reverse snow globe. A couple of lounge chairs and a table sat at the near end of the modest-sized pool, and another door led outside to a covered hot tub. She could picture him out there, naked, arms thrown up onto the sides of the tub, relaxing with one of the superhot females he was often pictured with in the tabloids…

Ugh, that was enough.

She found his bedroom opposite a home gym people would pay a mint to use. Who needed three different treadmills?

Or a bedroom the size of her apartment?

"Cyan!" Stryke's pained shout kept her from gawking.

She hurried into the bathroom—also huge. Just inside the door, a marble basket sat on the counter, filled with neatly stacked syringes, each containing 3 CCs of a reddish liquid. Assuming those were what he'd been talking about, she grabbed one and jogged back.

As she rounded the corner to the living room, she came to a shocked halt.

Welp. There's the superhot female from the hot tub.

A naked female straddled his thighs, her hands scrambling at his waistband. Stryke captured her wrists and shoved her away.

"I said no."

"You idiot!" Sitting back on his legs, she flung her arm toward Cyan in a furious gesture. "You have two females right here, ready to fuck you, and you choose a needle?"

"Whoa, whoa, whoa." Confused for so many reasons, Cyan held up her hands, the syringe dangling from her fingers. "I'm not ready to fuck him. Not even close. There will be no fucking." She paused. "Who are you, anyway?" She glanced over at the sliding glass door but saw no new tracks in the snow outside. "And where did you come from?"

The female jammed her hands onto her hips and stared down at Stryke. "Are you going to tell her?"

Ignoring the stunningly gorgeous, dark-haired, chestnut-skinned female with the mysterious accent riding his hips, Stryke thrust his hand out to Cyan. "Give me…" He took a couple of panting breaths. "The syringe."

Cyan folded her arms across her chest, keeping the syringe well out of his reach. "Not until you tell me what the hell is going on."

"Ha!" The female grinned, her emerald nose piercing glittering in the light from the antler pendant overhead. "I like her. Now, tell her."

He snarled like a feral animal and tossed the female off him. She rolled and came to her feet in a catlike surge as he sat up and braced himself against the couch.

"Cyan, this is Masumi." He hissed in pain, and when he spoke next, it was between clenched teeth and through shallow breaths. "She lives in that vase. She's a succubus species created specifically to service Seminus demons."

"Excuse me?" Cyan recoiled in horror. "She was *created* to screw you?"

"Not me. Not specifically." He rolled his eyes at what must have been an expression of disgust on her face. Yes, Cyan was a demon with murky moral boundaries, but she'd grown up in the human realm, and the idea that any female had been bred to please males made her sick. "Yeah, yeah, it's horrible, but what are you gonna do?" He wrapped his arm around his midsection and groaned. "We need sex, or we'll die. She needs sex with *us*, or she'll die. Sex with her species even gives us a couple of extra hours of relief versus any other. It's a mutually beneficial arrangement."

Okay, but still. Infuriating. "So, Masumi lives with you? Or with Mace and Blade? I've heard them talking about her."

Masumi snagged a pink satin robe from the arm of one of the leather recliners and slipped it on. "My other vase is in Stryke's old compound, where his brothers and some cousins live."

"You live in a vase? Do you travel between them, or do you exist in two vases at once?"

"Both at once," she said. "Stryke calls it an extradimensional, um, spheroid."

"*Inter*dimensional. And still wrong." Grimacing, he made an impatient give-me gesture at Cyan.

"No. You've explained precisely nothing." Cyan held up the syringe. "What is this for? And if you need sex, why aren't you having it with the succubus?"

"Those are good questions, Cyan." Masumi slid a meaningful look at Stryke.

"Just"—Stryke doubled over and moaned—"give me the shot."

"Stubborn fool." Masumi swiped the syringe from Cyan, uncapped it with her teeth, and plunged it so deeply into Stryke's thigh that he shouted.

Ouch. "That was a little overkill, don't you think?" Amusing, but still overkill, given that Stryke was clearly already injured.

"No." Masumi tugged her robe tightly around her. "He can choose to have sex, or he can take an injection that mimics the effects of sex. It gives him the lifesaving boost of chemicals without having to stick his dick in a female." She tossed the empty syringe onto his lap as he rested, slumped against the couch cushions. "Good night, *Master*."

He cursed softly as she strode away, her body disintegrating into a pulsing, shiny fluid that slid inside the vase.

That was some crazy shit.

Stryke cleared his throat. His color was better now, and some of the swelling in his face had even gone down.

"Does sex—and whatever was in that syringe—help you heal?"

"In a way," he said, sounding stronger. "The longer we go without an injection or an orgasm, the weaker we get, and the more our immune systems slow down. Once we get what we need, it boosts our bodies' healing ability." He pushed himself up off the floor and stood, steadier on his feet than she would have expected. "Thank you for helping me home. You can go now."

"Wow. Talk about whiplash. You couldn't have said that in any nicer way, huh? Didn't we go through this already?"

"Go now, *please*." He moved toward the liquor cabinet. "Better?"

She ignored his order and his sarcasm. "Why aren't you making use of a succubus who is willing to help you?"

"Why aren't you leaving?"

He had a point. She'd done her good deed for the day, and there was no reason to waste the rest of it with an ungrateful asshole.

"You know what? That's a good question." She pivoted toward the door but came to a stop when she saw that the entire front wall was one giant whiteboard. Equations in black and red covered it like graffiti. She was proficient in higher math and mechanics, but whatever he'd done on that board looked absolutely alien, and despite her annoyance, she wanted to smile.

He'd come to her college to speak once and had brought a portable whiteboard, which he'd used to explain why gravity differed in various locations inside Sheoul. She hadn't paid attention at all. No, at that time, all she'd seen was a handsome, confident, smiling twenty-one-year-old male who had been passionate about science. His confidence flirted with arrogance, which she'd found to be a bit of a turn-on. He'd filled her mind with inspiration, and her body with heat. She'd fantasized about him for years after that.

Not anymore. He was much more likable from afar. Like, in her distant memories.

"You're still here," he pointed out in a bored drawl as if she was just. So. Tiresome.

"Fuck you. No, wait." She wheeled back around. "I take that back. No *fuck you*. I wouldn't fuck you if you were dying, were the last man on Earth, *and* all the dildos were gone."

Practically spitting with fury, she stormed out. Shanea would have said she'd flounced.

Shanea.

Yet one more reason for her to despise Stryke. She just hoped he hated her as much as she did him. Nothing would make her happier than knowing she got on his nerves. No, wait. Right now, champagne would make her happy.

Enough to make her forget she'd ever tried to be nice to a self-avowed jerk.

Chapter 9

Every day, for as long as Stryke could remember—and he remembered everything that had happened since he was a year old—he woke at precisely five a.m., no matter what time zone he was in. He'd always been able to get a lot done in the early morning hours, from schoolwork when he was a youth to research when he was in college.

Now, as an adult, he got up, drank precisely eight ounces of water flavored with half a lemon, and worked out in his home gym until six. Every Monday, Wednesday, and Friday, he followed the workout with a forty-five-minute battle-training session with Ares, the Horseman of the Apocalypse known as War. Which was great because the guy was all about fighting and not talking.

Then he showered, dressed, and arrived at his office by seven-thirty, where, if it was a weekday, Kalis would have breakfast waiting for him. Always five pancakes with peanut butter and real maple syrup from Vermont. Four dry-scrambled eggs. A grilled tomato, saucy beans, and a bowl of berries…strawberries, blueberries, and raspberries. Except on Wednesday, when he wanted pineapple. If it was a weekend, he'd nuke a breakfast burrito she kept stocked in his office fridge.

But last night had been restless, plagued by erotic dreams of Cyan and nightmares about Chaos. He hadn't been haunted by replays of Chaos's death in years, but one had left him jackknifing up in bed, panting and screaming. Another had ended as he penetrated Popcorn Girl…except it hadn't been the human. It had been Cyan.

Rolling over in bed, his cock throbbing, he'd fumbled for the syringe on his nightstand and jammed it into his thigh. As the liquid did its work, he drifted back to sleep, only to be transported back into an erotic dream involving Cyan, except this time she was in his bed. Her hot mouth had taken him deep, drowning him in pleasure. And for the first time since Chaos died, he'd let himself enjoy the sensation of being sucked and licked. Of seeing the pleasure in her expression as she brought him to the brink of release.

There had been nothing but bliss as he rolled her onto her back and settled himself between her creamy thighs. The dream took them to various locations in his house and put them in different positions. In the dream—and in real life—he'd been on the verge of orgasm, a wet dream that would soak the sheets.

But he was a Seminus demon, and no matter how hot the dream was, he couldn't come unless he was inside a female.

Pain awakened him again. The fiery agony of orgasm denial, as if someone was simultaneously crushing and twisting his testicles while driving a red-hot poker through his gut. The pain had blinded him, locking his spine and joints. And in his thrashing, he'd knocked the tray of syringes onto the floor.

Then Masumi was there, and he'd felt a sting in his thigh. Sweet relief flowed through his veins and soothed his nerves as the medicine took effect.

Nausea came on its heels, and he'd barely made it to the bathroom before everything he'd eaten in the last five years came up.

Exhausted, he'd spent the rest of the night on the cold bathroom floor, his body racked by bouts of dizziness and cramps, which Eidolon said would happen more and more often if he didn't stop taking the injections.

And, as a result of a shitty night's sleep, he'd awakened at five-thirty instead of five.

Half an hour late.

He was never late to anything, but this was the second time in a week.

Thrown off his carefully plotted course, he skipped the workouts, showered, and went straight to his office. He was early, so Kalis hadn't put out breakfast.

Not that he was hungry. Nausea still held him in its grip. Besides, she probably wasn't even at the office yet.

It was another oddity in his day that would affect the rest of it. He didn't tolerate change well. Never had.

Taking a deep, centering breath, he flicked on his desktop building monitor, which showed the location of every employee in the building. StryTech operated twenty-four-seven, but here at HQ, during the local business hours of eight to five, the number of staff members increased by a third. Right now, at six-fifteen, there were two hundred and twelve workers in the building.

He scrolled through the 3D screen to the R&D department, and his heart skipped a beat when he saw that Cyan was logged in.

So, she's a workaholic too.

Of course, she was. She struck him as a hardcore Type-A.

She'd definitely been hardcore in his dreams.

His body heated as scenes from the dreams flashed in his head. Man, the things they'd done in his bed. His kitchen. His lab. She was so naughty in his fantasies. Was she like that in real life?

I wouldn't fuck you if you were dying, were the last man on Earth, and all the dildos were gone.

He knew she'd meant what she said as an insult, but all he'd been able to do after that was picture her pleasuring herself with a dildo.

Son of a bitch. This had to stop. His hours, days, and years were carefully scheduled and regimented, and there was no room for a relationship of any kind. And if he did someday find room, Cyan wouldn't be in it. She wasn't his type.

Come to think of it, he didn't have a type. He just didn't think about being with females at all. Males, either, so that wasn't the problem.

Not that he *had* a problem. Some people were into all people. Some were only into the same gender. Some were into the opposite gender. Some weren't into anything at all.

Stryke figured that if a shot could take care of what sex could, he didn't need to concern himself with having a type. Yes, he could narrow down his preferences to the female gender. And he did prefer humanoids. But aside from that, he didn't care. He didn't waste his time getting turned on by females. His brainpower was far too valuable and needed elsewhere.

He took another breath to center himself and flicked away the screen. He needed breakfast. And maybe another injection. Hopefully, minus the episodes of nausea that were becoming more frequent and debilitating.

His comms beeped. Grateful for the distraction, he swiped his wrist and sent the call into the air. StryTech's software ran the comms unit, so his company symbol, an intertwined capital S and T inside an atom, rotated two feet above his desk as the caller's information flashed beneath it.

ROSS, TARAN, Foreman of the oil platform *Sea Storm.*

"Answer."

The rotating symbol flickered away, replaced by a two-foot-tall image of Taran Ross, wearing a hard hat and a yellow rain slicker, hovering over his computer screen.

"Taran. Haven't heard from you in a while. What's going on?"

The guy didn't ever call to chitchat. The werewolf was as work-focused as anyone Stryke had known. Other than himself, of course.

"Comms have been unreliable," he said. "But we've got bigger problems. In my last report, I said one of the sensors monitoring the breach went offline."

Stryke nodded. "A new sensor is on its way."

"Yeah, well, weird shit has been happening ever since. One of my boys swears an oil slick climbed up a support beam and came after him. He burned it into a stain on the deck. Cameras didn't catch jack shit. Two days ago, another guy claimed he saw a merman holding a trident with a man's head stuck on its tines. He didn't recognize the face, seeing how it had been bitten off, but Rich Newland hasn't been seen since."

Shit. "Do you think the patch we installed over the breach is leaking near the broken sensor?"

"Yeah, but we didn't detect any activity on *any* sensor, so I don't believe any demons came through – at least, not then. I think we were experiencing leaked evil itself. It affected sea creatures that entered the bubble of leaked material. We've had sharks attacking the rig, and we had to spear an octopus that got inside the galley and tried to kill three people." He shook his head. "But today…"

"Today what?"

Taran's gray eyes turned grim. "Something else got onto the rig. Fucking forty-foot-long alligator-shark-demon thing. Never seen anything like it. Killed two of my men and wounded eight more before we put a flamethrower down its throat. Turned it into fucking sashimi."

"Sashimi is raw," Stryke said absently, his mind still trying to wrap itself around a potential disaster. "And you have a *flame thrower?* On an oil rig?"

"We ain't here to pump oil, boss." Taran adjusted his hat. "We're here to repair an opening from the hell realm and capture the demons that escaped during the initial breach. You're lucky we didn't bring nukes."

Stryke swore. Taran had a point, but flame throwers on oil rigs sounded like a future documentary waiting to happen. He could practically watch it unfold, news reports about how StryTech caused an ecological and demonological disaster with a massive explosion.

"Just...be careful," Stryke said, and Taran nodded. "I'll have a team on its way within the hour. What do you need?"

"We could definitely use a couple of medics. An engineer. Magic user. Maybe some extra muscle and weapons. And hurry. We're starting to pick up a lot of heat and movement down there. I'm not sure the seal will hold much longer."

Stryke clicked off the screen and started to call DART's senior technomancer, a Cyberis demon like Cyan, but his finger froze over the button. The guy was on leave. Shit.

That left Cyan, who didn't even work for him.

This day just kept getting worse and worse.

Cyan loved being in a laboratory. Even if it was at StryTech. And honestly, although she hated to admit it, she *loved* being in the StryTech facility. Her lab at DART was modern and well-equipped, but it had nothing on the high-tech equipment available to her here. From the newest-generation thermal cyclers and confocal microscopes to a Next-Generation Sequencer she was pretty sure wasn't even available to the rest of the world yet, she had the best of the best to work with.

Who needed sleep? Especially now that she was doing little more than tossing and turning in her apartment. She hated being there, but it would have been too weird to go to DART just to snooze on a cot, and she definitely wasn't sleeping at StryTech.

Today, she'd even been given access to StryTech's genetic library, which contained biologics from thousands of demon species. The technician on duty had been processing a new sample for inclusion in the company's DeTecht demon-detection software when she arrived.

"Where does the DNA come from?" she'd asked.

"Some is sent to us by various law enforcement agencies" the technician had explained. "But most comes directly from Stryke. No idea where he gets it."

Stryke probably paid thugs to hunt down demons and steal their genetic material. The jerk.

She'd thought about that on the way back to her workstation, but it didn't take long for her work to make her forget about Stryke and his mysterious method of collecting DNA.

"Cyan?"

She turned to see Parker walking toward her, his hands tucked into his white lab coat's pockets.

"Hey, Parker. I'm sorry I ditched you at the party last night. I wasn't feeling well, so I went home." It wasn't a complete lie. Even though she'd considered going back for champagne, she'd ultimately found herself at her apartment, drowning her sorrows in salted caramel gelato.

"It's okay," he said. "I'm just happy you took the hint when I said I've always wanted to see DART headquarters."

She laughed. He had practically begged for an invitation to the party.

She liked the good-looking, good-natured male who, despite the fact that he'd been bitten by a werewolf and lost his military career, managed to always be cheerful. He came closer, pausing to peer at the flasks of simmering ectoplasm another researcher was working with.

"Stryke is here to see you," he said.

"Send him in. It's not like he doesn't usually barge inside on a whim," she muttered.

"He wants to speak to you outside. In private."

Okay, weird. Why hadn't he summoned her to his office?

Her stomach fluttered a little as she walked to the exit. They hadn't exactly parted on good terms last night. Not that she cared. She just didn't like having to face him after her dramatic exit.

When she stepped out of the lab, he was standing at the end of the hall in front of the wall of windows, his gaze fixed on Sydney Harbor several stories below. He swung smoothly around to her, his broad shoulders filling out a tailored black button-down shirt, the sleeves rolled up to reveal his tan, thickly muscled forearms.

Her gaze climbed upward, and she drew in a quick breath at the intensity in his dark eyes. His chiseled jaw, bruised and swollen just last night, now looked as hard and perfect as ever. His entire face had healed…even the deep cut on his dark brow.

"I need a favor," he said. No *hello*. No *hi*. No, *sorry about being such a dick*.

She ground to a halt a few feet away. "You're kidding, right? Why would I ever do you a favor?"

He let out an impatient huff as if she was being oh-so-tedious. "Maybe I should have been, I don't know…more appreciative. Last night, I mean. But right now, I need your help."

His lame attempt at an apology amused her. He was so, so bad at it. Someone wasn't used to making amends, was he? Well, it was fun to watch him squirm, and she wasn't going to make anything easy for him.

"Sorry, I'm busy." She spun around, but he was suddenly in front of her, his big body blocking the corridor.

How had he moved so fast? Seminus demons were way more agile than she'd thought. It made her wonder what else she didn't know about his species.

"It's an emergency," he said. "And only a Cyberis demon can handle it."

Well, that was interesting, but hell if she would admit it. So, she merely gave a nonchalant shrug. "And what is this emergency?"

"I'll tell you on the way there." He turned toward the elevator and gestured for her to follow. "Come on. We're already taking longer than I'd like."

She wanted to tell him to take a hike, but her curiosity overpowered her better judgment. It was the story of her life, and the reason she got herself into trouble a lot. She stepped into the elevator and rode in uncomfortable silence to his office.

"Now what?" she asked as they exited the lift.

He quickly strode across the floor, clearly expecting her to keep pace. "We're taking the Harrowgate."

"Where?"

He waved her into the gate and followed her inside. "To Aberdeen." His fingers deftly flicked across the maps, and then he entered a private code. "Probably should have grabbed jackets."

"My species is tolerant to most temperature extremes."

"Excellent." The gate opened onto a dark airport tarmac, and they stepped out into stinging rain and shrieking wind. He took her hand. "Hurry!" he yelled against the roar of the weather as he led her across a helicopter pad to one of two waiting choppers.

Her feet splashed through puddles, but at least she'd chosen comfy flats today instead of heels. Still, it would take forever to dry them out.

As they approached the aircraft, an attendant opened the lead helicopter's side door and helped them out of the storm and into luxury.

Soaked and dripping, they took seats at a table sitting opposite each other. The attendant handed them warm towels, which Cyan took gratefully.

"Are you going to tell me what we're doing?" She patted her face dry as she peered out the window. The driving rain made it difficult to see much except blurry lights from vehicles and a nearby building.

"We're flying out to an oil rig in the North Sea." He ran the towel over his hair, leaving it messy...and strangely charming. She'd never seen him look anything less than perfectly composed.

Aside from the beating last night, of course.

She started wiping her arms. "You own an oil rig?"

"I took control of *Sea Storm* from a gas company after it drilled into Sheoul."

She froze, the towel at her elbow. "It drilled into Hell?" Gooseflesh prickled across her skin, and her mouth went parched at the very idea. She'd kill for a Perrier right now. "How is that even possible?"

His expression became as stormy as the weather. "We think they either discovered an unknown, inactive hellmouth or breached a weak spot in the membrane that separates the demon and human realms."

There were weak spots? Before Cyan could speak—not that she could get a word past the lump in her throat—another flight attendant appeared from the back of the helo with sparkling water for Cyan and an iced coffee for Stryke.

After she left, Cyan frowned at their drinks. "Is that what you wanted?"

He rattled the ice in his glass. "Yep. Why?" He gestured at her water. "Isn't that what you wanted?"

"I was just thinking that I'd die for a glass of sparkling water, and here it is."

"Oh, yeah. Delwhin can read minds. And her claws are poisonous, so if anyone thinks about killing me, she's got my back."

Ah. Of course. Didn't everyone have a poisonous flight attendant bodyguard on their payroll?

As the bird lifted off, bucking and jolting, she concentrated on keeping her mind from reeling and her drink from spilling.

The overhead speaker squealed, and the pilot's deep voice came on. "Mr. Stryke, we should be at the rig in approximately twenty minutes. We're flying into the storm, so things are going to get rough. Hold on and enjoy the flight. And try not to puke."

"He always says that," Stryke muttered over the rim of his glass. "I only did it once. Bastard."

"Why do you employ him if he's so annoying?"

Stryke put down his coffee. "He's an excellent pilot. And a luck demon. I figure the odds of me making it to my destination alive go way up with him on board."

"Hmm." She leaned back in her creamy leather seat. "Luck demons build up bad luck that has to be passed off. So, if you're getting the good luck, who gets the bad?"

"My enemies." His dark smirk was both sexy and chilling. "Behvyn isn't *just* my pilot."

"Nice." His ruthlessness was kind of hot. She took a gulp of seltzer to keep it from sloshing over the rim of the glass. "Okay, so the oil company drilled into Sheoul. I'm guessing we're going to try to plug the hole?"

"We plugged it a month ago." He gazed out the window. The clouds had broken up, allowing brief glimpses of whitecaps on the rough water below. "A few weeks ago, X-Oil contacted StryTech about some incidents on one of their rigs. Equipment was malfunctioning, the drill kept breaking, and then people started dying. They thought they were haunted."

"But they weren't."

"No." He took a drink of coffee. "We determined that the drill had broken into a body of water in the demon realm, and aquatic demons were spilling into our realm."

The helicopter banked hard enough for Cyan to white-knuckle the table with her grip, but Stryke barely seemed to notice.

"We bought the rig and sealed the breach with the help of a technomancer. I've got mercs hunting down the demons that came through the rift before we patched it, and I stationed mages on the rig to maintain a ward to protect the platform. It's been secure since." He glanced again at the rain pelting the window. "Or so I thought. My foreman called today to tell me that at least one demon got through the breach *and* past the mages. We need to figure out how to repair the breach before demons that can't otherwise leave the hell realm realize they have a way out." He paused, concentrating on the thrashing sea below. "Aquatic demons are especially hard to deal with."

"Why is that?"

He turned back to her. "Not much is known about them, even

inside Sheoul. They're hard to predict and harder to kill. Just a few could disrupt the entire planet's oceanic ecosystem. No more whales, sharks, or dolphins. Eventually, no more anything."

She swallowed dryly and wished she had some vodka to mix with her seltzer. He was describing some seriously apocalyptic shit. The oceans fed the world, and dead oceans meant dead everything. She might not necessarily want to help Stryke, but she couldn't say no to helping the planet.

Suddenly, the flight attendant appeared with two mini bottles of vodka and a fresh bottle of sparkling water.

"Oh. Um, thank you," Cyan said. The female nodded and disappeared. As she poured one of the vodkas into her glass, she considered the aquatic demon issue.

"Fire and air are often effective against aquatic lifeforms," she offered. She'd excelled in her Weaponized Biology class in college.

"So I've been told," he murmured.

The intercom chirped, and the pilot's voice rang out. "We're approaching the *Sea Storm*. Should be on the platform in a couple of minutes. Could be a rough landing, so if you're not wearing your seat belt, now is the time to buckle up."

The chopper slowed and started to descend, and she looked out the window in time to see the lights of a massive oil rig come into view in the distant darkness.

The janky landing made her glad for the harness-style seat belts and sturdy armrests. When she told Stryke as much, he seemed amused.

"This is nothing. I've been on a few flights I didn't think I would survive. Probably wouldn't have without Behvyn."

A few? All it would take was one like that, and she'd swear off flying forever. Fortunately, thanks to the Harrowgates, she didn't have to fly much.

Once the helo was safely on the platform, a big man in a yellow raincoat ran out to greet them. They ducked the rotors and sloshed through rain to the nearest door.

It was warm inside—relatively—and smelled like oil and chemicals. Although there was the faint aroma of something savory coming from the hallway off to the right.

The guy led them through empty halls, Cyan's shoes making squishing noises on the skid-proof floor until they reached the forward operating center. The room resembled the bridge of a ship, with massive windows overlooking the vast sea. Not that she could see much in the darkness and with the rain pelting the windows.

A couple of people monitored the flashing and softly beeping equipment while a male and a female stood at a table in the center of the room. A 3D set of platform blueprints hung in the air at eye level. On another floating screen, the female was resizing underwater images.

The big male came forward, his hand outstretched. "Stryke. Glad you made it."

Stryke shook the other male's hand. "The rest of the team is on the second helo. It should be here in a few minutes." He pivoted to gesture at Cyan. "This is Cyan, a technomancer on loan from DART. Cyan, this is my foreman, Taran Ross." He nodded toward the other female. "That is Twila Coppa. She's in charge of the cameras and imaging equipment."

Twila gave Cyan a dismissive nod, but Cyan barely noticed; her concentration was focused on one of the underwater images. She drifted toward it, drawn by the glowing symbols barely visible through some sort of dark, floaty stuff.

"How long have those glyphs looked like that?" she asked.

Taran shrugged. "I don't know what you're talking about, but those images are about an hour old."

She tapped her finger on one of the symbols. "I'm looking at those. They're broken. Some are peeling off whatever that surface is." She looked closer. A pipe, maybe?

"We aren't technomancers." Twila flicked the photo Cyan fingered off to the side and magnified the area Cyan had indicated. "We can't see what you're seeing."

Right. Cyan always forgot that others couldn't view magic that was as visible to her as printed text was to them. She looked closer at the drill casing and the odd bulge the glyphs were adhered to.

"Can you see the object connected to the drill casing?"

Taran nodded. "That's a nanomachine injector."

"A what?"

"It's new tech," he said. "It's doubled oil production at some sites."

She expanded the image and focused on the spherical casing. "How does it work?"

"The injector drops nanomachines into the well," Taran explained. "Once they reach the oil, they form vein networks to reach smaller pockets."

She was glad the injector created an electronics-adjacent surface for the glyphs, but the location didn't make sense.

"Wouldn't it be easier to inject the nanomachines from the platform instead of deep underwater?"

Stryke came up behind her and studied the image. "There's a minimum safe distance requirement. No one wants them to crawl back up the pipe."

"Crawl up the pipe? And do what?"

"They're programmed to drill," he said. "If they aren't contained, they could start drilling anything full of liquid. Like us."

That was incredibly disturbing. She side-eyed him. "I'm guessing it's a StryTech invention?"

"Hardly." Stryke shot her an offended look. "This tech is an abomination. Demonovation was reckless and irresponsible."

She could say the same about some of StryTech's products, but she had more important matters to deal with.

"Okay, well, then what I'm seeing on the casing is broken code. But it's not just broken." She frowned at the glowing, twisted outlines. "It's…rearranged. I don't understand it. Why would someone do that?"

"You think it was a some*one*, not a some*thing*?" Strike asked. "Maybe a whale hit it, or a seismic event—"

"It was intentional," she interrupted, a little annoyed that he'd questioned her. She knew her shit, dammit. And she also knew that now wasn't the time to get pissy, so, setting her irritation aside, she pointed out the telltale pattern in the images as if he could see it. "Definitely done on purpose. But who could have done it?" She glanced at Taran. "Stryke said you have mages on board?"

"Yes," Taran said. "But mage magic doesn't work underwater."

"Not usually," she murmured. "But that doesn't mean there isn't a workaround. They could be teaming up with aquatic demons who live in the human realm. Rusalkas or mermen." Although, as far as she knew, neither of those species was inherently proficient in magic, and whoever had done this was a master *and* a Cyberis demon. "You said you don't have another technomancer on board?"

Taran shook his head. "We haven't had one since the last time Quillax was here."

"When was that?"

"About two weeks ago." Stryke wandered over to the communications center, which seemed surprisingly high-tech for being on an oil platform. "He flew out to make sure everything was secure before he went on leave." Stryke pointed at a red light. "Why is that flashing?"

Taran let out a vile curse. "It means the comms are down." He crossed the room in half a dozen strides, punching a technician in the shoulder on the way by. "Why the fuck aren't you manning the radio?" He flipped a series of switches, and the screen went dark.

Cyan peered over him. "What are you doing?"

"Rebooting the system." Taran's fingers flew over the controls. A moment later, the screen lit up again, and he leaned into a mic. "Dire Wolf One, this is *Sea Storm*. Can you hear me?"

"Wolf One, affirmative, *Sea Storm*." Cyan recognized the pilot's voice. "We are on approach into Aberdeen after dropping off Mr. Stryke and passenger."

"Copy that, Dire Wolf One. Safe flight." Taran punched another button. "Dire Wolf Two, can you hear me?"

Cyan glanced at Stryke. "You named your helicopters after Dire Wolves?"

"I always wanted one as a pet." Stryke gave her a sheepish look. "I was jealous of Logan's hellhound."

Er...yeah. Neither sounded like a fun time.

"Dire Wolf Two," Taran said, more urgently this time," this is *Sea Storm*. Can you hear me?"

Static filled the suddenly tense silence.

"Dire Wolf Two. Can. You. Hear. Me? *Dire Wolf, this is Sea Storm. Come in.*"

"...*Storm*...Dire...Two."

Stryke swore under his breath, his frustration at a situation he couldn't control making the muscles in his jaw twitch. She got it. She didn't like being helpless either.

"Wolf Two, *Sea Storm*, say again. I repeat, say again."

"...lost...instruments...where are...storm?"

Cyan shouldered her way past Stryke and Taran, firing up her spellcaster energy.

"I can boost the signal." She activated her third eye, and the inner workings of the communications system—the wires, microchips, and switches—instantly appeared to her as a schematic overlay. And while she couldn't explain any of it, she instinctively knew how to manipulate its electricity.

"Wolf Two," Taran shouted. "Say. Again." He shot her a look. "Anything?"

"I'm working as fast as I can." She let out a frustrated breath. "The signal is being blocked and warped by a forcefield. Some kind of dark power." She cast a wave of magic to convert her commands into actionable spells. When the spell framework inside the comms device lit up in a series of symbols, she nodded. "Try now. I compensated for demonic energy."

Stryke smiled, a slow, sexy tilt of the mouth that inexplicably made her pulse spike a little. "Clever. I wouldn't have thought about evil interference from the breach."

"*Sea Storm!*" Dire Wolf's pilot shouted over the radio, his voice broken but still considerably clearer than before. "We hit a wall of... fog...storm...we lost...navigation...altitude. Mayday, mayday, mayday!"

"*Taran!*"

At Twila's shriek, they wheeled around to the forward window. A dim light in the sky pierced a veil of thick, undulating fog that hadn't been there just sixty seconds ago.

"It's coming in fast," Stryke barked. "Get down!"

Suddenly, he was on her, taking her to the floor as an explosion of sound and light detonated all around her. Glass and stinging rain pelted her face and arms, but Stryke's heavy body shielded her from the worst of it. Beneath them, the floor trembled.

Lights dimmed and flickered, things sparked, and Cyan dazedly tried to sit up. A strong arm forced her back to the floor.

"Stay down." Stryke shoved to his feet.

She did not stay down.

The devastation was incredible: wrecked equipment, groaning metal, tinkling glass. And the stench of smoke, fuel, seawater, and brimstone.

Stryke turned to her. "Are you okay?"

"Yeah," she said numbly. Her ears rang, and her stomach churned, but she wasn't injured.

Taran stumbled around the space, checking on his people as Stryke wrenched open the door, its twisted hinges creaking and groaning. She followed him out to the railing, holding her forearm across her face to shield it from the dark, oily plumes of smoke. Down below, burning, mangled wreckage and fuel created a debris field in the roiling sea.

"I see movement!" She pointed to what appeared to be someone swimming in the waves. "There! We need to help them!"

She looked desperately for a life preserver. Yes! Found one—

"Wait." Stryke grabbed her by the wrist. "Those aren't people."

Confused, she looked down. At first, she didn't see what he was talking about, but shapes slowly formed out of the darkness. Figures with slick skin and monstrous teeth and claws. First, just a couple. Then a dozen. Then the water churned with dolphin-sized creatures that screeched as they tore apart the aircraft's remains…and its passengers.

Horror crawled up her spine, paralyzing her as the reality of the situation sank in. Those poor people. And if this got worse, the poor planet.

"We got lucky," Taran shouted from behind them. He jogged up, limping and holding his elbow. "The mages can erect a shield to stop the wind and rain from damaging what's left of our operations center."

"Lucky?" Stryke asked quietly, but his voice somehow carried over the roar of the storm and the shrieks of the demons below. "We just lost a lot of good people."

"It could have been worse, sir."

Stryke stared down at the sea, which had claimed almost everything now. Even the fires waned.

"Oh, it'll get worse." His voice became distant. Haunted. "The initial disaster is just the beginning. The real carnage comes *after.*"

Chapter 10

Stryke led everyone back to the forward operating center. The mages had already constructed a magical dome, and now that the storm was no longer pouring in, damage assessments and repairs were underway.

"Sir…uh, Taran." A sandy-haired male with a scalp laceration and worry in his eyes looked between Stryke and Taran. "Mr. Stryke…"

Stryke made an impatient gesture at Taran. "He knows more about this operation than I do."

The guy nodded but still addressed them both. "Our communications are completely down—radio, sat phone, personal devices. We have no way to call for assistance."

Stryke automatically checked his wrist comms, and sure enough, there was no signal.

"A simple storm shouldn't have knocked out the comms. Radio, sure. Maybe satellite. But the tech in my comms device network is practically bombproof."

"But is it evil proof?" Cyan asked. She was staring out into the night, at the eerie, undulating fog that persisted despite the intense wind. It rolled and boiled like a living thing, unbothered by wind and rain that should have ripped it apart.

Evil. Of course. Why hadn't he thought of a disruption of that sort before? When he'd assigned the team to reinforce the network against any and all potential threats, they hadn't even considered demonic energy.

He wheeled around to Twila. "What kind of readings are you getting from the fissure?"

Gaze fixed on half a dozen screens in various states of functionality, Twila scrubbed a bleeding hand over her face. "The seismic equipment is broken, and I'm not sure the temperature readings are reliable. They're fluctuating wildly."

Cyan frowned. "Can I see the photos I was looking at earlier?"

As Twila brought up the images, Taran leaned close to Stryke. "Sir, can I talk to you? Alone?"

"Make it quick." Leaving Cyan to study the images, Stryke followed Taran to his office, just off the FOC. Once inside, Taran closed the door and turned to Stryke.

"I didn't want to say this in front of the technomancer, but all our problems began after Quillax recertified the magic that's sealing the breach." He jammed his fingers through his wet, dark hair, flinging droplets onto the lockers behind him. "It could be a coincidence, but the day after Quillax left, we lost one of the sensors. Right after that, we started getting seismic readings from beneath us. They were small at first. We logged them but didn't think too much about it. Geological activity has been reported in this area for decades."

"You mentioned the seismic readings in your last report."

"Yes, but then they got stronger. And each time, something weird would happen right afterward. The octopus, the sharks. Yesterday, when the demon-shark thing attacked, it followed an abnormally intense seismic event."

"Do you still have the body?"

Taran shook his head. "It disintegrated after it died."

"Which means it was a demon and not an Earth creature transmogrified by evil."

"Yeah. Who knows how many have come through?" He made a come-with-me gesture. "The creature disintegrated, but it left slime everywhere. We have samples in the lab-slash-secondary-emergency-care office."

When they entered, Stryke frowned. "Where's Dr. Arapago?"

Taran paused, then gestured to the covered body on one of the two exam tables. "He suffered a sudden catastrophic decapitation event."

Stryke wasn't sure he'd heard that right. "A what?"

Taran opened the door to the fridge. "The demon bit his head off." He took a Petri dish off one of the shelves and slammed the door closed. "We need a new doctor. A medic, at least."

"Where are the other injured?"

"They're in their quarters. We didn't have enough beds in here. Or a doctor who's still alive."

"The medical personnel were on that chopper," Stryke said grimly. "But I can look at your staff's injuries."

"You get some medical training from your uncle?"

Everyone knew Stryke's uncle was the famous—or infamous, depending on who was talking about him—founder of Underworld General Hospital. But most people didn't know that their species possessed innate abilities that affected the body or the mind...for good or bad. Stryke's ability was the same as his father's, whose gift was well suited to his work as a paramedic.

"All Seminus demons have one of three abilities. Mine doesn't heal, not like my uncle's, but I can stop bleeding and reduce pain, and I can boost the body's natural ability to heal."

He could also *cause* bleeding and pain, but he didn't see any reason to point that out.

"We could sure use you then—"

Cyan burst inside. "Hey, sorry to interrupt." She sounded breathless as she forced the door closed with her shoulder. It was an inner door, but two freshly torn openings in the outer doors created a wind funnel out there. Shoving her wet, windblown hair back from her face, she addressed Taran. "How did Quillax embed the spells on the drill casing?"

"He used the submersible pod."

Closing her eyes, she let out a little groan. "I was afraid of that." She turned to Stryke. "I need to go down there."

"Why? Can't it be fixed from here?"

She shook her head. "I tried."

"There's got to be another way." Stryke gestured at the single, tiny window and the swirling fog. "Using the submersible while evil is bubbling around us is too risky."

"We don't have much time." She wiped water from her cheek with the back of her hand. "The spell is disintegrating. And whoever wanted the rift open, wanted it to happen slowly. They weakened the mages' ward as well."

The rig rocked again, and Taran reached out to steady himself on the wall. "Sir, if the seal breaks wide open, thousands, if not hundreds of thousands, of demonic monsters will flood into the human realm.

These aren't demons that can be rationed with. These are animalistic beasts. They give other demons nightmares. It'd be like *Jurassic World*, except with dinosaur-sized demons that make even the velociraptors look like house cats."

Stryke knew all that. But he didn't want to lose Cyan. DART would freak the hell out if they lost another of their people because of StryTech. Stryke might freak out a little too, but only because she was proving to be a great asset on the Reaper project.

Yep, that was the only reason.

Liar.

Whatever.

"How much time do we have?" he asked her.

"Best guess?" Cyan blew out a breath. "Twenty-four hours. Maybe thirty, if we're lucky."

Damn, he'd hoped for double that. "Okay, let's use the time to come up with another solution. And we need a plan to make using the submersible safer. Taran, get your people on that. I'll go down to the crew quarters and do what I can for the injured."

"What do you want me to do?" Cyan asked.

"Work on getting communications back up. We need help." He felt around in his pocket for his injector. He'd need his next dose soon, which would leave him with three more doses. After that, he'd be in trouble if he didn't get off this rig or get a supply brought in.

He'd been stupid to leave without grabbing another one. But that was how he lived, wasn't it? Daring Death to take him and making it easy for the bastard.

Clearly, being a genius didn't mean he was smart about everything.

The communications were fucked. All of them.

No matter what Cyan did, she couldn't get any piece of equipment to operate, even with magical assistance. One of the crew, a hyena shifter named Ubundi, did his best to repair the machines that had been damaged in the helicopter crash. But according to him, the satellite had been destroyed, and the radio, while functional, seemed to be blocked by the malevolent fog surrounding the rig.

Cyan tried using magic to boost the signals, but nothing she did affected transmissions, which led her to believe that the fog had grown thicker.

"I think we're screwed."

Ubundi nodded. "I cannot do anything else here. I will make sure the submersible wasn't damaged."

Good idea. She hadn't thought of that. Without a way to get down to the enchanted glyphs, the seal on the breach would continue to weaken until it broke, releasing evil toxins into the human realm like radiation from a damaged nuclear reactor.

"Check the lifeboats too," she said. "They may be our only way to get out of here if worse comes to worst."

"I will do that." He took off.

"We got new images!" Twila shouted. "Yes!"

"The camera is working again?"

"Thanks to whatever you did."

Cyan had sent a generic repair spell into the equipment with few hopes of success. Thankfully, it had worked. The camera hadn't been physically damaged, but a power surge had killed it. Fortunately, the fine weaves in her spell had patched all the burned-out components. The fix was temporary but obviously enough to relay some updated images of the damaged glyphs deep below the surface.

She hurried over to Twila's station as the other female threw the images into the air like half a dozen big-screen TVs.

"How do the glyphs look?" Twila asked.

Cyan's blood chilled as she compared old images to the new ones. "They're degrading. Faster than I thought." She peered more closely at one that had begun to peel away from the pipe. If that one went—

The floor beneath her rocked so violently that Twila stumbled and would have fallen if Cyan hadn't steadied her. All around them, metal groaned and creaked as the platform shuddered. Outside, something screeched.

"We're running out of time," Cyan croaked, her throat clogged with terror.

Between the demonic danger and the threat of the platform collapsing into the sea, Cyan felt like she was on the verge of hyperventilating. Drowning in a dark body of water was her second biggest fear, right after being raped, tortured, and eaten alive by demons. All those things could happen on this death trap.

She needed to get down to the glyphs immediately.

The rig stopped shaking, but Cyan's nerves didn't. This assignment sucked.

Get it together. You've been through worse.

Absolutely. Losing loved ones was way, way worse.

Cyan used a trick her mother had called *emergency mode* to put her fear aside and get shit handled. Still, as rattled as she was, she made sure everyone in the FOC was okay and then made her way to the crew quarters. Stryke had said he'd be administering first aid until his *"juices ran dry."*

The guy had a lot of flaws, but no one could argue that he didn't care about his people.

Wind howled through the cold passages as she traversed the winding hallways. Pipes ran along the corrugated-metal walls, some finished with painted paneling, others paneled with naked wood or steel, none of which did much to muffle the screeches and growls that rose from the sea below. She'd had to dart outside twice to get from one building module to another, and she'd nearly been knocked off her feet both times by what she hoped were wind gusts and not the air displacement from really big demon wings.

Please let them be squalls.

The rain had stopped, but the fog clung to her in the form of damp, cold droplets. It weighed down her hair and made her clothes stick to her skin like wet sheets. When she opened the hatch to the crew quarters, the warm, dry air welcomed her like an embrace. She was so sick of being wet.

Rubbing her arms in a futile attempt to dry herself, she hurried down the hall to the first room, but the four bunks were empty. Two beds in the second room were occupied by two bandaged males lying prone in their bunks. All four of the bunks in the third room were taken up by injured guys, but there was no sign of Stryke.

"You looking for the boss?" one called out from where he was sitting on his bunk.

"I'm looking for Stryke."

"We heard a scream." The guy braced his elbows on his knees and dragged his hands through his mop of blond hair. "He ran outside to see who it was after the rig stopped shaking. We'd have gone with him, but he told us to stay."

A guy with about a dozen gashes across his chest and arms

nodded weakly. "If Stryke says stay, you stay."

Shit.

She didn't think about how stupid it would be to go back outside. She just did the stupid thing and ran out into the piercingly cold night.

A chill instantly spread across her skin, but it wasn't from the cold. The air felt heavy and sinister, seeping into her as she moved to the railing and craned her neck to check out the decks below and above. The mist thickened and thinned randomly, making visibility inconsistent...several yards in one direction and only a couple of feet in another. Sometimes, she couldn't see her hand in front of her face.

"Stryke?"

An eerie silence settled all around her. Even the crash of the waves against the metal structure seemed muted.

"*Stryke?*"

A loud crash made her jump. She wheeled toward the sound, wondering why she'd come out here without grabbing the ax mounted near the exit. Sounds of a struggle came on the echoes of the crash.

Heart pounding, she followed the sound of pained grunts and fists on flesh.

Crack.

That sounded like metal striking bone.

She slipped on the wet deck as she scrambled between equipment and beams, ducking at times beneath cables as thick as her waist. The fog thinned just as she heard a thunk.

She looked up to the level above her. Dark liquid dripped through the metal grating near where Stryke stood, holding a wrench, a slimy black thing twitching at his feet. He kicked at its body, shoving it toward the platform's edge.

Cyan mounted the stairs and reached him just as the demon tumbled over the side and into the sea.

"Stryke, are you okay?"

Gaze still fixed below, he nodded. "Thing killed Ubundi before I could stop it."

Shock sapped the moisture from her mouth. "Where's his body?" she croaked.

"Down there. He's gone."

She looked down at the churning sea and swore she saw something with tentacles and lots of teeth.

"Let's go inside where it's safe," she said, turning back to Stryke.

"You go. I'll catch up."

She stared at him through the dense tendrils of fog that swirled in the space between them. "I'm not leaving you here alone."

He didn't look at her, but she swore he said something like, "I couldn't save him."

Not so distantly, a sound like something wet slithering on metal sent a chill up her spine.

"Stryke," she said with growing urgency. "Let's go."

His head swung around, and she drew a sharp breath at the gleaming gold burning in his eyes.

"I can't," he growled. "It's not safe."

A warm wave of arousal washed over her, and instantly, she understood. "Did you bring your medicine?"

He reached into his pocket and pulled out a crushed injector pen. "This contained four doses." He closed his eyes. "Blade was right. I'm an arrogant asshole. I couldn't save him."

"Er…yeah." He wasn't making sense. None of this made sense. Maybe he was experiencing a nervous breakdown. Too much stress or something.

"You did everything you could for Ubundi," she said calmly, but his eyes popped open, and he looked at her like he didn't understand.

"Not Ubundi."

Not Ubundi? What was he talking about?

Something in the fog snarled, and closer, something hissed. She decided to worry about whatever was wrong with Stryke later.

"Okay, we'll deal with it inside." He didn't move, but he did open his eyes. Somehow, they glowed even brighter, a molten gold that made her feel like whiskey flowed through her veins. She burned in the best way. "Stryke." She extended her hand. "We *really* have to go inside."

The wrench clattered to the deck, but he still didn't move. Fiery turmoil as violent as the stormy sea filled his expression, drawing her in with a sense of almost morbid fascination. She wanted to touch that fire. See how badly it would scorch her.

She stepped closer, her heart pumping so hard she could hear it over the roar of the wind. Desire fluttered in her belly, even as her brain screamed that they were in danger. Screamed that *he* was the danger.

"Come on," she whispered, taking his hand.

His grip snapped closed on her wrist, and he wheeled them both around lightning-fast, slamming her against a huge tank. He pinned her wrists above her head and pressed his big, warm body against hers.

Teeth bared, his face inches from hers, he growled, a sound that relaxed her muscles and turned her core liquid. Oh, wow. So, this was why lust demons were so dangerous. Here they were in a situation that could get them killed, and all she wanted to do was strip off her clothes and let him do whatever he wanted to her. Right here. In the cold rain. Likely with demons stalking them.

"Go...inside," he gritted, even as he pushed his pelvis into hers, the hard ridge of his erection making her instinctively roll her hips against it. He sucked in a harsh breath, and the gold in his eyes swirled.

"I'm not going in without you," she said, her voice sounding more breathless than she'd like.

"Yes, you are."

Did he understand what he was saying? Did he really want to send her away? What the hell was wrong with him?

Her lust turned to instant fury, something she was far more comfortable with around him. She jerked angrily out of his grip. "What is your deal? If you stay out here, you'll get killed!"

"I know. But I won't make it easy on them, and I'll take out as many of those bastards as I can."

Oh, gods. He was serious. He really was prepared to fight to the death. And he wasn't even bothered by the idea. It was all just very ho-hum.

"Stryke, you don't have to die. Come inside."

He laughed, kind of a maniacal laugh timed perfectly with a flash of lightning. "Twila is mated, and you said you wouldn't fuck me if I was the last male on Earth." He turned back to the railing and looked out into the darkness. "It's okay."

Dammit. He was right, and he was being completely and frustratingly logical about it. Again, with the ho-hum.

She stepped next to him. "Yeah, I said that. I don't like you—"

"I'm well aware."

"Yeah? Okay, Mr. Smartypants, are you aware that I'm also incredibly turned on right now?"

She hated that she'd said that, but it was the truth. She didn't like him, but damn, he was hot. No doubt the lust pheromones he was putting out were to blame for a lot of what she was feeling, but she was also honest enough with herself to know that he was an attractive male no matter what.

And maybe the crush she'd had on him for years wasn't

completely gone. Also, she'd seen how he took care of his employees. He was a dick, for sure, but he wasn't a *complete* monster.

He inhaled, his broad chest expanding and making her wonder how his muscles felt under his soaked shirt.

"Yes," he rumbled, "I am aware." His gaze caught hers, holding her captive as he swung around to face her. "I can feel the throb of your pulse against my skin. I can smell the scent of your desire. It's like hot honey." His hands formed fists at his sides. "It's driving me insane."

Oh. His words drew pictures in her mind, explicit scenes of him kneeling between her legs while she gripped the railing and threw her head back in ecstasy, the wind lashing her skin as his tongue lashed between her legs.

"Then why...?" She paused, giving herself a second to think. To *try* to think. The level of arousal she was feeling right now had flipped a primal switch in her brain, and logical thought was losing the battle against her physical needs.

"Why...what?" he asked, the seething anger from earlier rising in his voice again.

"Why aren't you asking me to help you? You're dying, Stryke. Why can't you ask me to save your life? Why aren't you *begging* me to do it? Hell, I've heard your species isn't aversive to rape, so why aren't you throwing me down right now and taking me like the lust demon you are?"

He looked taken aback. "Is that what you want?"

Now *she* was taken aback. "No. Hell, no. I'd fight you tooth and nail, and I promise, my species isn't as delicate as we appear."

No, her species had learned to fight dirty. They'd had to, since they'd existed for thousands of years without any special gifts. They might as well have been humans. In fact, they had so much in common with humans that they'd bred with them, nearly wiping out their entire race. It wasn't until the invention of technology that their inherent spellcasting abilities had made themselves known.

"No," he growled, "you aren't delicate." His gaze raked the length of her body, growing hotter and darker. "You've stood your ground against me since the first time we met."

She shivered when his eyes locked with hers. His nostrils flared, and his chest heaved, and for a heart-stopping moment, she thought he might test her resolve to fight.

Then, with a blink and a shake of the head, he tore himself away, panting, his head hanging, his hands gripping the railing so tightly she feared he might crush the piping.

Damn him! Damn him for putting her in a position where she had to save his life. She'd wanted him dead more than once, had wanted him to suffer the way he'd caused so many other people to suffer. Now, she needed to save his arrogant ass because no one would make it off this rig if he was dead.

That's not the only reason you want to save him.

No, it wasn't. Part of her wanted him to live because she was angry. Angry that he was giving up the way her mother had after her father died. She couldn't watch anyone let go like that again.

"Damn it, Stryke! What the fuck is wrong with you? Do you not care whether you live or die?"

He didn't have to answer. She could see it in his eyes. There was so much pain in them—agony that went beyond the physical symptoms he must be feeling as his needs went unmet. Wrapping one arm around his middle, he doubled over, bracing his shoulder against the railing.

Suddenly, a shadow moved behind him. A shape took form in the mist, a massive, tentacled thing.

Stryke noticed it at the same time. In a jerky but fast motion, he lurched at her, catching her arm and dragging her toward the nearest hatch. The monster came after them, the wet slap of its tentacles on the metal getting louder with every frantic footstep.

They reached the hatchway with a second to spare. Stryke flung them both through and slammed the door on the tip of one of the demon's black, slimy limbs. A six-inch section of tentacle plopped to the deck as she spun the wheel, locking the hatch.

Outside, the thing screamed.

Terror, anger, and lust ignited, lit by an adrenaline dump for the record books, and she slammed her palm into Stryke's heaving chest. "You decided to live? Why?"

"I couldn't let someone else die."

His words, the rough delivery that hinted at soul-deep trauma, cooled her anger, but that only made more room for arousal.

"So, you're ready to let me help?"

"Are you going to make me ask again?"

"The way I made you ask for help the night of your mom's party?" Boy, he had not liked being made to ask nicely for a favor. "No. Just tell me what you need."

His fists flew at her, and she nearly screamed when they punched into the wall on either side of her head. His face was in hers, his body pinning her with its weight. He dipped his head, and for a second, she thought he was going to kiss her. But as she tilted her face up, he put his mouth to her ear, his hot breath caressing her skin, his damp lips tickling her lobe.

"What do I need?" His throaty voice vibrated through her, making her hormones dance. "I need to fuck you, Cyan. And, gods help me, I don't just need it. I *want* it."

Chapter 11

Sixty seconds ago, Stryke had been prepared to die. Deep down, a tiny part of him had *wanted* to die. Maybe then…maybe he could find Chaos. Because right now, as a breathing, corporeal person, he hadn't had any success locating his baby brother's soul. But as a soul himself, Stryke might have an advantage.

So, death had never been something to fear. He'd flirted with it over and over. Sometimes intentionally, other times recklessly, still more unconsciously. It wasn't that he yearned for death. It was that he just didn't care if it came for him.

But in this moment, he wanted to live. He wanted to taste Cyan's mouth. He wanted to inhale the metallic scent of her skin. He wanted to feel the slippery wetness between her legs.

He couldn't remember ever desiring a female like this, like he wanted to pour everything into her.

Desperate. That was the word for what he was feeling. Desperation for her. For an escape. From his head and this fucked-up situation.

They were probably all going to die, so he might as well go out with a bang.

"Come with me." He took her wrist and hurried them both to his private quarters, ignoring the crewmembers' curious stares as they passed.

Once inside the small, starkly appointed room, he slammed the door closed and faced Cyan.

Her hair, flattened to her skull by the rain, hung in her eyes as she watched him, her violet eyes sparkling. Literally sparkling as if they were tiny snow globes. He'd never seen anything like it.

"Your eyes." He stepped into her, catching her face in his palms as he studied them. "They're remarkable." Mesmerizing.

Her smile made the corners crinkle, and her lashes swept down almost coyly. "They do that when we're channeling our ability." She gestured to the door. "I locked it."

"Good."

He hadn't wanted to take the time to operate the electronic lock. He needed to be inside Cyan before Chaos made his appearance in his head and fucked everything up.

Two minutes. He'd give half his fortune to have just two minutes of mind-emptying freedom from everything except the feel of Cyan wrapped around him.

"Stryke." Cyan tapped his cheek. "You okay? It's like someone hit your pause button."

"It's all good," he said as she slid her palm along his jaw to the back of his head and pulled his mouth down to hers. Her other hand dropped to his belt and tugged.

He kissed her as he worked the buttons on her pants, his tongue tangling with hers in the hottest kiss he'd ever experienced. He'd never liked kissing; it seemed like an unnecessary and pointless act. But Cyan made it…interesting. Little nips and licks that made him imagine her doing that to other parts of his body. And when she caught his lower lip between her teeth and sucked gently, his knees nearly buckled.

Then she took him into her palm, and they did buckle.

Catching her around the waist, he dropped them both onto the bed. It was little more than a cot he'd never even slept in, but it was enough. He shifted to the side and worked her pants down her thighs as her hand worked his cock.

Firm strokes took him from the crown to the base and back up, and he groaned into her mouth. Her slacks, wet from the storm, bunched up at her ankles, but he didn't care. He couldn't wait a second longer. Not when his blood was on fire, and his pelvis was throbbing so hard he could feel it all the way to his teeth.

Dipping his hand between her legs, he tested her readiness for him, even though he already knew what he'd find. Hot honey coated his fingers as he slid them between her folds. Okay, maybe he could spare a couple of seconds to play a little.

He added his thumb to the game, circling her clit and then pinching lightly. Her soft cries stoked the flames shooting through his veins, making him so hot his damp clothes should be steaming.

How does she taste?

The thought shocked him so much that he glitched for a second.

He'd never wanted to taste a female. It was another of those pointless things people did during copulation.

He'd always been in it for the life-giving orgasm. A few pumps of his hips, and the shit was done. Masumi had offered to teach him to perform oral sex a million times, and he'd refused.

But suddenly, he wanted to go down on Cyan and make up for lost time.

Except it hadn't been lost because he'd used those pointless minutes to solve problems and make the world a better place.

"Stryke," Cyan moaned, arching into his hand. "Yes…oh, yes."

The sight of her, flushed and aroused, rocking into his touch, filled him with a sense of pride. Again, all his life, sex had been about one thing. Him.

But he was loving what his touch did to Cyan.

Her hand swept across the head of his cock, and then she tugged him closer. By his penis.

Holy…damn, that felt amazing, and if she wanted him closer, that worked. He needed to be inside her.

He rolled on top of her and pinned her legs between his. Her pants bound her ankles together, but there was enough room to rock his hips and bury his cock inside her slick heat. They both moaned as he sank deep.

"How are you doing?" he rasped. "You okay?"

"Yes," she breathed. "Hurry."

That was all he *could* do. She was too tight, and he was burning. She jammed her hands under his waistband and slid his pants to the bare skin of his ass, holding him against her as he pumped his hips wildly. He let ecstasy roll over him like a wave, drowning him in bliss.

And for a moment, a precious, glorious moment, there was nothing but pleasure.

Then he smelled popcorn.

Buttery fucking popcorn.

Chaos.

Mental anguish blew his world apart like a bomb. The fire in his blood became a cold sludge, even as his heartbeat went tachycardic, beating so fast he thought it might explode. Icy sweat bloomed across his skin as his baby brother's death played through his head like a movie.

Time had not blurred the edges of his memory, either. If anything, the images were sharper, the screams louder, the blood redder.

Please, no...

His body moved independently of his brain, seeking and finding the release it needed. But the pleasure was dulled by the nightmare in his head, leaving only a distant sense of physical relief.

Beneath him, Cyan cried out, her body writhing in ecstasy. She came hard, not even noticing his hasty withdrawal. That was the power of a Sem's ejaculate. She'd climax over and over until her body was wrung out and exhausted.

Few females complained about being tired.

Quickly, Stryke zipped up and ducked out of the room. He tried to tell himself he had shit to do so they wouldn't all die, but he'd never been good at lying to himself. And while time was definitely of the essence, there was more to his hasty exit.

He was running from himself again.

He was *always* running from himself. And soon, there would be nowhere to go.

Okay, so that was weird.

Cyan panted through what she thought might be her ninth orgasm. They were milder now, mild enough that she'd actually been able to pull up her pants during one.

Weakly, she made it to Stryke's private bathroom and cleaned up, the process of which made her come again. Wow. Just the slightest touch of the washcloth had left her moaning and weak-kneed. No wonder there was a market for arousal creams formulated with Seminus semen.

She took a deep breath and collected herself. Checked her watch. Damn, she'd lost fifteen minutes to—

She sucked air as another climax ripped through her. The mildest so far, it still left her wobbly on her feet as she fixed her hair, borrowed a dry denim work shirt from his closet, and made her way to the door. She didn't have time for this.

But wouldn't it be nice if I did? If I could just lie there with Stryke and bask in wave after wave of mind-blowing pleasure?

She immediately struck that thought. She wasn't going to have sex with Stryke again. That had been a one-time thing to keep him going so they could get off this wretched platform alive.

Hopefully, he was working on that right now. Why else would he have escaped from her as if she were a female Dire Mantis intent on devouring him after mating?

Still, he could have at least said goodbye.

Her fingers shook as she opened the door and slipped out into the empty hallway. No one saw her as she made her way to the bridge, where Taran told her Stryke was two decks below with the submersible.

The rain had stopped again, but fog engulfed her, wrapping her in a stinging, dark sensation as she took the metal stairs down, pausing once for another climax. She clung to the railing, acutely aware of how bizarre it was to experience pleasure while malevolent forces swirled around her. Worse, the vulnerability that came with it left her sweating despite the cold. Anything could climb out of the sea and drag her into the water while she was distracted.

When the pleasure passed, she hurried toward the submersible. The metal sphere hung suspended over a gap in the grating by a massive crane-like structure. Stryke stood next to it, discussing something with Taran.

As she approached, Taran nodded and headed away at a jog. Stryke waved her forward.

"We figured out a way to electrify the sub's exterior. It might not be effective against leviathans, but it should offer some protection against smaller demons and Earth realm animals affected by the malevolent radiation."

"Great," she said. "You wanna talk about what just happened?"

He shot her a look. "What happened between us? No. Nice shirt. Hand me that epoxy."

"It was dry, and I was freezing." She didn't care that it was too big and hung to mid-thigh. She passed him the tube lying on the deck a few feet away. "How long do you have?"

"Until I need sex again?" He shrugged as he wiped a section of the sub dry with his sleeve. "Four to six hours, but hopefully, we'll be off this thing by then."

"Then can we talk?"

He carefully applied a layer of glue to the dry spot. "No."

"No?" She stared at him in disbelief. "Excuse me, but you owe me."

"For saving my life?" He snorted. "Okay, thank you."

He. Was. Infuriating.

"Not that, you jackass. You wanna off yourself, I don't give a shit. What you owe me for is being here in the first place. And you owe me for getting me killed because that's probably what's going to happen."

He pulled a quarter-sized, crimson witchstone from his pocket and affixed it to the glue.

"Okay, fine. I owe you. What's so important that we need to discuss it right this second instead of, you know, saving the entire world?"

Damn him. He was right. She'd let her emotions reign when she needed to figure out how to repair the other technomancer's work before a rift between realms opened.

Setting her irritation aside, she studied the witchstone, a type of spell-absorbing stone that allowed magic users to extend the reach of their spells. Most mage magic didn't work underwater, but the witchstone would act as a slow-release capsule and, in theory, create a temporary barrier from evil.

"If you glue your comms unit to the side of the sub, I can use it to make a secondary protective barrier."

"Good thinking." He whipped it off his wrist. "I don't know how deep it'll go before it breaks, though."

"Anything will help." She gestured, and he tossed it to her. She whistled as she turned it over in her palms. The leather band, encrusted with what she was sure were diamonds, screamed money. "You want to remove the band first? It's gotta be worth ten grand."

"Thirty. And no, it's fine. The diamonds enhance the unit's performance."

Okey dokey. "I guess when you're a bazillionaire, thirty thousand bucks is nothing."

His gaze bored into hers. "If the watch was worth my entire fortune, I wouldn't care," he said. "What I care about are the people on this rig and on this planet who will die if we fail. Evil can't win, Cyan. I won't let it, and I don't care how much it costs."

And that fast, she felt like a jerk. She had no idea how to respond, so she concentrated on the inner workings of his comms, sending a spell into it to enhance the mage's barrier. When she was done, she handed it back to him.

He secured it to the craft, pausing every time something growled or screeched nearby.

"This is so creepy." A chill skittered over her skin as she looked around the platform and the tendrils of fog that slithered across the deck.

"It's nothing compared to what will happen if the breach breaks wide open and brings Sheoul to our realm," he said. "Ever been there?"

"Sheoul? Never. I was raised in the human realm, and I prefer to stay in it. Most demons are horrible." She eyed him. "Why? Have you?"

"Yep." He stepped back from the craft and admired his handiwork. "Been a long time, though."

"Does StryTech do business with demons in Sheoul?"

"We do," he said. "But I make them come to me, or I send representatives in my place."

The sound of footsteps drew their attention, and they turned just as Taran cleared the last step on the ladder down.

"We're good to go," he said grimly. "All that's left to do is pray to the deity of your choice. You're going to need every advantage you can get."

Chapter 12

The Thrones might have had a hard time getting Azagoth to respond to them, but Gabriel didn't. He and the being known as the Grim Reaper had known each other for thousands of years, and while they definitely weren't friends, Gabriel respected the cold bastard.

Gabriel used the portal designed specifically to access Azagoth's realm and breathed a sigh of relief when it worked. A new addition to Azagoth's island home, he had to turn it on for every guest, and if one tried to use it when it wasn't activated, the result was…painful at best, and fatal at worst.

Gabriel strode along the beach path to the mansion at the end, where Azagoth stood, clothed exactly as one would expect the Grim Reaper to be dressed: black leather pants and a hooded, black cloak with a flaming scythe in one hand. He'd pushed the hood back, revealing his face, and as Gabriel approached, he ditched the scythe. Apparently, he couldn't wear anything else, and if he tried, the Reaper clothes appeared instead. Punishment, apparently, for destroying Sheoul-gra.

"Jim Bob," Azagoth said, using the code name Gabriel had used back before he'd revealed himself to Azagoth. "To what do I owe this unexpected visit?"

"Pour us a drink, and I'll tell you."

Azagoth inclined his dark head in a nod and pivoted on his booted feet. "This way."

Gabriel followed Azagoth to the stone steps at the front of the house. "Nice place," he said, taking in the two courtyard fountains and colorful birds flitting from tree branches to broad-leafed plants and tropical flowers. "You got lucky. Pretty much every angel wanted your head on a pike. Instead, you got this."

"The beauty only lasts a few hours," Azagoth said. "After that, this realm is a nightmare." They mounted the steps, Azagoth's cloak billowing around his feet. "But it's more than I could have ever hoped for. Especially because it was my daughter who paid the highest price."

"That...was bullshit," Gabriel said.

Azagoth's dark laugh rang out, and the birds exploded from the bushes. "Isn't that what you guys are all about? Punishing people by hurting those they love?"

Gabriel couldn't deny that, but it really all depended on who was in charge of Heaven. It also depended on who was being punished. Sometimes, the only way to hurt someone—like a demon or fallen angel—was through their families.

"It's not a punishment I would have chosen," he said. "Raika should have been allowed to choose her fate, not have it handed to her in the form of a curse." He paused. "I hear she's doing a great job, though."

"She shouldn't have to spend her life capturing dangerous demons that *I* set free." He ushered Gabriel into the building. "But she takes her duties seriously. I'm thankful she doesn't despise me for her fate."

"Why would she? You saved her mother."

"And I don't regret what I did. But I regret that Raika paid for my choices." Gabriel took in the palatial setting as Azagoth poured a couple of whiskeys from the pub-sized bar. Beyond that, the entire back of the house was open to the outdoors, where two females in bikinis were lying in the sun near the pool. One was Azagoth's mate, Lilliana.

The other, a slender female with tan skin and hair as black as Azagoth's, stretched her arms high and yawned, arching her slender back and thrusting her plump breasts toward the sun. Holy shit, she was hot. And he was envious of the sunbeams that got to caress her—

Wait...was she...?

"If you stare at my daughter for another second," Azagoth growled, "I'll remove your eyeballs and serve them in your drink like olives in a martini."

Gabriel laughed, even though he had no doubt Azagoth was serious. He was pretty certain he could take the guy in a battle, but he wasn't sure enough to risk testing that theory. Azagoth was a ruthless son of a bitch, and crossing him wasn't wise, whether you were a demon or an angel.

He took the glass from the other male and turned away from the temptress by the pool. "What do you know about the Gehennaportal?"

Azagoth's eyebrows climbed up his forehead. "I haven't heard it mentioned in thousands of years. But I do know it was rendered inoperable when the Gaiaportal was shut down."

"You heard about Harvester, I assume."

Azagoth's emerald eyes turned troubled. "She went through the Gaiaportal and was killed. But why?" Azagoth asked. "The gate was inoperable. It was inoperable when *I* was in Heaven. I don't ever remember it being in functioning order. So why would she go through it? And why have several of my sons and daughters been missing since that day?"

"I can't tell you that." Zaphkiel had ordered Gabriel to keep his mouth shut about any and all Heavenly matters.

"Is that so?" Azagoth's voice was low. Dark. Roiling with malevolent undercurrents. "Then I can't tell you more about the Gehennaportal."

The glass in Gabriel's hand shattered. The shards pierced his palm in a dozen places. One thick piece penetrated all the way to the back of his hand. The whiskey must have been made from hellfire because it *burned.*

"You know better than to come to me for anything empty-handed, *Jim Bob.*"

Yeah, he did. Gabriel watched his hand heal, the bloody bits of glass falling to the floor. "I was hoping you might want to help me out of the goodness of your heart."

Azagoth laughed. "You sound like my wife."

"I hope you don't stab *her* with glass shards."

"Never. I only like seeing *other* angels bleed." He walked back to the bar and poured another whiskey bomb. "Tell me what's happening in Heaven, Gabriel."

If Gabriel hadn't been desperate, he'd have told Azagoth to shove that glass up his evil ass. He'd been dealing with the guy for thousands of years, and they'd mostly been on equal footing. But right now, Azagoth had him by the short feathers, and when Azagoth spied any opening, any weakness, he pounced with the ruthlessness of a hellhound after its prey.

Gabriel accepted the lowball—gingerly—and considered Azagoth's request.

Zaphkiel would be furious if he found out that Gabriel had spilled Heavenly secrets to Azagoth. He might even consider it treason.

But what would they do to him? Kick him out of Heaven? Not a chance.

"Heaven's gates are closed," he said. "Your children, and every angel who was in Heaven when the realm was locked down, are stuck there. I was only allowed out to talk to you." Gabriel's gaze drifted to the pool again, and he snapped his eyes back before Azagoth started looking for toothpicks. "The Thrones staged a coup. All Archangels and Reaver are imprisoned."

Azagoth was rarely surprised, but he stilled with his tumbler at his lips. "The Archangels are *imprisoned*?"

Gabriel nodded. "The battle to capture them is what led to Harvester escaping through the Gaiaportal, which activated the Gehennaportal."

Azagoth frowned. "The Gehennaportal was built at the top of Agony Peak at the south end of the Mountains of Eternal Suffering. The peak collapsed into the Demented Sea a thousand years ago. Maybe more."

"So, it was destroyed?" That was a relief.

"I don't know. But if it wasn't, any demons using it, at least at first, would be aquatic."

Gabriel thought about that. The Heavenly portal was connected to Temple Mount, while the Sheoulic portal had transported demons to a once uninhabited area of southern Norway.

"As far as I know," he said, "there haven't been any reports of dying aquatic demons in Norway, so it must not be active. If it is, it's either inaccessible or demons haven't found it yet." That was also good news.

"No," Azagoth said, his dark brow furrowed, "but the Genhennaportal's Sheoulic gateway moved when the mountain collapsed. What if the human realm's gateway location moved too?"

Well, that was a dropkick to the gut. Gabriel did not like the direction of this conversation.

Azagoth moved to his media display and brought up a 3D rendering of a news story.

"The day Harvester disappeared," he said, "an oil company reported a disturbance at one of its North Sea platforms. There haven't been any follow-up stories about it, but within a week, StryTech struck a secret deal and bought the platform. Very few know about this. They're trying to keep humans from freaking out."

Gabriel didn't have to ask how Azagoth knew. He had an extensive information network that had probably shrunk since he was no longer running Sheoul-gra, but he also ran in Stryke's family circle.

"You think the oil company drilled into the Gehennaportal? At the bottom of the North Sea?"

"I know they drilled into *something*. StryTech thinks it might be a weak spot in the barrier between the human and demon realms. Last I heard, Stryke had sealed the breach. But if what they drilled into was the Gehennaportal, their seal might not hold."

"Now you see why I'm here."

Azagoth swirled the amber liquid in his glass, his expression troubled.

"Leave it to Harvester to cause mayhem." Azagoth's daughter stepped inside, a towel draped over one arm, a pair of sunglasses dangling from her tan, slender fingers. "What did she do?" She eyed Gabriel up and down, her shrewd green eyes sizing him up. If she was as good as he'd heard, she'd already assessed his weaknesses and determined what weapon would work best against him. "And who are you?"

Azagoth smoothly blocked Gabriel from her line of sight. "He's no one."

"Oh," she said in a deep, sultry voice as she stepped back into his view, "I doubt that."

Visibly annoyed, Azagoth turned to his daughter. "Raika, have you heard of any demon incidents in Norway or near the North Sea?"

"No, why? Does this have something to do with Harvester? Have you figured out a way to bring her back?"

Gabriel blinked. "Bring her...back?"

Azagoth swung around to him, casually blocking his view again. "Apparently, her Grace never returned to Heaven. Instead, it found a human vessel."

Gabriel's breath caught. "A vessel? No angel has taken a vessel in centuries. Not for more than a few days, and not without a good reason." When an angel died in the human realm, their souls—their Grace—could either return to their Creator or enter a human. They couldn't stay for long lest they burn out the body. They mostly just hung out, but sometimes, they could communicate through their host or even influence their behavior. "Has she spoken through this vessel?"

Raika shifted back into Gabriel's view and gave her dad a

questioning look—a definite is-this-stranger-cool look—and waited for his nod before answering.

"Idess thinks Harvester may not be conscious enough to speak," she said, referring to her half-sister, one of Azagoth's many children with many angelic mothers, and one of Stryke's aunts. "The more traumatic a person's death, the longer it takes for them to adjust."

That certainly held true for humans. It could take those in Heaven years to come to terms with their deaths.

He had no idea about angels since little was known about what happened to their Grace—their soul and their power—after they returned to Heaven. Some believed the Creator reabsorbed them. Others thought their souls were recycled the way humans and demons were, reborn into another body.

A significant number of Celestials refused to consider that as a possibility because it would mean they had something in common with lowly humans and vile demons.

"So?" she asked. "Do you know how to reach her? Bring her out so she can speak through her vessel? We need to know what happened to her. Also, who *are* you?" She glared at her father. "And don't tell me he's no one. If he's not a high-ranking angel, I'll eat a bag of dicks for dinner."

"You most certainly will not," Azagoth said, and Gabriel had to bite back a laugh at the graphic image that must be going through his fatherly head right now.

"I'm Gabriel," He inclined his head in greeting. "Your father and I are old friends."

"*Friends* is a bit of an exaggeration," Azagoth said.

"True." Gabriel gestured with his glass. "A friend wouldn't explode a drink in their hand."

"Be thankful it was your drink and not your head," Raika said with a laugh. "This creepy guy a couple weeks ago? Messsssy." She looked him up and down. "Gabriel, huh? Archangel. Not what I expected. I have a lot of questions."

Not what she expected?

"Don't you have a bunch of demons to capture?" Azagoth asked.

She rolled her eyes. "That's why I'm not still in the pool."

"Going to be hard fighting demons in a bikini."

She snorted. "I can probably fight *better* in a bikini. Less restrictive." She crossed her arms over her chest, and Gabriel had to force himself to look away from the smooth swells of flesh barely covered by tiny triangles of black fabric. "Tell me why you're talking about Harvester and what she has to do with potential demons I might need to stop in Norway."

Azagoth's jaw tightened in frustration. "Put on some clothes."

She rolled her eyes again, but a second later, she was dressed in black tactical pants, combat boots, a black tank top, and a weapons harness.

If Azagoth thought getting his daughter out of a bikini would make her less hot...he was so fucking wrong.

Raika was a freaking goddess in warrior gear.

Azagoth seemed satisfied, though. "Harvester caused an ancient portal in Hell to open. It needs to be closed before demons discover it's active. Gabriel is here looking for information." Azagoth wandered over to a bookcase, where a miniature model of Sheoul-gra spanned an entire shelf. "The sorcerers responsible for creating the Gehennaportal also designed and built Sheoul-gra. Unfortunately, no one knows where they are or if they're even still alive. That's why it's taking Hades so long to rebuild Sheoul-gra. But," he said, "I do know that both Sheoul-gra and the Gehennaportal were fueled by eternal fire. If you destroy the fuel source, you destroy the portal."

Gabriel thought about that. "There's just the small matter of getting to the source. Most angels don't do well underwater."

"You might not need to get all the way to the eternal fire," Azagoth said. "Unleashing angelic energy just inside the portal should work."

"Maybe we could use Stryke's drilling platform to reach it."

Raika nodded. "You could drop an angelic power bomb down the shaft and extinguish the eternal fire." Her eyes glittered with dark amusement. She was so like her father. "Brilliant!"

He tore his gaze away from her with great effort. "So, I need to get in touch with Stryke, and I need to get onto that platform. "Is he still Primori, do you know?"

"I've never known. I'm no longer in that business. But," Azagoth said, "as powerful and influential as he is, I can almost guarantee he's Primori."

Which meant he was protected by a Memitim, a class of angel bred from Azagoth himself, and wouldn't die until he'd fulfilled his fate or Heaven had no more reason to keep him alive.

"Knowing won't help you," Azagoth said, "unless you're planning to kill him."

"Actually, it might. Primori are crucial to the timeline of existence in some way. He may play an important role in this. He probably does, and from what I've seen, his alignment tilts toward good, so he might be willing to cooperate with me." He might be *fated* to cooperate. "But he's notorious for not responding to Heavenly summons. I had to wait an entire year for him to answer me once."

Azagoth snorted. "You think a demon will be *summoned* by angels? That's your problem right there. After dealing with me for so long, you should know better than that, Gabriel." He glanced down at his drink as he spoke. "But Stryke isn't your problem. Revenant, if he gets out of Hell...*that's* your problem." Azagoth raised his eyes and grinned, flashing fangs. "Heaven's going to burn," he growled, "and it'll deserve it."

Chapter 13

What the hell had she been thinking?

Cyan peered down through the tiny hatchway of the submersible that was supposed to take her to the enchanted glyphs that needed to be repaired. The pilot, a friendly blond human from Norway, had already squeezed into the underwater deathtrap.

Stryke laid his hand on her forearm, halting her as she zipped up the jacket Twila had loaned her for the icy temperatures in the vehicle. "You don't have to do this."

She appreciated his concern, although it was easy to say she didn't have to risk her life when the truth was that it was their only option.

"You know I do."

He heaved a heavy breath. "Just remember to control your fear. Don't let it affect your judgment or performance."

Right. He made it sound so easy. "I'm not afraid," she informed him, although there was a bit of terror running through her. "I'm claustrophobic. And also, I work best under pressure. So, bite me."

No doubt her irritability went far in proving how well she did under pressure.

The dudes standing around to help looked at each other, expressions ranging from shock to curiosity. Obviously, they couldn't believe someone was talking to their boss that way.

Well, she didn't give a shit. He wasn't *her* boss. She could speak to him any way she wanted to.

"Just be careful," he said. "Kynan will be pissed if I get his head researcher killed."

"I'm sure Kynan's wrath terrifies you."

Not waiting for a response, she lowered herself down the ladder and into the submersible. She took deep, calming breaths and concentrated on the buttons and gauges inside the vehicle instead of on how tight it was in there and how she was going to lose her mind in the tiny thing.

She focused on breathing as the pilot prepared for submersion, constantly speaking back and forth to the team on the rig. She nearly jumped out of her skin when the hatch closed.

She was locked inside, unable to get out, unable to escape. Anything could go wrong, and she'd die in the dark, wet, cold sea.

Oh, gods, this was a mistake.

"Hey." Oskar, the pilot, gave her a look of sympathy. "Take a seat and buckle in. Close your eyes and play a song inside your head. Or recite a poem. Just keep your mind busy for a few minutes. We'll be down there and back up before you know it."

"Okay." She nodded. "Okay."

I can do this.

Calmly—at least on the outside—she sat in a very uncomfortable jump seat and strapped herself in. Then she threw her head back and summoned a song. Well, she tried to summon a song. *Shivers*, an Ed Sheeran classic. She'd just seen a video of him in concert. He was in his sixties now, but man, he could still sing.

But for some reason, her mind kept taking her back to a song she'd heard playing at Runa's party. A dark, moody piece from a recent movie's soundtrack, had rolled through the room like a riptide.

She's a beautiful heathen, a righteous bitch, and she'll take your soul into the darkness…

A clank startled her, then a jolt, and Oskar glanced over at her with a reassuring smile.

"All normal. We're starting our descent now."

"How are you two doing?" Stryke's deep voice came over the speaker, and something fluttered in her stomach. He'd asked her that during sex, and now her mind wanted to play that scene over and over.

"How are you doing?" he rasped. *"You okay?"*

"Yes," she breathed. *"Hurry."*

She couldn't stand the guy, but her hormones sure hadn't gotten the message.

"All's good," the pilot said. "I'll shift the camera so you can see us both."

She nearly groaned. It was bad enough that Stryke was watching any of it. He didn't need to see her struggling to prevent a panic attack. He didn't need to see how she'd just nearly jumped out of her skin when the submarine creaked.

"Hey, Cyan. See this?" Oskar pointed to a number readout on the dashboard of gadgets. "That's our depth. Focus on that."

"I don't think that's a good idea," she whispered as fresh stirrings of anxiety gripped her by the throat. "I don't like this. I don't like this at all—"

"Cyan?" Stryke's voice, a calm, resonant purr, instantly captured her focus. "Listen to me. Concentrate on my voice. Tell me something about yourself. Something I don't know."

She knew this trick. She'd seen her psychologist mother use it all the time. "How about you tell *me* something? Make me more interested in you than I am in how small this damned thing is."

"What do you want to know?"

I want to know why you freaked out during sex and ran away. Also, why is your voice so deep and sexy? "I think you can guess."

"Come up with something else."

Yeah, probably not cool to make him discuss something so intimate in front of however many people were listening. Closing her eyes, she did her best to ignore the fact that they were plummeting deep into the sea, and if this thing sprung a leak...

"What's between you and Blade?" she asked.

"Next question."

"Why are you such an asshole?"

Oskar nearly choked on his own saliva.

"Ah, an oldie but a goodie," Stryke mused. "There are many theories. None of which I care to share right now."

"Well, we have a problem then because there's nothing else about you I want to know."

"I see." She thought she heard a note of amusement in his voice. Great. She hoped he was enjoying this because she'd rather be fighting her way through Sheoul's Horun region with nothing but a pair of nail clippers than be sealed inside this metal coffin. "Why don't you tell me about your childhood then?"

Her childhood? Why did he care? Then she realized he *didn't* give a crap. He was just trying to keep her from trying to claw her way out of the sub.

What the hell? She inhaled deeply, closed her eyes, and thought about growing up in the Los Angeles suburbs.

"My dad worked for a tech company based in LA, and my mom was a psychologist. I went to school at Hellmouth Academy because my parents didn't want me to have to wear contact lenses or a glamour to fit in with human kids."

She had worn contacts anyway when she went out in public or hung out with her human friends, but at least she didn't have to wear them all the time. She could get away with sunglasses most of the time now.

"When were you at the academy?"

She was pretty sure he already knew the answer to that question. "Same time you were. We're the same age."

He laughed. "We're the same age, but I graduated six years earlier than you did."

"I know. You were twelve when you graduated, and then you attended college virtually."

"I see you did your research."

Obviously, he had done his as well. "You can find that factoid in every interview you've ever given. Plus, it's on the StryTech website." She knew because she'd read or seen every interview, and she had the StryTech website memorized. But not in a creepy way. Really. "Your parents didn't want you in college until you were old enough not to draw attention."

"A twelve-year-old kid in advanced physics classes would have drawn attention we didn't want."

"That didn't turn out well, did it? You're the most well-known demon in the world."

There was a moment of silence. "Things don't always turn out the way we plan, do they?" She got the feeling his question was posed more to himself than to her. "So," he continued, "what made you want to become a technomancer?"

The sub was deep. Was it supposed to be this deep? Oskar seemed unfazed, making her feel a little better. "It's what my species does."

"Not all of you have the gift of being able to manipulate technology."

"Only about half of us," she acknowledged. "My mom couldn't. It's why she went into psychology." The craft shuddered, and she took a moment to catch her breath. "My dad almost didn't take her as a mate because of it. He wanted to make sure his offspring would be *blessed with the gift.*"

There was another pause. Then Stryke's voice, laced with curiosity, crackled over the increasingly sketchy connection. "I find it interesting that your species went from being one of the most reviled to one of the most celebrated in the matter of a century."

Reviled was one word for it. As demons with no unique powers, her kind had learned to avoid Sheoul, where they were tortured and often eaten simply because they were weak compared to most demons.

"That's why so many of our holidays center around the discovery of electricity and the industrial revolution."

The miracle of technology had changed their lives. Even the weakest Cyberis technomancers were now in high demand in the demon realm. They had status, power, and seats in the Maleconcieo, basically the Sheoulic version of the human realm's United Nations. No one fucked with them anymore, and if they did, they'd better not be wearing—or be near—any kind of advanced technology.

Their power was also what made them feared and heavily regulated in the human realm.

"Where are your parents now?" he asked.

"You did research," she said. "You tell me."

"Your father suffered an accident on the job," he said. "Your mother died six months later, a result of your species being lethally affected by a broken mate bond."

"She didn't just *die*," she said bitterly. "She gave up." Yes, it was rare to survive a broken bond, but it happened. "And my father was killed by a faulty StryTech product."

There was silence. Even Oskar's soft breathing stopped.

"I'm sorry," Stryke said. There was more silence, and then, "I hate water."

"What?" She scowled at the speaker. "Did you say you hate water?"

"You asked me to tell you something about myself that you didn't know." There was a little static, and the craft bounced, but she barely noticed. She was too curious about where this was going. He might be trying to change the subject, but she got the feeling it was more than that. He was giving her a private, personal piece of his life, revealing a vulnerability, something she doubted he ever did. "Water feels weird on my skin."

That explained the invisible umbrella he was working on. "But you have a pool and a hot tub."

"They're for Masumi. I don't go in either."

If she had a pool and hot tub, she'd be in them every day. "How do you deal with showers?"

"They're tolerable, but I don't linger."

She could picture him in the shower, soaping up, scrubbing his chest as bubbles ran down his hard-cut abs and then lower to his—

"I'm sorry to interrupt," Oskar said, "but we're getting close to the nano injector. Keep an eye on the monitor."

Glad to have something more to do than fantasize about Stryke in the shower, she leaned forward in her seat, so close to Oskar she could smell his musky aftershave.

Stryke smelled better. Like dark chocolate and the smoky diablo peppers that grew in the blood-fed fields along the shores of Sheoul's River Scaldera. Her mom had brought some home once, and Cyan had never forgotten the spicy tingle in her nose. Stryke's scent caused a spicy tingle *everywhere*. Not that she should be thinking about what he smelled like or where he made her tingle right now.

Returning her attention to the monitor, she watched the craft's powerful light sweep along a massive drill casing. Oskar kept the craft steady, flipping switches, pressing buttons, and steering with practiced hands.

"You got to hear all about me and Stryke," she said to him. "What's your story?"

"Don't got one," he said, shooting her a sideways glance. "I'm human, but I work for anyone who pays me, and Stryke pays well."

"I do," Stryke interjected. "I'm willing to pay for quality. I want the best people in every field."

"And you always get them, don't you?" she said.

"No," Stryke replied, surprising her. "Not always. Some people won't work for a demon no matter the pay."

"And what? Your sparkling wit and charm don't win them over?"

He laughed. "That," he said, "has never happened. I have neither sparkles nor charm."

"Tell me about it," she muttered, and Oskar snickered. "There!" She pointed at the screen. "I see some glyphs."

Oskar shifted a lever, and the pod came to a gently rocking standstill. "I got a temperature spike," he said calmly into the microphone, clearly not speaking to her. "Are you reading—?"

"We're reading it," Stryke answered.

"A five-degree spike isn't unusual," Taran said. "But we're seeing spikes of twenty degrees a half mile to the south."

Cyan tuned out the chatter, trusting that Taran and Stryke knew what the data meant. Her job was to analyze the fractured spell and repair it.

She reached deep into the center of herself, into what her people with the gift called her *quanimas*, the part of the soul that could connect with the energy around it, including that from other dimensions. According to her people, everyone, including humans and animals, possessed a *quanimas*, but not everyone could access it. And yet, it was the access point for all magical and supernatural abilities, an organ unseen but capable of great power. Like the heart, except that it circulated spiritual energy instead of blood.

Warmth pumped through her body as her mind grabbed the glyphs and replaced them with a new weave, one that would spread a protective web extending from the man-made components of the rig across the floor of the ocean. The web, if woven correctly through the nanotechnology, would act as a butterfly bandage across the widening fissure through which Sheoul's realm was leaking.

One of the glyphs, frayed at the edges, got a quick patch job. But another, a broken link, was nothing but shreds. She replaced it, but she didn't spend extra time smoothing the edges. The tech who had placed the weave before her had been good at his craft, every element of the spell precise and clear.

She was a little messier, preferring to get the rough draft done before going back to strengthen and polish it.

Power flowed through her hands and fingers as she used them to shape and form glyphs while trying to ignore the occasional bumps of ocean currents against the craft.

Then the submersible rocked hard, nearly knocking her against the wall. "Hey, do you mind—?"

"More heat blooms to the south." Taran's voice stuttered over the connection. "I think you guys should hurry."

"This isn't something that can be rushed," she said irritably. She might be efficient under stress, but she was also grumpy as hell. "Your other guy might have been able to—"

The sub rocked hard, tossing her and Oskar around in their seats, held in only by the harnesses.

"Shit." Oskar flipped switches and cranked levers as an alarm screeched.

"What's going on?" she asked as she threw a glyph into the weave. Just a few more…

"Get out of there!" Stryke shouted, and her heart leaped into her throat. Stryke was not one to panic. "Hurry! *Go!*"

"Massive heat signature moving toward you," Taran barked. "Oh, man, it's big. Get up here. Get up here now!"

"Emergency ascend," Oskar said calmly, and she had to give him credit. She wasn't even sure she could speak right now, let alone speak in a soothing monotone. "Buckle in."

She was already buckled, so she held tight as the craft shot upward, its light shining on the rig's structure as they passed joints and bolts and other things she couldn't identify.

"There's another one," Taran barked. "Multiple heat signatures moving this way."

"How long?"

"You got about sixty seconds," Stryke said.

She glanced at the pilot, and her heart sank. The look on his face said they wouldn't make it.

"I'm guessing this thing isn't armed?"

He snorted.

Okay, so it didn't have weapons. But…the submersible was a giant piece of machinery with advanced technology. As long as she was on board, it *could* be armed, especially with the improvements she and Stryke had made to the skin of the craft.

Quickly, she formed the first defensive spell weave she'd learned and injected it into every bit of onboard electronics.

"What are you doing?" Taran asked.

Suddenly, the sub swung sideways and forward, crashing against a platform beam. The metal groaned and creaked, and then, through the metal walls, something screamed.

"Yes!" Stryke breathed. "Cyan, what did you do?"

"I sent a bolt of lightning through the water. We might only get one more charge out of it before it drains the sub's power, though."

"It's coming back—"

She looked at the camera just in time to see a massive set of teeth and long, creepy claws flashing in front of the screen before everything went dark, and they were tumbling through the blackness. The sound of rending, twisting metal, and furious shrieks blew through her ears until the pain became overwhelming.

And then there was no sound at all.

"Reel it in!" Stryke shouted at the top of his lungs as he raced from the FOC to the sub's launch and recovery platform. "Reel the fucking thing in!"

The crew was already on it, and he knew that. But panic had destroyed his logical thoughts. All he could do was act on instinct and fear—something he hadn't done since...

Fuck.

He charged down the metal steps two at a time, clearing three levels in mere seconds. He hit the platform at full speed, skidding across the wet surface until he managed to grab a railing.

Three technicians scrambled to bring the submersible the rest of the way to the surface, one watching the water, one operating the lift, and the other standing guard with a flamethrower. Above them on the two upper levels, several members of the security detail manned outposts, their various weapons aimed at the churning waters below.

Stryke's pulse pounded in his ears, and his heart hammered in his chest as the top of the little craft breached the surface. Blackened, twisted claw marks and mangled tooth punctures scored the sub's thick skin, and Stryke held his breath as the crew stabilized the craft and popped the hatch.

"Help me!" Oskar held Cyan in his arms, her unconscious body slumped against his chest.

Stryke's heart plummeted to his feet. He sprang into action, working with the crane operator to haul her limp body through the narrow hatch. Her face dripped blood from a gash in her temple, her head hanging loosely from her shoulders. Oskar pushed from below, but the craft suddenly wrenched hard. The crane operator lost his grip as Oskar lost his footing, and Cyan nearly dropped all the way back into the pod. Only Stryke's hold on her wrist kept her from hitting the deck.

The high-pitched whirr of arrows and other projectiles filled the air, joining the hellish roars of the creatures under the waves. A massive claw punched out of the water and caught the crane operator. The male didn't even have time to scream before he suffered a *sudden catastrophic decapitation event.*

Shit.

Stryke hauled Cyan up, her body slamming against the sides of the hatch as the craft bucked and rocked. She groaned, her eyes opening, flaring in groggy recognition. She seemed to understand the urgency and swung her empty hand upward to grip his arm.

A demon, black as night with glowing yellow eyes, its slick skin rippling and steaming in the cold air, flung itself out of the water and wrapped around the pod. Stryke leaped backward, taking Cyan with him. They landed in a pile as the demon attacked the pod's hoist with its teeth and webbed claws. Oskar tried to escape, the terror on his face stark and gut-wrenching as he desperately tried to claw his way out of the craft before the hoist failed.

In a groan of metal, the hoist collapsed and fell into the sea, taking the pod, the demon, and Oskar with it.

"*No!*"

Blood bubbled up, joining the crane operator's as it dripped over the side of the dock.

As the seas churned and arrows and crossbow bolts flew, Stryke gathered Cyan in his arms and charged up the stairs. Below, the demons screamed as they attacked the platform. It appeared they couldn't leave the water. The ones who breached the surface only did so for a moment, their skin steaming.

Consoled by that one small blessing, Stryke hurried to the med shack, a double-wide shipping container outfitted for basic medical care.

He shouldered open the door. "I need some help!"

Nothing. Of course. The doctor who had been stationed here had been killed. In his panic, he'd completely forgotten.

"Hold on, Cyan."

"I'm okay," she slurred. "Okay."

"No, you're not." He placed her on the patient bed, and when she tried to sit up, he gently palmed her shoulder and pushed her back down.

"Oskar…" She wiped blood out of her eye. "Where is he?"

"He didn't make it." Stryke charged his gift and sent it into her. He couldn't heal like Blade or his uncle Eidolon, but he could speed up her body's natural abilities to make blood and stop bleeding. He also tweaked her system to control her pain, and with a sigh, she closed her eyes and lay back.

The door burst open, and Taran stood there, his face smeared with blood, one sleeve shredded by what must have been claws.

"Demons are scaling the supports. Hundreds of them. So far, they haven't made it to the platform, but if they do, we're not going to be able to take them all out. We're outnumbered."

That left only one option. "Then we evacuate."

Taran shook his head. "Our escape pods are no match for those things."

"We die if we stay here. If we can put down all the pods, maybe one of them has a chance of making it to safety." He jerked his head toward the door. "At least prep for evacuation."

"Yes, sir." Taran took off.

"We're not going to get to safety on the lifeboats," she mumbled, sounding groggy. "You know that."

"And we're not safe here for much longer."

"Come on, genius," she said, her voice sounding stronger as he worked his healing magic. "Surely, you can come up with something. Something you missed. You developed the communications system. Maybe you can refigure it to use evil energy as a patch through the fog."

"It doesn't work that way. The fog is more than energy. It's biological. Alive. Anything that can penetrate it would have to be…" He trailed off as a thought occurred to him. What was the date?

What was the fucking date? He'd have checked his comms but it had been destroyed along with the submersible, and his spare was in his quarters. Quickly and frantically, he darted around the room, searching for a calendar.

She sat up. "What? What is it?"

"The date," he said hastily. "What's the date?"

"Ah…the fifteenth."

The fifteenth…okay, so the moon phase was…?

"The moon phase?" she asked.

Had he spoken out loud? Didn't matter. He did about a million calculations in his head, and…holy shit.

No. It was impossible. He couldn't be this lucky.

"Stryke?"

He wheeled away from her, his mind reeling. Could he? *Should* he? How would his brothers react? Strike that. Brother. If he did this, he wouldn't involve Crux or Rade.

He needed Blade.

Would Blade even *want* to help?

"Dammit, Stryke, what is it?"

He turned to her. "Did you know that Seminus demons are connected to their brothers? We can feel each other's intense pain. We know when they die."

"That…must be incredible."

"Incredible?" He gaped at her. "Incredible to feel your sibling die? Incredible is not the word I would use. Agonizing. Traumatic. Fucking abominable. Those are the words I would use."

"I didn't mean it like that," she said. "But to have such a deep connection to someone you love seems…special."

She knew nothing.

Nothing.

"The price is too high for connections like that," he said dismissively, his thoughts already jumping ahead. "But I also carry my mother's genetic werewolf material. As do my brothers. On nights of the full moon, we can communicate with each other. At least, some of us can."

"Some of us?"

"I had the links—all the links—between my brothers and me severed."

She blinked. "But…why?"

"Doesn't matter." It was a long story, and he didn't owe anyone the reason behind it. "What matters is that it's a full moon. If I can restore the werewolf link, I can get help."

She jackknifed up so fast he thought she might fall off the med bed. "You can do that?"

"No, but *you* can." He brushed his fingertips across the tiny NeuroTech implant in his temple, the comms chip nearly everyone in the world had implanted to use modern-day communication technology.

Technology designed by StryTech but manufactured by humans to ease fears of "*demonic devices.*" Those who didn't get the implant could wear an external device behind their ear, but at the price of some functionality.

Frowning, she peered at his temple. "A technomancer did it. I can see the spell now that I'm looking for it."

"Rewire it so I can get in touch with Blade."

"Just Blade?"

He nodded. Opening a line to Crux would only fill the kid full of hope, and Rade probably wouldn't give a shit. Plus, Blade, as a member of DART's special operations team, was in a position to get them help.

"Are you ready?" she asked, and he nodded again.

"Just be prepared to sever the connection when I tell you to."

She appeared taken aback. "You want to shut it down?"

"I'll have you reconnect it if I need it. In the meantime, can you do something to help keep the demons off the rig?"

"I don't know what. I can't do a general repellent spell because a lot of us working here are demons."

He thought about that. "The fog…it's malevolent. It's what allows the things in the water to exist out of it, even if only for a little while."

She sucked in a harsh breath, understanding now where he was going with this. "If I can repel the fog—"

"It might leave just enough space between the rig and the mist to limit the creatures that can attempt to get on the platform."

She nodded. "I'll head over to the engine room right away."

Chapter 14

"That's a big pile of body parts."

Blade looked over at his cousin and DART spec ops teammate, Mace, and snorted. "I don't know why you insist on piling up all the demons we kill. They disintegrate."

"Dude. This is a holy place. It's rude to leave greasy stains all over."

Scotty rolled her eyes at Mace. "You're so weird."

Totally agreed. Mace had some odd quirks. "He's just like his dad," Blade said in a low voice so only Scotty could hear.

She laughed. "Which one?"

"You know which one." Lore, the male who'd raised Mace, was a pretty level, down-to-earth dad. But Mace's biological father, Wraith, was an adventurous, impulsive son of a bitch who had always been everyone's favorite uncle. Blade glanced over at Scotty's sister, Aleka. "You done?"

Aleka blew out a frustrated breath as she looked between the map in her hand and the rough, earthen chamber walls. "Hardly. There has to be a vessel here somewhere. Harvester's blood didn't just disappear."

Scotty eyed the structure over their heads: the floor of the mosque above them. Most didn't know there were several passageways and chambers below, where Aleka was convinced the blood of the angel Harvester had flowed after the blood rain event a few weeks ago.

"Thank you for helping out, by the way," Aleka continued. "When I asked Kynan to borrow Scotty, I didn't expect him to send all of you."

"We're a package deal," Scotty said. "You need security? You get us all."

It was true. Blade, Mace, and Scotty had been inseparable since childhood, and they worked so well together that, when they joined the Demon Activity Response Team, Kynan had built an entire special forces department around them. Mace and Blade's aunt Tayla managed the twelve-person department, and while most of the others worked interchangeably as teams, Scotty, Blade, and Mace rarely went anywhere without one another.

"I didn't need security," Aleka said crisply. "I can take care of myself." She glanced at all the dead demons. "Usually."

Yeah, as the daughter of the Horseman known as War, Aleka was a capable fighter. She was not as capable as her younger sister, but then, unlike Scotty, Aleka had dedicated her life to research, not combat.

"So," Mace said, crossing his arms over his broad chest, his weapons harness whispering against his black T-shirt, "what happened between you and Sabre?"

Blade winced. Mace truly was incapable of tact.

"Nothing." Aleka ran her finger over a seam in the stone wall. "Subject closed."

"But you guys left Limos's party together," Mace said, referring to the get-together the day Harvester's blood rained down on just two places on Earth: here at the Temple Mount, and at the party. "And then we got home, and Sabre was drowning his sorrows and grumpy as hell."

She rounded on Mace, her long, red hair a few shades lighter than Scotty's, stirring the dusty air. Anger made her green eyes glow, and for a moment, Blade thought Mace was about to feel the burn of Aleka's summoned fire sword. Blade had experienced it only once, years ago, while sparring under Ares' tutelage. His ribs still ached sometimes. Charred bone took a long time to heal, and not even his uncle Eidolon could facilitate the process beyond a certain point.

"He was drowning his sorrows?" Aleka's lips turned up into a dark smile. "Good. Now, drop it and follow me," she said, heading down a narrow passage marked by layers of dust and cracked mosaics.

Blade fell in behind the others, taking up the rear, his eyes peeled for signs of danger. "Hey, if we—"

He missed a step as a wave of...something...washed over him. The feeling was subtle but powerful, strange yet familiar. A sensation he hadn't experienced in years.

My brother.

A spear of awareness shot into his very soul, and suddenly, Stryke was with him again, the way Rade and Crux were. The way Chaos used to be.

"Stryke," he whispered hoarsely, his emotions so out of whack he couldn't focus on walking, breathing, or even standing. He sagged against a pillar and did his damnedest to stay upright.

"Blade?" Mace's steadying hand came down on his biceps. "What's wrong? What happened?"

"I don't know. I can…I can feel Stryke."

"What?" Scotty was there too, concern putting a frown on her glossy lips. She rarely wore lipstick, preferring the shiny clear stuff. "He reestablished the connection?"

"I doubt it was intentional." He frowned as the tingle of awareness became taut. Unsettling.

"*Help.*"

Help? This had to be a trick. Some demon messing with him. Stryke wouldn't ask *anyone* for assistance, let alone Blade.

Mace's grip tightened. "Hey, man. Tell us what's going on."

"*I'm in trouble.*"

Whatever it was, it was probably deserved. If it was even him. Blade sent a mental "*fuck you*" back.

A blast of irritation came through the connection. Okay, yeah, it was probably Stryke.

"*The world is in danger. Tell Kynan. Need assistance.*"

"Okay, I'll bite," Blade returned. "*What's going on?*"

"*A rip in the fabric between the hell and human realms resulted in a malevolent Shoulic ejection. We're surrounded by a fog of evil and can't get out.*"

"*Where are you?*"

"*Oil platform. Tell Kynan he can get the details from Kalis. Talk to Dakarai about the diffuser prototype and the runic amplifier. Hurry. We don't have much time.*"

The connection dropped, and a unique anguish, an emptiness he hadn't experienced since the day Chaos died, made him sway. Scotty and Mace caught him as he went down and lowered him gently to the ancient tile flooring.

"Blade." Scotty went down on her knees next to him. "Talk to me."

"It's like he died," he rasped. "Maybe he did. Fuck. Just…fuck."

There was so much rage inside him, so much pain, and maybe a lot of hate. But he didn't wish Stryke dead. No, that bastard needed to live so he could spend his long life regretting what he'd done to their family when he cut them out of his life.

"What can we do?" Mace asked.

"We need to find him," Blade said. "He said the world is in danger. Some sort of Sheoulic breach."

"You're sure it was him?"

"Yeah."

"You think he's telling the truth?"

"Why would he lie about something like this?"

Mace shrugged. "Why does he do half the shit he does?"

Good question.

"Did he say where he is?" Scotty asked.

Blade tapped his comms device and sent a NeuroLink request to Kynan. "Some kind of oil platform."

He rubbed his chest as if that would fill the fresh hole put there by Stryke's reappearance and disappearance. It felt as if someone had taken a hole punch to his soul.

Again.

And he was getting really fucking sick of it.

Chapter 15

Cyan didn't know how long she'd been working in the platform's engine room, using her skills to disrupt the evil fog outside. She'd been able to create a narrow band of positive energy around the rig that kept the mist from touching it. The band was only about ten feet wide, but it was enough to discourage some of the malevolent creatures from getting onto the platform.

The catch was that if she didn't monitor her weaves, they unraveled the moment she left the engine room. But if she could get one of the mages to add their power to hers, she might be able to finally get out of this hot, stifling chamber.

The main door swung open, and Stryke and Taran burst through the hatch. "Between the mages and our weapons, we've beaten back the demons," Taran said. "But I don't know for how long. The heat signatures from the rift are getting bigger, and the crack is growing." He slicked his hair back from his face as he looked around. "Why is it so quiet in here? I usually need to yell to be heard."

"I got tired of the noise," she said. "I wove a silence spell into the machinery."

Stryke gave her an approving nod. "Nice." He started toward her. "We got new images of the rift you might want to see."

"Did you bring them? I can't leave unless you can get a mage in here."

Taran reached for the door handle. "Hold on. I'll download the images. Give me ten." He took off, presumably for the FOC.

Stryke held out a bottle of water. "You hungry? The cafeteria is actually serving some hot food. I can grab something for you."

She gratefully took the water and shook her head as she twisted off the cap. "No. I just want off this thing. I swear I'm never going near the sea or ocean again." She took a huge gulp. "Have you heard anything from Blade?"

"Comms are still down."

"Maybe you shouldn't have broken the link with him," she suggested, more than a little annoyed by his refusal to do the smart thing.

"Maybe it's none of your business."

"Excuse me?" The plastic bottle crinkled in her tight, irritated grip. "None of my business? You brought me here to fix a potentially catastrophic rift between the human and demon realms, and I'm probably going to die. So, yeah, it's my business when you endanger us all. I can't believe I fell for your bullshit," she snapped. "I can't believe I took you at your word when you said difficult answers require difficult decisions. You didn't make the difficult decision here, Stryke. You made the easy one because you didn't want to deal with your brother."

He went still. "What did you say?"

"Oh, don't get pissy," she spat, frustrated by his stubbornness. "It's obvious you don't want to deal with your brother."

"Not that," he ground out. "The difficult answers thing."

"Oh." She blinked. Sometimes, he was hard to follow. A little calmer now, she explained. "When I was in school, you came back to your alma mater to speak to my class. You talked about having to make difficult choices at such a young age."

"I remember that," he said, frowning. "I didn't think anyone actually listened."

"I listened." She remembered every word, every gesture, every detail of his lecture. "You were my hero, Stryke. And then after I saw you speak at my college, you became the reason I wanted to work for DART. You're the reason I want to expand the lab and create our own weapons and defenses. But thanks to the crap going on with The Aegis, our funding was cut."

"Thanks to my weapon, you mean."

"Take it as you will." She turned back to the wall of anti-fog glyphs only she could see, then realized she wasn't done. Hell, no. He owed her. She wheeled back around to him. "What happened to you, Stryke?

What changed? What happened to the cocky genius who laughed and shared his love of science with the world?"

For a long, tense moment, he stood there as still as a statue. His eyes grew haunted, and she swore she saw shadows writhing in their dark depths. The trauma lurking there made her regret her question.

"What changed?" he asked finally, his voice as haunted as his gaze. "What changed is that I killed my brother."

Cyan's expression slowly shifted from anger to surprise. And then disbelief.

Join the club.

Stryke couldn't believe he'd actually said that. With the exception of Blade's bullshit every couple of years or so, he hadn't spoken about that day since then. Well, until his dad came to his office the other day.

Stryke had kept that part of his life buried deep, unwilling to open up about it to anyone. And now, in the middle of a hazardous situation, he'd just blurted it out. Invited questions. Exposed his throat and made himself vulnerable.

What was it about this female that made him so stupid?

He wanted a do-over. Wanted to finally get started on inventing a time machine so he could go back and change this moment.

Dolt. If you invent a time machine, Chaos never has to die.

"I didn't know you had another brother," she said, bringing him back to the present, where time machines didn't exist.

A dull ache centered in his chest. "His name was Chaos," he said, his voice scratchy, a stranger to the topic. "He was Crux's twin."

"Crux?"

"The tall blond at the party the other night. The kid masquerading as Kynan's nephew."

Her pale eyebrows rose. "I remember him. But why the lie?"

"Because he hasn't gone through his transition yet. Anyone who knows anything about my species would realize how young he is."

"How young…" Her eyes shot wide as realization hit. "Oh, my

gods. Sheoul-gra was destroyed thirty-one years ago, shutting down the reincarnation of demon souls. He's what? Twenty-one or twenty-two? Which means he shouldn't have been born."

"Exactly. Now, you know why we keep his existence secret. Who knows what some psycho demons or human researchers would do with him. As far as anyone knows, Crux and Chaos are anomalies."

"That's...incredible." Abruptly, her fascination became concern. "And you don't worry that someone who knows will give up his secret?"

"Not really. My dad would kill whoever talked. Then I'd destroy their legacy, Rade would slaughter their entire bloodline, and Blade would bury the bodies. We've had it worked out pretty much since the twins were born."

"Ruthless," she murmured appreciatively, her voice a low, rumbling purr that went through him like a caress. Cocking her head, she gave him a questioning look. "How were the twins even born? Do you know?"

"There are a million theories," he said with a shrug. "I've done a lot of research into it, and I believe that when Azagoth destroyed Sheoul-gra, there were a handful of unassigned souls in the pipeline, ready to be reincarnated. Instead of being returned to the bodies they'd died in to fight Azagoth's war or being sent into waiting fetuses, they wandered around for a few years, searching for the right bodies for their souls."

And now, because there was nowhere for demon souls to go, Chaos was either a lost soul somewhere or was being held prisoner in a soul trap made by Stryke's company.

Fucking hell.

"Is it possible their souls were human? I mean, your mom is human."

He practically hissed at the wrongness of that. Seminus demons were *demons*. Not humans. "My mother is a warg," he said, using the term most werewolves used for their kind. "She's no longer human."

"But according to most experts, werewolves who were turned, not born, have human souls."

"It's still not possible," he said, shutting down that ridiculous line of thought.

She nodded thoughtfully. "So, is Chaos...is what happened to him why you're estranged from your family? Do they blame you?"

That wasn't something he wanted to talk about. Not now, not ever.

Something growled outside, and something else screamed, and he still thought he'd rather step into that malevolent hell fog than be talking about Chaos.

Yet the evil outside was the best reason to talk about it. If something happened to him, he wanted *someone* to know his story. Besides, he owed Cyan. Not that he'd admit that to her.

"I'm pretty sure Blade blames me," he said, feeling like the words were being forcibly dragged out. "The others say they don't, but how can they not? It was my fault. Chaos is dead because of me."

She took a drink of her water. "Is that why Blade attacked you the other night?"

His cheek throbbed in an echo of that fun little beating.

"We used to be tight." He looked up at the maze of different-colored pipes weaving along the ceiling. He wondered where they all went. "It was always Blade and me against Rade."

"Tell me," she said softly.

He'd said too much already, and his throat was starting to close as if he were having an anaphylactic attack. What function did each pipe serve?

"It was a long time ago."

"Maybe. But it's still affecting you all today."

He hated that she was right, but the fact was, it wasn't a new revelation. All that shit had gone down more than fifteen years ago, and it hadn't been dealt with since.

And most of that was on him.

"Please, son. Talk to us. Your mom and I are concerned about you. It's been nine months since Chaos died, and we still haven't talked about it as a family."

"Blade has talked about it enough for all of us." His brother's sharp words, as cutting as the weapon he'd been named for, sliced into him over and over, flaying him wide open.

You shouldn't have left the twins alone.

You should have asked someone to watch them.

You should have fucking been there!

"Stryke," Shade said, "Rade said you left him a message. You're giving your StryTech facility to your brothers and cousins?"

"I'm building a new complex in downtown Sydney. I'll live there."

Since the entire continent of Australia had been ceded to demons, much of it was unoccupied, especially in the business sectors. Demonic governorship in the human realm was going through some growing pains, and while the district Sydney was in was home to only Ufelskala One and Two denizens who had mostly lived secretly in the human world, they were, in fact, still demons. And demons had a tendency to rule, not lead.

The messy demonic politics had made it easy for Stryke to swoop in and claim abandoned ultra-modern, human-constructed buildings practically for free. Most hadn't been in use since the humans abandoned the continent, and those that were in use got emptied in favor of Stryke's rapidly growing business and notoriety. He'd assured the people in charge that he'd bring in money, humans, and legitimacy for Australia's government—which humans were still trying to accept.

It had been over a decade since the destruction of Sheoul-gra, when the human world learned about the existence of demons and angels, werewolves and vampires. And humans had reacted exactly how humans had reacted century after century to anything new: with fear and violence that eventually turned on themselves.

But Stryke's goal was to bring down the temperature on the planet and provide the humans with tools that would protect them from demons like those that had killed Chaos. He'd sworn to do that for his brother. To prevent anyone else from going through what Chaos had. What their entire family was going through.

"Might have been a good thing to tell us," Shade said. "You know, your parents. Who haven't seen you in six months."

"Guilt trip noted. That's why I'm here, Dad. I wanted to tell you myself. I'm expanding the company. The soul traps division has made millions, enough for me to branch out. I've got designs for upgraded communications tech and anti-demon weapons. But I'm most excited about working on demon-detection devices and software."

"I thought you wanted to work for NASA or some other space agency."

He had. And then Chaos died, and his entire life's trajectory had altered in an instant.

"Things change."

"Stryke—"

"I have to go."

"But your mom—"

"Tell her I'm sorry I missed her."

That had been over fifteen years ago, and he'd only seen his family a handful of times since. He'd seen more of his brothers, mainly because they'd moved into his compound, and Stryke had needed to keep in touch with them about that. But most interactions had been through holo-messaging and not in person.

"Stryke?" Cyan's voice jolted him back to the present, which was a much better place to be, even with the threat of imminent death.

"Yeah?"

"What happened?"

He'd dreaded that question. Knew it was coming and only wondered why she'd waited so long to ask it.

Sweat rolled at his temples as he looked back up at the pipes and began calculations on the number of hours it would have taken to design the layout. It helped to keep his brain busy so his emotions didn't get out of control.

"I was twenty-two. Only transitioned for eleven months." And three weeks, two days, and six hours. He kept track because he'd noted the exact time the hellish experience of transitioning into a mature Seminus demon had ended. "I was supposed to be watching the twins at a theme park. Long story short, I was fucking some park employee when demons attacked. Chaos…" He swallowed, hyperfocused on the maze of ceiling pipes. A human would have spent days designing that. AI? Six seconds. "He died."

"I'm so sor—"

"Don't." He shook his head. His heavily divided brain was starting to hurt. "I'm barely keeping it together as it is."

Her hand came down on his back, and he nearly jumped out of his skin. Instinctively, he shouldered her away, but she moved with him, and when she touched him again, her touch was firmer.

Comforting.

Beneath her fingers, his skin trembled. He wasn't used to this. He wasn't used to baring his soul. Or being on the receiving end of compassion. Or being touched.

He didn't know what to do. He only knew his system was on overload, shifting up into fight or flight.

Stop running away.

Blade's words rang through Stryke's head like one of the punches that had followed.

"It wasn't your fault."

"But it was," he blurted angrily. "I didn't want to watch the twins that day. I missed a lecture on quantum inversion theory because of it, and I was pissed. So pissed that I didn't plan for my needs well."

"You didn't have an injection?"

He swallowed the lump of shame in his throat. "I should have asked Blade or Sabre for one. But the popcorn stand girl was cute, and I hadn't learned to control my urges yet."

The first year after transition wasn't easy. Eidolon said it was similar to a human teen going through puberty, except condensed into one year and ten times more intense. Sexual needs raged, wiping away rational thought and logic. But that was no excuse for what he'd done.

And failed to do.

"I was doing the human when the attack started…my fucking pants were down, and I stumbled. I didn't get there in time." His gut ached, and his heart clenched as the memories slammed into him like Blade's fists but far more painful. "Then, afterward…I don't know. A lot of it's a blur."

Unfortunately, a blurry nightmare was still a nightmare. He might not remember much of the immediate hours that followed, but there were a few things he'd never forget. That left him sick and riddled with guilt.

His mom's soul-deep, gut-wrenching screams when she got the news stuck with him. He recalled how his father had, for months, been a mere shadow of the vibrant, larger-than-life male Stryke had known. Friends and family had been sober and sad, the very opposite of the lively, close-knit community they'd been for as long as Stryke could remember.

Crux had taken it the hardest. He'd shut down for weeks, curled into a fetal position on his bed, his blank stare focused on the wall. The entire family had taken turns bringing him food and liquids, which he'd eaten like a zombie before curling up again.

Blade had turned angry; his pain honed into a white-hot spear of rage that was always pointed at Stryke.

And then there was Rade. The brother who had been bereft of emotion since the day he was returned after being kidnapped by a vengeful demon as an infant. He hadn't shown any feelings, but his red-rimmed eyes had said it all. Not that they'd needed to. Stryke had felt the depth of his agony, so buried that it could barely even be labeled a smolder. But every once in a while, a burst of heart-wrenching suffering would escape Rade and take Stryke to his knees.

That was when he'd found Quillax. Stryke had practically begged the male to find a way to sever the connection he had with his brothers. He couldn't handle his pain, let alone theirs. And for the good of them all, he'd cut his thread and freed them from everything he felt.

Cyan squeezed his arm. "So, you've just been living with all of that alone? For all these years?"

"I've had my work. It's the most important thing. Without it, Chaos's death means nothing."

"That's why you create the things you do," she mused. "Weapons and traps and detectors. Now, it all makes sense."

"Glad I could help you solve the puzzle."

She didn't seem to notice the sarcasm. "Yes, and...*oh.*"

"Oh, what?"

"Sex," she breathed. "You associate what happened to Chaos with sex. That's why you try to avoid it. I'm right, aren't I?"

Only partly. "I avoid it because it's a waste of my time."

She offered a thoughtful nod. "I can understand why you'd think that. But I still think I'm right. I saw you with Masumi. You chose an injection instead. I saw you in the storm with the demons, and you damned near chose to die out there with them rather than have sex with me. And then when we finally did do it, you ran out of there like you were on fire."

"I needed to get to work," he said, knowing it was both the truth...and lame.

Of course, she called him on it.

"Bullshit. Something happened. It was as if a switch turned on. I saw it, Stryke, so don't try to tell me I didn't."

Closing his eyes, he just stood there, too tired to argue. Besides, it was pointless. She'd figured it out. Lying would only insult them both.

"You're right, but we're done talking." His brother should arrive soon. "We need to prepare for Blade."

The door at the far end of the engine room opened, and Taran called out. "I've got the images. I'll be right there. I need to check some gauges really quick."

Cyan turned to Stryke as Taran disappeared behind a wall of equipment. "You never told me what you said when you contacted Blade."

For the first time ever, he was glad to change the subject to that particular brother. "I told him to bring some prototypes from StryTech labs. A diffuser powered by Heavenly material that I hope will disperse the fog and an amplifier that might allow you to fix the glyphs remotely."

"Really?"

He nodded. "Quillax helped the devs design it after he did the oil platform job. He hated going down in the sub."

"Has it been tested?"

"Unsuccessfully," he admitted. "Quillax gave it a trial run the last time he was here. According to him, it wasn't powerful enough, but my people have been working on it, so there's a chance it'll be sufficient for your needs now."

She scowled, her gaze turned inward. He liked how she looked when she concentrated: like a sexy professor or a scientist pondering a complex equation. Did she ever wear glasses? Because he'd like that even more.

He'd never been one to fantasize about females, yet suddenly, he was picturing her in front of a DNA sequencer as she explained, in seductive, scientific terms, how it worked. And she was wearing nothing but a lab coat, glasses, and high heels.

Stop it! The world was in danger, and his Seminus instincts chose *now* to suddenly thaw from the deep freeze he'd put them in? Inconvenient and unacceptable.

"Hmm." She tapped her chin thoughtfully. "Maybe that's what happened to the spells. Maybe it wasn't intentional, after all. If he attempted to use the device on them, it's possible the *failure* actually caused the deterioration."

That made a lot of sense. More than thinking Quillax had intentionally messed with the glyphs.

"Hopefully, you can make it work this time," he said. "We need to get your spells into the depths without actually going down there."

Cyan was quiet for a long time. "And if we can't?"

Then we might be very, very fucked.

Leaders didn't say that kind of shit, though. Ares was fond of saying, *"No matter how badly the war is going, if you can't withdraw, you tell your troops the battle is worth it and that there is always hope."*

So, instead of telling Cyan they were all probably going to die, he said, "Blade will get us off this thing. I know him, and I know Kynan. They have a plan."

"That's great," she said. "But escape means leaving the breach unsealed, right?"

Behind them, the sound of the door opening announced Taran's arrival.

"Yes." There was no way to sugarcoat what that meant. Not even Ares would be able to find hope. "And without a miracle, the planet will face a disaster of Biblical proportions."

"So...just another day on planet Earth."

Her delivery was deadpan and perfect. Gallows humor was the best kind. Especially when it was so fitting.

One second, Cyan thought she had Stryke figured out. The next, he blew her away with some new revelation. He'd exposed his soul and flayed hers when he revealed his past, agony, and...vulnerability.

She got the feeling he didn't do that easily or often, and for some reason, he'd brought her into a circle of trust that was, no doubt, very, very small.

She contemplated the significance of that as she looked over the images Taran had left with them. She couldn't imagine the burden Stryke carried or the difficulty of being a sex demon who needed—but hated—sex. Had he ever sought help? Counseling?

She wished her mom was alive to ask for advice. But she wasn't. Because she'd died of a literal broken heart when the bond between her parents broke. Because of a StryTech device malfunction.

It was getting harder and harder to hate Stryke for that, though. Especially after hearing what he'd gone through with his family. He was already punishing himself to extremes, and she had to admit that it disturbed her to see beneath his cold, hard, asshole exterior to his desperately broken interior. And maybe she had too much of her mom in her because she felt the desire to help.

Help the male she'd sworn to make miserable.

"It's so weird," she murmured.

"What? The glyphs?"

"No. Well, yes, but that's not what I'm thinking about."

He seemed to weigh whether or not to press. As if he normally didn't care enough about anyone to ask follow-up questions.

So, naturally, she got stupid warm-fuzzies when he said, "What are you thinking about?"

However, just because she was inwardly smiling didn't mean she'd forgiven all his behavior. "Nothing."

He gave her the side-eye. "I sense you're attempting to teach me a lesson."

She grinned. "You really are a genius."

Amusement softened his expression as he gestured to the

holoimages. "What do you see?"

"Nothing good," she admitted. The glyphs had frayed faster than she'd expected. "Maybe you should connect with Blade again—"

"Not yet."

"But, Stryke—"

"I said no. How much time do we have?"

Unbelievable. She'd have argued, but he had that this-conversation-is-over tone that made them both prickly. And, frankly, they didn't have time to fight.

She did a quick mental calculation. When she finished, her gut was churning.

"Cyan?"

She looked up, hating this. "If my calculations are correct,' she said hoarsely, "We're down to maybe eight hours."

Chapter 16

Stryke spent the next three hours preparing for Blade's arrival, taking inventory of the life rafts, making sure the crew was ready to evacuate, and calculating the odds of success.

They kind of sucked. Sucked hard.

He hoped Cyan, who was still maintaining the fog repellant in the engine room, would be able to get the StryTech amplifier to work. Everything came down to that.

He checked his comms for the time as he reached for the engine room door. It had been five hours since he'd relieved his urges with Cyan. At most, he had another hour before his balls started cramping as if they were in a vise. An hour and a half before he was delirious with pain. Two to three hours, and he'd be actively dying. Of course, by then, the seals protecting the breach would be close to breaking, and *everyone* on the platform would be actively dying.

Where the hell was Blade?

"Hey." Cyan looked up from the table where she was sketching designs he wasn't familiar with. "What's up?"

"A mage will be here in half an hour to take over for you."

"Good. I simplified the spell. Hopefully enough that a mage can maintain it. They don't have to be able to see the glyphs I put down." She dropped the pencil onto the table. "You didn't come down here to tell me about the mage, did you?"

He both hated and loved how observant she was. "I'm just thinking

Blade's arrival might be getting down to the wire."

"I know. I'm hoping to get a new set of images of the glyphs soon. We'll get a better idea of timing then."

"I wasn't talking about that."

She frowned, and then her lids lifted in realization. "Oh, *that*." Catching her bottom lip with her teeth, she studied him. Again with that sexy-professor way of hers. His dick stirred. "You sure you want to risk waiting? What if Blade doesn't show up?"

"He'll be here," he said gruffly, the topic of his brother settling his dick down. "Blade might hate me, but he doesn't want me dead."

"But what if something happens? What if they can't get through the fog? Or—" She inhaled, obviously deciding against saying, "*What if he's injured or killed?*"

"He'll be here," he repeated. "Blade won't pass up a chance to ride in and save the day." To be fair, though, neither would Stryke. If he could be the hero *and* make his brother look bad, it was a no-brainer.

She was still thinking. "It's just...I have an idea."

"What kind of idea?"

"Well, you said you avoid sex. You wait until the last second."

"Yeah. So? Are you ever in a rush to do something you despise?"

She looked at him with pity, and suddenly, he was twenty-two again, Chaos was dead, and people either pitied or hated him. It had taken years, but he'd finally built an empire that ensured no one pitied him ever again. Hate, sure. He got that. He was a selfish shitbag.

But man, he hated pity.

"Okay," she said with a decisive nod. "I get it. I mean, not in the same way as you, obviously, but I've been known to put off getting cavities in my teeth filled half a dozen times."

"See, we both avoid drilling."

She laughed. "Oh, my gods. You actually have a sense of humor."

"I've mastered all the coping mechanisms," he said dryly. That said, when it came to coping, he usually went with avoidance. Humor took too much effort. And all that smiling.

"Has it always been that way?" She moved around the table, coming closer, and he wondered what she was up to. "Like, even before what happened to Chaos?"

Yeah, for the most part. He'd learned from Blade and Mace how to flirt, but Stryke had done the bare minimum required to get laid, and then he'd been all about skipping to the end. The females didn't mind a lack of foreplay, not when the finale involved dozens of orgasms. They got off for up to half an hour, and he got to go back to work. Win-win.

"Always," he admitted.

"Why?"

"You tell me. You're the one psychoanalyzing me."

"Hmm." She pressed her lips together in thought and then nodded decisively. "You seem like the type who resents *having* to do anything."

Impressive. And as much as he admired her accurate insight into his behavior, he wasn't sure he liked how easily she read him.

"That," he said, "is not wrong. Sex is like food. Something the body needs and that consumes far too much time. If I could get all the nutrients and sexual chemicals I need from pills or injections, I'd never eat or fuck again. Like sex, I hate that I need to eat."

Her mouth fell open. Snapped shut. "Wait. Food? You hate *food?*"

"I don't *hate* food," he told her, "I resent having to eat. There's a difference. Eating simply isn't a priority."

"My belly aches for you." She slapped a hand across her stomach, and he regretted not bringing her a meal from the galley. "Do you enjoy *any* food?"

"I can appreciate good food. And I'll try anything once. But in general, eating is boring and a waste of time. Like sex, I hate that I need it."

"Oh, man." She folded her arms across her chest and shook her head. "That is...I don't even know what to say."

He shrugged. "No one does. It's okay. Not even my family knows how to deal with me."

In that way, he'd always felt a certain kinship with Rade. No one understood him, either.

The difference was that Rade's trauma hadn't been of his making, and he didn't remember any of it.

"What if sex wasn't something you needed?" she asked.

Pure. Bliss. "I'd give up half my company for that. But I don't follow."

She wheeled around and then paced back toward him, her brow wrinkled in thought. "Well...since Chaos's death, you wait until the last second to put off experiencing the negative associations and side effects. But all that's doing is reinforcing them. What if you *want* sex instead of needing it?"

"But I don't want sex."

She huffed and rolled her eyes. Then she unbuttoned her shirt. *His* shirt. Knowing it was his filled him with an unexpected primal possessiveness he'd never experienced before. He kind of…liked it. She could wear anything of his she wanted.

The oversized denim work shirt peeled open to reveal her two perfect breasts cradled in a black satin bra. When they'd fucked earlier, he'd determined that the left was slightly larger and heavier than the right by a few grams, and that was perfect to him.

"What are you doing?"

She unbuttoned her pants. Slowly. Far slower than necessary. Especially considering they were in a time crunch to save the world. Was she trying to seduce him? It wouldn't work.

His cock twitched like it wanted to argue otherwise.

She dropped her pants to her feet, so she was standing there in nothing but her matching bra and panties, the harsh lights above bathing her creamy skin in a cool radiance. His pulse kicked up as he dragged his gaze up her long, slender legs that stretched from high-arched feet to a tight bubble ass.

He'd always liked a little junk in the trunk.

Not that he really cared. Sex was sex, and he wouldn't partake at all if he didn't have to. But that didn't mean he couldn't appreciate the female form or have favorite parts of it. He was, after all, male. And a lust demon. Lusting for what only a female could give him was part of the deal.

He cleared his throat. "If you're attempting to seduce me—"

"I'm not." She came closer, invading his personal space, her breasts rolling gently with every step. "I'm attempting to get you out of your head."

He barked out a surprised laugh. "Good luck with that."

"My mom was a psychologist," she said, a touch of defensiveness in her tone. "I know a little about it."

"And? My dad is a paramedic. I couldn't tell you how to intubate someone." Actually, he could, but only because he'd read all of his father's medical manuals when he was a bored kid. But knowing wasn't the same as doing. Hands-on experience was invaluable. Even he knew that.

"I'm going to look forward to your apology," she said, reaching out to trail one long nail up his back as she walked around him. He admired her confidence, so he'd play her game. "What am I touching?"

Strange question. "You're touching me."

"What body part?" Her tone was sharp. She wasn't messing around. "Be specific."

"My shoulder," he said warily.

She dug her nails into his skin, and he sucked in a sharp breath at the unexpected yet...pleasant sting. "More specific."

"Yes, ma'am," he rumbled. "Right deltoid muscle." The muscle twitched beneath her fingertips as if excited about being singled out.

She stepped in front of him and brought both hands up to the collar of his shirt. Her fingers were nimble, making quick work of the buttons.

He considered stopping her, but now he was curious to see where she was willing to take this.

Also, his cock was becoming curious, too, and it had been a long time since that'd happened. At least since it had happened naturally: arousal *for* someone and not the sudden, desperate need for release demanded by unmet Seminus requirements.

She pressed her warm palm against his chest. "Now, what am I touching?"

"Outer dermis. Beneath that, my right and left pectoralis major. And in the middle, my sternum."

"Wow," she said, one eyebrow arching high on her forehead. "You know your anatomy."

"When I was five, I went on a reading bender of my dad's medical texts." He shrugged. "One of them was a book on human anatomy."

Her startled gaze flew up to meet his. "When you were five? And you understood it?"

"Every word. When I was done, I read Eidolon's demon anatomy books. All four volumes."

"How long did it take you?"

"An entire week." He'd holed up in his room and read for hours on end. Best days ever. "I could have finished sooner, but my parents kept making me stop reading to go play with my brothers."

"The horror." She gasped dramatically.

"*Outside,*" he said. "Too full of people."

She laughed. "I felt the same growing up. And I've seen those books. It would take me a week to just read *one.*" She dragged her finger down his abs to his waistband. "Do Seminus demons have any unique body parts or organs?"

"Yes. As a matter of fact, we have several."

She unzipped his pants, and his cock popped out, all "*Hey, good to see you.*" "I'm guessing they are all specialized for reproduction?"

"They are..." He trailed off as she skimmed the palm of her hand across the sensitive tip of his shaft. A lightning bolt of pleasure zipped through him, shocking him as much as an actual electric zap would. "What are you doing?"

"I told you what I'm doing." She gave him an exasperated look. "I thought you were smart."

"Ha. Ha." He opened his mouth to tell her exactly how smart he was, which put him among the top ten in history, but then her hand dipped inside his pants, and all he could do was gasp.

"What am I touching?"

"My balls."

She rolled said balls between her fingers. "Be specific." She pinched the skin between them so hard he groaned in both pleasure and pain. "I won't tell you again."

Oh, fuck. Her touch was amazing.

"My scrotum. Inside that, my testes. Inside them, glands unique to my species called *paratestes.*" Her fingers slid upward, skimming across the skin of his shaft, tracing the veins and sending shivers up his spine.

"And what do they do?"

"They produce the chemical..." Oh, hell, yes...her touch was magic. "That triggers multiple orgasms in females."

"Nice." Smiling, she pressed her lips to his as she shoved both her hands around to his ass. Instinct had him pumping his hips into her, his cock cradled by the curve of her pelvis. Suddenly, she stepped back and shoved down her panties, then removed her bra. "Where are the glands that produce the pheromones that make females like me crazy?"

He dropped his pants and pressed his fingers to both sides of his groin. "Here."

Slowly, she eased to her knees, and his pulse shot up a few points. "Are they sensitive?"

"Very...ah...fuck..." He bucked as she kissed the tender skin.

She moved her mouth lower. "What am I kissing now?"

"The adductor brevis," he breathed. "Maybe the adductor longus...I can't think."

She swiped her tongue up his inner thigh, and he lost his damned mind. Thinking was the last thing he wanted to do. And yet...she was right. This was keeping his mind from going other places. Right now, every thought was with her. Her questions. The feel of her lips on his skin. The feathery touch of her fingers.

Her mouth opened over the head of his cock, and when she took him inside her warm, wet depths, he shouted in ecstasy. Her tongue flicked lightly across the crown, and then she sucked him deep—so deep he could feel the back of her throat. Shit, this was…amazing.

He looked down at her just as she looked up at him, her gemstone eyes bright as she smiled around his shaft with the enthusiasm of a hellhound sucking the marrow out of an angel's femur bone.

"What do you want me to do?" she asked, her voice saucy and teasing. She knew what he craved, but her game right now was all about making him say it.

Their gazes locked so fiercely that the air between them threatened to combust. He growled. "Suck it."

He watched her, his entire body on edge, practically trembling with the need to come inside her. He usually avoided oral sex, but right now, all he wanted was for Cyan to swallow him whole and give him new memories. New experiences. New neural pathways that could rewire his fucked-up brain.

Still looking at him, she kissed the tip. "Suck it how? Slowly?" She took him into her mouth and took her time going down and back up. He could barely contain a groan. "Fast?" Her pace increased, her head bobbing, her mouth working him into a frenzy. When she stopped, he blew out the breath he'd been holding. "Hard?" Again, she swallowed him, but this time, she applied firm suction that damned near blew his head off.

"Yes!" he barked. "*That.*"

She stopped and looked at him, her eyes glazed with passion that humbled him. "Tell me. Explicitly." Lowering to his cock, she paused with her mouth open. "Waiting."

Gods, she was incredible. As much as he wanted to take her to the floor and ravage her like the lust demon he was, he wanted this experience more.

"Suck me," he commanded, and she shivered as she took him into her mouth. "Hard and fast."

He shouted as she obeyed, gripping him firmly in her fist as she gave him the best blowjob anyone had ever had in all of history. Her mouth was magic, her tongue a weapon, and when she squeezed his sac, it was the last straw. He came with a roar. He thought he said her name. Maybe a curse word. Maybe both.

Pleasure rode him in waves of intensity as he came over and over until he was drained. Nothing but a dried-out husk. Cyan rocked back on her heels, her face flushed, her eyes glazed.

"Oh," she said as she reached between her spread thighs. "It's true.

It *is* an aphrodisiac. I'm so…" She groaned as she touched herself. "Aroused."

So was he. Watching her circle her clit with a fingertip lit him up again. Another new experience. Usually, when he was done, it was done.

But this time, it was just the beginning.

Cyan buzzed with lust, her body quivering, her sex soaked. And it went next level when she focused on Stryke, how sexed-up he was, panting, jaw clenched, eyes drilling into her.

She needed him inside her. Right. This. Second.

"Stryke," she rasped, "I need—"

She broke off as he hauled her off the floor, cupped her ass, and deposited her on some sort of machine casing. He stepped between her legs, the tip of his cock positioned at her aching sex.

"Need," he asked, his voice husky and low, "or *want?*"

"Both." She arched into him, gasping as the head slid inside a fraction of an inch. She was on the verge of orgasm right now. If he so much as breathed—

He breathed.

She screamed.

Pleasure *destroyed* her. Ecstasy was a firestorm that came in wave after wave, so intense she registered nothing else. She was dimly aware of Stryke churning between her thighs, caught in his own maelstrom of lust.

Her body demanded everything he could give her, and when he claimed her mouth in a hard, hot kiss, it triggered another series of platform-rocking orgasms.

She lost track of time. She lost track of her freaking *mind*. And when the storm finally eased, the orgasms coming less frequently, she couldn't believe fifteen minutes had passed.

And Stryke had held her the entire time, his powerful arms caging her against his hard body, his cock filling her over and over.

"Are you okay?" he asked, his voice wonderfully exhausted.

"Oh, yes," she murmured against his shoulder. "You?"

"I was thinking."

She looked up at him. "You weren't supposed to be thinking."

"I was thinking about you."

"Then that's okay." She dropped her head back down to his shoulder and inhaled. He smelled like seawater and machinery, but beneath it was the dark, sensual scent unique to him. "What were you thinking?"

"That you were right. I need you to re-establish the connection with Blade," he said. "My stubbornness is irrational when the fate of our lives and the very world is at stake."

Pleasantly surprised by his change of heart, she reached up to touch his temple. "There."

He gasped, and she knew he felt his brother.

"I can't tell where he is, but I can feel that he's alive. Just a second." Closing his eyes, he concentrated. She had another orgasm.

When he opened his eyes a few seconds later, he looked tired. "They're almost here. We might just make it out of this alive after all."

Chapter 17

"This is fucking epic," Mace shouted as the military Rigid Hull Inflatable boat plowed through waves on its way to the coordinates Kynan had given them after talking with Stryke's assistant. "We've never done a water mission before."

"I've never even seen an aquatic demon," Scotty yelled back over the roar of the engine. Her flaming red hair, pulled back into a tight braid, whipped in the wind as she kept a watchful eye on the vast expanse of water all around them. "This is gonna be cool!"

Mace looked over at Blade, whose calm expression didn't match the turmoil writhing in his dark eyes. Blade had always been the most reserved of the three of them, the voice of reason, the one who liked a plan, when Mace and Scotty preferred to rush into a situation and rely on instinct instead. He was rock-steady, reliable, the guy who pulled you out of the trouble you got yourself into.

It took a lot to rile Blade, but he hadn't been the same since the first contact with Stryke a few hours ago. The contact had left him as tense as Mace had ever seen him.

Kynan had managed to arrange transport to a U.S. Naval warship with a helipad just two miles from the target, but it had taken time to acquire the gear, the platform schematics, and have a briefing before sending the three of them on this mission, and Blade was probably a lot more jittery on the inside than he appeared.

Normally, Mace enjoyed a good family drama, but he didn't dare ask what was going through Blade's head. His relationship with Stryke was a sensitive subject, and BFFs with Blade or not, Stryke was one topic Mace avoided like a super-spreader spiny hellrat plague. Especially since Mace's relationship with his biological brother, Talon, was shaky at best—and a subject best left alone.

"Holy shit," Scotty breathed. "Look at that."

Mace peered through the darkness, his natural night vision giving him a clear view of the sight up ahead. And yeah, holy shit.

He'd expected to see an oil platform and maybe some fog. What he hadn't expected was what appeared to be a solid wall of writhing, boiling darkness. And were those...*faces* in it? Screaming, tortured faces. And tentacles. Claws.

"I've seen some scary shit in my life," Scotty said, her pale face seeming even paler as she stared at the phenomenon, "but that...is *terrifying*." A sword appeared in her hand, and Mace doubted she even realized she'd summoned it.

"Let's just hope this contraption of Stryke's works." Blade held up a device that resembled a blowhorn with a trigger that, once pulled, would blast a wave of Heavenly energy to displace evil energy.

The technician who'd shown them how to use it had said it didn't work on solid demons, but it should dispel or repel malevolent souls, invisible demons, and demonic weather events—whatever those were.

Mace hoped the fog they were closing in on counted.

"Get it ready," Mace said as he slowed the boat. "That scientist dude said to activate it within fifty yards."

"We're about there." Blade made his way to the front of the boat and held the device in front of him. "Damn, that shit is creepy."

"Ready," Scotty said, her gaze flicking between the fog and her comms as she measured the distance. "Ready...almost...now!"

Blade pulled the trigger. At first, nothing happened. But as they approached the writhing, twisting dark cloud, a hole formed, widening and deepening. By the time they reached the anomaly, a boat the size of a small yacht could have fit through the tunnel it formed.

"I can see the platform ahead," Scotty shouted over the shrieks and bloodcurdling growls coming from all around them.

"Keep that trigger pulled, man," Mace said. "We don't want—"

Scotty screamed, and as Mace wheeled to her, she slammed backward over the edge of the boat, a spiny tentacle wrapped around her waist.

"*Scotty!*" Mace bolted to the edge where she'd gone over. "Scotty!"

"Help—" She disappeared, blood bubbling up all around her.

Terrified in a way he'd never been, Mace made a desperate lunge. His fingers slipped against hers, and she went under.

No!

Her hand thrust upward, and he grabbed it hard with both hands. He wasn't letting her go this time. No way.

He yanked with all his strength, and she breached the surface, sputtering and coughing, her eyes wide with terror.

Blade dove across the boat and grabbed her other hand. "We got you!"

Some sort of fishy thing with a million teeth and no eyes burst out of the water and fastened onto Mace's forearm. Pain screamed from his fingertips to his shoulder, but he kept hold of Scotty as he and Blade struggled to haul her onto the boat.

The moment she was lying on the deck, blood spilling from deep, ragged gashes that exposed tendon and bone—and maybe an organ or two—Blade buried a seven-inch blade in the demon's skull. It hissed, releasing Mace's arm before slithering back into the sea.

The mist closed in. "Blade! The fog! Shit!"

"I know, I know!" He snatched up the device from where he'd dropped it and swept it in a circle, forcing the heavy mist into retreat. "Can you drive?"

Mace didn't want to leave Scotty, but they needed to get to the safety of the rig, and they needed to do it fast. She was losing a lot of blood. She might be immortal, but that didn't mean she was unkillable. Under the right circumstances, everything died.

His left arm screaming with pain and practically useless, he scrambled over to the controls just as a set of clawed hands reached over the stern. Glowing red eyes and a gaping maw full of fangs popped up on the port side. That was enough dawdling.

He gunned the engine and took them toward the platform at top speed. Unable to hang on, the demons dropped off the boat, but shit, how many of those fuckers were there in these waters?

Waves crashed against the massive metal support beams as they approached. Things were looking up. Scotty's father said that aquatic demons generally avoided the violent action of the waves against rocks and piers. Dude had been fighting demons for thousands of years and knew his shit. Ares knew his shit so well that he ran a battle academy of sorts, and all three of them had spent countless hours training with him—twice a week since the day they learned to tie their shoes.

We must prepare for the Apocalypse.

The guy said that all the time. Constantly.

"My species has a five-hundred-year lifespan," Mace had once argued. Because, yeah, he wanted to be a badass. But Ares took fighting lessons to the extreme. Even Mace's biological father, Wraith, who lived to fight and was proficient in every fighting discipline, thought Ares was a little too obsessed. "We won't be around when Satan's prison sentence is up in…what, nine hundred and fifty-something years?"

"Do you want to survive to your full lifespan?" Ares had growled. "Yes? Then train."

Right now, Mace was glad he'd been pushed into being the best he could be. No, he didn't have Scotty's immortality or her ability to summon weapons, but he was stronger and faster than any human, he healed quickly, and he'd been honed into a lethal weapon by not just Ares but *all* the Horsemen, Wraith, and even a couple of angels.

Thanks for being a pain in my ass, Ares.

"Ky said the dock will be on the south side," Blade shouted back.

"I see it." He steered the craft up alongside the dock.

Shade tossed a rope and leaped onto the structure. While he tied up, Mace shut down the craft and scooped Scotty into his arms. She was barely conscious, but she flopped her arm around his neck and clung tightly.

Tentacled and clawed things, and things with no eyes or skin, reached for them as they ran toward the stairs. The metal steps vibrated as they took them two at a time to the upper levels.

"There!" Blade pointed at a door. "The forward operating center."

They ran over to it. Locked.

Blade pounded on it, and almost immediately, a muffled "Who is it?" could be heard.

"Stryke called us. We're from DART!"

The door whipped open, and a tall, blond guy greeted them. "Thank the gods. Come in. Sorry about the lock. Demons."

Mace only half-heard as he shoved past the guy and lowered Scotty onto the floor. Blade was right there next to him, and before Scotty was even fully laid out, Blade's arm lit up like a torch as his healing power surged into his fingertips and then into Scotty's body.

Mace fired up his gift and powered it into her too. Blade could repair her torn vessels and sliced muscle, while Mace could control her pain and tweak her body so it would produce red blood cells at an accelerated rate.

"This is pretty bad," Blade murmured.

"Nah," she moaned, already looking better. "You guys have healed me from worse."

"Like that time you got jumped by six Nightlash demons, and they tried to peel you like a grape?"

She snorted. "Yeah. Like that."

That had been a clusterfuck. But this was worse. Blade knew it too. The intensity in his expression, the worry in his eyes…it said a lot. Mace knew the guy well enough to know that, right now, he was regretting not spending more time with their Uncle Eidolon. Blade had chosen to hone his fighting skills rather than his healing ones, and times like this made him kick himself for that choice.

Blade reached over and took Scotty's hand in his, giving it a comforting squeeze. She flashed him a grateful smile.

And right then, for the first time in Mace's life, he felt the stirrings of jealousy.

Shocked and irritated beyond belief, he stimulated her pituitary gland and sent a rush of pain-relieving endorphins through her. She rewarded him with a grin, and his jealousy melted away. It was stupid to be jealous of Blade. They'd sworn a blood oath long ago that neither of them would ever hook up with Scotty. Not ever, under any circumstances. She was a friend. Their best friend. And no way would any of them fuck up their friendship.

"You guys are both so awesome," she said, almost drowsily.

"We are," Mace agreed, grinning down at her.

She swatted at him, but he easily caught her wrist. "Nice try, Princess," he said, using the nickname they'd used to annoy her when they were kids. Her father liked to say she'd been a tomboy from the cradle, and being called a princess was the ultimate insult.

"I take back what I said about you being awesome."

"But *I'm* still awesome, right?" Blade asked, cracking a smile for the first time since the contact with Stryke. It was a sign that he felt better about Scotty's injuries.

"For now," she said. "Until you do something stupid."

"I give him an hour," Mace said.

Blade shot him a give-me-a-break look. "I give *you* five minutes."

The door swung open, and Stryke and Cyan burst inside. Blade's smile slid off his face like butter off a hot knife.

Stryke nudged Cyan toward the holographic images hanging near a couple of destroyed windows, his intimate, gentle touch so discreet

Mace would have missed it if he'd blinked.

He's fucking her.

Interesting. Also, what the hell? She'd brushed off Mace's flirtations for years, but she was doing Stryke?

Wait, it actually made sense. They were both Type-A brainiacs. They probably solved math equations as foreplay. Really, Mace had dodged a bullet.

"Finally," Stryke said, sounding relieved. He looked them over and then quickly scanned the room. "Where's the equipment I asked for?"

The shadows flickering in Blade's eyes grew agitated as he shoved to his feet. Uh-oh. Mace and Scotty exchanged shit's-gonna-start-up glances.

"Oh, hey, hi, Stryke," Blade said, sarcasm and anger dripping from every word. "I must have missed your thank you. Also, yeah, we're all okay, except Scotty was almost disemboweled and dismembered while coming to save your sorry ass, but thanks for fucking asking."

Mace wasn't sure if he should cringe or laugh. This would either be the worst or the best assignment ever.

Chapter 18

Oh, hey, hi, Stryke. I must have missed your thank you. Also, yeah, we're all okay, except Scotty was almost disemboweled and dismembered while coming to save your sorry ass, but thanks for fucking asking.

Yep, this would be fun.

"Scotty?" Stryke glanced over at her as she sat on the carpeted floor, her shredded clothing dripping water and blood onto the already-soaked surface. "You okay?"

She nodded and accepted a towel from Taran. "Blade was being dramatic. All the equipment you asked for is in the boat."

Stryke gestured to Taran, who took off to gather the equipment before the sea demons got a hold of it.

"How thick is the fog?" he asked, his gaze flicking between the three DART agents.

Mace had been peering out the window at the mist; now, he turned back to Stryke. "Three hundred meters, maybe."

Not good news. "You're sure? It's that thick?"

"We were too busy trying not to die to get an exact measurement," Mace said.

Scotty came to her feet with a wince. If she'd taken a wound in every spot her clothes were ripped, Blade hadn't been exaggerating. She looked like she'd barely survived a date with Freddy Krueger.

"What's going on, Stryke?" she asked. "Is this a rescue mission, or are we here to help fix this rift? Because I gotta be honest and say I don't know how to seal a rift between realms."

Blade, leaning casually against the map table, looked around the operating center, studying everything except Stryke. "Oh, I'm sure my brother has all the computations figured out."

"Yeah. I do." He gestured to Cyan, his heart skipping a beat when she slid him a brief smile from where she was studying the newest images from the underwater monitor. "She's going to use the amplifier you brought to seal the rift from here instead of underwater. If that fails, we'll use the diffuser to get everyone off the platform before the rift blows."

"*Blows?*" Mace had been casually flipping a dagger, but now he went still, and the weapon hit the floor. Cursing, he swept it up in his fist. "It can blow? What happens then?"

"Aquatic demons will fill the Earth's seas and oceans," Stryke told him. Told all of them. "The fog will spread. I don't know how far, but if it reaches land, it'll support aquatic demons for miles inland. Billions will have to evacuate or will be killed. The oceans will die. The planet will suffer a slow, agonizing death that would likely hit its crescendo when Satan is released from his prison, and Armageddon arrives."

There was a long, heavy silence.

Scotty finally broke it, her voice uncharacteristically grave. "Wow. That was, uh, stark."

"So, this is save-the-world-type stuff, right?" Mace popped off. "Because A, talk about bragging rights, and B, I'm trying to beat Wraith's record."

Blade punched him in the shoulder. Stryke would have gone higher. Scotty gave her teammate a scathing you're-a-dumbass look and turned back to Stryke.

"How can we help?"

"We could use your security and combat skills. Help us keep the demons off the rig. While the mages hold the fog at bay, Cyan will do her thing." He turned to one of X-Oil's senior crewmembers who had stayed on after Stryke bought it. "Put together an evacuation plan. We may need to make multiple trips through the fog to get everyone off the platform."

"Yes, sir." Jackson took off, and Stryke turned back to the agents. "What do you guys need?"

"Our weapons are still on the boat," Blade said.

"My people are getting everything out of it right now." He looked between Mace and Scotty, ignoring Blade's cool glare. "What else?"

"We need to know what kinds of demons you've been fighting," Mace said, snapping into pro mode. "We also need to know what is and isn't effective against them."

"When Taran gets back, he can brief you. What else?"

Blade pushed off the table. "I want to know how you caused this."

"I didn't. Anyone else got a stupid question?" He could practically feel Blade stewing but wisely kept his mouth shut.

The door banged open, and Taran burst inside with two heavy duffels and three black backpacks slung over his shoulder. Behind him, a deckhand Stryke didn't know carried the diffuser device and a metal case that contained the runic amplifier.

"Taran, they have some questions." He took the case from the deckhand. "Cyan, you need to figure out the best place to work from."

She nodded. "I'll need the platform's schematics."

He gestured to Twila. "Can you bring those up?"

"Sure thing."

He looked around at all the expectant faces, people who trusted him to get them out of this. He wouldn't fail them. He couldn't.

"We've got this," he said. "We're all the best in our professional fields, and I need you to give it your all. Let's get to work."

Everyone jumped into action, but as Stryke went to join Cyan at the blueprints, Blade's hand came down on his arm, stopping him in his tracks.

"You never said how this happened."

It wasn't an unreasonable request, but Blade had turned it into a dickish demand.

"Short version? An oil company drilled into Sheoul. StryTech bought the rig to seal the breach. But it sprung a leak, and here we are."

Blade seemed satisfied by Stryke's answer, but he didn't budge. "It must have been hard for you to call me for help."

"You really want to get into this now?" Stryke snapped. "Jesus, Blade, for all you throw shit at me for being a fuckup, your hatred of me makes you stupid and puts everyone around you at risk. So, take your hypocrisy and shove it up your ass."

"Are you kidding me?" Blade asked, incredulous. "You're the one who hates *me*. You think I forgot that time we got into that fight at Underworld General, and the sentry attacked you?"

"The sentry?" Cyan asked.

Scotty leaned over and spoke quietly, but even over the angry roar of his pulse in his ears, Stryke heard her say, "It's a statue inside the hospital that senses when someone wants to kill. It bites and paralyzes that person long enough for the staff to restrain them. Very painful."

Cyan frowned. "Isn't Underworld General covered by an anti-violence spell that prevents fights?"

"Our family is exempt," Mace said. "We get to fight with each other all we want."

"Stryke didn't want to *fight*," Blade said in an angry, accusatory tone, his gaze locked hard with Stryke's. "He wanted to kill me."

Son of a bitch. Stryke was sick of this shit. He was sick of letting Blade treat him like a punching bag, no matter how much he deserved it.

"I didn't want to kill you!" Stryke roared, his hands clenched, his temper finally erupting. "It wasn't about you! Not everything is fucking about you!"

"Yeah, who then?"

Everyone stared, the crewmembers shrinking back from what probably looked like the start of a brawl. Blade would like that. Screw Blade. He wasn't getting any of Stryke's blood today.

Releasing his fury, he barked out a bitter laugh. "Fuck off. It doesn't matter. I'm out of here. Cyan, meet me in my office with your decision." He stormed out the door and headed for his office, but he only got a few yards before the sound of running footsteps came up behind him.

"Stryke?" Cyan's hand caught his and pulled him to a stop. "You okay?"

Sighing, he swung around to her. "Fighting with Blade isn't anything I haven't done before."

She pursed her lips and slid her gaze to the wet deck before looking back up. "Was he right?" she asked quietly. "Did you want to kill him?"

"Back then? No. Right now? I'm entertaining the idea." He wasn't serious, but damn, his brother could use a broken jaw.

"Who was it, then? Who did you want to kill?"

Inhaling a deep, ragged breath, he looked out at the boiling wall of fog a few meters away. Hideous faces and horrific images formed in the mist, and the sounds that emerged...he suppressed a shudder. He would not look forward to trying to get to the other side of it.

"It's not important," he said. "It's in the past, and no one died."

She didn't appear to have heard him. "Someone close to you? An enemy?"

Both.

"I mean, if you—"

"Me, Cyan," he blurted suddenly. "I wanted to kill myself."

She stood there, stunned, but no more than he was. He'd never told anyone that. Not even Masumi, and she probably knew more about him than anyone did.

"Wow," she murmured. "Because of what happened to Chaos?"

Man, she asked a lot of questions. And for some fucked-up reason, he kept answering them.

"Yeah." Painful memories flitted at the edges of his mind as he looked out at the fog. "We didn't know what'd happened to him—his soul, I mean. No one can find him. I thought...I thought that if I was dead, it would be easier to locate him."

She nodded as if she understood, but she didn't. She couldn't. She hadn't killed her baby brother and ruined many lives.

Something in the mist screamed. Fat, crimson veins began to spread through the fog, pulsing and squirming, growing more agitated as if sensing his mood.

"Look," he said, "we have shit to do and not much time to do it in."

"You're right." She nodded decisively. "We can save this for later."

"We're not saving anything." He started toward his office but heard her quiet snort and knew there *would* be a later—and she was definitely saving for it.

Cyan was still rattled by Stryke's confession when she returned to the forward operating center, where Taran was catching Blade, Mace, and Scotty up on events. The team armed themselves as Taran spoke, pulling weapons and tools from their packs, stuffing them into pockets and sheaths, and strapping them onto different body parts.

He'd been so desperate to find his dead brother that he'd been willing to die. Holy shit. How much agony had he been in to consider such a thing?

Focus. You have a job to do.

Shaking her head to clear it, Cyan studied the blueprints, searching for the perfect location to activate the amplifier. Ideally, near electronic machinery, but she also wanted to be as close to the water and broken glyphs as possible.

"Boss." Jackson gestured to his equipment screen. "We got another heat signature. Headed this way fast."

"What's that mean?" Mace asked.

"It's either a big demon, a mass of small demons, or a blast of evil atmosphere that'll hit like a storm and add to the fog." Taran tapped his wrist comms, and the speakers on the bridge clicked on. "*Sea Storm*, brace for impact or attack. Mages, fortify the shield. *Incoming.*"

Suddenly, the platform trembled. Something hit the only window with no cracks, and the thing nearly shattered. The fog closed in, seeping between the smallest gaps in the glass and metal. A moment later, the mages must have regained control, and the mist retreated from the rig.

"This is so fucked up." Blade lowered the handheld crossbow he'd aimed at the window. "Leave it to Stryke to kick off the start of the end of the world."

"Stryke didn't start this." Cyan zoomed into a center section of the schematic. "The oil company did. Stryke is trying to fix it."

Blade shot her a look of disappointment. "So, you're on Team Stryke."

"I'm not on any *team*, Blade," she said, unable to contain her irritation.

She was starting to understand why there was so much tension between the brothers—and in the entire family. She'd also seen how deeply Stryke was affected. He didn't need Blade's guilt trip when he was drowning in his own.

"I definitely wasn't Stryke's biggest fan when I started at StryTech," she admitted. "But now…" She shrugged. "Now, I see another side of him."

"The side of him without clothes, I'm guessing," Blade muttered.

"*Excuse me?*" She snapped her head around to glare at him because, hell no. She wasn't putting up with that shit. Furious, she wove a nasty shock spell into his wrist comms and triggered a jolt that made him yelp. "My opinion of him isn't based on orgasms." She shocked him again, turning up the intensity. This time, he leaped backward with a curse. "Say something like that again, and I swear I'll train you to sit pretty and roll over on command. And I'm not in the mood to show mercy." An image of Blade beating Stryke flashed in her mind, and she zapped him once more. *That was for Stryke*, she thought, feeling grimly amused when Blade clenched his teeth and took that one like a champ. "You got it?"

"Buddy." Mace tested the edge of a blade before disappearing it up his sleeve. "Stow it. I hate to agree with Stryke because he's such a dick, but he was right. We're in a fuckton of trouble, and your beef with him is turning your focus to shit. Now's not the time for this. Stop being an asshole and team up."

Scotty thrust out her fist. "Team up."

Blade, his expression stormy, looked over at the petite redhead. "So, you agree with Mace?"

"Yup," she said, "and you're lucky he said it before I did. I wouldn't have been as nice. You're *way* out of line, and Cyan went too easy on you. She should have laid you out. Deal with your personal shit on your own time."

The shadows in Blade's dark eyes writhed angrily, but they gradually disappeared, and he gave his teammates a resigned fist bump.

"Team up." He shot Cyan a sheepish look. "That was uncalled for. I apologize."

"We're cool. Thank you."

As if nothing had happened, the trio went back to arming themselves and discussing the mission.

Their ability to work together in sync, almost as a single organism, was practically legendary at DART. Now, Cyan saw why. Blade had gone off the rails, but Mace and Scotty had quickly gotten him back on track and on mission. Cyan had to admire the way he'd taken his teammates' harsh criticism without getting angry or defensive.

"Well," Twila said, bringing Cyan back to the unfolding crisis. "Where are you going to set up?"

Cyan pointed to a controller apparatus at the very center of the rig. It was two floors up, but it was directly above the deep-water glyphs.

"Right there." She started toward the door. "Wish me luck!"

A chorus of well-wishes followed her as she hurried down the corridor to the outside exit. She used her comms to tell Stryke where she was going. To her surprise, he was there already, his dark hair slicked back and grooved by his fingers, an ivory column the size of a small banana in his hand.

"I figured you'd choose this spot," he said.

Of course, he had. She gestured to the object. "So, what is it? And how does it work?"

"It's an artifact I purchased from an underworld dealer who specializes in rare sources of power." He hefted it in his hand. "This was carved from the horn of a *brojibeast*."

"Wow." She stared in awe at the smooth, featureless rod, a treasure so rare they were almost mythical. "Those are coveted by all magic users. With that, someone could turn a poison gas spell with a ten-foot radius into one that could engulf a full city block." She looked up at him, her nerves quivering with excitement. "The mages could use it to push the fog back half a mile or more!"

"Which wouldn't help us. We'd still have to get through the wall of mist. But as a last resort, they can use it to fight demons that get onto the platform."

She didn't like the last-resort talk. "So, what has StryTech been doing with it?"

"Mainly, we're trying to replicate it. Imagine if DART spellcasters and Underworld General healers had access to something like this."

Oh, the amazing things they could do. But powerful objects were often used in less honorable ways. Her excitement died a painful death.

"And imagine if the bad guys had access to it too."

His gaze sharpened at that. "Like all of StryTech's products, there would be strict controls."

"Strict controls didn't save Shanea and Draven," she shot back before she could stop herself.

Shit. She'd just done exactly what Blade did; she'd brought a personal grievance into a dangerous situation. Swallowing her pride, if not her anger, she reluctantly apologized.

"Sorry. We should give this a try. I'll warn you, though, my kind of magic doesn't usually work with amplifiers that aren't electronic."

"Which is why," he said as he turned it upside down, "we had a microchip embedded into it. This is what might have screwed up Quillax's glyphs. We've done some upgrades to the chip since, but we haven't tested it yet."

"Yeah, you mentioned that. So, I'm the guinea pig?"

"Congratulations."

The clang of multiple footsteps on the walkways joined the thrashing of the sea against the rig's giant supports and the creepy noises coming from the fog and water. Several of the crewmembers, armed to the teeth, lined the railings to watch. At three of the corners, Blade, Mace, and Scotty looked on, their watchful gazes darting between Cyan and the surroundings.

"Good luck," Mace shouted down. "No pressure. It's only our lives and maybe the whole planet."

As she took the device from Stryke, she considered rigging Mace's comms with an electronic zapper like Blade's.

"Taran, what is this thing?" She gestured to a big box with gauges and a control panel.

"That monitors oil flow, pressure, and emissions."

"Do the power lines that run through it also run down to where the glyphs are?"

"The lines aren't directly connected, but they're on the same circuits."

Okay, good. Maybe they had a shot at this. "Oh, one more thing. The rig isn't operational, right? I won't accidentally cause an oil spill or anything, right?"

"You shouldn't. It's been shut down for almost two months."

Excellent. Closing her eyes, she channeled the powers that allowed her to weave electrons from all sources into spells. She wove a long thread into the device and then into the control panel, where it shot through the platform's electrical grid, seeing the line that would take it to the glyphs.

She gripped the artifact tightly. Its power assist wasn't needed yet, but as the thread began to travel below the water's surface, her power started to fade.

In her fist, the device sparked a glow. Dim at first, its eerie green-white light intensified as it pushed her energy thread deeper and deeper. In her mind's eye, she could see the depth as a set of numbers and could even read the temperature and pressure as the existing line transferred data.

The device's glow became so bright she had to turn away from it. Others shielded their eyes. Mace, Blade, and Scotty popped on sunglasses they'd pulled from one of their dozens of pockets.

Keep going, keep going...

The thread stretched, inching down.

There! She could see the uppermost glyph. Fragments of it, anyway.

Almost there...

The thread stopped.

No!

Clenching her teeth and fists, she strained, drawing on every drop of her abilities. The artifact grew hot in her palm, its glow spreading through the rig as far as she could see, breaching even the darkness beyond the railings, where flying things flitted at the edges, screeching when their leathery wings touched the light.

"You can do it, Cyan." Stryke's deep voice, smooth like good whiskey and just as warming, gave her a much-needed boost.

The thread stretched farther until its tip brushed the top of the glyph, and she could see the rest. Hopefully, that was enough.

She imagined the fix, allowing the spell to form through electrical currents. Hope filled her—

The spell sparked, fizzled, and the thread receded.

"No!" she cried, desperately trying again. And again.

But the glow around the artifact was fading, and so was her power. She'd exceeded her limits, and the more she tried to reach into the well for more, the weaker she became.

Hope turned to despair.

"I failed," she whispered. "I've doomed us all."

Chapter 19

Gabriel soared across vast oceans and wide swaths of land as his internal homing system guided him to the North Sea. The coordinates of the *Sea Storm* had been easy to find, and his built-in GPS had done the rest.

Outfitted in gold armor forged by an ancient, now-extinct race of fae, he zipped through space and time, circling the globe, wondering if he was doing the right thing.

No doubt, destroying the portal was the right thing. But what if it resulted in a very wrong thing?

What if, by destroying the Gehennaportal, its twin, the Gaiaportal, was also destroyed? Once, it had been the sole means by which Celestials could travel between Heaven and the human realm…and the demon realm, if needed. It had been shut down for millennia, but now that Heaven's barriers had been erected once again, perhaps it should be kept functional.

One never knew when one might need to escape a tyrannical rule.

What if he could merely shut down the Gehennaportal, leaving it intact instead?

He drew to a stop a hundred miles from the platform, hovering in clear skies over another oil rig, its blowout preventer pumping out gases. He was pretty sure Stryke's platform was no longer operational. It made him wonder how much StryTech had paid the oil company for it. It also made him wonder why Stryke had bought it. Was it genuinely a save-the-world thing, or would StryTech somehow benefit from the proximity to the Gehennaportal?

Not much was known about Stryke's alignment on the scale of good and evil. He appeared to be siding with humans against demons, which was why Heaven had chosen to take a wait-and-see approach to him. Until Stryke, it had been unthinkable for Heaven to allow a demon to have so much power and influence over humans, but so far, he'd helped mankind far more than he'd hurt it.

His first mistake, however, would probably be his last, even if he was Primori. Especially now that the Thrones were in charge and Reaver wasn't around to defend his demon friends and family. After all, Celestials had, in the past, reassigned Memitim guardian angels in order destroy Primori before their time.

But there were always consequences. One of those, the Third Servile War, had ended in Spartacus's defeat, the crucifixion of six thousand men, and a dozen angels being expelled from Heaven.

"Greetings, Gabriel."

Instinctively, Gabriel summoned a fireball in his right hand as he wheeled around to the owner of the voice.

"Hutriel?"

He didn't extinguish the fireball.

Hutriel, angel of punishment and the Prime Celestial Enforcer, hovered a couple of feet above him, his great lavender wings spread wide, their tips buffeted by the wind.

"I won't let you take me," Gabriel said, holding his power at the ready, prepared to lob Hut out of the sky if necessary. "I haven't finished my mission."

"I'm not here to return you to Heofon," he said, using the ancient pronunciation for Heaven. The Adonis-faced angel was an Old Celestial...not necessarily because of his age but because he, like many of the stuffiest of angels, clung to the traditional ways and had spent little time in the human realm. "Yet. I'm here because we determined that the Gehennaportal is located beneath the very oil rig you've been circling. I'm here to assist."

"One, I already knew that. And two, I don't need assistance."

"That is not your call to make." Hutriel's salt-and-pepper hair ruffled, seemingly as annoyed as Hutriel. "The situation in Heofon has changed. A minion of Hell entered through the Gaiaportal."

Gabriel couldn't contain a shocked gasp, his fireball fizzling out. "There was a demon...in Heaven?"

"It was a water fiend, and it died before it fully emerged, but now you see the import of our situation. We must destroy the Gehennaportal." He cleared his throat imperiously. "The Forsaken One," he said, using one of many antiquated nicknames for Azagoth—and doing so with a sneer. "Did he disclose how to do the deed?"

"He did. And then we reminisced about how he stole Lilliana from you and kicked your pompous ass so hard you were pulling your feathers out of it for a month. Anything else you want to know?"

Hutriel's periwinkle eyes nearly bugged out of his head. A storm cloud formed behind him, and Gabriel dared the bastard to try zapping him with a lightning bolt. But a moment later, the cloud dissipated. Smart move.

"If Azagoth told you how to destroy the portal," Hut ground out, "why haven't you done it already?"

It was a good question and one he'd been asking himself. At least he had a believable answer, even if it wasn't the *whole* answer.

"Because I've been planning the best approach angle through the fog."

"Fog? What fog?"

Gesturing for him to follow, Gabriel shot toward the platform, Hutriel keeping pace with ease. Within seconds, the massive, seething cloud of darkness surrounding the platform became visible. He slowed at the edge of it, every angelic sense he had screaming a warning.

This was bad. Really, really bad.

"I don't like this." Hutriel hung back, regarding the phenomenon with wary eyes. "The evil emanating from it…it's like nothing I've felt before."

Gabriel agreed. And he'd been inside Hell once or twice.

"Different parts of Sheoul contain different concentrations of evil," he said. "There are places we can't enter because of it. This… abomination must have seeped into this realm from one of those areas of concentrated evil."

Hutriel shrank back a little more. "I'm having a very strong reaction to it."

A very strong reaction to it? The idea of penetrating that inky storm put dread in the very pit of Gabriel's soul. His gut churned, and every drop of self-preservation warned him that the mist was something akin to poison.

"The one thing we have in our favor is that the dome isn't very thick," he said. "The platform is close."

Hut looked at him. "What if it is not a dome? What if it has engulfed the platform? We cannot survive in that kind of environment for long."

Yeah, that would be a problem. Hopefully, Stryke had done something to push the shit back. Gabriel's armor should provide a measure of protection, but Hut-boy was on his own.

"See why I haven't been really anxious to dive in?" He looked at the writhing mass of evil, the sounds of suffering ringing in his ears, and then he shrugged.

What the hell?

He crashed into the writhing darkness.

Instant regret.

Every muscle seemed to lock up, his arms and legs hanging uselessly as he flew through the fog like an out-of-control airplane. His wings drooped, every flap feeling like he was flying in some sort of evil Jell-O.

Things clawed at him, a slow-motion attack that made his exposed skin burn with even a mere graze of a slippery tentacle or serrated tooth.

Behind him, Hutriel hissed in pain and cursed the "fiends from Satan's playground."

Every breath was agony as if teeny, malevolent bacteria penetrated Gabriel's lung tissue. Blood dripped from his nose, and his eyes felt like they might be melting. He tried to engage his powers, but the fog absorbed or corrupted the energy of every weapon he summoned. His fireball fizzled at the tips of his fingers. His ice storm created hail that shredded their shriveling wings.

Where the hell was the platform?

There!

Finally, the massive metal structure appeared, and they popped into sweet, non-evil air a few meters from the rig.

Weakened by the struggle to get through the fog, the abrupt change in atmosphere sent Gabriel into an uncontrolled tumble of wings and limbs. He cartwheeled onto the deck and skidded across the grating. Hutriel didn't fare much better, crash-landing in a heap of feathers next to a metal chest.

Holy...

Through blurry vision, he watched the other angel writhe, his blood dripping between the deck slats. His wings were mangled, the feathers curled and melted, and the right one might be broken. Slices and chunks of flesh had been ripped out in a dozen places.

Gabriel didn't even want to see how badly he was torn up.

"Hey, assholes!"

Groaning, he looked up to where four armed males had weapons drawn and trained on them.

"Who are you?"

"I need...to speak to...Stryke." He paused, trying to catch his breath, but his lungs were still burning as if cooking him from the inside. "Tell him...tell him it's Gabriel."

One of the guys took off, and Gabriel flopped back onto the platform to let his body start healing. Angels healed quickly, usually instantaneously under the right circumstances. But the more intense the evil, the worse the damage, and longer the injuries took to mend.

Closing his eyes, he felt the sting of wounds as they knitted together and thought his lungs felt a little better. His eyes rolled around under his lids as they healed, and son of a bitch, it hurt.

The muffled sound of footsteps rang out. He sensed someone stopping next to him and opened his eyes.

"Stryke," he croaked.

Stryke looked down at him, his head cocked. "Never thought I'd ever say I was happy to see an angel."

"Glad..." He coughed. "Glad I could make your day."

Stryke jacked his thumb at Hutriel, who had managed to sit up and prop himself against the chest. "Who's that?"

"Hutriel. He's here to babysit me."

Stryke raised an eyebrow at that but said nothing. "Let's get you inside before creatures start climbing onto the platform again." He signaled his men over.

"Does this fog ever come closer?"

"It has. I've got mages holding it back right now."

Gabriel hoped they were good because if their magic failed while he and Hut were still injured, they'd be too weak to get back through the fog. They could end up falling into the sea, where they'd be torn apart by demonic creatures in an endless, living hell. Some things were worse than death.

Stryke's men helped them into the platform's forward office. Cracks spiderwebbed both windows, and buckets had been set out to collect water from leaks in the walls and ceiling.

"So," Stryke said. "How bad is all of this if Heaven sent angels?"

"It's as bad as it gets, Stryke. As bad as it gets."

Chapter 20

Sea Storm's conference room, an austere, windowless office space, had seemed cramped before everyone took their seats at the ten-person table. Now, it was a sardine can where Cyan sat next to Stryke as everyone got caught up.

And there was a lot of catching up to do.

The angels' revelation that the drill had breached a massive portal that could open into not only the human realm but also Heaven itself…had left them all in shock. And it made their mission to fix the problem more urgent, especially if demons were accessing Heaven through the legendary gateway.

And then there was the fact that she was sitting at a table with two angels. Two freaking *angels*. And one of them was an *Archangel*. From the *Bible*.

No one else seemed fazed, but then Scotty not only grew up on an island with Memitim angels, but her grandfather, Reaver, was the most powerful angel in existence. Blade and Stryke were no strangers to angels either and had trained with them their entire lives. Mace's mother, one of Azagoth's daughters, had been a Memitim angel born to watch over Primori, making him one-quarter angel.

So, chatting with an Archangel must have seemed like just another day for all of them. Cyan, meanwhile, couldn't decide if she was awed or terrified.

Gabriel turned to her, his fabulous, multicolored hair swirling around the shoulder plates of his dented armor. It was said that his hair consisted of all the colors of humankind, and she didn't doubt that.

"If you can access the original glyphs," he said to her, "can you repair them and seal the breach?"

"We're not sealing it." Hutriel slapped his hand on the table, the ear-shattering crack making her jump. "We're *destroying* it. Azagoth told you how."

Gabriel swung his chair around to the other angel. "Think about it. We don't know what demolishing it will do to the Gaiaportal. Destroying one will probably destroy the other."

Hutriel was unmoved. "The Gaiaportal is a relic from an earlier time. Its usefulness is over anyway."

"Is it?" Tiny, angry lightning strikes turned Gabriel's brilliant blue eyes into plasma globes, and Cyan wondered if anyone else could feel the tension crackling in the air. "Right now, ninety-nine percent of Heaven is in lockdown."

Lockdown? Cyan exchanged glances with the others, and they seemed as stunned as she was.

Hutriel went apoplectic with outrage. "Are you suggesting we *re-open* the Gaiaportal?"

"I don't know," Gabriel said. "Maybe. The Thrones have lost their minds. We're all trapped. You're in charge of security. Doesn't it make sense to have an escape route?"

"You're walking a treasonous line, Gabriel," Hutriel said, his voice dripping with warning. "And you're doing it in front of *demons*, making your offense more egregious."

Treason? What was so treasonous? And why were angels trapped? Also, the way he'd said *demons* was incredibly offensive. Probably wasn't the best time to point that out, though.

"I'm beyond caring." Gabriel's voice got louder, and Hutriel's face grew redder. "We should temporarily seal the rift instead of going scorched earth. Give everyone time to consider the consequences of total destruction."

"I have my orders, and so do you," Hutriel snapped. "End of discussion, especially in front of these…hellspawn. We can't trust them with *any* of this."

Mace snorted with amusement, Blade seemed to be sizing Hut up for a coffin, and Scotty studied her nails.

Stryke shot to his feet, clapped his palms on the table, and leaned toward Hutriel. "Let's get something straight. These *hellspawn* saved your asses. This is *my* rig. *My* equipment. *My* people. I'm about as happy to be working with you dickhead halos as you are about working with us lowly demons. Get fucking over it." He gave Blade a meaningful glance before shifting his gaze between Hutriel and Gabriel. "We need to work together to survive this, so stow your baggage and focus."

Cyan thought Stryke's tirade was damned hot, but Hutriel clucked his tongue in dismissal. "You did not *save our asses.*"

"Yeah," Stryke said, "I did. I didn't throw you overboard to the demonic sharktopus while you were too weak to do jack about it. You can thank me later." Mace barked out a laugh as Stryke turned to Gabriel. "I'm not taking any chances with this fucking portal. I don't give a hellrat's ass about Heaven's problems and what will happen to the Gaiaportal. We're destroying this fucker. End of discussion. How do we do it?"

Gabriel's eyes flashed with fury, and a fiery aura flickered all around him. Their gazes locked like two rival dire wolves plotting their attack, and for a heart-stopping moment, she thought the Archangel would slay Stryke where he stood.

"My powers are limited in the water," Gabriel finally said, "but I can create a life-sustaining bubble for myself and Cyan. I can get her to the glyphs or as deep as she needs to be. Once there, I can use my powers to supercharge hers. Together, we should be able to destroy the portal."

Stryke considered that. "What are the risks?"

"As I said, right now, Heaven will be at risk—"

"To her," Stryke broke in, gesturing to Cyan. "I told you I don't give a shit about your Heavenly civil war. I want to know what the risks are to *her.*"

Aw. She had unexpected warm-fuzzies. Shanea used to say she felt warm-fuzzies whenever Draven said or did something that showed how much he loved her. Which was pretty much daily. They'd been so in love.

She automatically glanced at Stryke, expecting the stab of anger that manifested every time she thought about Shan. This time, it didn't happen. There was only the ever-present grief that, somehow, felt a gram lighter.

Gabriel considered Stryke's question. "As long as I'm safe," he finally said, "she's probably safe."

Cyan did *not* like the sound of that. "Probably?"

Gabriel sat up straighter in his chair. "It's not like I have a lot of practice battling demons in the water. Aquatic demon incursions are extremely rare. I haven't been in a sea or ocean in thousands of years. You see one whale, you've seen them all, you know?"

"We need to prepare for worst-case scenarios." Scotty rocked idly in her chair, her arms crossed over her breasts. "Give us some idea of what kinds of things could go wrong."

"You *are* your father's daughter, aren't you?" Gabriel mused.

"I'll take that as a compliment."

Smiling, Gabriel inclined his head. "As it was intended. You've come a long way since the last time I saw you training in the arena, trying to keep up with the older boys." He lost the smile, his expression becoming serious as he addressed everyone. "Worst-case scenarios? We could get swallowed whole by a leviathan, in which case I could fight my way out, but Cyan would likely not survive. Or my bubble could burst, in which case Cyan could be crushed or drowned before I made it back to the surface."

"She's not going," Stryke announced. "You're angels. You can do this by yourselves."

"Perhaps," Gabriel said slowly. "I came here intending just that. But having Cyan's help increases the odds of success. The price of failure is too much to risk."

Cyan's chair creaked as she turned to him. "I have to do it, Stryke. You know I do. We're out of time and down to a Hail Mary."

She was right, and he knew it. He didn't argue. He couldn't have, not with the way he'd locked his jaw so fiercely the muscles in his face and neck twitched.

"I'm going with you," Hutriel said. "In my own bubble, of course."

Gabriel nodded at her. "Are you ready?"

"Wait." Stryke held up a hand. "I need to talk to Cyan for a minute." He cocked his head toward the door. "In private."

Once alone in the hallway, she turned to him. "What is it?"

He glanced back at the door, probably to make sure no one was listening. "I don't think you should do this. I don't trust them."

She doubted he trusted anyone. "I thought you knew Gabriel."

"I know a lot of angels. That's why I don't trust them. They will sacrifice anyone and anything in the name of a cause," he said, darkness settling into his tone. "I've only met Gabriel a couple of times, both brief, but I wouldn't trust him even if we were best buddies. He was involved with Azagoth at the time of Sheoul-gra's destruction, and I don't know how or why."

Whoa. Many people, both demon and human, had died as a result of Azagoth's actions, but even more consequential was its impact on the very course of history. Humans had become aware of the existence of underworlders because of it.

"Why would an angel want Sheoul-gra destroyed?"

"I don't know," he admitted, his brow furrowed in a scowl. He hated not knowing something. He'd once said in an interview that unanswered questions often became obsessions for him, and he could go down research rabbit holes for weeks at a time.

Before he could obsess, she laid her hand lightly on his arm. "I know you're worried. But unless you have another plan, we have to use Gabriel's. We don't have a choice, Stryke. You know it. We both know it."

"Yeah, yeah," he muttered, following it up with a curse. "But promise me you won't turn your back on them. Angels don't work with demons unless they have an agenda, and they make sport of killing us. Don't trust any of them."

His gaze captured hers, the intensity in his eyes making her breath catch. She used to think his eyes were cold, bottomless, and empty. But now she saw nothing but naked emotion under a veneer of indifference. He came across as not caring about anything, but she knew the truth now.

He cared about *everything*. To distraction. To the point where he'd erected a barrier to protect himself.

Stryke's problem wasn't that he didn't have enough feelings.

It was that he had too many.

Then there was the issue of him being an asshole in general. But she was kind of starting to appreciate it, especially when it was directed at someone other than her.

"I don't like this," he said softly, one hand rising to cup her cheek.

Heart pounding with sudden urgency, she froze in the moment, shocked by his tenderness and her response to it. He'd just stripped away all her barriers with a mere touch.

Suddenly, something jolted the platform. The tiles beneath their feet buckled, and they careened into the wall, only Stryke's strength keeping them from going down. Still, he smashed up against her as her spine hit the plaster wall.

The pain didn't even register. There was nothing but shaking and trembling, and the two of them. His eyes locked on hers. Another jolt, and he dipped his head, capturing her mouth in a brief, passionate kiss.

When he pulled away, his gaze was scorching hot, and she felt herself wanting to be burned. "Be careful. DART needs you."

A thread of disappointment filtered through her. "Just DART?"

A smile curved one corner of his lips. "StryTech too."

She smiled back because she didn't hear, "StryTech too," she heard, "*Me, too.*"

"Do you really think this will work?" Hutriel, his expression a mask of doubt, shifted his gaze from Gabriel to peer over the platform railing at the waves below.

Not really. I give it a 50/50 chance.

"Absolutely," Gabriel said. "I'm confident."

Hutriel turned back to him, his wrecked black-and-crimson armor creaking. "I don't trust Cyberis demons."

"I don't trust *any* demon. But Cyan is our best hope."

"Yo, angels." Cyan glared between them as she placed herself on the boat dock near Gabriel. "I can hear you. So, tell me again why you can't do this by yourself?"

Her sarcasm flew right over Hutriel's head. "We can. But we aren't Sea Celestials, so our powers don't extend very far underwater. And your magical abilities can compensate."

Gabriel frowned. "Why *didn't* the Thrones send a Sea Celestial for this?"

"Because the only angels who preside over water are the Principalities," Hutriel said. "They might have sided with the Thrones in their bid for power, but the taint of Satan's rebellion remains. They can't be trusted in a matter such as this."

Their powers were also weak compared to Gabriel's—and even Hutriel's. But it still would have been wise to send one. The Thrones were idiots.

"Exactly," Cyan said. "See, you need me. So, if you can't be nice, at least stop talking about me like I'm something you scraped off the bottom of your shoe." She glanced at Stryke, who stood, tense as a rod, on the platform a few yards away. When she turned back to Gabriel, she gave him a decisive nod. "So, how do we do this?"

He liked this demon. He didn't trust her, but he liked her. Hutriel, meanwhile, was probably plotting to kill her after her usefulness ended. He'd probably want to kill all of them.

"I'll encase us in a bubble of air. We'll be able to speak, but try not to touch the sides or they'll leak."

"Okay." White-knuckling the flashlight she'd brought, she blew out a long breath. "Let's do this."

He came up behind her and gripped her shoulders. Once the bubble surrounded them like a clear eggshell, he launched them up and away from the platform before lowering them into the water.

An instant, muffled silence surrounded them. Cyan's flashlight provided enough light to guide them to the drill casing, and he began a rapid descent.

"Will that provide light all the way down?" he asked.

"As long as the batteries hold out." She angled the flashlight down a little. "Taran said some of the beasts use a kind of electric pulse as a weapon, and they sometimes short out batteries. Why? Can't you make light?"

"I can," he said. "But angelic glow attracts demons. Damned inconvenient."

"I'll say," she muttered, glancing at her wrist comms' depth sensor. "Seventy meters. We're getting close."

Gabriel couldn't feel the pressure increasing on the surface of the bubble around them as they descended, but he somehow felt more confined. He'd hated tight spaces ever since he got trapped in a cave a few thousand years ago, and this was growing more and more uncomfortable. The sounds he was picking up with his angelic hearing—distorted, muffled groans and shrieks—didn't help his comfort factor.

"Stop. I see the glyphs," Cyan said. "Tell me what I need to do. I'm guessing we're going to attach angelic energy to mine and turn the nanomachines into a trillion little Heaven bombs. Am I right?"

That would be brilliant. If she could get the nanomachines to the eternal fire, they could douse it with the power of Heaven. Which would destroy the Gehennaportal and keep Revenant trapped.

But it could also destroy the Gaiaportal. And keep angels trapped.

Damn.

"Gabriel?"

He hesitated. The noises were getting closer. His mind spun, plotting out all the courses of action available to him, all the repercussions, all the scenarios. More eerie sounds...and a big shadow to his right. They needed to hurry.

"Gabriel!"

"Yes. We'll do that. No, wait." Indecision left him paralyzed in a way that rarely happened. As a powerful angel—formidable even by Archangel standards—he rarely doubted his decisions. Who would dare question him?

But with the Thrones in charge, a wrong move here could affect his upcoming Ordeal. Worse, leaving the rift sealed but the Gehennaportal operational could end *very* badly.

"Gabriel! *Helloooo.*"

Damn it! "We're not destroying the portal," he practically yelled. "Repair the breach."

"But I thought—"

"Repair it!" he snapped, hating his decision but knowing he'd hate the other equally. "Hurry!"

His heart tapped rapidly against his chest wall, and his mouth went dry. This needed to be kept secret until he could trust someone else with the information. But who? Reaver was comatose, Metatron was being held under guard, and all the other Archangels were imprisoned inside their heads. Not that Gabriel was allowed to talk to anyone anyway.

How long would he have to keep this to himself? Well, himself and Cyan. Cyan presented a problem.

I have to kill her.

Strangely, he didn't like that thought. Generally, he enjoyed killing demons. They were abominations deserving of torturous slaughter. But he'd also been around long enough to know that some deserved to live, even if their usefulness would eventually come to an end.

Cyan struck him as one of those. Low on the evil scale, just wanting to live her life. And she was, currently, on the right side of the war between good and evil.

"How's it going?" he asked.

She remained still, her focus on the glyphs he couldn't see. "I'm almost done."

"Cyan?"

"Yeah?"

He was about to make another risky move. "I'm going to need you to lie about what happened down here."

"Excuse me?"

"Keep working," he said calmly, even though his pulse was racing. "There are…things coming toward us. We don't have much time." Next to them, Hutriel was pointing animatedly at the things.

"I *am* working. Keep talking."

"We're going to tell everyone that we destroyed the portal."

Silence. Then, "Why?"

Here was where he should tell her that he was an Archangel, and she didn't need to know why. But she was a scientist, a technician of magic, and she wouldn't lie for no good reason. So, he'd go all-in with this demon and trust her.

I am such a fool.

"Because I believe that destroying it will do more harm than good. We can always come back and destroy it later."

She went taut, a subtle stiffening of her upper body he wouldn't have noticed if his hands hadn't been on her shoulders. "Of course."

She didn't trust him, and he didn't blame her. Why would an angel not want to destroy something so evil and with so much potential to cause widespread destruction?

It sounded insane to him too.

He might have made a catastrophic mistake.

"You need to trust me."

"Do I? What team are you on, buddy? And what are you willing to do to keep your secret? Given that I'm the only one who knows, I'm guessing I'll meet with an unfortunate accident on the way up." She blew out a breath. "I'm finished."

"You're not finished. I'm not going to kill you."

"No, I mean, I'm done. With the repair—"

Something slammed into them. They tumbled, hitting the bubble's walls with brutal force. The violence knocked the flashlight from Cyan's hand. It punctured the bubble walls and fell into the deep, its light gone in an instant. Water poured through the shield, several gallons before Gabriel could repair it.

Darkness surrounded them, and when he turned on his glow, he almost wished he hadn't. The sea teemed with demon fish, their grotesque, semi-transparent bodies writhing on the edges of his light, their razor teeth flashing.

Suddenly, the school of nightmares parted, making room for a nuclear submarine-sized monster with eyes that glowed like lava.

"I'm taking us up!" He shot upward. The thing sped after them.

He broke the water's surface, and right behind him, the toothy demon broke it too. It snapped at him as he twisted and banked toward where Stryke and the others were waiting. A massive splash as the beast fell back into the water nearly took Gabriel out, but he clung tightly to Cyan and managed to right himself and continue on course to Stryke.

To his left, Hutriel soared behind the platform, some sort of spiny-finned thing with wings chasing him.

"Remember," he growled in Cyan's ear as they approached the waiting *Sea Storm* team, "not a word to anyone. Not even Stryke. Not unless he resumes drilling operations or wants to sell the rig. This is important, demon. The current ruling body in Heaven will execute him."

It probably wasn't true, but Gabriel doubted Cyan would care about *his* plight. She wouldn't give a shit that Gabriel was already in trouble and this could get him not just imprisoned but imprisoned on an isolated planet on another realm, where no one would ever find him. A fate reserved for the worst offenses…that hadn't quite reached the level of being booted out of Heaven or executed.

No, thank you.

Unceremoniously, he plunked Cyan onto the deck in front of Stryke and flew upward on a draft, his fiery sword in hand. He couldn't see Hutriel's battle with the flying demon, but he could sense it.

Time to spill some blood.

Chapter 21

Stryke grabbed Cyan as she hit the deck. Gabriel flew off just as a long-necked, nightmarish creature leaped out of the water, steam hissing off its pointy scales. The whoosh of crossbow bolts whispered past his ears, and the heat from a flamethrower singed his arm hair. The demon took the full force of the bolts and flames, screeched in pain, and dropped back into the sea.

"Is the portal destroyed?" he asked her.

"Ah...yeah… Shit, behind you!"

They both ducked as the thing's tail whipped into the supports and walls, crumpling them before disappearing beneath the waves.

"Stryke!" Taran came down the ladder two rungs at a time. "Temp at the breach is normal. No heat signatures at all. I think the breach is sealed. But now these demons are stuck here."

Stryke shouted up to the security people lining the platform's walkways. "Stay alert. There might be more before this is over."

Explosions, screeches, and godawful roars rose from what sounded like the other side of the platform.

"Gabriel," Cyan blurted breathlessly. "It has to be."

They took off, rushing toward the sounds of battle. Streaks of lightning and black clouds full of red sparks roiled overhead, but as they approached the helicopter landing pad, everything went quiet.

Deathly quiet. Not even the things in the fog made noise.

Then, a sound broke the silence. *Drip. Drip. Drip.*

Blood. Dripping off railings and pipes to the blood-drenched deck, where a dozen gouged chunks of demon flesh quivered like small boulders on a game board. A massive, mangled wing, its feathers strewn about, dangled from the roof of the superstructure.

"Gabriel!"

The angel stood near the far railing, his sword in hand. It was no longer aflame and the tip rested on the deck. The weapon looked too heavy to hold as he stared vacantly down at the body at his feet.

"Is that...a head?" Cyan skirted a bloody object.

"I think it's Hutriel's," Stryke said.

Sure enough, as they got closer to Gabriel, it became obvious that the one-winged, headless body belonged to Hutriel. A couple of yards away lay the Land Rover-sized severed head of the demon that had chased Hutriel to the helicopter pad.

"What happened?"

Gabriel looked up, blood matting his hair and streaking his armor. "That thing...ripped him apart."

"Stryke!" He wheeled around. Cyan gestured into the distance as the security team and the three DART agents came to a sudden, shocked halt at the top of the ladder.

The fog thinned, folding in on itself. Dim, filtered light seeped through the evil veil. Creatures no longer writhed and screamed in the mist's depths, and the sea below no longer thrashed. Within a minute, the fog was gone, and a cloudless blue sky lit the platform.

Yes.

"Taran," Stryke shouted. "Check on the comms system and get StryTech on the line. I want all non-essential and injured personnel off this thing."

"I can't wait to get back," Cyan said. "I'm going to stuff my face full of pizza and drink an entire bottle of wine."

That sounded good to him too. But asking her to join him right now didn't seem appropriate. He might not have great social graces, but he did know one didn't ask someone on a date while standing on the blood-soaked site of a massacre.

"Gabriel," she said, turning to the angel. "I'm sorry about your friend."

"What?" Gabriel looked up, startled as if he just realized where he was. "Oh. Hutriel." He looked back down at the body. "Don't be sorry. He was going to kill you all."

With a wave of his hand, the corpse rose into the air, its severed noggin with it. A moment later, Gabriel and the dead angel were gone, blinked back to Heaven or wherever they were going.

Hutriel had planned to kill everyone on the platform?

He and Cyan exchanged apprehensive glances as the DART trio jogged toward them.

"Did you see Hutriel's neck?" he asked.

She leveled a troubled look at him. She'd seen it.

A clean cut.

As if made not by a demon's claw or teeth but by a sword.

Chapter 22

Most angels re-entering Heaven popped out in the same place.

The Sun Terrace, a round, golden-tiled platform that floated over the crater of a crystal volcano. From there, if you weren't stopped by security forces, you could flash to anywhere in the realm you wanted to go.

Gabriel had hoped to flash home before reporting to Zaphkiel, but as luck would have it, a Throne named Petulas was waiting for him, a Ligorial in his hand.

"Zaphkiel expected you back days ago," Petulas said, holding out the metallic silver bracelet for Gabriel to slip into.

"Days?" His surprise overcame his annoyance at being restrained, his powers blocked. The Ligorial might look like a plain piece of jewelry, but it both restricted the use of angelic powers and would also, with a single thought from its owner, wrap around the wearer's body like a python.

"Nearly a week has passed in the human realm. What took so long?"

A week? The evil fog must have leaked into the Earthly realm from a region of Sheoul where time ran faster, trapping the *Sea Storm* in its time warp.

"Just take me to Zaphkiel."

Petulas craned his neck to look behind Gabriel. "Where is Hutriel? We were told he would be accompanying you."

Gabriel schooled his expression, summoning the cool, superior nonchalance all Archangels had perfected. It wasn't hard. He was numb right now. Everything was great. Just great. Fucking peachy.

"Hutriel's not coming." Hutriel was *never* coming.

The toady looked at him but said nothing as they flashed to Throne HQ. Gabriel entered Zaphkiel's chamber, where he was seated on a dais with two other high-ranking Thrones.

Zaph stood, his formal purple robes swaying around his jeweled slippers. Man, Gabriel missed Metatron. He usually wore breezy, casual clothes and wasn't a douchebag.

"Finally," Zaphkiel said. "What news have you?"

Gabriel chose his words carefully. "The Gehennaportal is no longer a threat."

"So, you destroyed it?" At Gabriel's nod, Zaphkiel's mouth pursed. "Did Azagoth willingly give you the tools to do so? And where is Hutriel?"

A shadow passed over Gabriel's soul at the mention of the other angel's name, twisting and writhing as it wove itself into his very being.

"He was killed," he said. "In battle."

"Killed?" Morasha, the female on Zaphkiel's right, flowed to her feet, her crimson robes swishing. "How?"

The scene came back to him in slow motion and with crystal clarity. Demon teeth, flashing swords, blood, and feathers. His normally iron stomach roiled.

"Demons attacked the platform." He swallowed. "Hutriel...fought valiantly."

"What of his body?"

An image of Hutriel's body sinking beneath the waves flashed behind his eyes and brought bile to his tongue. "Lost to the seas."

"This is unfortunate," Morasha said. "He was one of our greatest warriors." She narrowed her eyes at Gabriel. "Were there any witnesses to his death?"

He pegged her with a hard stare and summoned Archangel attitude. "Are you questioning my account?"

"I'd simply like to know exactly what happened. He was my friend."

"He was my friend too," Zaph said. "We'll get to the bottom of it. But first, I want to know everything that happened while you were gone. Who you talked to. What Azagoth said. What his residence looked like, right down to the color of his walls. Understand?"

"And then what?"

"Then you will be returned to your cell until your Ordeal."

No. He had too much to do and few ways to accomplish it. Absolutely nothing would get done if he was imprisoned. But how could he—?

"I want to see Reaver first," he blurted.

"Reaver?" Zaph looked startled. "Why? He's not responsive."

"It's my pre-Ordeal right to see anyone I want. I choose Reaver."

The idiots looked between each other and finally shrugged. "We will agree to that *if* our laws allow that person to be unconscious."

"Agreed. Let's chat."

Like most Heavenly prisons, Reaver's was featureless, endless nothingness. He floated about four feet off the floor…if it could be called that. Technically, there was no floor, no ceiling, no walls. Just… space. It was both complicated, yet unbelievably simple.

And even though Gabriel didn't need his wings to hover next to Reaver's resting form, he kept them out and low in deference to the angel.

Reaver was…a legend.

And a total jackass.

But lying there in a shimmering white robe trimmed in bronze, his gleaming hair hanging like a molten gold waterfall, he looked regal, like a king in repose.

At least he wasn't being held captive like he'd been immediately following the Thrones' coup. They'd cleverly used the restrained Archangels as power banks to contain Reaver.

But now, he was a prisoner inside his own body.

"Hey," he said, trying to sound chipper and not like his entire world had gone to shit. "It's Gabriel, your second favorite Archangel."

Maybe. Reaver didn't like any of them, save his uncle Metatron, who'd raised him. He treated the rest with disdain and disrespect. But then most of Gabriel's brethren treated Reaver the same way. They constantly argued over whether he was deserving of his status as a Radiant.

In Gabriel's opinion, he deserved it. The guy had literally gone to Hell and back, had sacrificed himself over and over. Gabriel might not like him much, but he respected him. Anyone powerful enough to lock an Archangel in a prison with Satan deserved to be held in high regard. And maybe a little awe.

"Look, I hope you can hear me because I'm going through some things." He blew out a long breath as he questioned every move he'd made lately. "I gave up a chance to speak to someone who could actually help me so I could catch you up on the situation outside your thick skull."

His attempt at humor fell flat, even for him. There was too much going on, and he was in too much trouble.

"You probably already know all the Archangels are being held in stasis. Only Metatron and I are conscious. I'm only free"—he held up his wrist, the restraining bracelet rattling—"if you can call this free, because they're trying to punish me for what happened with Azagoth. Metatron is still around because they need him until they can find someone else who can give voice to the Creator. Not that we've heard anything. We have no guidance, and things are getting…bad. The Thrones are in charge and have no idea how to govern except through heavy-handed control. Heaven is on lockdown, and everyone thinks everyone else is a spy."

He paced, starting to regret his choice of pre-Ordeal counsel. Not that he was *too* worried. But he wanted the least severe sentence possible. He did *not* want to be banished to another realm or planet or end up like the other Archangels, who could be held like that for centuries until they were needed in the Last Battle against evil.

"From what I can see, your family is doing good. Whatever's going on in your head, be eased by that. And…I have news of Harvester."

He watched closely for a reaction. Any reaction. That was why he was here. Reaver needed to be brought back. If he could escape and somehow free the Archangels…

It was a long shot. Absolutely. But Reaver had faced greater odds and emerged victorious.

He'd also failed miserably a few times.

And had paid dearly.

Reaver didn't stir. Not so much as an eyelash.

"I know you can't feel her anymore," Gabriel said. "I'm sorry."

He couldn't comprehend the level of pain Reaver must be in. Gabriel had been in love a few times over the centuries, but he'd never felt the desire to take a mate. His purpose in life made him feel as though he was on a different path, one headed toward greatness somehow. Yeah, it sounded arrogant, but deep down, he felt as though he would make a difference—a critical difference—in the fate of the world. Taking a mate wasn't part of that.

"You know Harvester went through the Gaiaportal," Gabriel said, which was stupid because, of course, Reaver knew. His current condition was a direct result. "Well, not only did it kill her and sever the bond between you, but it also activated the Gehennaportal. She stirred up a lot of shit. So, when you think about it, she went out the way she lived."

He smiled fondly, which was curious since Harvester had not been likable in the least. She'd spent so much time as a fallen angel, faithfully serving at her father Satan's side, that darkness was part of her—even after she'd returned to the light.

"But here's the thing, Reaver." He stopped next to the Radiant's head and leaned in close to his ear. No one was supposed to be listening to any of this, but Gabriel wasn't taking any chances with information this sensitive. "Harvester's Grace never returned to the Creator. She found a host vessel in your grandson's female, Eva."

Nothing. No change.

No…wait. Did Reaver's eyeballs move beneath his closed eyelids?

Excitement stirring, Gabriel leaned in again. "Did you hear me? She's not gone. But that human body can only contain her for so long. She needs you, Reaver. Especially if the Thrones learn where she is. They could rip her from Eva. You know that can be fatal. Or worse." He paused for dramatic effect. "Poor Logan."

Yeah, he was milking this, but he wasn't lying. Reaver needed to be reminded of all consequences.

"And what will they do once they have her? I doubt they'll release her back to the Creator. They'll imprison her somehow. Maybe put her inside another host so they can use her for intel that only she, as Satan's daughter, can provide for the Last Battle. They could torture her."

Reaver's eyes flew open.

Gabriel nearly jumped out of his skin. "Hey. You there? If so, you need to close your eyes. You can't let anyone know you've got even the tiniest awareness right now."

Very slowly, Reaver's lids lowered, his long lashes leaving shadows on his skin.

Yes! Excitement made Gabriel's hands shake as he laid them on Reaver's arm. "If you are capable of anything more than opening your eyes, flex your biceps."

Not even a twitch. Nothing. Reaver was probably on the very edge of awareness. Which meant he could slip backward, or he could gradually come around.

Gabriel would make him come around if it was the last thing he ever did.

"Listen to me, Reaver. My Ordeal is happening soon. It'd be great if you exploded back into consciousness and started cracking heads before that. And it's not just because I want to avoid some bullshit punishment. A lot of people need this. Your family. All of Heaven. Harvester."

A gong rang, signaling that his time was up.

"Don't let us down, Reaver," he said hastily. "Armageddon draws near, and we need Heaven to be in order with our best warriors ready. We're counting on you." He inhaled deeply and released the breath in a slow, controlled flow as if to counter the heavy feeling in his gut. "I feel a darkness descending on us. On...me." His voice trembled, and he lowered it again, almost to a whisper. "I've done something terrible, Reaver. Something that turns the soul black. I need my choice to have been the right one, and that'll only happen if the Archangels are restored to power." He almost laughed at his delusion that everything he'd asked and hoped for would be possible. "So, you know, wake up and save Heaven and Earth. Again." He headed toward the exit, turning around at the doorway. "But no pressure."

No, the pressure was all on him now.

Chapter 23

They completed evacuation from the platform in a couple of hours, but Stryke remained behind to deal with the aftermath and find the way forward. Apparently, he'd had his suppressants delivered, and he'd sent Cyan on her way through orders from Taran without telling her goodbye.

Sure, he'd been extremely busy. With all communications restored, he'd been bombarded with communiqués. They all had.

But still. He could have at least...what? Kissed her? The way he'd kissed her before she'd gone into the water with Gabriel?

Warmth flooded her at the memory. His intensity, his passion...she shivered, wondering how that passion would translate if they weren't in danger, were alone, and in a bed. Or on the floor. Or wherever.

Would he even be interested now that he no longer needed her? It certainly wasn't as if they were in a relationship.

She laughed at the very idea as she opened the door to her apartment. A relationship with Stryke, billionaire CEO of StryTech and the world's most eligible bachelor? How ridiculous.

Stepping into her apartment, her amusement faded, replaced by a sudden loneliness. The place felt empty without Shanea, certainly. But as she closed the door behind her, what she felt struck her as something new. A different kind of loneliness.

Or maybe she was just overly tired. And she was. She was *exhausted*. Physically *and* mentally.

An Archangel wanted her to lie about a highly dangerous, monumentally important bit of information. How was she supposed to function with that weight on her shoulders? How would she keep asking Stryke about his plans for the *Sea Storm* without looking suspicious?

Could she even trust the angel? The one who might have beheaded his buddy?

Shivering with a sudden chill, she made a beeline for the shower. The hot steam both relaxed and revived her, making her think about Stryke's aversion to water. And sex. And food. Some of the greatest pleasures in life. What *did* he do for fun?

She took her time under the cleansing spray, and by the time she'd dried her hair and put on sweats, she almost felt like a new person.

Someone with the fate of the world in her hands. No big deal.

She scrounged in the fridge for something to eat, her belly protesting when she didn't find anything that wasn't spoiled or moldy. Which left her with a choice between oatmeal, ramen noodles, or boxed pasta using water instead of milk.

Ramen would be the quickest, so ramen it was. Resigned, she slammed the fridge door just as the doorbell rang. The mounted kitchen viewscreen revealed Parker in the hallway, peering into the camera.

What was he doing here?

"Door open," she called out, wistfully eyeing the package of dried noodles on the counter.

The door swung open, and Parker stepped in, holding up a couple of bags. "Hey, welcome back. I figured you might be in need of a good meal."

Her stomach growled at the aroma of hot roast beef and frites, and she had to stop herself from snatching the bags and ripping into them with her teeth. "Parker, you're my hero."

He gave her a sheepish grin. "You've been gone for a week, and I got stuck on the project. Figured I'd run it by you really quick while we eat."

A week? There was no way. A couple of days at most.

She checked her wrist comms, and, sure enough, seven days had passed. Time must have worked differently inside the anomaly. Interesting. She'd have to study that when she had a chance.

"You okay?" he asked, watching her with concern. "We didn't get the whole story, but what we did hear sounded bad."

She really wasn't in the mood to talk, despite her loneliness, but she was starving, and Parker had brought her food, so she figured she could manage a few minutes of conversation.

"I'm fine, thank you." She gestured to the kitchen table. "I have beer and seltzer. I think I might have a bottle of wine somewhere…"

"Seltzer is fine," he said, putting down the bags. "And don't worry, I won't stay long. You gotta be tired."

That was putting it mildly. "What have you heard?" she asked as she opened the fridge door.

"That there was some sort of doorway to Hell beneath an oil rig." He spoke while he pulled food containers from the bags. "Most people at the company didn't know what was going on with the platform, so hearing that it was engulfed by a leak from Hell was big news." He dumped condiments onto the table and set aside the bags. "So…what happened?"

Cyan gave him the basics as she opened a couple of bottles of sparkling water and fetched dishes.

"Damn," Parker said, sounding a little stunned as they took seats at the table. "That's some insane shit. Dakarai said a DART special ops team picked up a couple of prototypes to take out there, but he really didn't know the full situation."

"It was…an experience." She took the sandwich he offered and nearly moaned at the first bite of the roast beef and cheddar on a warm roll.

"So, is the portal destroyed?" he asked. "Or just sealed?"

She nearly choked. "What?"

"You said you and the angel stopped the leak. You didn't say how." He washed down a big bite of his sandwich with a swig of seltzer. When he was done, he shook his head and swore. "I can't believe you worked with an *angel*. And not just any angel. An *Archangel*. Holy shit, Cyan! Were you freaked out? I mean, angels aren't known to leave demons alive."

She dragged a frite through one of the sides of mayo. "Yeah, well, Gabriel did tell us the other angel wanted to kill us." She shrugged. "He was pretty cool. The other guy was a douche."

She was glad Gabriel had killed him. *If* that was what'd happened. It was entirely possible the demon really had managed to take the guy's head off with a super clean cut.

Super clean.

"So…how did you solve the problem with the breach?" Parker repeated.

Dammit. She hadn't prepared for an interrogation. And Parker wasn't stupid. He wouldn't buy a lame story or another evasion.

She dabbed her mouth with a napkin, buying time. "First, I repaired the glyphs that kept the breach sealed. But just before I repaired the last one, he sent some sort of angel-powered bomb down the pipe and into the breach."

Parker nodded idly, considering her answer as he chose a fat, well-done frite. "Why didn't he do that to begin with? Why did you need to repair the glyphs first?"

Damn him and his curious mind. "Because if the breach was mostly sealed, the explosive energy would be contained rather than losing some of the power to the sea."

"Ah. Makes sense." He popped the frite into his mouth and chewed. "How did you confirm it was destroyed?"

"Why are you so interested in this?"

"You kidding?" he said, picking up his sandwich. "Who wouldn't be? The Gehennaportal's existence has been the subject of debate since, well, always."

"Really? I'd never even heard of it until a few days ago."

"Eh, I go down some rabbit holes of knowledge sometimes." He took a bite of his sandwich, chewed, and swallowed. "So, here's the thing. According to what I've read, when it comes to Heaven and Hell, there has to be a certain symmetry. That's why there are evil people and good demons. It's why Heaven has a Radiant Angel and Sheoul has a Shadow Angel. When they made the Gaiaportal as an angelic gateway between Heaven and Earth, they created the Gehennaportal as a demonic gateway between Sheoul and Earth—back before there were hellmouths and Harrowgates."

"Yeah, I know all that already."

"Okay, but here's the thing." He leaned forward, his voice taking on a conspiratorial tone. "You said a demon got into Heaven, right?"

"Yes," she said slowly, unsure where he was going with this.

"Don't you see? It doesn't make sense." He waved his frite around, punctuating his words. "Why would the Gaiaportal's makers allow demons to come through it?"

He had a point. She thought about it for a second. "Maybe they overlooked the possibility," she offered. "Maybe that's why they shut the thing down in the first place. We don't know."

"Hmm. Maybe." He frowned down at his sandwich for a moment, then shook his head and looked up. "Just...you'd think angels wouldn't fuck up something like that."

"Well," she said, piling her garbage inside a container, "we have no way of getting answers, so how about we talk about whatever problem you came here to discuss?"

He gave her a reluctant nod. "It's not nearly as interesting," he said, tossing his napkin aside. "But we have an issue with the thermal infuser…"

Where the hell was Cyan?

Stryke paced in front of the monitor that gave him a view of the Reaper project lab, and while he'd had an eyeful of Dakarai and Parker all morning, Cyan had been absent.

She was probably sleeping and taking some well-deserved time off, but she could have at least messaged him.

Not that he was obsessing over it. He'd been too busy playing catch-up after being away from the office for a week.

A freaking *week*.

Apparently, time inside the evil dome had run slower than time in the normal human realm. What had seemed like twenty-four hours had been seven days. Fortunately, his body hadn't fast-forwarded when the time shift occurred, and he'd only had to take three injections since the last time he and Cyan had sex.

And for the first time ever, as he'd injected himself for the eight millionth time in his life, he almost wished for the real thing instead of a cold needle.

Almost. Now that things were back to normal, and he was no longer subject to the intensity of life-or-death struggles, he wasn't sure if being with Cyan would be the same.

And now that they were back in their normal lives, would she even *want* to have sex again?

It was a question that had driven him to distraction from the moment he watched her fly away on Dire Wolf One. He'd wanted her to stay, but he'd had no plausible reason to keep her on the rig. All he could do was watch and wave as the bird lifted off.

He had to stifle a groan at the memory of how awkward he'd felt the moment the emergency was over. It was like being back at school, smarter than everyone, including the teachers, an excellent if reluctant athlete, and comfortable in an educational setting. But social situations had *not* been his thing.

It wasn't that he experienced much anxiety. His main method of coping—and making things more interesting—was to hang out inside his head. Once, at a school dance, he'd spent so much time in his head that he'd solved the problem magic users experienced when they mixed elemental air and fire spells at extremely high elevations without first tempering the fire with earth. The magic community still thanked him for that one.

And Maysea Childress had nearly messed it all up by asking him to dance.

He'd said no. Awkwardly, like when he'd waved at the helicopter, knowing Cyan probably hadn't even looked back. The difference was that he hadn't liked Maysea since the day she spilled a soft drink in his lap in the cafeteria. Cyan? She could do anything she wanted to do in his lap.

Kalis's voice rang out. "Sir, you have a call from Kynan Morgan. Do you want me to put him through?"

"Yes, please."

"Have you seen the message log yet, sir?"

"Yes, and thank you. Put Kynan on." He didn't need to be prodded by his assistant about the damned messages.

There were a *lot* of messages. None of which he'd addressed because he'd been busy obsessing over Cyan.

He was such an idiot.

Counting on Kynan to get him back in the mental game, Stryke pushed a button on his desk comms, and Ky's life-sized hologram appeared on the floor in front of him, legs spread, hands locked behind his back like a general addressing his troops.

"Stryke," Kynan said. "Glad to see everything worked out. I'd love a briefing as soon as possible. I got a summary from my team, but I want your take. Sounds like you have some insight into what's happening in Heaven."

Stryke nodded. "A little. The angels didn't say much, but it looks like Heaven's in some sort of political upheaval. It's apparently shut down, and no one can get in or out."

"Which explains why the Horsemen haven't been able to summon

Reaver." He gave a quick, dismissive shake of his head. "Well, it's not our problem. But the Gehennaportal *is*. Are you sure it's been destroyed?"

"According to Gabriel and Cyan, yes."

"Thank God." Kynan shifted his stance, relaxing slightly. "That could have been an apocalyptic disaster. I'll inform the WCSG. They've been breathing down my neck for days."

Stryke didn't doubt that. Half the messages he was ignoring were from the Council.

"Don't worry about contacting them," Stryke said. "I have a feeling I'll be talking to them within the hour."

"Better you than me," Kynan muttered. "How is Cyan?"

Cyan is…amazing. "She took today off to get some rest."

"Good. And the project?"

"I haven't talked to my people yet. I'll get back to you as soon as I have an update."

"Great. Thank you. Let's schedule another meeting soon."

"I'll send you some potential dates."

With a nod, Ky disconnected. Ten seconds later, Stryke took a call from The Aegis. After that, the WCSG called, just as he'd said they would. He spent an hour staring at four pompous dumbasses as they sat around a monstrous table and pounded him with questions.

What do you plan to do with the platform now that the danger is over?

Will you sell it back to the oil company?

Will you drill for oil yourself?

He had no idea. He'd barely had time to catch his breath, let alone consider the future of the *Sea Storm*. One thing he knew for sure, though: He wasn't selling the thing. It may never produce oil again, but its value could prove immeasurable, providing countless research opportunities. He already had his people hunting and recording new demon species that'd escaped the breach and analyzing a sample he'd taken of the fog.

He'd kept that information out of his briefing with the WCSG dumbasses.

He fielded a dozen more calls, turned as many more away, including a call from his uncle Eidolon, who probably wanted to ride his ass about the injections. But the thing was, he actually felt better. After being with Cyan, his body seemed to have done a reset. How much had he healed? He had no idea, but the energy boost, mental clarity, and general mood lift made it clear he was healthier than he'd been in a long time.

Sure, the last injection had made him a little dizzy, but only for a minute.

As he disconnected the last communication, a meeting with the CEO of China's largest security company, a message popped up on his wrist comms.

From Cyan.

His heart thumped, and he sank into his chair, his skin flushing hot and his stomach fluttering oddly. Maybe the injections were affecting him more than he thought. He hated the sensation.

Sort of.

He'd never felt this before, and he loved experiencing new things. And truthfully…the sensation was maybe a little…pleasant.

Stryke, can we talk? How about I meet you at your place for dinner? I'll bring the food.

It was funny because his first instinct should have been to say no. He liked to conduct all business on his terms. Setting the date, the time, the place, and the activity. Had the message been from anyone else, he'd have said he'd get back to them with options.

Instead, his instant reply reeked of desperation.

Hi, Cyan. That sounds great.

That sounds great?

Lame and desperate.

And the flutters in his belly only got worse.

Chapter 24

Cyan hadn't been this nervous in her entire life. She didn't even know why she felt this way. She'd spent a lot of time with Stryke at this point, so it made no sense why the pending dinner with him should make her so anxious.

He'd sent her a code to enter his office and another to operate his office Harrowgate to his Canadian home. It made her wonder what it had cost him to get a private Harrowgate like that.

And who he'd paid. Only the highest-level demons had the authority to authorize personal Harrowgates.

She clutched the bags of food and stepped out of the gate and onto his deck. He'd cleared the snow, but light, dry flakes swirled around her as she walked. She'd always loved the cold weather, especially when she could be out in it.

And being out in it…was part of her plan for tonight.

The door opened automatically as she approached. Stryke stood there, still in his black work slacks and a tailored black button-down. He'd gone casual, though, with rolled-up sleeves and his shirt partially unbuttoned.

He was so freaking hot her hormones practically vibrated.

He took the bags from her. "What is this?"

She followed him to the kitchen, admiring how his pants hugged his backside. "Since you don't like eating, I thought I'd bring something you are *guaranteed* to like."

He laughed, then sobered, looking at her as if she was a dumbass. "You're kidding."

"Not. At. All." She unpacked the appetizers and handed him the plate. "Try one."

Cocking his head, he studied the little wafers. "What are they?"

"Just try one."

He narrowed his eyes at her. "Why?"

"Eat one of the wafers, and I'll tell you."

Now, his eyes narrowed to slits. "And if I *don't* eat one?"

"Then you'll never know how this experiment turns out," she said glibly, taunting his innate curiosity.

As predicted, he appeared intrigued, one eyebrow arching and a spark lighting his dark eyes. "This is an experiment?"

Kind of. "Do you know Azagoth's daughter Suzanne?"

"Who doesn't? She has a show called *An Angel in the Kitchen*. She uses her angelic powers to infuse food with emotion." He glanced down at the wafer in his hand. "Is that what this is?" He put it back on the plate and shoved it at her. "I don't want artificial feelings—"

"That's not how it works. No spells or trickery involved. It's more like...you know how laughter is infectious? Or when someone you're with is in a good mood, it can help lift yours? It's like that. Give it a try."

"No one infects me with laughter, and my mood isn't dependent on—"

She grabbed his hand and plopped a wafer into his palm. "Just try it."

He shot her a petulant glare that made her smile, but took a bite. A nibble, really. Stared at it. Took another bite, bigger this time.

"Huh. It's not bad."

"See, it's already working."

He popped the rest into his mouth. "What's it supposed to do?"

"It's going to help me rewire your brain."

He froze mid-chew. "What?"

She laughed. "Don't worry, it's basic psychology. It's going to help you associate positive feelings with things that are currently negative."

Taking a deep breath as if the air contained courage, she stripped off her sweater and hoped she wasn't making a huge mistake. She'd seen a different side of Stryke over the last few weeks, and especially during their time on the *Sea Storm*, and somehow, she'd gone from hating him to wanting to help him. She wanted to see the villain be redeemed, to become the good guy like in her favorite movies. She wanted to see the

Grinch get a big heart. Severus Snape to reveal his loyalty and love. Darth Vader to choose his family over the dark side.

And, she had to admit, her scientific curiosity was killing her.

"See, after you eat that," she said, "we're going to go for a swim and have sex."

Stryke barked out a laugh. "You seriously think eating this is going to *change my brain*."

"It's not a magic pill," she said as she shoved down her jeans. "But, yes, absolutely. My mom always used to talk about the brain's capacity to rewire itself. She even conducted a few breakthrough studies."

"You're talking about neuroplasticity. The ability of the brain to change, adapt, and heal."

"Exactly. Your brain can create new neurons and pathways with repetition and positive associations."

He appeared to consider what she'd said as he studied the plate of wafers. Then, with a shrug, he took the one he'd put down and popped it into his mouth.

"I guess we'll see." He eyed her. "Did you bring a swimsuit?"

She shrugged out of her bra. "No. Is that a problem?"

Gold flecks glittered in his eyes as he watched her step out of her panties. "Not at all." He glanced out at the pool. "But I don't think I'll be joining you."

She grinned. "We'll see about that." With that, she sauntered to the sliding glass door, feeling his hungry gaze following her.

She didn't have to look back to know that he watched as she stepped into the warm water, but when she did look back at him, she laughed.

He was eating another wafer.

Suzanne's wafers were fucking phenomenal. Savory, spicy, and sweet. He didn't enjoy eating, but if he had to, that was the type of food that intrigued him and awakened his taste buds.

He didn't feel any noticeable effect from eating them, though.

Maybe Suzanne's talent was a scam. Or the effects were psychosomatic. Because he felt the same as he had before he'd eaten the cookies.

Well, that wasn't entirely true. He was seriously turned on, but that had more to do with the naked female swimming in his pool than some cheese biscuits with pepper jelly.

Because, damn, Cyan was something else. Her long, lithe body cut through the water like a shark as she swam from end to end, barely even creating a ripple on the surface. He could watch that all day.

And it wasn't just because she was naked. He'd come to admire her in so many ways. She was smart, unafraid to speak her mind, and as curious as he was. She wanted to know how things worked and make them work better. From spells and weapons to, well, him.

The thought filled him with a pleasant, effervescent sensation that was almost…euphoric. How long had it been since anyone besides Eidolon wanted to make him better? To help him get past the shit that had weighed him down for almost half his life?

How long had it been since he'd allowed anyone to get close enough that they would *want* to do any of that?

Yeah, he bore some responsibility for how people reacted to him. Bore most of it. Like, ninety-nine percent of it. And he hadn't cared. Up until right this minute, he hadn't cared.

Suddenly, he did. He wanted to let Cyan into his life. But…maybe not all the way. He wasn't ready for that.

He may never be ready for that.

She dove beneath the water's surface, her slinky body outlined in the glow of the dim pool lights. He held his breath in solidarity and let it out in relief when she did a porpoise, flinging water everywhere as she shook her head and wiped her eyes.

Rivulets streamed down her face and neck, disappearing in a gentle current that swirled around the tops of her breasts.

He wanted to do that with his tongue.

His pants grew uncomfortably tight, so he whipped them off. His shirt went next, followed by his boxer briefs, and then he found himself at the edge of the pool, his hungry gaze glued to Cyan.

She swam over with a grin. "Hey."

"Hey."

He had no idea why he suddenly felt so awkward, like a newly transitioned male talking to his first female.

"Come on in," she said. "Water's nice."

"Of course, it is. I keep it at body temperature."

She rolled her eyes. "Come on, Mr. Literal. Get in."

He'd never been in the pool. Once a year or so, he'd dip his feet in to see if his feelings about swimming had changed.

Nope. They never did.

So, he didn't expect anything different when he stepped into the slightly cool water. And, sure enough, by the time he was in the pool to his waist, his skin was crawling, and he was wondering what the hell he was doing. Then Cyan swam over, her gaze locked on his. When she stood in front of him, her wet skin glistening under the light of the moon overhead, she was a goddess, and he couldn't move.

"Hi," she said, her lips wet and curved into an adorable, kissable smile.

"Hi," he said lamely.

So. Fucking. Lamely. He really was that post-transitioned dork all over again.

She moved closer. Slowly. Seductively. Her fingers teased the water playfully as she came within inches.

"Wanna get wet?" she purred, reaching out to trail one finger down his sternum to his navel. He reached for her, but she fell back into the water with a splash and a laugh. "Come get me," she called out.

She didn't look away as she started a lazy backstroke toward the deep end, her breasts breaching the water, her hips sinking just beneath the surface. So tantalizing.

With a growl, he dove in after her, some predatory instinct awakened, demanding he catch her. No, not awakened. His inner predator had always hunted, but it had focused on making demons pay for their evil. On bringing down powerful people who fucked with him. He'd used his power, wealth, and killer instinct to bring entire countries to their bony knees.

But now…now, all he wanted was to bring one female to her knees. Preferably in front of him, with her mouth warming his cock.

And then it wouldn't be long before he would be on his knees before her, using his mouth and tongue to make her scream his name.

Laughing, she swam harder, squirming out of his reach every time he nearly had her. She was a natural in the water, unlike him, who had only learned to swim to keep from drowning.

But where she was agile and fast, he was relentless. He stalked her around the pool, slowly wearing her down.

"You know I'm going to catch you."

"I'm going to *let* you catch me."

He stopped in chest-deep water, confused. "Then why are you dragging it out?"

She rolled her eyes. "It's called foreplay, Stryke."

Foreplay. Obviously, he knew what that was. He'd just never engaged in it. Not ever.

Waste. Of. Time.

"Come on," she said, crooking her finger at him from the shallow end of the pool. "I'm right here."

"You're just going to swim away. I know your game."

"Yes," she said. "The game is called foreplay."

"And how long must we play it?"

"Until I say so."

"And why do you get to make the rules?"

"Because I'm the one who is going to make you come."

His cock jerked in anticipation, so on board with that. But his brain...his fucking brain had to be contrary, putting on the brakes as it gave itself time to process all the new sensations and experiences.

"But I don't *need* you," he pointed out. "I have Masumi. And injections."

For a split second, her eyes flashed with hurt. Or anger. He wasn't sure. But he did know that he'd fucked up.

Cyan swung away from him and splashed up the steps.

"Wait!" He swam to her, catching her by the elbow as she reached the top step. "I'm sorry. That didn't come out right. I didn't mean to make it sound like—"

"Like you don't want me and are basically doing me a favor by having sex with me?"

"Ah, no. Definitely not. I'm saying that I don't *need* you. Not for sex. I still have a couple of hours until my next injection. But I *want* you."

The tension in her body melted away, and a slow smile curved her lips, a naughty grin that stole his breath. She sank down so she was sitting on the edge of the pool, legs spread wide, and feet braced on the top step.

"Show me. Show me what you want."

So much. There was so much he wanted to do that he'd never done before. But where to start?

"If you're having trouble deciding," she said, "a kiss would be a good place to begin."

A kiss.

One of those things that had always seemed unnecessary but he didn't mind doing with Cyan. In fact, as he stared at her full mouth, his watered. Inside his chest, his heart pounded in excitement, and maybe a little anxiousness. He wanted to learn, but he didn't like looking like a fool.

His hands shook as he braced them on the ledge on either side of her hips and leaned in.

She lifted her face to meet his, her violet eyes reflecting the twinkling stars in the clear night sky.

Slowly, nervously, he lowered his mouth to hers.

The sudden sensation of her wet, warm lips on his sent a jolt of lust into his groin. That probably wasn't unusual, but the deep, soothing heat that flowed through him in a wave of affection was. For him, anyway.

He'd never experienced anything like it. It was even better than the belly flutters.

With a breathy, sexy moan, she arched into him, her breasts pressed against his chest as she deepened the kiss. Her tongue met his, tangling and licking as she sucked gently and clamped her inner thighs against his hips.

His shaft, mere inches from her center, strained to get to her. Always before, he'd have taken her by now, sinking deep to get the shit over with.

But right now, all he wanted was to revel in these new, exciting sensations.

Like little waves lapping at his legs. Cyan's skin rubbing against his. Her teeth nipping at his bottom lip.

Somewhere nearby, wolves howled, their songs vibrating through the icy night.

This was perfect, something he hadn't known he wanted. Now…he *wanted*.

Backing down the steps, he kissed a trail on her skin as he went. He laved her neck all the way down to her collarbone. His kisses turned to nibbles when he reached her breasts, and she moaned when he sucked one berry-colored nipple into his mouth.

Her thighs clenched around his waist, but he broke her hold and licked his way lower, lapping water from her skin in long, slow sweeps. Kneeling on the bottom step, he admired her as she watched him, anticipation gleaming in her eyes. She smirked and spread her legs wider, giving him a cock-blowing view of her glistening, pink center.

His mouth watered.

Heart pounding with excitement, he probed her gently with his tongue.

"Yes," she whispered, throwing her head back. Her spine arched, thrusting her milky breasts into the night, the glow of the moon bathing her in a milky light.

She was perfect, a goddess he could worship all night long.

He licked her hungrily, pressing the flat of his tongue firmly against her smooth flesh, taking note of the textures, the flavors, the *responses*. Hearing her sharp breaths and deep moans made his blood heat, and his cock throb.

Damn, he liked this. So much time wasted because of his hang-ups. So. Much. Time.

But he wouldn't change anything. Cyan was the right person to introduce him to true pleasure. To help him get out of his head and into the moment.

He flicked the tip of his tongue across her clit, and she cried out, the sound joining the wolves' song. Something stirred deep inside, something feral and elemental.

His mother was a werewolf, and even though he'd been immunized to prevent his animal nature from taking control, his DNA remained unchanged. Part of him reached out to the beasts, recognizing their calls to family. To mates.

With a low, deep growl, he penetrated Cyan with his tongue before sweeping up her cleft. He couldn't wait any longer. His need to claim her now, in the dark night under the light of the waning moon, had become a primal directive—not because the lust demon in him *needed* it…but because the beast in him *wanted* it.

Wanted Cyan.

Lunging, he slid inside her. Tight, wet flesh clenched around his cock, rippling up and down his shaft in powerful waves. He barely pumped his hips; the sensations were so strong. And he wasn't ready yet—

He came with a roar that made the wolves stop howling. Pleasure so intense it bordered on pain ripped through him, spreading from his cock to his toes and to the top of his head. He could practically feel his brain synapses sparking from the overload.

It was incredible. Mind-blowing. And, as his orgasm waned and Cyan's hit another level, he realized he hadn't thought once about that day at the amusement park. His body hadn't locked up, his stomach hadn't roiled, and for once, the dampness on his skin came from something other than cold sweat.

Cyan bucked, taking him deep again as she moaned, triggering another firestorm of pleasure. It went on and on, orgasm after orgasm wrecking him.

As a lust demon, this was the way sex should have always been. A cascade of erotic responses instead of one torturous mix of mild pleasure, physical discomfort, and mental anguish.

"Cyan," he breathed as he dragged her into the water so they could just float and feel the bliss.

"Mmm," she hummed. Then she moaned, arching into him as another orgasm took her.

"You're so beautiful." He drew back just enough that he could watch her as she convulsed in his arms, water licking her breasts, her lower body wrapped around his waist.

Her eyes were closed, her head thrown back, and he'd never seen anything so erotic in his entire life. He wanted to see her like this every day, several times a day. And night.

Resting between bouts of pleasure, they floated like that for fifteen or twenty minutes. Stryke lost all sense of time, something he'd always been acutely aware of. But right now, he just didn't care.

When the pleasure finally stopped, he lifted Cyan into his arms and carried her to the shower to rinse. Her sated smile and sultry voice had him wanting to go again before they'd even dried off, but she was tired, and so was he.

He gently tucked her into bed and went to fetch her a cup of chamomile tea, but by the time he returned, she was snoring softly, her body curled around her pillow.

Very carefully, he climbed into bed next to her and was out in seconds.

But not before he kissed her on the cheek and thanked her for coming into his life.

Chapter 25

Cyan woke to the aroma of coffee.

Yawning, she looked at her wrist comms. Five-fifteen in the morning. She blinked. Looked again.

Five-fifteen in the morning? On a freaking Sunday?

Swinging her feet off the mattress, she groaned at the ache in her muscles and the tenderness between her thighs. She and Stryke had gone several more rounds during the night, the sex both leisurely and urgent as he discovered everything he'd been missing out on his entire life.

"Teach me," he'd growled into her ear, his deep voice rumbling all the way to her core. "Keep my brain busy."

She'd taught him, all right. He was a quick, eager student too. He was a practice-makes-perfect kind of guy, and once he mastered something, he used that knowledge to devastatingly erotic effect.

Only once had things taken a dark turn. They'd both gotten up for a glass of water, and after they'd quenched their thirst, they'd ended up with her against the kitchen wall and him between her legs. Pumping his hips in slow, grinding circles, he'd brought her to the brink—

Then stilled. Shadows crept into his eyes as the color drained from his face.

She'd quickly reached up and brought his mouth down to hers, then wrenched him away from the wall and took him to the floor.

"Fuck me, Stryke," she'd growled as she rolled her hips and lifted until only the tip of him was inside her. Then she slammed back down.

He'd gripped her waist and lifted her up and down, his gaze fully engaged with hers again, the moment of distraction forgotten.

Afterward, he'd said the position had brought back his time with Popcorn Girl, and his body had sort of shut down. He'd thanked her for yanking him out of it and making their time on the floor something new for his brain to process.

So, yeah, they'd had a busy night. But he was up at too-dark o'clock, making coffee.

Yawning, she reached for the black satin robe he'd given her. Apparently, he kept one in every closet for Masumi. She tried to work out how she felt about the succubus as she slipped into the garment, but truthfully, she wasn't sure. She hardly had the right to be jealous, not when Masumi had kept him alive for years. She'd supported him, cared for him, and given him doses of truth he needed to hear. Cyan should be grateful, and she was. But that didn't mean she wanted him to be with Masumi going forward.

She put the Masumi issue aside and padded down the hall toward the kitchen, where she found a cup and a note next to the coffee maker.

There's coconut creamer in the fridge.

Wow. He really had done his research on her.

Impressed by his thoroughness, she prepared her brew to a rhythmic pounding coming from the open stairway just off the kitchen. When she was finished, she took the steps down and halted at the bottom so suddenly she nearly spilled her drink.

Stryke had an amazing laboratory down here. And, off in a well-lit cove, a second but smaller state-of-the-art gym, where he was destroying a punching bag.

"You know it's Sunday, right?"

He shot her a glance before pummeling the bag with a jab-cross-jab combo. "I'm aware."

"So, you don't believe in sleeping in?"

"I have to go to work."

She sipped her coffee. "Why? Is there an emergency?"

Jab-jab-uppercut. "I work every day."

Ah. "Why am I not surprised?"

Jab-hook-slip. "Because it's in keeping with my workaholic personality."

"It's also in keeping with your need to keep your mind busy and off other things."

He stopped mid-strike. Stepped back from the dummy and dropped his hands.

She peered at him over the rim of her mug. "You know I'm right."

For a moment, his jaw and fists clenched as he worked out the truth of what she'd said. So much of his life was about avoidance, but he actually seemed honest with himself about it.

"You're right," he acknowledged. "But I *am* obsessive about work. I have to be doing *something.* I've never been good at doing nothing."

"Then why don't you take today off? We'll do something you've never done." Silence. Just more clenching. "You don't like your routine disrupted, do you?"

He smiled, and her heart hitched a little. Gods, he was gorgeous when he did that. "You know me too well."

"I recognize the issue. My mom was like that," she said. "She liked structure and routine. It's where I get it too. Just…not to your extent."

"So, what do you propose we do?"

She thought about that for a minute as she looked idly around his lab. The equipment was interesting, sure, but she'd worked with most of it and was familiar with the rest. No, what caught her interest were the personal touches.

Nowhere else in the house had them, aside from maybe the liquor cabinet and the dart board in the living room. But even those didn't reveal much about him.

But down here, in his obviously beloved lab, he'd revealed a lot.

Like the chess board. Maybe she should challenge him to a game. She was pretty good.

"How are you at chess?" she asked.

"Very few people can beat me." He worked at removing his boxing gloves.
"And by few, I mean only one."

She laughed and then realized he was serious. "Okay, but I don't recall seeing you on the list of world chess champions."

"I don't want the attention." He carefully placed his gloves on a rack near a set of free weights. "But I've played with every living champion, and I've beaten them."

She gaped. "Every one?"

He shrugged. "Money gets private games."

Wow. "Who is the one person who can beat you?"

"Ares," he said. "He can take a game off me now and then. But he's also thousands of years old and a master tactician."

So…chess was not an option. She kept looking.

One wall featured all his degrees and awards, interspersed with framed magazine covers. But the other three walls, lined with shelves, held a wide array of items, from a crystal skull...probably one of *the* crystal skulls...to models of NASA space shuttles and rockets. What appeared to be ancient artifacts from all over the world and Sheoul took up a lot of real estate as well.

Maybe they should visit a museum. He'd probably been to them all, though. Her gaze moved back to the space shuttle.

"I saw pictures of you at NASA headquarters a long time ago," she said, remembering the photos of him surrounded by security that had been plastered all over the cover of a sleazy tabloid. The hit piece had questioned why a government entity with highly secret tech and sensitive information would allow a demon anywhere near one of its facilities, let alone work with one. "Is that where you got the models and patches?"

He strolled over to the shelf and ran his finger fondly over one of the rockets. "The NASA director sent them to make up for not hiring me. Or paying me for my designs and research. They couldn't be seen collaborating with a demon, you know."

"You sound a little bitter."

One shoulder twitched in a dismissive shrug, but he couldn't hide the wistfulness in his expression. "Growing up, it was my dream to work there. But that was a long time ago, and I have more money than they do, so that takes a lot of the sting out of it." He smiled before dropping his hand to his side, his expression turning sad. She knew he was thinking about Chaos. "Besides, my life went in a different direction."

She hated that he'd had so little joy in his life. A couple of months ago, she'd have thought his existence was basically nothing *but* joy. He had money, fame, power. Females wanted him, and males wanted to be him. He had everything.

Everything except happiness.

Meanwhile, she'd led a charmed life, but her recent losses had made her focus on her grief instead of the joy of the years before.

She wanted that joy back, and she wanted it for Stryke too. But how?

She contemplated the model rockets. Obviously, she couldn't get him on a real one, but she did have an old friend at Kennedy Space Center who owed her a favor. A big one.

And Cyan was ready to call it in.

"I can't believe you've never been on a private NASA tour," Cyan said as they arrived at her apartment.

"I can't believe you have a high-level contact who owed you a favor," he said. "What did you do to earn that big of a payback?"

"I helped her bury a body." She eyeballed the biometric scanner.

"Seriously?"

"Yep." Her door whooshed open. "I told you we went to college together," she said, and he nodded. "Well, one night we were working late on some research, and Jamie went home before I did. I only lived a few blocks away, so I always walked, and I was almost there when I heard someone sobbing behind an old house. I found her in a shed." She ushered him through the doorway. "She was naked and bloody and scared to death, and the guy who assaulted her had a hatchet buried in his rib cage and was taking his last breath."

"I'm glad he's dead," he growled as the door clicked shut.

Instantly, the scent of winter holiday spices dulled his anger and filled him with comforting warmth, one of the few scents that didn't annoy him and he associated with pleasant childhood memories. His family, close *and* extended, loved the holidays, and they went big. Lots of gatherings at the Four Horsemen's places, and lots of festivities and feasts at his parents' house. Unlike his brothers, Stryke had never cared much about the food, music, or games, but he'd enjoyed the feeling of family. The closeness. The laughter.

He…missed that. For the first time in over a decade, he actually missed it.

"I don't know if you heard," she said as she dropped her purse onto the entryway bench, "but I told Jamie that NASA should be consulting with StryTech a lot more than they are."

"Once they hear about my newest project, they will be." Hell, NASA and every other space agency, private or government funded, would soon be clamoring to be involved.

"And what's that?" she asked as she started toward the kitchen.

"I'm funding an operation to colonize the moon."

She stopped dead in her tracks and swung around. "Are you serious?"

"You know Armageddon is coming, right? It's not a vague concept anymore. There's an actual timeline."

"A timeline that's kept from the public."

"For good reason. People would panic if they knew there's only nine centuries left."

"Actually," she said as she resumed her mission to the kitchen, "I would argue that after an initial panic, things would die down. Humans don't seem to care about generations to come. They'll just put off the problem until it has to be dealt with. And by then, it'll be too late. Don't need a crystal ball to see that one."

"Hmm." He hadn't considered that. Humans baffled him sometimes. "You might be right."

"So," she said, "you mentioned Armageddon. Are you saying you want to put a population in space in case it doesn't break our way, and the planet is taken over by evil?"

"Yep."

"That's pretty cool. Why not Mars?"

He looked around her apartment as he spoke, committing everything to memory and taking note of anything that might help him understand her more. And to his dismay, he understood that she liked bright colors and fluffy pillows.

"Mars is far less inhabitable than Earth's moon," he said, wondering what all the boxes were about. Was she moving in or out? "And the distance and logistics involved make it unfeasible, given the short amount of time we have to get it done."

"Got a timeline?" She pulled a couple of Belgian beers from the fridge. "Like, during my lifespan?"

"Your lifespan is similar to mine, right? Five hundred years or so?"

She fetched an opener from the drawer. "Give or take. Can you reserve me a spot on the first rocket off this shithole?"

He laughed. "I think that can be arranged. We can make the trip together." He kind of stumbled over that, seeing how he'd just implied that they were a couple. A thing. And that they would still be in the estimated two hundred years he needed to establish a colony.

Fortunately, she didn't seem to notice, or if she did, she ignored it, sparing them both an uncomfortable moment.

"Thank you for bringing me home," she said as she popped the tops off the bottles. "You didn't have to do that. I'm only a block from the Harrowgate."

He took one of the offered drinks. "I wanted to see your place."

She gave him a you're-full-of-shit look. "You wanted to see how I live."

There was no point in denying it. "You can tell a lot about someone by what they keep in their personal space and how they treat it."

"And what does my personal space say about me?"

He used his ale to gesture at the pile of boxes. "Are you in the middle of moving?"

"Shanea was."

Of course. Shanea had been her roommate. Now, he had no idea what to say, and he wasn't usually left speechless.

Finally, he managed a soft, "I'm sorry."

He expected a snarky reply or, at the very least, a hateful glare. Instead, she just stared at all the moving materials and looked sad. "I miss her."

Unsure how to respond, he checked out the books on her shelves—mostly scientific and engineering texts, as well as a lot of spell books and tomes about magic. Completely expected. There were pictures of people he assumed were her parents, as well as a couple of college photos and lots of pictures of her with Shanea and her fiancé, Draven.

And, on the floor, were some torn-up pictures of Stryke. Magazine articles. She'd also done a confetti job on an aerial photo of the StryTech facility.

She came over and looked down at the mess. "I was really pissed at you."

"I see that."

"I told you; I admired you, Stryke." She looked over at him, her cheeks flushing an adorable pink. "I mean, okay, maybe I was a little obsessed with you for a while. You were my rock star crush, you know?"

He hated that he'd let her down the way he had everyone else. And he hadn't even known her when it happened. It was quite the feat. Stryke really was good at everything, wasn't he?

"And then I disappointed you." Fuck. Stryke stood there, feeling dazed. He'd spent most of his life knowing he was different. Above average in a lot of ways. Enviable for his looks, intelligence, power, and wealth.

And yet, an utter failure in so many other aspects of his life.

He was socially inept in situations where he wasn't in charge. He didn't care what people thought of him. He was okay with being an asshole. So, yeah, he failed basic personhood.

Why would anyone consider him their rock star crush?

He wasn't sure how what to think or say, and uncertainty made his chest tighten, and his head throb.

"I'm, ah…" He jacked his thumb toward the front door. "I'm gonna go. It's getting late."

"You don't have to—"

"No, no…I do." He set his bottle on the kitchen island. "My brain feels like it's about to malfunction."

"Have you tried turning it off and back on?"

Her attempt at tech humor made him laugh, releasing some of the turmoil. He liked how she could do that to him so easily.

"I had a good time today," he said, meaning it to the depths of his soul. "It's been a long time since I did anything fun."

"That's because you're so busy taking care of the world that you don't take care of yourself."

"I take care of myself," he protested.

"Really?" She rocked her head toward the door. "So, just right now, were you planning to leave, take an injection, and then work in your lab for a few hours instead of stripping me naked and actually enjoying yourself?"

Guilty as charged. He'd injected himself once during the time they'd been at NASA, and he'd need either sex or an injection within the next hour.

For the first time ever, he envied Blade. Blade would know what to say right now. He'd know what to do. But this was all new territory for Stryke. His idiot brother might not know the difference between a neutron and a kangaroo, but he knew his way around the females.

So, yeah. *Look who's the idiot now.*

"Look," he started before pausing, hesitant to reveal how little he knew about relationships. "I'm comfortable in my lab. I'm comfortable being alone. I'm *not* comfortable in unfamiliar situations. Like now." He shoved a frustrated hand through his hair. "I don't know what's going on between us. I've never done this before. I don't even know what *this* is."

"That makes two of us," she said, making him feel a little better. "What do you want it to be?"

He had no freaking clue, and it left him unsettled. He hadn't had time to process the last few days, let alone his feelings about them.

"What do *you* want it to be?" he asked, hoping she was better at this than he was. Which made him realize he knew nothing about her past relationships. Now, he wanted to. What kind of males was she attracted to? How many had she been with? Had she ever been in love?

Had she slept with Parker?

The idea made his jaw clench and his blood steam. Maybe he didn't want to know about her past after all.

Bracing one hand on the counter, she appeared to consider his question. "I don't know. My feelings about you have changed, and I'm not sure how I feel about that."

They were so alike in that way.

"Maybe," she continued, "we should just play it by ear. You know, see how things go for the next couple of weeks. I've got a lot of work to do in the lab, and I'm sure you have a mess to deal with between the Gehennaportal, the WCSG's investigation, and your company. Let's wing it."

"Wing it?" Fucking *wing it?* He was wrong about her. They weren't alike at all. "I don't *wing* anything."

"You did today," she pointed out. "You played hooky from work and went on a last-minute boondoggle. It was all very spontaneous."

Sure, he'd give her that. But he was willing to adapt to changes under certain conditions. Like the fact that it was Sunday, and he didn't *have* to go into work.

And he'd wanted to spend time with Cyan.

"But I get it," she said. "You need some structure."

"And rules."

Her skeptical expression amused him. "I didn't think you followed rules."

He grinned. "I don't. But I need to know them, at least."

"I can respect that." She folded her arms across her chest and settled in for what looked like a negotiation. Those, he was comfortable with. "Okay, how about we agree to meet at least once a day?"

Sounded reasonable. "Agreed. Are we exclusive?"

"That would make us an official couple. Are you ready for that? Because I don't think I am."

He didn't see himself being with any other female, but the idea of being in an official relationship was too much. "Agreed."

She nodded. "Good, because I'm supposed to meet Parker for dinner sometime this week."

Jealousy burned a hole in Stryke's chest, and when he spoke his voice sounded warped. "Are you dating him?"

"Nah." She waved her hand in dismissal. "We're just meeting to discuss a few aspects of our project over a pizza. I owe him for bringing me food the night I got back from the *Sea Storm*."

The male had been *here*? Inside her apartment? Sudden, possessive anger flared hot, and Stryke had to tamp it down before he did something stupid. Like fire the guy. Or have Behvyn blow some bad luck his way. That was always amusing.

"So, are we good to go?" she asked.

Stryke could live with the agreement. But her dinner with Parker had better be her last. "We are."

"Good." A slow, naughty smile made his groin tighten as she stripped off her shirt. "Now, let's make it official."

Chapter 26

Stryke paced anxiously in his office, the way he did before every meeting with Cyan.

After over two weeks, he'd have thought his physical and emotional reactions to her would have eased, but nope. If anything, what he felt for her was becoming more intense. He couldn't wait to see her every day, and when it was time for one of them to leave, he felt like his world was being watered down.

Sex with her was amazing, the most incredible experience. But so was just being with her. They enjoyed the same movies and books—science fiction, mostly. She also liked romcoms, which she said Shanea had introduced her to. Neither of them was fond of outdoorsy things like camping or hiking, and they would both happily spend their lives locked inside a library or research facility.

He couldn't wait to tell her he'd secured a private tour of the newly built, hyper-modern astrology lab in Germany. It would be their first real *date* out in the world since the NASA tour, and he wouldn't have to deal with the hassle of bodyguards. He hated being in public. If he could get a place to shut down while he was there, he did. And he was willing to pay anything. Just two days ago, he'd arranged to shop at Harrods, completely alone except for his personal security team, for an hour while he purchased Christmas gifts.

Usually, he sent Kalis or Leilani to do his shopping—and he *had* sent them for most of it, but he'd wanted to get Cyan something himself. She claimed to dislike the human holiday season, but the pictures of her and Shanea dressed as Christmas elves said otherwise.

So, for the first time ever, he'd gone shopping and decorated his house. It was completely over the top and ridiculous, but he had to admit that his log cabin worked well as a Christmas canvas. He'd even found himself smiling a couple of times as he admired the lighted garland and perfectly symmetrical tree he'd decorated with handmade glass ornaments from Italy.

He couldn't wait for Cyan to see it after their tour of the astro-lab.

He glanced at his wrist comms. Where was she? She was never late.

"Tech Comms," he said, and the building's AI assistant clicked on. "Where in the complex is Cyan?"

"Cyan is currently in the Newton Library."

A virtual screen popped into the air and zoomed in on Cyan. She was walking toward the exit in a hurry. Parker, that asshole, joined her, said something, and she laughed. They exited the building, chatting. More laughing.

"Sir," Kalis interrupted, "you have an urgent missive from Taran Ross."

Stryke swiped away the camera feed. Fucking Parker. Also, he could do without the sharp pain stabbing his brain. He'd had a mild headache all morning, but it suddenly decided to go from an annoyance to painful enough to make him wince.

"Thanks, Kalis. I got it." He tapped his desk comms, and Taran flickered into view in front of him, his jaw tight and his mouth a grim slash. "Taran. What is it?"

He winced through another stab and another pain in his gut. Maybe he'd eaten something that didn't agree with him. He'd eaten a lot of new things since he and Cyan started seeing each other on a regular basis. And he always looked forward to eating with her, even if he still hated the hassle of eating when he was alone.

"Nothing, I hope." Taran turned, gesturing to the wall of new or restored monitoring screens. Repairs had gone well so far, and last time Taran talked to him, he'd said the forward operating center would be secure in a couple of days. "Everything's been quiet since the Gehennaportal was destroyed. But a few hours ago, we got a strange temperature reading. I thought it might be an anomaly, but it happened again. And again. There's a pattern."

"A...*pattern?*"

"Yeah. And here's the thing. I went back through all our old readings, and I found the same pattern. We just missed it because there was so much else going on. But it's back. This is going to sound crazy, but I get the feeling it's kind of a...heartbeat."

Stryke gripped the back of his chair as a wave of nausea washed over him. "A heartbeat for what?"

"The Gehennaportal," Taran said. "I don't think it was destroyed after all."

"That's impossible. Cyan verified it."

Taran averted his gaze, clearly hesitant to speak. But he was a professional, and he didn't beat around the bush, which was why Stryke had hired him. "I think Cyan lied."

"No way," Stryke said, his voice sounding mushy, like his tongue was too big for his mouth. "She wouldn't have lied." He reached for a tissue and wiped the sweat off his brow. Maybe he had food poisoning. "If the gate is functional, it's not because of anything she did. I'll see her in a few minutes. I'll ask her—"

He broke off as pain spiraled through his body. Squeezing, twisting pressure racked his insides as if all his organs were cramping.

"Stryke?" Taran's voice sounded distant. Muffled. "Stryke! What's wrong?"

His lungs...wouldn't work. Stumbling for the emergency button under his desk, he gasped for air, his vision fading and legs collapsing beneath him.

"*Stryke!*"

He wasn't going to make it to the button. He wasn't...going...to...

Cyan was in love with Stryke.

After two and a half weeks of meeting him daily, mostly in his office and sometimes at his log home, she couldn't deny it anymore.

The first couple of days had been a little strained, and clearly, he was jealous of Parker, tensing every time she mentioned her coworker as part of talking about their project. Stryke never asked about Parker, though, respecting the boundaries they'd put in place.

She wouldn't have minded if he'd asked since nothing was going on between them. She hadn't even seen Parker outside of the office since their pizza night. He'd asked her out a couple of times, but she'd politely declined.

Parker was the kind of guy she'd have been interested in if not for Stryke. He was smart, funny, and sweet. Shanea would have pushed Cyan at him.

But no, the only male on her mind was Stryke, who did something special every time they met. Sometimes, he gave her a gift like gold-plated chocolates from Paris or a signed copy of one of her favorite books about the role of technology in the future. Other times, he made dinner—a Suzanne recipe that guaranteed anyone could make it delicious—or had food brought in. Once they met in his basement lab and conducted an experiment to test the effects of his *Sea Storm* fog sample on cell specimens from demons of varying moral alignment.

Cells from evil beings thrived in the fog. Specimens from less evil beings fared far worse. His tiny sample of an angel feather shriveled.

He'd definitely seduced her with science.

But what she loved most was that, for the last week, all their meetings had been about the Moon project. And sex. But after the sex, he'd asked her opinion on everything from where to build the facility to where he should go to headhunt the best employees.

But…as much as she loved working with him on such a mon-umental project, she was also concerned. His energy seemed to be growing frantic, and she suspected he wasn't sleeping much. He appeared more and more distracted.

Not that she wasn't distracted too. Her team had hit a snag on the Reaper project, and it was taking a ridiculous amount of time to solve the issue. She'd become increasingly exhausted, so much so that she'd gone home early a couple of times so she could nap. Even her appetite became a victim of her stress and exhaustion. Yesterday, Stryke noticed and commented on it after she'd shoved her plate of Chinese food aside during dinner.

She was starving at the moment, though, so maybe she could talk him into having pizza delivered when she got to his office. There was a new, werewolf-family-run Italian joint in New York she wanted to try, and they even delivered via Harrowgate. She'd seen one of the delivery people pop out of the company gate just outside the courtyard.

She smiled and nodded to everyone as she traversed the long, sterile hallways to Stryke's offices. Folks at StryTech had been guarded around her at first, but they'd largely come around. She'd even been invited to a get-together at the Sydney home of one of the scientists from the NeuroLink division.

"Coming through!" someone yelled from behind her.

Startled, she leaped up against the wall as paramedics ran past, their black uniforms and duffle bags identifying them as Underworld General personnel. But where were they going? Surely, not—

They were headed toward Stryke's offices.

Sudden fear made her gut plummet. Panicked, she ran to catch up, her heels clacking, her pulse pounding. Ahead, Kalis waited at the elevator, her face pale and lips pressed into a thin, grim line.

"Kalis!" Cyan stopped in front of Stryke's assistant as the medics stepped into the lift. "What's going on?"

"I'm glad you're here," Kalis said, taking Cyan's elbow and guiding her to the elevator. "Something's wrong with Stryke. He was talking to Taran and collapsed. If Taran hadn't alerted me…" She trailed off, her voice quivering as the door slid closed.

One of the medics, a Seminus demon, exchanged worried glances with his ginger-haired partner.

"Are you related to Stryke?" Cyan asked.

"Distantly." The guy gestured to a spiral symbol woven into his *dermoire* near his elbow. "But his dad is my boss, and his uncle is the Big Boss."

"We don't want to fuck up this call, that's for sure," the other one growled as the doors slid open.

Stryke. She gasped in horror at the sight of him lying near his desk, his chest heaving, body twisted in agony. She didn't remember running across the endless expanse of flooring, didn't register the pain of hitting the floor next to him with a crack of kneecaps. He moaned, but she didn't think he was aware of her presence.

The ginger Seminus medic crouched beside her and gripped Stryke by the shoulder. The black lines of his *dermoire* lit up as his healing energy surged through his arm. A moment later, he looked up at his partner. "We need to get him to UG. Now."

"Come on," she said, shoving to her feet. "I can operate his private Harrowgate."

The two Sems hauled Stryke into the gate, and the moment the door closed, she pressed the lit symbol representing the famous demon-run hospital. Almost instantly, they emerged in Underworld General's Emergency Department.

Cyan had only been here once, decades ago as a child, when she broke her wrist during an ice skating lesson. She remembered the chaos, the mix of demons and humanoids, and the strange writing on the walls.

What she hadn't remembered were the gutters that ran with blood or the strange medical devices hanging on the walls and from the ceilings. The place was truly creepy.

The medics barked out a bunch of medical terms Cyan knew but wasn't ready to think about as a tusk-faced female in scrubs directed them to an empty room.

Terrified and overwhelmed, Cyan held Stryke's hand as the medics laid him on the bed. Instantly, there was a swarm of people and activity and medical jargon, but she tuned it all out. She couldn't take her eyes off Stryke's face, so handsome, but so shadowed and sunken.

"Stryke," she whispered. "Please. Talk to me."

He didn't open his eyes. Didn't even moan.

Desperate, she swung around to the medical staff. To anyone who would listen. "What's wrong? Help him!"

Eidolon broke through the crowd, and a sense of relief helped her breathe. If anyone could help Stryke, it was him.

"Someone get Shade," he barked. "And I want Talon too. Hurry!" He turned to one of the nurses. "Start a line and prep a crash cart."

A crash cart? The blood drained from Cyan's face. This sounded bad. Really bad.

"Doctor?"

He wheeled around to her. "Cyan, right?" When she nodded, he continued. "Are you with him?"

"With him?" she asked, confused. She was standing right there. Of course she was with him.

"I mean, are you fucking him?"

Her mouth fell open at the blunt question. "I don't see how—"

"Yes or no," he said. "I need to know when he last had sex and when he last used an injection."

Oh, of course. The doctor wasn't being a perv. He was asking medically relevant questions.

Feeling like a fool, she said, "I don't know when he had his last injection. I know that we were, ah, intimate about twenty-three hours ago."

"Thank you." He gestured to the door. "I need you to leave."

"But—" She broke off as Shade burst through the doorway, his expression a tortured mask of devastation and fear that made her heart break. Maybe it would be best to wait outside. This was family stuff, and she wasn't exactly that.

But right now, in this moment, she wanted to be.

Terrified and feeling lost in a way she hadn't felt since Shanea died, she slipped out as Talon, another of Stryke's cousins, entered, looking every bit as worried as his uncles.

Chapter 27

The world was blurry and tasted like vinegar.

Stryke blinked up at the ceiling overhead. Why were there chains? And what was that infernal beeping?

Confusion left him dazed. And why couldn't he see any colors? Just shades of black and gray.

"Stryke?"

He blinked, trying to recognize the voice. It sounded like his dad—maybe—but the buzz in his ears made everything distorted.

"Son." His dad's face filled his vision, and to Stryke's left, Eidolon's got too close for comfort. At least they were in color. "You're awake. Thank the gods."

Now the chains on the ceiling made sense. He was at Underworld General Hospital. But how had he gotten here?

"What—?" He coughed, wincing at the tightness in his chest. "What happened?"

His uncle and father exchanged glances before looking down at him again. Eidolon gripped his wrist, and Stryke felt the warm vibration of the doctor's healing power flowing into his body.

"Remember I told you what would happen if you kept taking the suppressants?"

Oh, yeah. That. Shit. He would never hear the end of this.

"What the hell, Stryke?" Shade growled. "What were you thinking?"

He ignored his dad and focused on Eidolon. "Give it to me

straight."

"I've *been* giving it to you straight, and you haven't listened. Maybe now you will." The doctor stepped back and folded his arms across his broad chest, covering the caduceus symbol on his black scrub top. "Your organs are shutting down," he said bluntly. "You experienced a cardiac event that would have been fatal if you'd gotten here five minutes later."

"Oh, my God." The new voice—his mother's—left a pit in Stryke's stomach. "A cardiac event? He could have died?" Runa rushed over, and his dad made room for her to get to the head of the bed. "How is he now? Can this be reversed?"

"I'm cautiously optimistic that it can. His organs are regenerating, and function is returning. He might have some temporary memory loss, but for now, he's stable."

"See?" Stryke said, taking his mom's hand. "It's not that bad. I'm fine."

That earned him scathing glares from his dad and uncle, but at least they kept their mouths shut. They didn't want to upset Runa more than she was.

His mom's bloodshot, dark-crescented eyes tore at him. He'd never liked seeing her upset. As a child, he'd always been the one to run outside to pick a flower to cheer her up when she was sad. He'd been free with his hugs when she was mad. And he'd smiled when she was happy.

He hadn't given her a reason to be happy in a long time, had he? She was wearing his necklace, though. Hopefully, that made her happy.

"I'm sorry I scared you," he said, relieved when she smiled, the tension fading from her expression.

"It wasn't just me you scared," she remarked. "You have a lot of concerned friends out in the waiting room."

Friends? Not likely. "I don't have any friends," he muttered. "Why are you lying?"

She laughed, the last traces of tension disappearing. "I'm not. Blade and Rade are here too." He nearly groaned. The last thing he needed right now was Blade and his attitude. "Blade said you two worked together on an oil platform."

They'd cooperated. Stryke wouldn't say they'd worked together. But he couldn't dash the thread of hope in his mother's voice, so he nodded politely.

"He and his team took out a lot of demons." He glanced behind her at the door. "Is Cyan here?" He hoped he didn't sound too eager. Or worried that she wasn't out there in the waiting area.

"She came in with you," his dad said. "You want me to send her in?"

Badly. For some reason, Stryke needed to know that she was okay. Which was ridiculous since he was the one in the hospital bed. Maybe she could help explain how he'd gotten here.

"Please. Thank you, Dad."

Stryke struggled to sit up in bed until his mom raised the head with a push of a button. Feeling a little foolish, he looked down at his pink and yellow bunny-spotted hospital gown and cursed silently. He'd bet anything Talon had been responsible for that. He and his physician cousin had pranked each other a lot as kids, and up until now, Stryke had been up by one.

Eidolon adjusted his stethoscope around his neck and moved toward the door. "We can talk about your condition and treatment later."

His uncle and father slipped out of the room. The moment the door closed, his mom reached over and raked her fingers through his hair.

"Mom!" He tried to stop her, but she slapped his hand away.

"Your brother also said he thinks there's something going on between you and Cyan. Sit still. I'm trying to make you presentable." She frowned. "You always had that one curl that refused to behave…"

Presentable?

"Mom." He caught her hand and gently pushed it away. "Enough. Cyan's seen me in worse shape." He looked down at the bunny gown. "Mostly. Also," he added, "Blade needs to learn to keep his mouth shut."

"He didn't mean anything by it." Her voice had a distinct *mom tone* to it. "He likes Cyan. I do too. Is it serious?"

Yes. "I really don't—"

The door swung open, sparing him further awkwardness. He didn't want to talk about this with his mom. Didn't want to talk about it with anyone except Cyan. It felt serious to him, but how did she feel? What if she wasn't where he was emotionally? Did he even want to know?

Son of a bitch. He hated the uncertainty. Hated the lack of control over his feelings. Relationships were nerve-wracking.

Cyan stepped inside, and his heart beat a little harder against his tender rib cage. She was all elegance, from her black heels and shimmery leggings to the flowing white blouse with a midnight rose print.

And she was still wearing her lab coat. Man, she was ridiculously beddable, and he was suddenly glad for the thick blanket across his lap.

Runa engulfed Cyan in a hug before she made it halfway to the bed. "Thank you for bringing him in," she said to Cyan as she drew back. "You saved his life."

"I can't take any of the credit," Cyan said. "I didn't do anything except help the medics navigate the office Harrowgate. They did all the work."

"Well, thank you anyway." Runa looked back over her shoulder at him as she reached for the doorknob. "I'm going to have some food sent up. I'll see you in a little while."

"Thank you, Mom," he said, hoping he sounded as sincere as he felt. "For everything."

"Of course. You're my son," she said simply. She gave them both a farewell nod and stepped out into the hall.

The door whispered shut as Cyan came over, concentrated concern putting lines around her eyes. "I was so worried," she said, taking a seat next to the bed.

"I'm fine," he assured her. "They wouldn't put a bunny gown on someone who was in serious condition."

That made her smile, but it didn't take the concern from her gaze. "What happened?"

"You tell me," he said, flopping his head back onto the pillow to stare at the ceiling. What *did* they use those chains for? "I don't remember much. I know I was in my office. I was supposed to be meeting you." He looked over at her. "Are you the one who found me?"

She shook her head. "I got there with the paramedics. Apparently, you were talking to Taran. He's the one who alerted Kalis."

He searched his brain for that memory, but the file seemed to be missing. "I don't remember meeting with him, but Eidolon said I might have some memory lapses." Hopefully, that file would be restored soon. Changing the subject so he wouldn't obsess over it, he gestured to the door. "Mom said there are people out there. I'm guessing from work?"

But really, why *had* he been talking with Taran?

"Parker and Dakarai came as soon as they heard. I've been updating Kalis."

Parker. Great. Just great. The guy was probably disappointed that Stryke was still alive. On the upside, his mind was off Taran. Jealousy and a hot bolt of possessiveness took over instead.

"Have you been seeing him?" he asked, hoping he sounded calmer than he felt.

"Who?" She reached up to adjust one of her three silver hoop piercings in her right ear. "Parker?"

Stay cool. Blade used to tell him that, back when Stryke was learning to flirt with females. *Chicks can sniff out desperation.*

Stryke shrugged, like it was no big deal if she was dating Parker. Except it was. He would *destroy* the guy. Right after he got out of this bunny gown.

"You had dinner with him, but you never said how it went."

She crossed her legs and sat back in her chair a little defensively. "That's because we agreed not to ask about other people."

"No," he said, "we agreed to non-exclusivity."

She folded her arms across her breasts and arched a pale eyebrow at him, daring him to argue. "Not asking questions about other lovers is implied."

Made sense, he supposed. He didn't argue, deferring to her knowledge of relationships.

"I haven't asked you about Masumi," she pointed out, and he thought, for just a heartbeat, there'd been the slightest hint of jealousy in her voice.

"You could have. I haven't been with her since before we went to *Sea Storm.*"

She blinked. "Really?" He liked that she sounded pleased. "So, it's just been me and your injections?" When he inclined his head, she scowled. "Why didn't you tell me? If I'd known that, I could have been there more. Those shots can't be that healthy for you."

No shit.

Suddenly, she leaned forward, her eyes narrowed. "What are you not telling me?"

"What are you talking about?"

"You got that shut-down expression when I mentioned the suppressant not being good for you."

How was it possible that he both hated and loved how easily she read him?

"Spill." She crossed her arms again and waited.

Crap. He might as well tell her. She was bound to find out anyway.

"The suppressant is why I'm here." He inhaled, the twinge of tenderness in his chest punctuating his words. "Apparently, it's killing me."

"Excuse me?" She stared at him as if trying to figure out if she'd heard him right. "Killing you? Did you know it was dangerous?"

"Yeah." He shifted to face her, pushing through the soreness that seemed to permeate every cell of his body. "Eidolon warned me about it a few weeks ago."

"A few *weeks ago*? And you kept using it? What the hell, Stryke? You have Masumi! Why would you not be with her if you knew the suppressant was killing you?"

He caught a whiff of her anger, a hint of smoke mixing with her clean, metallic scent, and his entire body flooded with warmth and arousal. He loved being near her. Loved what being near her did to him. Even when she was angry at him.

"So, you want me to be with Masumi?"

She shoved angrily to her feet. "No. I don't. I admit it. But I also recognize your biological imperatives, and we agreed to non-exclusivity, so I have no right to be jealous—"

"You're jealous?"

"Oh, please, you know I am," she snapped. "And wipe that smirk off your face."

He laughed and caught her hand. "I don't want to be with Masumi," he said. "Ever since we got back from the *Sea Storm*, the thought of it feels like a betrayal. But it felt like a lot to ask of you if we weren't exclusive."

There was a long pause. "Then maybe we should be," she said quietly.

A pang of desire and something deeper and stronger centered in his chest. He'd always gotten what he wanted, and there was nothing he wanted more, right in this minute, than to call this female his.

"Are you sure?" he asked, his voice rough. "It's a lot—"

He broke off as she leaned over and slanted her mouth over his, silencing him in the best way.

"I'm sure," she murmured against his lips.

He wrapped his arm around her and hauled her up onto the bed so she was lying on top of him, her legs tangled with his. He arched his pelvis into hers, making his erection blatantly known.

"Oh, my," she breathed as she shoved herself up onto her elbows. "Just let me lock the door…"

They made it quick. At least, as quick as it could be, given that, for fifteen minutes afterward, Cyan had to lay there and muffle her moans every time a climax rolled through her.

"Everyone is going to know what we did," she said against Stryke's throat as she panted through another one.

"Don't worry about it." His voice vibrated through her, deep and comforting, and she snuggled in closer. "For my people, sex is no different than breathing. Everyone knows we're breathing in here, and they don't care, you know?"

She'd never really thought about it that way before. She'd grown up in the human world, where sex was often stigmatized, shamed, and even regulated. But for Stryke and his family, it was just another aspect and requirement of life, as vital yet mundane as eating, sleeping, or breathing.

Still, she wasn't looking forward to facing everyone in the waiting room.

Stryke's fingers, which had been stroking her arm as they lay there, went motionless. His chest rose and fell in deep, even breaths, and a couple of purring snores slipped between his full lips.

Good. He needed the rest.

Once the orgasm storm blew over, she cleaned up and dressed in the private bathroom. A few minutes later, she tiptoed out of the room and walked down the long, gray hallways to the private waiting room.

Runa looked up from her book the moment Cyan entered, looking tired and worried. "How's he doing?"

"He's resting." She looked around at all the empty chairs. "Where is everyone?"

"They went to the cafeteria." Runa put aside her book. "Do you want anything? I can message them."

"No, thank you. I'm fine."

"Maybe some water? You look a little flushed, and you must be tired."

Heat seared Cyan's face. Of course, she was flushed and tired. Her body was a wrung-out noodle. And Runa knew exactly why. "I, ah…"

Runa patted the seat next to her. "There's nothing to be embarrassed about. I'm just happy you're helping my son through this."

Smiling, Cyan took a seat. "I'll bet you were a great mom." Runa struck her as patient but firm, loving but not a pushover. A mama bear who didn't let anyone screw with her kids. Or, more accurately, a mother werewolf, which was far more terrifying than a bear.

Runa laughed. "Those boys tested me every single day."

"I can imagine." Cyan shifted on the cushion, appreciating the comfortable touches in the waiting room built specifically for hospital staff and their families. "So, what was Stryke like when he was little?"

Glancing in the direction of Stryke's room, Runa smiled fondly. "He was happy. Always inquisitive. When his brothers wanted to watch cartoons, he wanted to watch documentaries. When they wanted ice cream, he only wanted to know how the ice cream was made."

Cyan had been much the same. Except she *did* want the ice cream. "When did you realize he was gifted?"

"Pretty early." Someone in scrubs walked by and waved, and she returned it before turning back to Cyan. "We knew something was different about him when he was reading fifth-grade-level stories to his brothers at the age of three. At four, he not only knew the name of every dinosaur that ever existed but could spell their names as well." Shaking her head, she let out a little laugh. He was always either wanting to learn new things or telling you about the things he'd learned. He was so damned smart."

"And stubborn, I'd imagine," Cyan muttered.

"Ha! You have no idea," Runa said. "We didn't know how to handle him half the time. Not even Eidolon could help." She waved to someone else. "I remember we once had to leave a state fair because of the loud noise. Stryke said the music tasted like lemon rinds and he couldn't stop throwing up. Eidolon had no clue how to help him. We finally learned to carry earplugs everywhere." She sighed. "And getting him to eat was always a challenge. Up until the time he was twelve, I had to set a timer in the morning so he'd finish his breakfast. I still worry that he doesn't eat enough."

"I've found that if the food is interesting enough, he'll eat it. But no, food is definitely not a priority."

Runa studied her, her pale eyes making Cyan sweat a little. She felt like a bug under a magnifying glass. In the sun.

"You're the first female of his we've met."

Cyan had to force herself not to squirm. She'd dated, sure, but she'd never actually met any of her boyfriends' parents. Nothing had ever gotten that deep. So, this was…uncomfortable.

"We're not…I mean, it's not that serious."

Runa arched a brow. "I saw the way he looks at you. He's let you in, Cyan. He's never let anyone in. Not even his family."

She closed her eyes and thought about what Runa said. He'd told Cyan that he'd never been in a relationship before, and she'd absolutely gotten the impression that he'd never opened up to anyone before.

"Was he always so private and closed off?"

"Private? Yes, but I would say that it was less about privacy and more about being unable to engage with others on the same level. Even as a kid, he didn't enjoy playing with other kids. He did enjoy combat training, though. It gave him a chance to talk to his trainers about similar interests, and it got him out of his head." She smiled sadly. "But he became closed off after we lost Chaos. He just sort of…left us."

Cyan's heart broke for her. And for Stryke. "I think he worries that the sight of him brings the family more pain."

"He's so wrong." Runa's eyes grew misty, and Cyan's eyes stung. "What brings us pain is his absence."

So heartbreaking. Cyan had no idea what to say, and her mouth felt too dry to say anything anyway. She stood, intending to find the nearest water fountain, but suddenly, the room spun.

"Cyan?" Runa caught her arm, steadying her before she fell. "Are you okay?"

"I don't know." Cyan sank back into the chair. "I think I'm just tired."

Frowning, Runa put the back of her hand to Cyan's forehead, checking for fever. "Maybe Eidolon should take a look at you."

"It's nothing," she insisted. "I'm probably dehydrated."

Runa gave her a no-nonsense look. "Maybe Eidolon should take a look at you," she repeated more firmly this time, and Cyan couldn't help but smile.

Her mom would have said the same thing.

Chapter 28

"What are you doing?"

Stryke looked up at his uncle as he buttoned his shirt. "What's it look like? I'm getting dressed."

"You're not ready to be discharged."

"I feel great. It's fine."

Eidolon slammed his clipboard down on the counter loud enough to make Stryke jump. "Listen to me, you arrogant ass. I'm tired of your shit. I'm tired of everyone walking on eggshells around you because they're afraid you'll retreat from them even more." He jammed his finger into Stryke's sternum and pushed him backward until the backs of his legs hit the bed. "You're going to sit your ass down and listen to me."

Stryke gaped. Arrogant ass? His uncle had never spoken to him like that before, and it was enough of a shock to have him sitting down, just like Eidolon said.

He'd gone toe-to-toe with genocidal dictators and faced demon emissaries who ate the flesh of their enemies while they were still alive. He feared little and respected few.

And his uncle just put him on his ass like a spoiled child.

"You almost died," Eidolon barked, jabbing into Stryke's sternum again. "Do you know what that would have done to your family? Do you know what that would have meant to the entire world? What you do is important, too important to entrust it to someone else. But you have a fucking death wish" —he thrust his finger in Stryke's face when he opened his mouth to argue—"and don't even *try* to fucking deny it. Do *not* take me for a fool any longer, Stryke."

Eidolon stepped back, his fists clenched, anger putting gold flecks in his eyes. "The suppressant's killing you. You know it, and you keep using it. Knock that shit off. You might think you're invincible, but you're not, and—"

"It's not about being invincible," Stryke protested, even though the truth wasn't much better.

"You're right," Eidolon said with a nod. "It's about not caring if you live or die."

Bingo. Stryke hadn't cared about much outside of work since Chaos died. But lately…things had changed. Cyan had helped him find interests outside of work. He even enjoyed the pool now.

As long as she was in it too.

"I care, Eidolon," he argued. "There was a time when I didn't. But I do now."

Skepticism flickered in the angry gold glitter in Eidolon's eyes. "Good. Your parents have been through enough."

"Agreed." Stryke was done with this conversation. He started to stand, but Eidolon slammed him back down.

"We're not finished." He breathed deeply as if bracing himself for what he was about to say. "StryTech's demon-detection software is leaps and bounds ahead of the closest competitor's. You probably outsell everyone ten to one."

"Twenty to one," Stryke shot back in a flare of temper. His uncle was treating him like a child. Worse, Stryke wasn't sure what to do about it. He'd rarely been treated like a child even when he'd *been* a child.

"Yeah, why is that?"

"It's because my tech is far superior." Stryke met his uncle's gaze, daring him to find fault with his company. "The number of demon species in our database is three times that of Demonovation's. Four times the number of Ufelskala Five demons."

"And how," Eidolon began, his gaze locked with Stryke's, aggressive tension thickening the air, "did you manage to acquire the genetic material for that many species?"

Oh, shit.

Stryke's gut took a dive all the way to his feet. His uncle had walked Stryke up to the edge of a trap and let him spring it himself for maximum humiliation.

He knew.

Eidolon wheeled away from him and looked up at the ceiling. "We recently upgraded our security, data, and storage software, and it created some strange glitches in the hospital's DNA library. We brought in a specialist to identify the problem." He shook his head, hands locked behind his back as he turned to Stryke again. "Turns out someone hacked our original software and added code that alerted them every time we logged a new species. After a little more digging—"

"Spare me the forensics," Stryke said, shame making his voice gruff. "You got me."

The disappointment in Eidolon's expression shredded him.

"Dammit, Stryke." Dismay weighed down Eidolon's voice. "You've been stealing from me for years. Why? Why not just ask me? I'd have given you whatever you wanted!" He threw up his hands and cursed. "You remind me of Wraith when he was young. You take what you want because you can. Too proud to ask for help. Using your pain as an excuse to be toxic to everyone around you." He threw open the door. "Get your shit together, kid. Your family needs you, whether you believe it or not."

Stryke snarled and leaped to his feet, but Eidolon slammed the door closed before Stryke could defend himself. Yeah, he'd taken the samples from the hospital, but he hadn't exactly *stolen* them. He'd just mapped the genetics and duplicated them.

Okay, maybe he should have asked, but he hadn't wanted to put his uncle in a compromising position with the WCSG, which was already wary of Underworld General. Finding out there was a secret demon hospital beneath New York City had freaked them out so much that UG's existence hadn't yet been revealed to the human population.

Fuck. Angry, hurt, and full of self-loathing, Stryke strapped on his wrist comms just as it vibrated.

Taran.

Had it been anyone else—other than Cyan—he would have ignored it. But he'd apparently been talking with his foreman when he had his *event*, and he had questions.

He threw Taran's hologram into the room and finished dressing while they talked.

"Boss," Taran said. "I'm glad you're okay."

"Yeah. About that." He tucked his shirt into his pants. "I don't remember anything. What happened?"

Taran shrugged. "One minute we were discussing the

Gehennaportal, and the next, you were on the ground."

Stryke stilled as he tugged on his belt. "Why were we discussing the port—?" The memory hit him like a brick to the face. The portal was possibly still active. "Never mind. I remember. Has anything changed?"

"No, but I took the liberty of showing the newest casing images to Quillax. He wasn't happy about being interrupted during his leave. Very grumpy. Anyway, he said the glyphs have been repaired, but he also said they aren't destruction spells. They're containment spells."

"So? They would have needed to contain Gabriel's destructive energy inside the breach."

"That's what I said. Quillax insisted there would have been another glyph alongside the seals. A backup of sorts in case destruction rattled the seals loose. It's like I said, the Gehennaportal is intact, and there's no way Cyan wouldn't have known that."

Stryke couldn't believe it. Refused to believe it. Cyan had told him the portal was destroyed. Why would she lie to him?

He thought about all the times she'd quizzed him about *Sea Storm*. He had thought she seemed oddly interested in its operations and what he planned to do with the rig. Restart it? Sell it? Use it for research?

He'd told her more than once that he planned to hold onto it. Who knew what kinds of residual effects they'd see after the incursion. Sheoulic elements could have been introduced to the sea floor or water. Aquatic demons may yet be lurking in the depths, breeding with native species. It was even possible that the portal's destruction had caused a weakening in the membrane that separated the demon realm from the human one. The site needed to be monitored for decades. Centuries, maybe. And Stryke wanted sole control of it.

Had she been as curious as she was because she feared the breach would open again?

"Boss?" Taran's voice brought him back to the present.

"Yeah. I heard you. I'll talk to Cyan about it. Is that all?"

Taran nodded. "Just glad to hear you're okay."

He was not okay. He'd been spanked by Eidolon, and the female he lov—no, the female he *felt strongly about* might have duped him.

He disconnected with Taran and got the hell out of there. He didn't want to see anyone right now. This was all too humiliating. Rock-bottom shit. Time to drown himself in work, numbers, and anything that would keep him from feeling the crush of emotions he didn't know how to process.

Fortunately, the halls were empty of anyone he knew, but as he passed the private waiting room, he saw his family. He stopped. Backed up. Peeked inside.

His mom, Blade, Crux, Parker...they were all gathered around Cyan, who sat slumped in a chair. Blade's *dermoire* was lit up as he gripped her forearm.

What was wrong with her?

Panic shot through Stryke. Cyan was pale, her skin damp. He needed to be at her side—

"Holy shit, Cyan." Blade stared at Cyan, wide-eyed. "You're pregnant."

Stryke froze in mid-step. *Pregnant?* Impossible. Well, almost impossible. Crux and Chaos had been born during this offspring-less time for demons. But still. Blade had to be messing with her.

She rolled her eyes. "Real funny, Blade."

"I'm serious." He kneeled next to her, his *dermoire* lit, pulsing gently as his power connected with Cyan's body on a level not even Stryke could. "I can sense fetal tissue."

Stryke's heart stopped, and his lungs locked up hard. She couldn't be pregnant. Stryke wouldn't be fertile until *s'genesis*. So, if she was pregnant...

It wasn't his.

Parker.

Parker was a turned werewolf, so the child could have a human soul, and therefore bypass the no-demons-born-since-the-destruction-of-Sheoul-gra thing.

Stryke's heart shriveled as Parker reached over and took her hand. How gentlemanly of him.

The male was going to die.

Icy cold rage spread through every cell. If the hospital wasn't under an anti-violence spell, he would have pounded Parker into the ground.

Stryke didn't care that he and Cyan weren't officially a couple at the time of conception. The logic of the situation didn't matter right now. Right now, there was only pain and bitterness and a sense that his life was one gigantic pile of shit.

As if in a dream, he watched his family—and Parker—gather around Cyan. He could no longer hear what they were saying, maybe because his pulse was beating so loudly it echoed through his head like drums in a canyon. Oxygen became precious, and he panted, sucking in shallow breaths as he slammed his palms against the sides of his skull, covering his ears.

This was too much. Things were breaking inside him, like his organs were cracking open. Especially his heart. That sucker was being raked up and down a cheese grater.

Sensory overload. *Sensoryoverloadsensoryoverload*...his head swam as he tore away from everything going on in that room and stumbled to the Harrowgate. His vision faded and wavered, but he somehow managed to operate the gate's interface and get home.

He entered a house that had never felt empty before. Now, it was too quiet. Too still. It was a dark void.

Just like his soul.

Cyan sat, stunned and baffled, with half a dozen sets of eyes staring at her.

"I don't...Blade, that can't be."

Blade shrugged and waved Eidolon over. "We need a second opinion."

Eidolon approached, the intensity in his expression reminding her of Stryke. "On what?"

"Her pregnancy."

One dark eyebrow arched. "Cyan, would you rather do this in private?"

Splotches of pink spread across Blade's cheeks, and he gave her a sheepish look. "Oh, yeah...hey, I'm sorry. I didn't mean to blurt it out like that. There's a reason I work for DART and not the hospital."

"It's okay." She sighed. "You're wrong anyway." She offered Eidolon her hand so he could do his glowy thing. "Go ahead."

Eidolon gripped her wrist, and his *dermoire* lit up. No worries. He would find that Blade was wrong, and this was all a silly mista—

"You *are* pregnant," Eidolon said, and she nearly choked on her own breath. "Your species gestation is similar to that of humans, so I'm guessing you're no more than three weeks in."

Which would have put her on the oil rig. With Stryke. Shock left her swaying in her seat, her brain short-circuiting.

"That's not possible," she rasped. "None of this is possible. I haven't been with anyone." Her cheeks burned. "I mean, except for Stryke…"

"Stryke isn't fertile," Blade said. "Not for another sixty-five to seventy years."

"I know. So, it's impossible for me to be pregnant." She looked frantically at Eidolon. "Right? I mean, no demon female has gotten pregnant since Sheoul-gra—"

"That," Eidolon interrupted, "isn't entirely true."

"Okay, I know about…" *Crux and Chaos.* She gestured to Runa, but he shook his head.

"Those rare exceptions aren't what I'm talking about."

Runa reached over and took Cyan's hand. Then she waved away all the males except Eidolon.

"Give us a minute, okay?" Once the guys moved off, she turned back to Cyan. "I know this is difficult," she said. "I know you've only been with Stryke." She paused, and when she spoke again, her voice was soft. Understanding. Compassionate. "But is it possible that you were drugged at some point? Have you felt like you've lost any time?"

"No." She shook her head vehemently. "I remember everything from the last month clearly. I was never the victim of a spell, or drugs, or anything."

"What about your dreams?" Eidolon took a seat across from her. "Some species of lust demons are known to fill your sleep with erotic images so they can impregnate you while you're dreaming."

She shuddered. Her parents had raised her with a healthy fear of demons that were threats to their kind, and she'd always thought that the ones who assaulted you and *didn't* kill you were the worst.

"I haven't had any dreams like that." On the verge of tears, she buried her face in her hands. "This can't be happening."

"Let me run some tests," Eidolon said gently. "If we can identify the father's species, we can go from there."

The father. She shuddered again. It had to be Stryke. *Please, let it be him.*

Lifting her head, she blinked back tears. "Where is Stryke? Still in his room? I need to talk to him."

"He discharged himself against my orders," Eidolon said, irritation lacing his voice. "He's pretty furious with me."

Looking as alarmed as Cyan felt, Runa turned to him. "Why?"

"Because I injected him with a large dose of truth."

"Well, I'm sure he needed to hear it," Runa said, but Cyan had questions.

Unfortunately, she didn't have a chance to ask any because Eidolon stood and held out his hand to Cyan. "Are you ready?"

To learn if she was carrying a monster inside her? Sure. Who wouldn't be?

Still, she couldn't imagine being in better hands, and it was a relief to let Eidolon take charge. She just wished Stryke were there.

Resigned, she took the doctor's hand and allowed him to help her up.

"I'd be happy to go with you if you'd like," Runa offered.

"I appreciate it," Cyan said, touched by the concern. "But I'll be okay. I just need to know how this happened." And then she had to sort out how she felt about it.

Runa gestured to her chair. "I'll be right here if you need me."

"You really don't have to—"

"Cyan." Runa gave her a stern look. "How long have we worked together? You're part of the DART family. And now, you're part of Stryke's life. So, I'm staying until I know you're okay. Got it?"

Tears welled in her eyes. "Yes, ma'am," she croaked, unable to contain the emotion starting to surface.

She might be carrying the spawn of Satan for all she knew, but at least she had a support system, something she felt she'd lost after Shanea died.

Now, she realized, it had been there all along.

Chapter 29

Stryke didn't sleep that night. At all. He just sat in his living room going over materials from *Sea Storm*, trying to figure out how to destroy the Gehennaportal. Well, he spent about half the time doing that. The rest had been spent thinking about Cyan. Why had she lied to him? Did Gabriel know the portal hadn't been destroyed?

And she's pregnant with another male's spawn.

Frustrated, angry, and still humiliated after Eidolon's dress down, Stryke jammed the heels of his palms into his eyes and roared. He let out everything he'd held in all night…and maybe for his entire life. Why was everything such a shitshow?

He shoved to his feet but then just stood there. Where was he going? Maybe he should talk to someone. His Seminus needs had been rapidly approaching, so he could summon Masumi. She was always trying to get him to talk.

She was always trying to get him to have sex too, and he wasn't ready to be with anyone but Cyan.

There was no way he was calling *her*.

"Wouldn't kill you to call Crux more often. He misses you."

The last thing Blade had said to him before the DART team evacuated from the *Sea Storm* popped into Stryke's head. They hadn't said proper goodbyes. Blade had bypassed Mace and Scotty as Stryke thanked them for their help, and then, halfway to the bird, he'd spun around and told Stryke to call Crux.

Blade was an asshole, but he wasn't wrong. And Stryke could use a few minutes to get his head on straight.

He sent a missive, and a moment later, an image of Crux seated in a gaming chair with his VR glasses on popped into Stryke's living room.

"Hi, Stryke!" Crux called out. "Just a second. I'm shooting demons."

All around Crux, the room turned into a battle, explosions and lasers everywhere. Crux took out a couple of dire leeches, and then the image faded away. He took off his glasses and grinned.

"Hi!" he repeated.

"Hey. I see you're playing the new game I sent."

His blond head bobbed enthusiastically. "It's awesome. I'll beta test for StryTech's gaming division any day."

The gaming division was Stryke's most recent acquisition after buying out an entertainment developer, and so far, he'd been pleased with the results. He hoped, after Crux finished with his software engineering degree, that he'd come work for Stryke to develop a game that would prepare humans to fight demons without them even knowing it. That goal was why he'd bought the company in the first place.

"Did you get the drone too?" he asked.

Crux slumped in his chair. "Mace took it away for a week."

"Why?"

"I used it to spy on him through his bedroom window," he muttered.

"You what?"

"I was just messing around," Crux protested. "I wanted to use the projector to make him think there was a hellrat in bed with him. How was I supposed to know he had those two females in there?" He grimaced. "Gross. I know we're supposed to like doing all that stuff, but I don't see how." He made a disgusted sound. "I can't unsee what I saw."

Stryke forced himself not to laugh. Poor Crux. And he'd have paid money to see Mace's reaction to a projected demonic rodent between his sheets. StryTech had worked hard to make the technology hyperrealistic.

"You'll understand after you go through your transition," he told Crux, struggling with every word to keep the amusement out of his voice.

"I don't want to go through it," Crux whined. "I asked uncle Eidolon if he can stop it." He huffed. "For the record, he said no, and that it would be dangerous to try."

That sounded like Eidolon, all right. "Don't worry, it'll be fine."

Crux seemed unaffected by Stryke's attempt to console him. "Masumi keeps coming to talk to me. She said it's so I'll feel comfortable with her when the time comes." He looked around and lowered his voice, leaning in conspiratorially. "It's not working. And why does she keep changing her appearance?"

This time, Stryke couldn't contain the smile. He'd hit the jackpot when he found Masumi. She truly cared about his family.

"She's monitoring your reactions to get an idea of your type," he explained.

"My type?"

"Yeah. She wants to know what kind of female turns you on. Blond, redhead, dark skin, light skin, thin, curvy, fangs, claws, scales, fur…"

"*What?*"

"Wait until she starts testing your kinks." Crux looked like he was ready to crawl into a hole, so Stryke dialed it back. "Hasn't anyone talked to you about all this?"

"They've all tried," Crux said miserably. "But I tell them that someone else already did it."

Stryke wished he could reach out and hug his brother, but right now, the best he could do was offer advice and an ear. "Hey, listen. Do you want to talk about it?"

Crux shook his head.

"Are you sure? I could have Masumi—"

"I'm sure!" Suddenly, Crux threw down his glasses and bounded to his feet. "Just leave me alone, okay? Why do you suddenly care about me after all these years of being gone? Back off, Stryke! *Everyone* needs to back off!"

The screen shut down.

And wasn't that just the fucking cherry on top of Stryke's shit sundae?

Cursing, he threw himself back against his couch cushions. His wrist comms indicated an incoming message, but he ignored it, just as he'd ignored every message for the last six hours. Instead, he dug into his pocket for his suppressant injector pen.

He had a choice to make. Summon Masumi, call Cyan, or take an injection.

Of course, there was an Option D, none of the above.

You have a fucking death wish. Eidolon's voice echoed in his ears.

Sure, that might have been true at one point. But things had changed. *Stryke* had changed.

Because of Cyan.

Dammit!

He sat on his couch, holding the injector pen, his body aching as his need increased.

The suppressant is killing you.

Fucking Eidolon. That guy's voice would *not* get out of his head. He was like an ear worm, except instead of a catchy tune playing relentlessly over and over, you got an obnoxious lecture.

His wrist comms vibrated again for the tenth time in twenty minutes. He finally looked down. His NeuroTech implant activated, bringing up a screen of the last twelve hours of missives.

Two calls from Ear Worm Eidolon. Two calls each from his parents. Two from Kalis.

Thirty-one from Cyan. The last ten calls had been hers.

"Stryke?"

He looked up at Masumi. She stood in front of him, naked except for a pair of high heels.

"I don't need you," he said.

"You're lying. I can sense it."

His fingers tightened around the injector. "I'm fine."

Slowly, sensually, she lowered to her knees in front of him. He went taut, waiting for her to go for the fly of his pants. Instead, she folded her hands in her lap and watched him.

"Where is Cyan?" she asked, and damn if that question didn't form a knot of acid in his belly.

I don't know." *Probably with the father of her baby.*

"Blade told me what happened. That you almost died." She gestured to the injector. "Because of that."

"Blade has a big mouth."

"Do not be angry with him." She jabbed a slender, gold-manicured finger at him. "You are the one holding the object that nearly killed you, prepared to do it again. Be angry with yourself."

"Oh, believe me," he growled. "I am. I put my trust in someone who lied to me. Betrayed me."

She laid her palms on his thighs. "I won't do that," she murmured, rising to nuzzle the side of his neck. "Let me help you."

He should. He didn't owe Cyan anything. She'd lied to him and put the entire world in danger with that lie. She was also pregnant with another male's spawn.

Pain and jealously zapped him in the heart like an electric shock. Extra shocking because he'd never wanted children. They were annoying little time-sucks that would take him away from important work.

But right now, he'd give anything to be the father of Cyan's baby. His child wouldn't be a time suck. It would be an opportunity for him to learn, teach, and atone for his mistakes.

And what *the fuck* was wrong with him? Wanting to be a father? Maybe his cardiac episode had come with a side of brain damage.

Masumi's hands slid up his inner thighs as her lips nibbled his neck, and for once, his libido didn't spin up, even though his body needed sex. If anything, he kind of…deflated. Not his cock…that bastard was aching.

No, what deflated was his initial thought that he should let Masumi help him. He couldn't. He didn't want her. He only wanted Cyan, that lying, traitorous—

"What the hell is going on here?"

He cranked his head around in shock at the sight of Cyan, standing in his doorway in jeans and a black blouse, snowflakes swirling around her, her hair whipping in the cold wind. Her eyes, normally a deep, rich amethyst, were now glowing with reddish-gold spokes, and anger had turned her expression into a hard-cut mask.

"*Cyan?*"

She stepped inside, and the door closed behind her with a bone-jarring slam, which was bizarre because he'd programmed it for complete silence.

"How did you operate my Harrowgate?" Surprise and anger made his voice harsh. "How'd you get past my security measures?"

"I'm a fucking technomancer, you ass!" she shouted. "I'm one of the most powerful Cyberis demons in the world. You think I can't counter your tech and magic-based measures?"

He lifted Masumi to her feet as he came to his in a surge of temper. How dare she break into his house and accuse *him* of wrongdoing? "You have no right to be mad at me—"

"Are you kidding me?" She tossed up her hands, gesturing furiously as she went off. "I've been trying to get ahold of you for hours, knowing you needed me. Knowing you wouldn't be stupid enough to use an injection again. But you didn't answer any of my missives, so I came here, thinking maybe you were in trouble again…and here you are with a fucking injection in your hand and Masumi in your crotch!" She waved at Masumi, her expression contrite. "Sorry, Masumi, I'm not angry with you. He's the one being a self-centered ass who isn't thinking of anyone but himself." She rounded on him again. "People are worried. They're scared, Stryke! And you can't bother to let anyone know you're not dead?"

She might have a point, but he wasn't ready to acknowledge it. Not when *he* took the trophy for justified anger.

"You have no right to be angry about *anything*!" He snatched up one of the photos of the *Sea Storm's* drill casing and threw it at her. "You lied about the portal, Cyan. You lied to my damned face and put the entire world at risk! I took you into my confidence, and do you know how often I do that? *Do you*?"

The fury drained out of her face. Her mouth fell open. Closed.

He pounced while she was still taken aback. He'd found that people were the most honest when their brains weren't working.

"Nothing to say about that?" He wheeled around and thrust his hands through his hair, needing something to do with them before he punched a wall. "Dammit, Cyan, why? Who are you working for? Do you know what's going to happen when Heaven finds out? When Gabriel, a fucking *Archangel*, finds out? How am I going to keep you safe?"

"Keep *me* safe?" She blinked at him, bewildered. "*That's* what you're worried about?"

"Well, yeah," he shouted, dropping his hands to his sides. "I'm not going to let Heaven assassinate you. I'm an asshole, but I'm not a monster, and I'm your best shot at staying safe." She stared at him in disbelief, which made him hit another level of furious. "What? You think Parker can protect you from Heaven?" He swore. "I'm really pissed off right now, so answer my questions. Why did you leave the Gehennaportal intact, and why did you lie to me about it?"

"Okay." She held her hands out in a calm-down gesture that did *not* calm him down. "Okay. I didn't want to lie to you, I swear. Gabriel made me. He said that if this got out, you could be in danger. I was only supposed to tell you the truth if you decided to drill or sell the rig."

It was his turn to stare at her in disbelief. "Gabriel *knows*?"

She came closer, bringing her sexy, copper-silver scent with her, and his body, already throbbing with need, responded with a fresh wave of lust. For a moment, his brain short-circuited, filling his mind with erotic images of Cyan in his bed.

Her voice brought him back, but he didn't know how much longer he could remain rational.

"...when we were underwater," she was saying. "Once we got to the site, he told me to repair the breach instead of destroying the portal, but he didn't say why. I'm sorry, Stryke." The plea in her voice, in her eyes, stabbed him in the heart. He'd always enjoyed when people groveled, but dammit, not Cyan. She shouldn't be groveling in front of anyone, least of all him. "Gabriel's an Archangel. I had to believe he knew what he was doing."

In his opinion, the fact that Gabriel was an angel was a good reason *not* to believe the guy. But Cyan couldn't have known that. She'd been put into an impossible situation and had done her best with the information she had.

Frankly, he no longer cared about the damned portal. Or Gabriel. Or anything but the female in front of him. Right now, all his blood and energy had been diverted from his higher brain to his basest instincts. It was this response that he'd always hated. He disliked any core need that took him away from using his mind, but this one was the worst.

At least, it had been until now. Now, he just wanted to be with Cyan. He wanted to let his brain rest and his heart and body do all the work.

Out of the corner of his eye, he saw Masumi slip inside her vase, leaving him alone with the only female he'd ever wanted to be with.

"Stryke?" Cyan came even closer, her hand up as if she wanted to touch him but wasn't sure how he'd respond. "I'm sorry. I never meant to betray you—"

He shut her up with a kiss. He didn't need her apology. He needed *her*.

And he needed to make sure she understood *exactly* how much.

Masumi smiled as she shrugged into a body-hugging pair of tactical pants and a shimmery black sports bra.

Stryke had found his match in Cyan, and it was about time. He'd needed someone to help him navigate not just his feelings, but also his life. As intelligent as he was, he was dumber than a stoned orc when it came to taking care of himself.

She felt him deep in her chest, their bond telling her he was on the verge of orgasm, and she smiled even bigger. For far too many years, she'd been his sole source of sex. Everything else had come via his injections.

He deserved this, and she was happy for him.

Another sensation pulsed inside her as she tugged on her boots, the reason she was dressing the way she was. Blade liked his females in workout or combat gear. He liked them physical. Strong. Able to withstand his appetite.

Because as caring and attentive as he was, he also liked to dominate, and he liked it a little rough. He'd taught her to fight, and sometimes they'd spar for an hour before finally peeling out of their sweat-soaked clothes and finishing in the shower.

Distantly, she could feel Sabre and Mace too, but their needs were hours away. She hadn't been with either of them in the last couple of days, but Rade and Blade had kept her sated, using her exclusively of late.

The sensation of her home being moved swept through her, and a moment later, Blade's summons tugged at her very being. Automatically, her physical form became another type of matter, a "viscous, Non-Newtonian fluid," Stryke called it. The sensation of being transported from her home into Blade's bedroom was almost erotic, leaving her breathless when she fully materialized next to her secondary vase he'd placed on his bedside table.

"I'm wearing your favorite outfit," she purred.

His smile was predatory, his voice husky. "Yes, you are."

He watched her, his gaze dark and hungry as she sauntered up to him, dressed in his own combat gear. Except he actually used his. He smelled of sweat, and smoke, blood and fury.

"I thought you might want to spar, but it appears you've been fighting already," she said as she trailed her finger down his chest. "With Mace and Scotty?"

His eyes flashed the way they always did when she mentioned Scotty. Sometimes, when they fucked, when he was wild, so deep into it he lost control, he called out Scotty's name.

And he wasn't the only one.

Mace had called Masumi by Scotty's name once, just before he sank his fangs into her throat and came so hard and for so long he'd failed to seal the punctures in her vein and she'd soaked the sheets in blood.

Blade didn't answer the question. "Have you seen my brother?"

"Rade?" she asked, knowing full well he was talking about Stryke. Sometimes, she liked to work him up before sex. His dark side was always so unexpected from someone who was usually so level. "A couple of hours ago. And don't ask what we talked about. He says very little."

He growled deep in his chest, the vibration so tangible she felt it between her legs, and she nearly moaned. "Not Rade."

"Crux, then?" She tapped her chin, pretending to recall her last meeting with Blade's little brother. "I talked to him yesterday. I believe his change is near. He's moody, skittish, and his pulse was erratic during my last couple of visits. Also," she said, "and this is curious, he's popping a slight hormonal spike when I wear a superhero or anime-style outfit, no matter my skin tone, hairstyle, or body shape. Interesting kink."

"Not. Crux," Blade ground out, his patience wearing thin as he pitted his body's growing needs against his need to get a straight answer from her. "Stryke."

She fluttered her lashes, loving how easy it was to tease him. "You know I can't say anything about what Stryke and I did."

"I don't care what you did. I want to know..." He trailed off with a curse, wheeling away from her, his hands balled into fists at his sides.

"What?" She slipped around in front of him and tenderly took his right hand in hers, playtime over. "What do you want to know?"

He looked up at the colorful painted pipes running across the ceiling and cursed again. "He almost died, Masumi," he said, his voice uncharacteristically thick with emotion." I want to know if he's okay."

She thought about how she'd left him with Cyan, the only female he'd ever let into his heart. Not even Masumi could claim to have been allowed inside that cold stone fortress.

"He is now," she said, feeling the truth of that in a wave of relief. She'd feared for him for years, watched him teeter on the edge of self-destruction he couldn't even see. But Cyan seemed to have the magic touch, able to call him on his shit *and* somehow bring him down from the precipice.

Blade's shoulders sagged in relief. "Thank gods. I never wanted him dead, Masumi. I'm just so...angry. I want him to know what he did to us."

"I know." Reaching up, she cupped his jaw. And then, using the seductive powers of her species, she altered her hair color, turning it wavy and fiery red. She made her eye color hazel with flecks of emerald green. Her skin paled, and she summoned a smattering of freckles.

Blade's gaze grew hotter, his despair fading as his libido won the battle over emotion. Reaching behind her, he caught her around the back of her neck and tugged her close. She bumped against his chest and brought her lips up to meet his.

His eyes bored into hers, flames of lust flickering in their depths. "What do you look like when you go to Stryke?"

"I've tried every female combination under the sun," she said, her lips so close to his she could feel their heat. "And he never showed any preferences." Until Cyan. "But I bet he's now as partial to short platinum hair and violet eyes as you are to sassy redheads with hazel eyes."

With a low growl, he captured her mouth and kissed her hard, one hand fisting her hair at the nape of her neck, the other hauling her ass up so she could wrap her legs around his waist. She purred in delight. Tonight was going to be frenzied and furious.

Tonight, he'd definitely call her Scotty.

Chapter 30

Yawning, Cyan stretched on the living room floor in front of the roaring fire and then snuggled deeper into the fluffy blankets Stryke had wrapped them in. They'd spent hours tangled with each other, drowning in erotic bliss. She still hadn't recovered from the last round, their cries breaking with the dawn streaming through the massive picture window.

The scent of coffee drifted to her, and she opened her eyes as Stryke knelt on the floor, two mugs in his hands.

Moaning in appreciation, she propped herself up against the back of the couch. "Thank you," she said, taking one of the mugs. "I'm going to need this after last night."

His naughty smile made her heart beat a little faster. "I'd apologize, but you didn't seem to mind the lack of sleep."

"Totally worth it." She wrapped her hands around the mug and let the warmth seep into her. "But do you mind if I make an observation?"

"As long as it's not a critique of my performance," he said, getting comfortable on the blanket, "go for it."

She laughed. "Your performance was exemplary."

Holding up his mug in salute, he gave her a cocky wink. She laughed again.

"You did seem a little extra...intense, though," she said, getting a little more serious. "It felt like you were trying to keep busy."

He studied the contents of his mug, his brow furrowed. "That's what I like about you," he said after a moment. "You see me. All of me, including my faults."

"Of which you have many," she said, teasing, expecting him to argue.

To her surprise, he agreed. "I do. And running away from my thoughts is one of them. I'm a self-centered asshole, Cyan."

"I do believe we've covered that topic," she said, still trying to keep things light, afraid he'd slide down a dark hole. They had things to talk about, and she needed him in a mentally sound place. "More than once."

He actually laughed but sobered quickly. "My company has been my sole focus since I started it. I was desperate to save the world from demons and spare people the pain that Chaos's death caused my family. Such a noble cause, right?" He laughed again, but this time it dripped with bitterness. "I justified everything I did in the name of saving the planet. Most of it I wouldn't change, but the pain I caused…I'd take it back. I regret all of it."

She was almost afraid to ask, but she had to. He needed to talk. Needed to lance an infected emotional wound, as her mother would have said. "What do you regret?"

Those dark eyes drilled into her, measuring her. Assessing her ability to handle his answer.

Her reaction to his next words would matter to him. A lot.

"I stole from my uncle Eidolon."

Holy shit. "What did you—?"

She inhaled sharply, recalling the conversation she'd had with one of StryTech's lab techs. He'd said that Stryke's acquisition of their DNA samples was a mystery.

"DNA," she breathed. "Of course! That's where you've been getting the genetic material for your DeTecht machines."

His gaze fell away, fixing on the fire. "Eidolon called me on it. And then I talked to Crux, who wanted to know why I suddenly gave a shit about him, and it hit me that Blade's right. He's such a dick—gods, he's a dick—but he's right. I hurt my family and called it the price of saving the world, when what I was really doing was running from my own pain."

"I understand," she said, looking down at her cup of coffee, the brew as dark as Stryke's eyes. "I've been doing the same thing. It was easier to hate you than it was to process my pain. Heck, I haven't even opened the bridesmaid gift Shan gave me because I'm too much of a coward."

Steam rose from her mug as she lifted it to her lips. Was coffee okay for pregnant Cyberis demons? She'd forgotten to ask Eidolon how much her body chemistry would change.

Lowering the mug, she wished her mom was around to help her navigate this.

A profound sadness threatened to overwhelm her, but for the first time, thoughts of her mom brought fond memories instead of agonizing ones. The pain of losing her parents, while still there, seemed to have dulled like the hate she'd had for Stryke.

"*When you let go of hate, you open your heart.*" Another mom-ism.

Thanks, Mom, but why couldn't you have left some bit of wisdom for when you have to tell the male you love that you're pregnant? Yep, she could use some motherly advice right now.

"Cyan?" Stryke rested his hand on her knee. Are you okay?"

Not by a long shot. "Uh…" She set the mug down without taking a single sip. "I need to tell you something."

He looked at her over the rim of his cup. "I know you're pregnant."

What? Incredulous, she stared as he calmly took a sip of coffee. "You *knew*, and you didn't say anything last night?"

"Things got busy."

Well, yeah, but it still hadn't crossed his mind during one of their breaks to say, "*Hey, I know you're pregnant?*"

"But how?" She shook her head, unable to comprehend any of this. "Who told you?"

"Nobody told me. I was looking for you at the hospital and overheard Blade."

It still was not making sense. And now she was annoyed that he'd left after finding out. "If you knew, why didn't you stay?"

She swore the temperature in the room plummeted. "Because," he said, his voice so cold she shivered, "I would have dragged Parker out to the parking garage and killed him."

Parker? What did he have to do with anything? Unless…no. Stryke did *not* think she'd slept with him. Did he? "You think I slept with Parker?"

"You didn't?"

He seemed so surprised…surprised that *she hadn't slept with a damned coworker.*

"No, you big jerk." She scrambled out from under the blankets and searched for her panties. Oh, there, hanging from the corner of the TV. Angrily, she snatched them up. "And I haven't slept with anyone else, either. No one but you in over a year." She stepped into them. They were torn, and now she looked ridiculous. "And Eidolon ran about a million tests to make sure I wasn't roofied or a victim of demonic possession or dream sex…shit like that."

Looking baffled, Stryke shoved to his feet. "What are you doing?"

"I'm getting dressed," she shouted.

"Why?"

"I don't know!" she cried, tears welling up from out of nowhere. "I'm just…I'm confused and scared." She stood there in her ruined underwear and nothing else, sobbing and feeling about as vulnerable as she'd ever felt in her life.

Then Stryke wrapped his arms around her, and she suddenly felt *safer* than she'd ever felt in her life. He'd thought she was carrying Parker's baby and still wanted to protect her.

"It'll be okay," he said. "Eidolon's the best in the world." He ran his hand up and down her back in long, soothing strokes. "Did you get the test results?"

She nodded. Sniffed. "There's no evidence of any kind of violation, physical or mental. The father is a Seminus demon. I don't know how, but it has to be you."

He went taut, every muscle locking up so hard he didn't even breathe. "It's not possible."

She stepped back and grabbed her shirt off the floor, giving him some space. A moment or two to process what she'd said. Hell, she was still processing.

He ran his hands through his hair as he paced in a tight circle, the muscles in his bare upper body flexing. How many times had she felt those muscles rippling under her fingers and lips last night? He'd been insatiable, and she'd reveled in it.

"It doesn't make sense," he said. "How can I be fertile? I'm at least sixty years away from *s'genesis*."

"There's an easy way to find out if you're fertile, you know." She gestured to the doorway near the kitchen. "You have a lab."

"My species can't jerk off."

"Yeah, I know." Sometimes, he could be really dense. "Hello, blowjob."

For some reason, he still seemed reluctant, as if he was afraid of the results. Sometimes, not knowing was the easier option. She got that. Sometimes, you didn't want to know what the dead thing in the box was.

Another fun mom-ism.

No problem. She knew Stryke's buttons now. "Think of it as a blowjob for science." She casually slipped on her shirt, leaving it unbuttoned, her breasts playing peekaboo with the silky fabric. "I'll be your lab assistant." She shifted, exposing her nipples. "Your *eager* lab assistant."

His head swung around, his gaze heating. "Let's do this, then," he said. "For science."

Stryke's legs were still shaking from the most amazing blowjob he'd ever had. He wasn't sure how he'd managed to get anything at all in the sample cup since he'd gone half-blind with pleasure.

Cyan continued to lave his shaft with her tongue as the last few spasms wrung him dry and filled the cup. Her fingers played with his sac, squeezing and rolling his balls, extending his climax to a new record.

"Damn," he breathed as he pulled away from her, too sensitive for even her gentlest touch. "Might have to get samples more often."

She came to her feet in a fluid, lithe surge and stepped over to the sink to wash. She was stronger than she appeared, something he was reminded of often. "You just like getting off in your favorite place. You should have a bed brought in."

He pulled up his sweatpants. "What, and miss out on the adrenaline rush of hoping we don't knock a vial of Ebola onto the floor while we're fucking on the counter?"

"Exactly." She dried her hands and started the process of putting his specimen under the microscope. "But I hope you're kidding about the Ebola."

"I wasn't kidding, but I was inaccurate." He moved to the sink, talking while he cleaned up. "It's DEbola. It's the demon version of Ebola." At her horrified glance, he chuckled. "The virus isn't active outside the demon realm."

"Yeah, well, demonic hemorrhagic fever doesn't sound like something we want to knock onto the floor," she said as she stuck the slide under the microscope.

He dried his hands and wandered over to her, hoping the dampness in his palms was residual moisture and not liquified anxiety. But damn, he was nervous. His logical side said that there was no way his sample contained live sperm. But the side of him that loved Cyan wanted it to.

I love her.

Holy shit, he did. Now wasn't the time to tell her, but—

"I see swimmers."

Swimmers. Live sperm. He stood there, paralyzed by the impossibility. How? How had this happened?

"I know this is a lot to absorb," Cyan said, looking up from the microscope. "We're both going to need time to figure out what this means." She straightened, and her hands shook as she fiddled with the buttons on her blouse. "I just...I don't know how much time we have."

Time? Because Heaven might be after them both for knowing that the Gehennaportal was still, technically, functional if not active?

His feet moved before his brain, and suddenly, he was in front of her, his hands on her shoulders, his face in hers.

"I won't let anything happen to you," he swore. "We have all the time in the world. This child is—"

"Not going to be born," she whispered.

He stepped back—stumbled back to be more accurate. "You're... getting rid of it? But you know it's mine now—"

"I'm sorry." She captured his hand, her voice pleading, her eyes damp. "Getting confirmation that you're the father makes knowing so much worse."

"Knowing what?"

"Something Eidolon told me." She took a deep, rattling breath. "It's true that no known demons except Crux and Chaos have been born since the destruction of Sheoul-gra. But what most people don't know is that the pregnancies haven't stopped." She laid her other hand lightly over her belly. "Just the live births."

Chapter 31

Please answer. Please answer. Answer, dammit!

Stryke held his breath, his chest constricting more with every unanswered ring of Eidolon's comms. Five rings in, and it hadn't even gone to techmail.

Six. Son of a bitch.

Seven. Shit.

Eight. *Shit!*

Stryke deserved Eidolon's cold shoulder. But fuck that. This was about Cyan. He'd hunt his uncle down and do this in person. He didn't care if the guy was in his office, in surgery, or in the fucking shower. All that mattered was Cyan.

Just as he was about to disconnect, Eidolon appeared a few feet away in his office, life-sized and wearing scrubs. A surgical cap hid his dark hair, and a mask hung off his chin. He looked annoyed.

"Stryke," Eidolon said, using his detached-doctor voice instead of his slightly less stern uncle voice. "This'd better be important."

Apologize.

He knew he needed to do it. He just…wasn't very good at admitting he was in the wrong. Because he wasn't wrong often.

He opened his mouth, but the words wouldn't come. Eidolon didn't make it any easier, just stood there waiting, his dark gaze drilling into him.

"It's about Cyan," Stryke said. "How long before…?"

Most of the ice in the doctor's eyes melted away. He knew what Stryke was asking.

"It seems to depend on the species." Eidolon tugged down his mask. "But generally, by the end of the first trimester."

"Do you know why? Most miscarriages are the result of fetal abnormalities, but how does that play into the destruction of Sheoul-gra?"

"I've run extensive tests for years and never got an answer," Eidolon said. "So, I consulted with Azagoth." He whipped the cap off his head, leaving his hair flat and plastered to his scalp. "He believes the reason for the miscarriages is the absence of a soul."

Whoa. Okay, interesting.

"Apparently," Eidolon continued, "unlike human fetuses, which aren't given souls until shortly before birth and it's certain the baby will be born alive, demon fetuses are ensouled by the end of the first trimester. It helps them absorb more evil and be born with ruthless survival instincts."

So unborn demons were evil sponges?

He must have spoken out loud because Eidolon nodded. "But how much they absorb is location dependent. The more evil they're exposed to *in utero*, the more evil they'll be. It explains why some species of demons seek out the worst parts of Sheoul to spend their pregnancies. It's also why demons born in the human realm are generally less malevolent than their Sheoul-dwelling brethren."

Stryke loved that his uncle was a living, breathing, vault of knowledge.

"Obviously, you've talked to Cyan," Eidolon said. "How is she?"

She was currently on her way to Stryke's office. The security system was tracking her and notifying him of updates.

"She's as confused as I am," Stryke told his uncle. "But we do know who the father is."

One curious eyebrow climbed up Eidolon's forehead. "Who?"

"I am. Apparently, I'm fertile." Not that it mattered. The baby wouldn't be born. Without a soul, it wasn't even a baby.

But the heaviness in his heart didn't care about the facts and logic. Which might be the first time ever.

The familiar lure of a mystery lit Eidolon's eyes. His dedication to science and knowledge had made Eidolon one of his idols growing up, and Stryke felt another twinge of guilt and sorrow at having let his uncle down by stealing from him.

"Have you determined how that's possible?" Eidolon asked.

He nodded. He and Cyan had spent hours working with theories, finally coming up with an answer.

An answer he really didn't want to share with Eidolon.

"It's the sexual suppressant my company developed," he said, shifting his gaze to a window to avoid a told-you-so look from his uncle. "You used pre-*s'genesis* Sems to create yours. I used post-*s'genesis* males, figuring their fertility would make my formula stronger. It did, but I believe it also made me fertile." He held up his hand, staving off Eidolon's next question. "Yes, I pulled it off the market."

"Does this mean you won't be using it anymore?"

Stryke nodded as the elevator doors opened and Cyan entered, looking exhausted but beautiful in worn jeans, tennis shoes, and a loose purple-and-white-polka-dot blouse. He couldn't help but picture her in a maternity top, but the image faded away as reality intruded.

"Hi, Eidolon," she said.

"How are you doing, Cyan?" Eidolon asked in a totally different voice than he'd been using with Stryke. Gone was the disappointed uncle, and in his place was a caring, soothing doctor. "Stryke told me you got your answers."

She shrugged, but Stryke knew she wasn't as nonchalant about it as she appeared. "Not that it matters."

A wave of possessiveness washed over him. Possessiveness and determination. This shouldn't be happening to either of them. The laws of nature, physics, and the entire universe be damned. Surely, there was *something* StryTech could do. Or maybe he knew someone who could help. He had a lot of powerful friends and family members. He had contacts who were Princes of Heaven and Hell. He also had blackmail material on pretty much everyone.

"Why don't you make an appointment with me for next week?" Eidolon said. "We'll help you through this, okay?"

Cyan's eyes grew misty, and she nodded. A moment later, Eidolon disconnected.

"Hey." Stryke went to Cyan and pulled her into his arms. He wasn't used to hugging or giving comfort, and even as he held her, his brain was in overdrive, searching for ways to fix this.

Maybe he could somehow help Hades get the new Sheoul-gra up and running. If Hades could start recycling souls again, maybe—

"Excuse me, Mr. Stryke." Kalis's voice filled the room. "There's an angel named Gabriel here to see you. He says it's important."

Gabriel? Here?

Instant alarm shot through him. What if this was about the Gehennaportal? Or the dead angel. Stryke didn't want Cyan anywhere near those conversations. Gabriel could be trying to cover his tracks, which could put her in danger.

On the other hand...Gabriel was a top-tier angel. Perhaps he could help Cyan somehow.

So, basically, either the timing was great, or really, really bad.

Gabriel was *in the building?*

No. No, this couldn't be. Did he know Cyan had told Stryke the truth about the Gehennaportal? Was he here to punish her or kill Stryke?

"I need you to go to my place," he said, snagging her hand and practically dragging her toward the Harrowgate at the rear of his office.

"Excuse me?" She planted her feet and refused to budge. "I'm not going anywhere. If this is about the Gehennaportal, I need to be here too."

"This is non-negotiable—"

Suddenly, the elevator doors slid open, and Gabriel, along with two other angels, filed inside. Gabriel, dressed in what appeared to be a burlap sack, stared daggers at the others, who swept to the center of the room, gem-encrusted blades in their hands.

Stryke released her, only to casually step in front of her, shielding her from the newcomers. "How did you get in here? I didn't give Kalis permission. Security should have stopped you."

"They tried," the dark-haired guy said, his dove-gray wings flaring, his voice a perfect imitation of Kalis's. A tremor of terror crawled up her spine at the realization of what that meant. This angel had announced Gabriel, not Stryke's assistant. "They were all such nice people."

"*Were?*" Stryke's lips peeled back from his teeth in a feral snarl. "What did you do?"

Gabriel hung his head, but his eyes, shifting back and forth between the others, sparked with pure defiance. "Thrones have no honor."

The other angel, his golden mane flowing hypnotically over his shoulders, stepped forward. "We need information."

"You can go fu—" Stryke choked, clawing at his throat as an invisible force threw him across the room. He slammed into a bookcase and landed in a heap on the floor.

"No!" Cyan rushed toward him, but Dove Gray caught her by the arm.

"Tell us what happened on the oil platform and what happened to Hutriel," he snapped, shaking her so hard her teeth rattled. "Tell us now."

"I don't know anything," she yelled, struggling to free herself from his iron grasp. She opened herself up to her gift, prepared to weave a defensive spell into the nearest tech.

But there was nothing there. Not even a spark of magical energy.

"What are you doing to me?" she screamed, struggling even harder, but she might as well have been trying to fight a statue.

"My touch negates a demon's power," he said calmly and then backhanded her so hard she saw spots.

A furious roar vibrated the room. "*Release her!*" Stryke stormed toward them, his *dermoire* glowing, his eyes crimson pools of rage.

Golden Mane intercepted, throwing up a translucent shield. "What if I told you I have something you want."

Stryke slammed his fist into the shield, the impact making it vibrate. "What I want is for you to die."

As if Stryke's fury was no more bothersome than a gnat, the bastard calmly held up his hand, a little ball of light bouncing at his fingertips. "Do you know what this is, demon?"

Stryke sneered. "A Heavenly lantern? An angelic anal bead? I have no idea."

Dove Gray snorted and jerked Cyan roughly. "There will never be a time when I won't hate demons."

Yeah, well, she was rapidly learning that angels were no saints either.

Golden Mane tossed the orb into the air and caught it again. "This," he said, holding the ball of light up to study it, "is a soul. Beautiful, isn't it?"

The crimson rage in Stryke's eyes faded, and Cyan wondered if she looked as confused as Stryke did. "What's your point?"

"You," Golden Mane said, "are a much-debated topic in my realm.

How much power and influence should you be allowed to have? What should we do if the weapons you create to kill demons are used against humans? And there are entire tomes written about how your past shaped you. It's fascinating. Really. No sarcasm intended. I wrote one of those tomes. That's why the Thrones sent me. I'm kind of an expert."

"Maybe you could sign a copy for me," Stryke said. "Before I cause you a whole lot of pain."

Golden Mane laughed and looked over at her captor. "He's cute, isn't he? I told you he'd come up with an empty threat."

Cyan held in a snort. This douche thought he was an expert on Stryke? Moron.

Stryke didn't make empty threats.

The douche turned back to Stryke. "A long time ago, you got your baby brother killed," he said, and Stryke's face paled. "You must have wondered where his soul went, given that he was born during this unprecedented and glorious period of no demon births. Was his soul demonic? Human? Otherworldly?"

Oh…oh, gods. Cyan stared at the luminous orb with growing horror, her knees quaking.

Chaos. That orb was…Chaos.

Golden Mane rolled the orb across the back of his hand, weaving it in and out of his fingers. "Tell us how Hutriel died."

"I don't know." Stryke stared at the glowing ball, sweat beading on his brow. "I wasn't there."

"What *do* you know?" Golden Mane released the shield, clearly no longer concerned about a physical attack. "Very few beings have the power to destroy souls," he mused, holding up the orb again. "Do you think I'm one of them?"

"If you do anything to that soul," Stryke said, his voice warping with rage, "I promise I will find a way to destroy *you*."

"I believe you'll try."

"If you've done your research," Stryke said in a voice as cold as a grave, "you'll know I'll succeed."

Golden Mane didn't appear too concerned. "I don't have to destroy it. I can do other things to it." A flame appeared on the tip of his finger. Smiling, he held the flame to the orb.

Stryke screamed, a soul-deep, bloodcurdling sound that tore Cyan's heart to shreds. He lunged at Golden Mane, but Dove Gray released her and flashed behind Stryke. In a hard, fast motion, he slammed Stryke to his knees.

"Stop!" she shouted, rushing toward him.

Gabriel appeared in her path, blocking her. "Don't," he warned her. "They *will* kill you."

Golden Mane doused his finger, his smile grim as Stryke struggled against his captor's hold.

"Tell me how Hutriel died," he repeated.

"Chaos," Stryke rasped, his gaze glued to the glowing orb. "Please, don't. Don't hurt him again. I swear I don't know anything."

Golden Mane eyed him with skepticism. "What of the Gehennaportal?"

Oh, shit. Cyan's heart leaped into her throat, clogging it so badly she could barely breathe. What was the right answer for these guys? What had Gabriel told them?

They were going to die today, weren't they?

Stryke's expression was impassive now, completely stone-faced. "What of it?"

Dove Gray cuffed him in the ear. "Was it destroyed?"

Stryke's split second of hesitation cost him. Cost Chaos. Golden Mane put the orb to the flame again.

Stryke screamed in agony. "Stop! The portal is—"

Suddenly, Gabriel crashed into Golden Mane. Taking advantage of the moment of confusion, Cyan swept a stapler off Stryke's desk and hurled it at Dove Gray's head just as Stryke power-jabbed his elbow into the angel's groin.

Cyan didn't see anything else. Everything spun as she was catapulted backward, tackled to the ground by—

Gabriel?

"Listen to me," Gabriel hissed into her ear.

He spoke so quickly it seemed impossible, but she heard it all, and she dropped to her knees in shock.

"Countermeasure," Stryke shouted distantly. "A-Four, New-F!"

Fog spewed from vents in the ceiling and floor, boiling and writhing, and Cyan's shock turned to horror. She knew that fog.

A malevolent heaviness filled the room, and the angels began to wheeze. They moved as if suspended in gelatin as the weight of pure evil bore down on them from all sides.

"Countermeasure," Stryke shouted again. "A-Two!"

A glowing red ball appeared in the center of the room. Golden Mane's eyes shot wide. He tried to reach it, but he moved in slow motion, his white wings dragging like sodden towels on the floor.

Too late. The ball burst, and a concussive wave hit all the angels on a level Cyan couldn't feel but that slammed them into the air, their bodies vibrating and contorting. And then they disappeared. Just... winked away.

"Cyan!" Stryke rushed over to where she sat against the wall, dazed, one hand draped across her belly.

"Cyan—"

"I'm okay," she assured him. "I just need...to catch my...breath." She sat up straighter as he went down on his haunches in front of her. "Using the evil fog was brilliant."

"I got the idea while we were on the *Sea Storm*." Closing his haunted eyes, he rested his forearms on his legs and bowed his head. "If that bastard hurts Chaos—"

"He can't." She reached out and gripped his wrist. "Gabriel made sure of that."

His head whipped up. "What?"

Gabriel's words rang like musical notes in her ears. She couldn't explain it, but when he'd spoken to her, she'd experienced a strange kind of peace, as if his voice had struck a frequency that tapped into infinite joy. And what he'd told her...it changed everything.

"He protected me. He protected all of us," she said. "When he attacked that golden-haired bastard, he took Chaos's orb."

"So, he has it? Then why did he attack you?"

"He didn't attack me," she said. "He knew I was pregnant and needed me clear of the fight." She tapped her belly, her eyes stinging at the momentousness of what was just now sinking in. "He gave me Chaos's soul. It's in me. It's in the baby. He's safe, Stryke. Chaos is okay."

"He's safe," Stryke breathed. "I can't..." He fell back on his ass, staring at her in stunned disbelief. She quickly crawled over to him.

"Listen to me, Stryke. Gabriel also said that Chaos's death wasn't your fault. Something about Primori. I didn't understand that part. But he made it clear that Chaos was fated to die that day. There was nothing you could have done to stop it. Nothing."

He still just stared, blinking, his brain processing. Gently, she reached up and tipped his face to hers.

"Did you hear me? It wasn't your fault."

"I can't believe it," he whispered, his eyes filling with tears.

His big body shuddered, and she wrapped herself around him, letting him release almost twenty years of trauma.

She held him so tightly she felt every breath, sob, and beat of his heart. Finally, he pulled back from her, his eyes bloodshot but the smile on his face lighting the room.

"I still can't believe it."

She looked down at her belly, reveling in a moment of joy after so much tragedy. "Chaos is getting a second chance."

"So am I, Cyan," Stryke rasped. "So am I."

Chapter 32

Gabriel was in a lot of trouble.

Oh, he'd gotten out of the mess at StryTech thanks to Stryke's anti-angel weapon that had exploded Matrius and Darniel's organs and given them a touch of amnesia. Gabriel had only been spared the worst effects because he'd been able to summon his golden armor at the last millisecond. And because he'd been largely unaffected, he'd told the Angelic Council a story that made him a hero. He'd actually *saved* Matrius and Darniel from their own clusterfuck.

Sure, some doubted his story, but it was all they had. So, no, his trouble didn't stem from that.

It came from a total sham of a trial, which Gabriel realized from the moment the Ordeal began in the Great Colosseum of Justice.

Most of the evidence against Gabriel was circumstantial at best, witch-trial-ridiculous at worst. One jackass, a Virtue named Furiel, claimed he had evidence that Gabriel helped Azagoth destroy Sheoul-gra. The *evidence* was that he'd once overheard Gabriel tell Reaver that Azagoth was right. Right about *what*, he couldn't say. But it was enough that Gabriel agreed with Azagoth on anything, apparently. It was also convenient that Reaver was comatose and couldn't dispute the account.

Joreem, a longtime friend of Gabriel's, stood next to him in the center of the judicial process arena as they awaited the verdict, his curly black hair shining in the sunlight.

"It's going to be a slap on the wrist," Joreem murmured.

Gabriel noticed Joreem didn't say, "*They'll find you innocent.*"

"So, you believe I'm guilty?"

Joreem looked at him like he was an idiot. "Come on. You know you are. What I don't know is why." He held up his hand. "It's okay, you don't have to tell me."

Yeah, well, Gabriel hadn't planned on it. Because sure, he'd helped Azagoth, but he hadn't known the extent of the Grim Reaper's plans. Gabriel thought the guy just wanted to break out of his prison.

But he definitely hadn't known he would destroy the prison and release billions of souls back into the realms. It would have been the equivalent of Reaver destroying the human part of Heaven, sending all of them all back into their previous bodies and providing no place for the souls of the departed to go. Human spirits would drift aimlessly on the spirit plane, unable to find peace or be reborn into new bodies. No babies would be born, and chaos would reign.

"What kind of slap on the wrist do you think I'll get?" he asked.

Joreem shrugged. "A century of soul-sorting, maybe? Or service in the Akashic Library. If they're really mad at you, you'll get stuck with counseling newly arrived souls."

"So...torture. Mind-numbing, monotonous torture." He shook his head. "Nah. I think they're going to throw me down into the pits with my brethren."

"They can't keep all the Archangels locked down for much longer," Joreem said in a low voice, even though no one was near them. The arena seats were packed, though. Gabriel had drawn quite the crowd. "People are starting to notice their absence."

Suddenly, the buzz in the colosseum hushed, and thirty-six red-robed justices, the Angelic High Court, filed in, taking their places standing on a crystal lens that rose into the air. It hovered above the arena so they looked down upon Gabriel.

Next to them, but separated by a few feet, Metatron stood in regal blue robes, his head bowed, his hands bound by a Ligorial.

The First Justice, Tsadkiel, stepped forward. "Gabriel, Celestial of the Archangel Order. We have reached our verdict." He paused, and in the heavy silence, Gabriel could hear his pulse in his ears. "We do find that you aided in the destruction of Sheoul-gra. We do pronounce you guilty of treason."

Treason?

The crowd exploded all around him. Some cheers, some boos, and a lot of shocked gasps.

Joreem shot him a stunned look, surely matching Gabriel's. Treason was a strong word, associated with only the most heinous of Heavenly crimes.

"Gabriel, have you anything to say?"

Oh, yeah, he had a lot to say. But Joreem jabbed him in the side, cautioning him against telling these bastards what he really thought.

"Just that you're wrong," he said in a powerful voice that resonated through the justice facility. "I believed in Azagoth's mission to help maintain a balance of good and evil souls between the human and demon realms. And I shared his opinion that he hadn't been treated fairly by Heaven. But I did not knowingly assist him in destroying Sheoul-gra."

"Noted." Tsadkiel inhaled deeply and addressed the crowd. "Gabriel has served Heaven as one of the Creator's most treasured, most trusted sons. His accomplishments over the millennia take up endless rows of tomes in the Akashic Library. He is a beloved, prominent figure in human lore and tales. We must carefully consider punishment, balancing his worth with his actions."

"Don't worry," Joreem whispered under his breath. "They can't do much to you."

No, they couldn't. Heck, this humiliation was far worse than whatever punishment they would come up with.

"So," Tsadkiel continued, "for the grave offense of treason against Heaven, we sentence you, Gabriel of the Archangel Order, to expulsion."

Expulsion?!

"No!" he yelled. "No, this is—"

Armed guards surrounded him, shoving Joreem away and grabbing Gabriel by all four limbs.

"Your wings will be torn from your body," he said as Gabriel struggled against the guards, "and you will be hurled into the human realm, where you will live as a pathetic Unfallen angel with few powers and little hope of redemption."

"No!" he screamed as they dragged him toward the platform where his wings would be torn—not even sliced!—from his shoulders.

"Or," the guy continued, "enter Sheoul and become an irredeemable True Fallen and turn your back on Heaven forever. So it shall be."

"So it shall be," all the justices intoned, their command falling with the finality of a guillotine blade in the silent colosseum.

Agony like Gabriel had never known ripped through him, shredding his body, his muscles, his very soul. Blades dug deep into his back as his attackers sought his wing anchors. He felt their fingers clawing, felt the blood streaming down his back and flank.

He screamed, gurgling blood as his bones snapped, his wings twisted and wrenched by powerful hands. They held his arms and legs so he was spread-eagle and then pulled as if he were to be drawn and quartered. He screamed into the ground as his right wing separated from his body. Then his left.

And then there was nothing but darkness.

Chapter 33

Stryke had survived a lot of hazardous situations in his life. And while he was confident he'd survive this one, there was still a risk of bloodshed.

He stood in the kitchen that used to be empty and sad when he lived here. Now, the compound on the outskirts of Sydney, where he'd first developed StryTech, belonged to his brothers, and they'd filled the living quarters with life.

And food. They had a lot of food in this place. At least one of them bought pints of cookie dough ice cream by the case.

"They're all inside," Cyan said, peeking in from the living room. She looked amazing in strappy red sandals and a red-and-green sundress. Perfect for a Christmas Eve get-together. The first family event he'd been to in years.

"Even Blade?"

"Even Blade. And I put Masumi's vase on the bookshelf. You ready?"

No. But his family had waited too long for this as it was. "Yeah."

"Are you going to tell them about…?"

"Chaos?" He blew out a breath. He'd waffled on that decision for three days in every spare minute he had while dealing with the memorial services for Kalis and the other angels' victims. He hoped those bastards were dead. Except Gabriel. He owed that angel everything. "I think it's best if we tell everyone later. My parents and brothers should hear it first." Maybe tomorrow, where he was having them to his cabin for the very first time. Blade was a wildcard, but he always was.

She smiled. "I agree."

He gave her a kiss, and they both walked down the short hallway to the living room, which was packed with his entire extended family. His parents, brothers, uncles, aunts, cousins…yep, they were all staring at him expectantly.

Except Blade. He sat in a chair, legs spread, looking between them at the floor.

"Thanks for coming inside," Stryke said. "I won't keep you from the barbecue and kegs for long."

"Don't worry." His dad waved his hand in dismissal. "The Horsemen will keep the grills going."

Stryke glanced out the back doors at the Horsemen and their families making use of the manicured lawns, tennis court, and pool. Scotty cannon-balled into the deep end, and he was surprised she wasn't in here with Mace and Blade, even though she wasn't technically family. Generally, where they went, she went.

Inhaling deeply to quell his nerves, he addressed his family.

"I just wanted to say that I owe you all an apology. I've been a terrible brother," he said, looking at each in turn. Blade met his gaze, but he was impossible to read. Then he looked at his parents. "I haven't been a good son, either." They both shook their heads, but he didn't give them time to protest. "I've also been an awful friend." This time, he looked directly at Eidolon. "I've been arrogant and selfish. I hurt the people I love and justified it in the name of protecting the world. I took risks with my life that were irresponsible and stupid." He closed his eyes, drawing in a cleansing breath. He'd been afraid to bare his soul like this, to admit to so much wrongdoing, but there was something freeing about being honest with himself. "I removed myself from your lives and said I was protecting you from me. From the pain my presence would cause. But it was a lie. I know that now. I wasn't protecting you. I was protecting myself."

He looked over at Cyan, who gave him an encouraging smile. Gods, he was thankful she was in his life. He was happier than he'd ever been, and none of it would be possible without her. Now, he had to make sure she never got away from him.

He had a plan for that.

Blade took a swig of the beer in his hand. "You still think you're smarter than everyone else."

"I am," he said, throwing in some snark because Blade had a way of getting under his skin. "But only in some ways."

Most ways. But Cyan had told him he didn't have to voice every single thought.

"Blade, you're a tactical expert," he pointed out. "I can't do what you do." Nor did he want to. "Rade, you know more about the mind than I ever could. In fact, I'm working on a couple of projects that could use your input." He tucked his hands into his jeans pockets. "What I'm trying to say is that I'm sorry."

"You're sorry?" Blade shoved to his feet. "You left us when we needed you the most! You cut us out of your life, Stryke. You severed our fucking *blood* ties."

"Stop it, Blade!" Crux leaped up from the couch, spilling his bowl of potato chips on the floor. "It's okay now. He's apologizing. Everything's okay."

Shit. Stryke hated seeing his little brother so upset and desperate for everyone to heal. The kid just wanted his family to be whole and happy.

"Crux, no, it's not okay," he said gently. "Blade's right. And you were right the other day when you accused me of not being there. I haven't been. It's going to take some time to rebuild trust. With all of you. That's why I'm going to restore our mental connection." He glanced at Rade and Blade. "If it's all right with you."

Blade cursed. "I'm done with this. You guys do what you want." He headed for the party, slamming the door behind him.

"Dammit," Shade muttered as he watched Blade storm toward the pool bar. "I'm sorry, Stryke."

"Me too," his mom said as she engulfed him in a hug.

"It's fine." Stryke welcomed his mom's comforting embrace, something he hadn't realized he'd missed until the night of her birthday party. "I knew this wouldn't be easy."

Rade moved over to him, and Stryke braced himself for anything from a blow to a chewing out, so he was surprised when he said simply, "I want the connection."

"Me too." Crux hurled himself at Stryke and their mom so he could hug them both. "Does this mean we'll see you more now?"

"Yeah. A lot more." Blade would be *thrilled*.

He pulled away from the group hug and picked up Masumi's vase. Its weight was heavy and comforting. He was going to miss her. She'd saved his life more than once, and he was one of the few people he trusted.

"You're sure you want to do this?" Cyan asked, and he nodded.

They'd discussed it last night, and he'd been surprised when Cyan had summoned Masumi to be part of the conversation.

"Masumi, how would you feel about having your bond transferred to one of Stryke's brothers or cousins?"

Masumi, who had emerged from her container dressed like a sexy Santa's elf, seemed confused. *"Why would you ask about my feelings in the matter?"*

"Because you aren't an object to be passed around," Cyan said. *"You are a person, and you should have a say in your future."*

"That is very kind." Masumi shifted, making the little bells on her outfit jingle. *"But I would think you would want me gone."*

"Oh, I do." Cyan sat next to Stryke on the couch and placed a possessive hand on his thigh. *"I'm grateful for all you've done for Stryke over the years, but he's mine now, and it turns out that I'm more territorial than I thought. But like I said, you're a person, not an object, and you deserve a voice."*

Masumi smiled over at Stryke. *"I like her so much. Don't fuck this up."*

"I won't," he swore. No way. He would always cherish this incredible female.

"Good. Then I approve of my bond going to one of your brothers or cousins." Now, if there's nothing else, I must return to Mace's party."

"Wait." Stryke stopped her before she could dematerialize. *"Any preference?"*

"I love them all. Let them decide."

So, in accordance with Masumi's wishes, Stryke held her vase out to Rade. "This is for you and the guys. You'll need to decide who I can transfer her bond to."

Rade gave a slow nod and carefully took the vase. They didn't need two in the compound, but an extra gave Masumi security. If one was destroyed or stolen, she still had another, and given that her species would die within an hour of losing their home, an extra was basically an insurance policy.

He would be curious to know who they chose. Crux was too young. Mace was too…Mace. Blade would take excellent care of her, but so would Sabre. Rade took responsibility seriously, but he was intensely private and didn't like being poked or prodded, something on which Masumi thrived.

Stryke would put his money on Sabre. The guy was a rock, like his dad.

Rade headed upstairs to put the vase away, and everyone took that as a sign to head back out to the party. His cousins, Talon, Sabre, and Mace fist-bumped him on the way out, and his aunts, Tayla, Idess, and Serena gave him hugs. His uncle Wraith clapped him on the shoulder and told him he was proud of him, and for some reason, that made

Stryke smile.

His uncle Lore invited him to see UG's new Medical Examiner office. As a kid, Stryke had loved assisting Lore during autopsies, so it would be cool to check out the new setup and equipment.

The room was nearly empty now, save Cyan, Eidolon, and Stryke's parents. Eidolon came up and offered his hand. "That took a lot of class."

Stryke accepted the handshake. "I'm sorry, Eidolon. I took advantage of our relationship, and it was shitty of me. I don't expect you to forgive me—"

"You're forgiven," he said. "But if you really want to make it up, we could use a sizable donation for the new facility in Johannesburg."

"Exploiting my guilt?" Stryke said approvingly. "I like it. I'll make it happen. But only if you name it after me."

Eidolon laughed. "You got it." He eyed Stryke critically, his demeanor sobering. "How are you doing?"

Stryke knew what he was asking, and he was grateful for his uncle's concern. "I'm good," he said, glancing over at Cyan. "I'm finally... good."

"I'm glad." Eidolon gave him a fond pat on the back and went outside to join his mate.

"That couldn't have been easy," his mom said, looking after Eidolon. "None of this could have been easy."

"No," he admitted, "but it was necessary."

His dad nodded. "This was a big step in the right direction."

"Tomorrow will be an even bigger one." And he was as anxious about it as he'd been about today. "It'll be our first Christmas together in more than ten years."

"I just hope Blade will be there," Runa said. "You'll be there too, right, Cyan?"

Cyan nodded, and he could see how hard she was trying not to look absolutely radiant and excited. His parents still thought her pregnancy was a huge tragedy, and neither he nor Cyan could wait to share the recent developments.

They spent a few more minutes talking to his parents, and then, finally, he was left alone in the living room with Cyan.

Taking his hand, she faced him. "How are you feeling?"

He reached up and scratched his neck. "Light."

"Light?"

"Yeah. Like there's nothing weighing me down." He paused, trying to pinpoint what, exactly, was different. When it came to him, he sucked in a surprised breath. "My mind," he whispered. "It's quiet."

"What do you mean, it's quiet? Like, it's not running at a million calculations per second anymore?"

He shook his head. "No, it still is, but it doesn't feel frantic. It's like how I felt before Chaos died." He scratched his neck again. Felt like something was crawling across his personal symbol.

"Oh, my gods." Cyan grabbed his hand and pulled it away from his throat. "Holy shit. Your symbol." She tugged him toward the mirror on the far wall. "Look."

Tilting his head, he checked out the lame square he'd gotten after his transition.

Except...

It had changed.

Cyan threw a screen up into the air from her wrist comms. A symbol hung there, a knotted square nearly identical to the one he now sported on his neck.

"It's called a Mpatapo," she said, reading from a text box beneath the glyph. "A symbol of peace after conflict."

Astonishment left his voice shaky as he read the rest of the description. "It also represents reconciliation and forgiveness."

He turned back to the mirror, marveling at the fluid lines. As a general rule, he didn't do well with change. He'd gotten used to his stupid square, telling himself it meant stability, even though it wasn't really true.

But now, he understood.

The square had merely been a frame. It had been empty because *he* had been empty. It hadn't been complete, because *he* hadn't been complete.

He glanced out at his family in the backyard and then looked at Cyan, his heart filling with warmth. No, he was definitely no longer empty.

Chapter 34

Standing in the middle of Stryke's cabin's living room, Cyan wrapped her arm around Stryke as his parents and brothers filed out the doorway onto his deck.

"I think that went well," she said once the door had closed. "Except for Blade."

He watched as they entered the Harrowgate and disappeared behind its shimmery doorway. "Actually, Blade handled it better than I thought he would. He only insulted me a couple of times."

"I was talking about him leaving."

Stryke nodded. "I think hearing that you're carrying Chaos's soul inside you overwhelmed him."

It had overwhelmed everyone. Tears everywhere. Happy tears, certainly, but man, a whole lot of emotion had spilled at the breakfast table.

He turned into her. "I don't know how long it'll take to mend fences with Blade, or if it's even possible. I just hope my relationship with him doesn't affect yours."

"I rarely see him at DART anyway. He works in a different department, and he's always out in the field."

"What if you didn't work at DART?"

She narrowed her eyes at him. "Do you know something I don't?"

"No, and this would totally be up to you, but I'm going to need someone to head the magical science division on the Moon project. I want the best, and the best is you."

"Wow." She pulled away from him to fetch her mug of hot cocoa. "That's an incredible offer. Can I think about it?"

"Sure," he said. "But you should know that I'm willing to pay anything, and I always get what I want."

She smiled at him from over the rim of her mug. "Your mom said you were always relentless."

"When did she say that?"

"While you were showing your dad and brothers the lab." Cyan took a sip of her cocoa, leaving her with a whipped cream mustache. "She wanted to let me know what to expect with the baby. She's really excited."

"So am I. And it's not only about Chaos. It's about being a father."

Taking a seat on the couch, she patted the cushion next to her. "Tell me about Chaos. We've never really talked much about him."

Stryke smiled, and it occurred to him that talking about Chaos no longer brought soul-crushing pain. Yes, he would forever mourn the boy who had died too soon, but he would always be grateful for the chance to love him again.

"He was a lot like Mace," he said, sinking down next to her. "The kid was always looking for trouble and dragging Crux along with him. It was funny because poor Crux was the exact opposite. He was the voice of reason and the one who would take the blame for the trouble Chaos caused."

"Sounds like he was a handful."

"That's definitely the word most associated with Chaos," he said. "If he loved something, he was obsessed about it. If he hated something, he let you know. And he definitely had plans for the future."

"Really? What kinds of plans?"

"He planned to either rule the world or serve with Revenant in Sheoul. He wanted to get mated at exactly ninety-three years old, name his first kid Chasm, and swore he'd be the first openly demon person to scale Mt. Everest."

"Wow. He had ambition." She laughed. "Serve with Revenant?"

"Yeah. He thought that if he cozied up to the King of Hell, he'd have street cred with his friends."

She laughed again. "That's adorable." She looked down at her belly and placed her hand over it. "You know, we haven't talked about what we should name the baby. It's not like we have to decide soon, but there's an elephant in the womb."

His heart stuttered for a second. "You want to know if I think we should name the baby after him."

She nodded.

Would naming a child after themselves be weird? More importantly, would it be right? This baby might be born with Chaos's soul, but he'd be his own person. He probably wouldn't even remember his past life.

"No," he said. "I'd like to find a better way to honor him."

"Well," she said, "what about Chasm? He obviously loved the name, and he never got a chance to use it."

He drew in a quick breath. "Chasm is perfect."

He waited for the sense of guilt to overtake him, but instead, there was only acceptance. He thought of the words Gabriel had said once during a training session in Ares' combat arena.

"Guilt is an emotion designed to teach you a lesson. Not destroy you. Guilt will make you suffer, as intended, but once you learn your lesson, make amends, forgive yourself, and become a better person. Live a good life and never forget what it taught you."

At the time, Stryke had been bored, his mind working on other things instead of listening to Heavenly propaganda. But even though Stryke had been one of seven students, it had seemed to him, even then, that Gabriel had been speaking directly to him.

And he had, hadn't he?

Gabriel had known what was going to happen to Chaos.

The realization blew his mind, and yet, it made so much sense. So much of his life was starting to make sense, and it had all happened because of Cyan.

Do it. Do it now.

He couldn't think of a better moment. Reaching into his pocket, he drew out the little velvet pouch he'd been carrying around all morning.

He shifted, turning to her, his pulse pounding with excitement. And maybe a little terror. What if she said no?

"I love you, Cyan," he blurted. "I want you to mate me. I'll give you anything you want."

She seemed amused, which was better than some of the alternatives. "Is this a business transaction?"

"It is if you want it to be. That's how much I want you. If you need contracts and lawyers, I'm okay with that. But I don't. I just want us to be a family." He emptied the pouch into his palm. "Before you, I thought I had everything. Now, I realize that I had nothing worthwhile. I had possessions, but with you, I have a life." He held up the diamond ring he'd had enhanced to amplify Cyan's abilities. Even if she refused to mate him, he wanted her to have it, anything to keep her safe. "Cyan, you've given me a reason to live that isn't about guilt and hate. Before you, everything was about me. I was trying to save the planet for *me*. Not for humans and the handful of good demons. It was all about me trying to assuage my guilt while fueling my self-loathing. I treated people like shit because I felt like I deserved their hatred. But you made me a better person. I like who I am with you."

Her gorgeous eyes misted over as she held out her hand so he could slip the ring on her finger. "And I like who I am with you. Let's do the mate thing." She paused as she studied the ring. "Wait. What does it involve? Pain? Human sacrifice? Animal sacrifice? I am *not* killing a goat."

"But you'd be okay killing a human?"

She shrugged. "Depends on the human. There's a lot of scum out there."

"I love your ruthlessness," he said with a growl. "But nothing so dramatic. There's just a little blood and a lot of sex. And then an unbreakable bond that will bind us together for life so we can't make love with anyone else ever. So, yeah. Nothing dramatic."

Her laughter filled his heart. "Let's do it. I love you, Stryke."

And he, her.

Cyan stepped inside her Brussels apartment for the last time.

The movers had packed and stored everything except the clothes and things she wanted at Stryke's cabin. Now, the place was empty, just waiting for her to make one more pass-through.

The cleaners had done a great job too. The flat looked better than it had when she moved in with Shanea.

She walked around, smiling at all the memories. The parties, the dinners, the quiet movie nights when she and Shan would make popcorn and watch a sappy romantic drama or a silly romcom.

The little bag containing the gift from Shanea dangled from Cyan's fingers as she moved from room to room. She still hadn't been able to open it, so she'd brought it with her, figuring this would be the perfect place to finally face that one last hurdle that kept her from fully healing. The bag had sat on the bathroom counter at Stryke's place for weeks, pretty much just torturing her every time she saw it. It had been Stryke who finally shoved it into her hand and told her to stop punishing herself. And as an expert on punishing oneself, he'd insisted.

After she'd inspected every nook and cranny, she stopped in the living room and closed her eyes. She couldn't put this off any longer.

Open it.

Stomach churning, she reached into the bag and pulled out a tiny white box with a violet ribbon. Very carefully, her fingers trembling, she opened the gift.

Inside, lying on a bed of white satin, was a bracelet, its intricate silver links made to resemble flowing water. It was beautiful, but what caught her eye, and her breath, was the purple charm dangling from a tiny loop.

"Oh, Shan," she whispered.

The bracelet, a new tech device that could connect with NeuroTech implants, was outrageously expensive. Shanea could have paid for her honeymoon with what the bracelet had probably cost.

Hands still shaking, the big rock on her ring finger glittering in the light, she slipped the jewelry onto her wrist, where it sparkled against the *dermoire* that had appeared after she and Stryke completed the mating ceremony. A perfect replica of Stryke's, from her fingers to her throat, it was a constant, comforting reminder that he was hers.

Reassured by the faint awareness of her mate, she pinched the bracelet's charm between her fingers.

Instantly, she found herself at the birthday party Shan had thrown for Cyan right in this apartment. Their friends were mingling, and Shan was cutting cake. The scene changed, but they were still in their apartment. They were making spaghetti in the kitchen, and Shan had spilled the sauce all over herself and the floor. Cyan slipped, and they'd both sat in the mess, laughing until they were sick.

The scene changed again and again, taking her to two dozen of her best memories with Shan, from karaoke night at the local pub, to surfing in Hawaii.

The last one, though...it wasn't a memory. It was a message.

Shanea stood before her in her wedding dress, but Cyan could barely see her through the tears.

"Hey, girl. Imma make this quick because you just went to get the fitting lady and you'll be right back. I just wanted to tell you how much I love you and that there's no one else in the world I'd want to be my maid of honor." She looked down and then back up, and her eyes were misty. "I know you're going to miss me when I'm gone, but don't worry, you're always welcome at my new place. Draven doesn't even care that

I'm calling the spare bedroom your room." She smiled. "I worry about you being by yourself, though. I know how you get, and I don't want you to wallow in your lab. There's more to life than work. Get out there and live, Cy. Be happy, okay?" She looked toward the door and hastily reached for the recording device. But before she shut it off, she whispered, "Love you!"

The feed shut down, and Cyan was standing in the empty apartment again, all alone, sobbing.

Suddenly, the door blew open, and Stryke stormed in, the tendons in his neck standing out starkly beneath the new tribal-patterned mate band encircling his throat. "Cyan! What's wrong?"

She dashed away tears and scrambled in her purse for a tissue. "Nothing, I'm just…why are you here?"

"We're bonded, remember? I could feel how upset you were."

"And you came running?" Smiling through her sniffles, she patted him on the arm. "That's so sweet."

"Are you okay?"

She inhaled, blew out a long breath, and gave the apartment one last look. "I am," she said, and she meant it.

Shanea had reminded her of something very important. She reminded her that memories weren't bad. And she'd reminded her to live.

So, as she and her new mate walked out of the apartment, she didn't cry when the door closed softly behind her.

Because another door had opened, and it led to new memories.

And a new life.

Epilogue 1: Gabriel

Sewers reeked, but they were safe.

Mostly.

Rats were usually the worst of the things that bothered Gabriel, but they didn't bother him for long. Their blood and flesh nourished him. Before he'd fallen from Heaven, he'd have been disgusted by the thought of eating a raw rat. But now, he had fangs and a mild craving for blood, so…whatever. He figured he only needed to eat another fifty or so to be at full strength.

Not that full strength for an Unfallen was anything to be excited about. Most Unfallen had no powers, their connection with Heaven severed. A few could tap into a little power if their wing anchors hadn't been completely destroyed during the removal of their wings. And some used magical or cursed items to gather evil energy around them so they could have at least some measure of defense against those who would give anything to drag an Unfallen into Sheoul against their will, turning them evil beyond their wildest imaginations.

Anger and hatred scoured his veins like acid. How dare Zaphkiel do this to him? The shock of it still sat in his chest, often leaving him numb before the anger took over.

He shifted against the stone walls of Jerusalem's ancient sewer system, wincing at the sharp pain in his back. He didn't know how many days he'd sat in misery after stumbling and crawling his way here from the top of Mount Megiddo, but it seemed like he should be more healed than he was.

A dull ache radiated from his wing anchors through his upper body and all the way to his head. Fever racked him, and every bone ached.

He'd been injured before, far worse than this, but he'd healed nearly instantly, a couple of hours at the most. But this...was this how humans and animals felt when they were sick or dying? Because it sucked.

Maybe he should try to get to Underworld General. But first, he needed to find a Harrowgate. He'd never used one before, but if demons could operate them, he shouldn't have a problem.

Correction, he thought as he fell flat on his face while attempting to stand. *First, I need to be able to stand up.*

He groaned and pushed up to his hands and knees. His arms and legs trembled with the effort it took to do even that.

Another surge of fury intensified the fever in his blood, and sweat rolled down his face and neck. Those fuckers! Did they not know what they'd done? The End of Days was coming, and Heaven would be short one very powerful warrior. Worse, they risked him becoming a True Fallen and fighting on the side of evil.

Fools. He would survive this, and he was going to destroy every one of those bastards. He just had to either earn redemption the way Reaver had, or hope that Reaver and the Archangels escaped their prisons and overthrew the Thrones.

Rage gave him the strength to shove to his feet. His head spun, and he lurched up against a wall, bracing himself as he retched. All that rat coming back up made him sick again, and again, until he was racked with dry heaves.

"Ooh, what have we here?"

The female voice made him jump, and he wheeled around, his unsteady legs barely holding him upright. He squinted through watery eyes, pain making for narrow tunnel-vision.

She stood in shadows thrown by bends in the sewer channel and streams of light from overhead cracks and grates. Tall, curvy, and dressed in black, she watched him with glowing red eyes. Power pumped through the air like a pulse, tapping on his tender skin. Oddly, the waves of pressure both hurt and tingled pleasantly. The tingle, in fact, filled him, becoming almost...arousing.

"Who are you?"

"I'm someone who can help you." Her velvet voice flowed over him like a caress, and he cursed, shaking his head as if to clear it.

"The only demon who can help me is a doctor. So, unless you can deliver me to Underworld General, begone foul beast."

Man, without his angel power, his command fell flat, and she laughed. "What is your name, Unfallen?"

"What makes you think I'm Unfallen?"

"Do you think you're the first disgraced angel to drag their broken bodies to these sewers after being yeeted from Heaven? I find a couple of you assholes every few months. You're lucky I found you before someone worse did."

"I don't need your help."

"Mmm. What did you do to earn expulsion?"

"Nothing. It was political."

"That's what they all say.

"Yeah? Well, this time it's the truth."

"They say that too." She moved with him, lingering in the shadows. She must be hideous. "What did you do?" She moved closer. "Gabriel."

His heart skidded to a halt in his chest. He hadn't been afraid in a long time. A really long time. But for the first time in his thousands of years of life, he knew bone-chilling terror.

This female was powerful, and she knew his name. He, on the other hand, was as helpless as an infant, and he had no idea who this bitch was. He wracked his brain for the names of the most powerful fallen angels, but there were too many to count.

"Gabriel? The *Archangel?*" Another female voice came from the shadows. Her delighted laughter echoed in the tight space. "Looks like we hit the jackpot today."

Oh, shit. In his poor physical shape, dealing with just one fallen angel would have been bad enough. He didn't stand a chance against two. Casually, he glanced at the entrance to the sewers. If he could get past the newcomer, and if any humans were nearby, the fallen might let him go rather than risk being seen in public.

Then again, now that humans were aware of their existence, underworlders had grown bolder.

"Who are you?"

"I'm hurt that you don't recognize me." The first female, the one with the sultry voice that sounded like midnight lovemaking, stepped out of the shadows.

And no, she was not ugly. She was so beautiful it was almost painful, with long, black hair that cascaded over bare breasts. Her plump crimson lips parted, and he had visions of those lips swallowing his shaft—

He roared in fury as the images flipped through his brain. She wasn't a fallen angel. She was a fucking succubus.

"Lilith," he hissed.

"It's been thousands of years, hasn't it?" She reached out and trailed a long nail over his forearm. "You somehow escaped my bed. It's time we remedy that."

He lurched away from her. "Never."

"It's adorable that he thinks he has a choice," the other female said.

He turned to look at her, wondering what monster would be working with Lilith, the cruelest, most infamous female demon in history.

The female moved toward him, her leathery black wings arched low, barely clearing the top of the sewer tunnel. Definitely a fallen angel. She looked familiar, but why? He blinked in an attempt to clear the haze of pain from his eyes.

She was gorgeous. Black hair, fiery orange eyes, curvy body in warrior armor. Then her appearance changed, and she became a tall blond with eyes as blue as the clearest sea. She smiled, and he gasped.

"I know you," he breathed. "You're—"

She swung, and the last thing he saw was the silver glint of a slashing blade and the glistening white tips of her fangs.

Epilogue 2: Chasm

Twenty-two years later...

Chasm dragged himself out of the wrecked bed, the blood, sweat, and semen-stained sheets tangled around his feet, and made it two steps on wobbly legs before they gave out, and he hit the floor.

His knees bore the brunt of the impact, and then his wrists when he lurched forward and almost took a header. Several seconds went by as he tried to catch his breath and gather his strength to get to the bathroom.

His blurry eyes were barely capable of focusing, but when they did, just for a second, he gasped.

His hands...his *arms*...they were so...big.

He knew his body would change during his transition into a mature Seminus demon, but to actually see it? It didn't seem real.

He had *muscles* now.

Not that they worked. His olfactory senses seemed okay, though, because the aroma of the potato soup, beef sandwiches, and German chocolate cake on the TV tray made his dry mouth water.

His stomach growled in agreement. How long had it been since he'd eaten? Masumi had tried to get him to eat...at least, he kind of remembered her shoving burgers, chicken strips, and french fries at him. He'd been in too much pain and too exhausted to eat, though. He did remember being parched and taking massive gulps of water. Sometimes, it even stayed down.

Every inch of his body felt drained and bruised, and damn he needed a shower. But he needed food first.

Groaning, he crawled to the tray and reached for a sandwich. Coordination, however, was not a thing, and he only managed to spill the soup everywhere. Finally, he got a hold of the extra-thick roast beef hoagie. His hand shook as he shoved it into his mouth, and by the time he finished, he was wearing at least half of it.

But he already felt better. His trembling eased as he shoveled two hefty slices of cake into his face. He was pretty proud of himself for only dropping a few crumbs and one glob of frosting into his bare lap.

And, oh, hey, look at that. His penis no longer looked like a cocktail wiener. Nope, that was a freaking summer sausage.

He grinned at the comparison, something Mace had once said.

"Kid, you're gonna love the transition. After it's done, I mean. The actual transition is possibly the worst thing you'll ever go through. But when you come out on the other side? Say goodbye, cocktail wiener, and helloooo summer sausage."

Mace was awesome. And now that Chasm was transitioned, he could join Mace at DART. He'd dreamed of battling demons as part of DART's spec ops teams, and he'd been training his entire life. But now that he had actual muscles and had grown a few inches, he might actually be worth something.

But what gift had he been given? He couldn't wait to test it out. He hoped he got the mind-altering one. Fucking with people's heads like his uncle Rade sounded like fun.

He'd gained something else during the transition too, something unique.

A personal symbol at the top of his *dermoire*, just above his father's Mpatapo glyph.

The personal symbol was, perhaps, the most anticipated—and feared—of all the changes brought about by the transition. What if you got something super lame, like the worm Tavin had been stuck with until he mated? Or Zhoin's unfortunate scribble that looked like a pile of dog shit.

Not that it really mattered, he supposed, since most Sems' symbols changed following an important life event. Usually, it happened after bonding with a mate, but he'd heard of a male whose symbol changed from a spoon to a shepherd's crook after he saved the life of his sworn enemy. His own father's had gone from a square to a symbol of forgiveness and peace after he got his life together.

His heart pounded as he contemplated getting to his feet and walking to the bathroom mirror. What would he find there? What would he look like, and what was going to be etched into his skin?

Absently, he stroked the area just below his jaw where his symbol would be.

Stop stalling. Go look.

Yeah, it was time to grow a pair. The thought made him chuckle, because he *had* grown a pair. Looking down, he smiled. A big pair.

Awesome.

The memory of Masumi stroking him, her every move and word meant to help ease the process, came back to him in a sweaty rush, and his groin grew heavy. Thank the gods he was *actually* feeling arousal because, with the exception of the very last time they'd fucked, every time his cock got hard, all he experienced was pain. His body had driven him to take Masumi over and over…and over and over. But even as his body was churning and frothing, his mind had been screaming, knowing what was to come.

Pain like a thousand acid-coated needles shooting through his shaft.

With the exception of the last time, he'd passed out afterward, the agony too much to bear. But now, he felt like he could go another round…and enjoy it.

Later. Right now, he had to see what the Fates had chosen to slap onto his neck.

He could still feel Crux's presence somewhere in the house as he eased to his feet, relieved that his muscles were strong enough to lift him. His uncle Crux, who used to be his brother, had insisted on being nearby in case his proximity could help Chasm through the transition. He'd said that having Chasm nearby during his own ordeal had helped, but Chasm didn't see how. Yes, they shared a unique connection, but it seemed to be stronger on Crux's side. He always knew when Chasm hurt himself, but Chasm had never experienced anything more than a vague awareness when Crux was nearby.

Standing, feet planted wide for stability, he tested his new body, swinging his arms above his head, rolling his shoulders, touching his toes. Energy filled him. Colors seemed brighter, his vision was clearer, sounds were crisper.

He'd never noticed that ticking sound from inside his computer before.

He took a step. His legs didn't buckle, so that was a win.

Two steps. Knees didn't even wobble.

Three steps. He wondered if this was what toddlers felt like. At least his mom wasn't here to watch this time. She was probably downstairs with his dad and the rest of the family, though. Transitions were family events, part celebration for the passage into maturity, and part gloomy deathwatch since it wasn't unusual for Sems to die during the process. Everyone stressed out until it was over, and then the party began.

He made it to the bathroom and only bumped into the wall once, so again, he'd call that a win. It would take some time to get used to those size giant feet, though. He kept kicking his own heels when he walked.

"Light on," he called out, and the bathroom lights blinked on. He braced his palms on either side of the sink and ignored the mirror on the wall. Instead, he focused on the drain, because at least then, he wouldn't be focusing on his throat.

What was his symbol going to be?

Taking a deep, bracing breath, he looked up.

And froze.

The male staring back at him...wasn't the same one he'd seen when he brushed his teeth before getting into bed with Masumi for the first time. The one who had been cocky and ready to take on the world and prove that every Seminus male before him had been a wuss when it came to their transitions.

He'd been wrong. He'd been such an idiot. And thankfully, the male staring back at him in the mirror was not that idiot.

This idiot had cheekbones. A hard, sharp jawline. And tendons that supported thick, ropy muscles through his neck, shoulders, and chest.

Still, he hadn't shifted his gaze to his *dermoire*. His peripheral vision gave him a glimpse of a new shadow, maybe a wavy line or a flame?

He couldn't look.

Dammit, look! You've waited your entire life for this.

Sucking in a breath, he tilted his head and studied the new glyph.

Holy shit.

He backed away from the mirror so fast he slammed into the wall behind him. *Holy shit!* He stared at himself in shock. He knew that symbol. It had been the first one he'd ever known. One that he'd known on instinct.

The glyph sitting just above the symbol of his father's was the symbol of chaos.

Chasm had known the story of Chaos since his parents sat him down and explained everything from his death to an angel stuffing

Chaos's soul into the fetus his mother carried. Chasm's fetus.

So, logically, Chasm knew that he was Chaos reborn, and that his father used to be his brother. But he remembered nothing of his last life.

Inhaling deeply, he leaned back into the mirror and studied the symbol. Chaos. He couldn't decide if that was cool or creepy. But what he did know was that he'd gotten a second chance. In this life, he was going to make a difference. Like his father, he was going to put his stamp on the world.

Still gazing at the glyph of chaos, he grinned.

He would do that symbol proud.

Also from 1001 Dark Nights and Larissa Ione, discover Legacy of Temptation, Bond of Passion, Bond of Destiny, Reaper, Cipher, Dining With Angels, Her Guardian Angel, Hawkyn, Razr, Hades, Z, and Azagoth.

Read on for a sneak peek of book three, *Legacy of Desire...*

Legacy of Desire
By Larissa Ione
Coming October 7, 2025

"I think it's time to lose my virginity."

Blade wheeled around at Scotty's announcement, the concealed doorway in the basement of the abandoned church forgotten. His cousin and DART teammate, Mace, popped upright from where he'd been bent over the body of a demon, his knife dripping with the monster's blood.

Mace glanced over at Blade. "Did she say what I think she said?"

"You heard right." Scotty made her summoned sword—also dripping with greasy, black demon blood—disappear. "My birthday is only two weeks away. I don't want to be a thirty-year-old virgin."

Unsure what to say, Blade and Mace just stared at her as she stood in a sickly beam of light that squeezed between the slats of a boarded-up window. They'd been sent to root out a nest of demons causing trouble for the church's new owners, but given the rundown condition of the building, Blade figured the demons were the least of their concerns.

Huffing, Scotty jammed her fists onto her hips, her bare, muscular arms streaked with gore. She looked like a badass in black leggings, combat boots, and a form-fitting black tank. A weapons harness and various sheaths crisscrossed her body, ensuring she always had a killing tool at the ready in the event that her ability to summon a sword failed...which didn't happen often.

"Well?" she prompted. "Will you guys help me?"

Help her? Joy sang through Blade's body. He'd fantasized about being with Scotty for years, and what she'd just asked for was basically his dream come true.

Except that, years ago, they had agreed that neither Mace nor Blade would ever—*ever*—have sex with their best friend. The three of them had been tight since they were kids, first playing together, then training together, and now working together, and their bond was too important to fuck up with sex.

But he couldn't help imagining what it would be like to be with her just once, to agree to her shocking request. His hands would probably shake as he peeled off her clothes, and his heart would race at the sight of her toned, hard body. He'd seen her in a bikini a million times, but he'd sell his soul to see what secrets she hid under the stretchy fabric. Were her breasts sprinkled with as many freckles as her nose and cheeks? Was she smooth between her thighs, or were her curls as red as her fiery mane?

Would she let him worship her with his mouth and tongue before sinking into her willing body?

Or would Mace be the one who got to be with her for her first time?

A hot surge of jealousy tore through him, followed by instant shame. They'd sworn their pact for this exact reason, and he was a jackass for hoping for something that couldn't happen.

He looked over at Mace, who slowly, carefully, wiped the blade of his knife on his pants and slipped it into the sheath at his hip.

"Scotty," Mace said, his voice low and rough, "we swore an oath. We can't help you."

She blinked, confused, and then laughed. "Oh, my gods. I wasn't asking you guys to help me like *that*." She made an *ick* face, which was kind of insulting. "I want you to help me pick the right guy. Maybe someone from DART, but not our Brussels office. If things don't work out, I don't want to have to see them all the time afterward, you know?"

Okay, so that was a knife to the heart. Blade had wanted Scotty for so long and had suffered through watching her date, even though she'd never actually slept with any of the guys. Now she wanted him to find someone for her to fuck? To take her virginity?

Hell, no.

"Uh…" Mace swallowed. The male was never at a loss for words, but he looked absolutely gobsmacked. "I don't…I mean, shouldn't you make that decision?"

"Come on," she said with a roll of her green eyes. "I have the worst taste in males. You've seen the idiots I've dated. Remember Chance? And Adam?"

Oh, yeah, Blade remembered. She'd met Adam, a human, at a grocery store and liked that he hadn't known who she was. When she told him, three dates in, he'd freaked out and ghosted her. On the other hand, Chance had known full well that she was the daughter of Ares, the

Horseman of the Apocalypse known as War. They'd met at a friend's party, and as a half-demon who ran a vodka distillery, he'd been enamored with her. Unfortunately, his fascination had turned to obsession, and it had taken a visit from Blade and Mace—and a few broken bones—to convince him to leave her alone.

Blade waffled. "I don't know, Scotty." On one hand, it would kill him to know that he'd played a part in selecting a guy to fuck her. On the other, he could make sure the guy wasn't an asshole. She deserved someone worthy. Caring. Someone who would cherish every second with her.

Someone Blade might not be tempted to kill afterward.

Nah, who was he fooling? He'd want to destroy any male who took what Blade desired.

Scotty jammed her fists onto her hips again. "What's the matter? You owe me. I've hooked you guys up with a million females. You both did my friend Marie. Once you even did her at the same time. She said it was the best night of her life."

"Ah, Marie." Mace grinned. "She was always game for anything. What happened to her?"

"She got married last year," Scotty said. "Now, back to my problem. Are you guys going to help me, or what?"

No way.

But, man, she had that muley look on her face that said she'd get what she wanted one way or another. Mace saw it too, and his expression was resigned as he glanced over at Blade.

Shit.

"Yeah," Mace said as he delivered a brutal kick to a dead demon's skull. "I'm in."

Not wanting to seem petty or raise questions, Blade nodded. "Same."

Scotty grinned. "You guys are the best."

Mace practically preened at the compliment. Dude soaked up flattery like a sponge. But Blade only felt sick to his stomach.

His dream female was going to plunge him right into his worst nightmare.

Sign up for the Blue Box Press/1001 Dark Nights Newsletter
and be entered to win a Tiffany Lock necklace.

There's a contest every quarter!

Go to www.TheBlueBoxPress.com to subscribe.

As a bonus, all subscribers can download
FIVE FREE exclusive books!

Discover 1001 Dark Nights Collection Eleven

DRAGON KISS by Donna Grant
A Dragon Kings Novella

THE WILD CARD by Dylan Allen
A Rivers Wilde Novella

ROCK CHICK REMATCH by Kristen Ashley
A Rock Chick Novella

JUST ONE SUMMER by Carly Phillips
A Dirty Dare Series Novella

HAPPILY EVER MAYBE by Carrie Ann Ryan
A Montgomery Ink Legacy Novella

BLUE MOON by Skye Warren
A Cirque des Moroirs Novella

A VAMPIRE'S MATE by Rebecca Zanetti
A Dark Protectors/Rebels Novella

LOVE HAZARD by Rachel Van Dyken

BRODIE by Aurora Rose Reynolds
An Until Her Novella

THE BODYGUARD AND THE BOMBSHELL by Lexi Blake
A Masters and Mercenaries: New Recruits Novella

THE SUBSTITUTE by Kristen Proby
A Single in Seattle Novella

CRAVED BY YOU by J. Kenner
A Stark Security Novella

GRAVEYARD DOG by Darynda Jones
A Charley Davidson Novella

A CHRISTMAS AUCTION by Audrey Carlan
A Marriage Auction Novella

THE GHOST OF A CHANCE by Heather Graham
A Krewe of Hunters Novella

Also from Blue Box Press

LEGACY OF TEMPTATION by Larissa Ione
A Demonica Birthright Novel

VISIONS OF FLESH AND BLOOD by Jennifer L. Armentrout and
Rayvn Salvador
A Blood & Ash and Fire & Flesh Compendium

FORGETTING TO REMEMBER by M.J. Rose

TOUCH ME by J. Kenner
A Stark International Novella

BORN OF BLOOD AND ASH by Jennifer L. Armentrout
A Flesh and Fire Novel

MY ROYAL SHOWMANCE by Lexi Blake
A Park Avenue Promise Novel

SAPPHIRE DAWN by Christopher Rice writing as C. Travis Rice
A Sapphire Cove Novel

EMBRACING THE CHANGE by Kristen Ashley
A River Rain Novel

IN THE AIR TONIGHT by Marie Force

LEGACY OF CHAOS by Larissa Ione
A Demonica Birthright Novel

Discover More Larissa Ione

Legacy of Temptation: A Demonica Birthright Novel

The legacy continues…

It's a gritty new world.

Three decades after the events of REAPER, the world is a different place. The secret is out. The existence of demons, vampires, shapeshifters, and angels has been revealed, and humans are struggling to adapt. Out of the chaos, The Aegis has risen to global power on the promise of containing or exterminating all underworlders, even if that means ushering in the End of Days.

Standing in their way is the next generation of warriors, the children of demons and angels and the Four Horsemen of the Apocalypse.

See how they become legends in their own right.

Legacy of Temptation

Eva Tennant, like everyone at The Aegis, hates demons. But she loves her job as Deputy Spokesperson for the global demon-slaying organization, and she's excited to be in the running for Chief Spokesperson. All she has to do is not screw up the two-week exchange program with The Aegis's rival agency, the Demon Activity Response Team. But things go horribly wrong when a murder turns her into a fugitive from justice and puts a demonic target on her back.

Logan, son of the Horseman of the Apocalypse known as Death, has dedicated his life to fighting demons alongside his colleagues at DART. He loves fighting, females, and his pet hellhound, Cujo. What he doesn't love is The Aegis, whose leadership attempted to slaughter him at birth. Understandably, he balks when he's ordered to protect an Aegis Guardian responsible for the deaths of his friends. Really, he'd rather feed her to Cujo.

But when an old enemy rises from the ashes, Eva and Logan find themselves giving into temptation even as they sacrifice the things…and people…they love the most.

Bond of Passion: A Demonica Novella

He was an assassin. She was his lover.
And his victim.
Now, years later, she's back from the dead and looking for vengeance.

Thanks to an unexpected and fortuitous disaster, Tavin's contract with the underworld's Assassin Guild was broken decades early. But instead of freedom, he's suffocated by guilt and regret. In many ways, he's more trapped than he was before. In an attempt to numb his pain, he works at Underworld General Hospital, saving people instead of killing them. But nothing can diminish the memory of assassinating the female he loved…not even the knowledge that he'd done it to spare her an even worse fate.

Deja remembers all of her dozens of former lives, and she knows that she only found love in one of them…until her lover murdered her. As a soul locked inside the nightmarish boundaries of demon hell, she stewed in hatred until a single, fateful event gave her one more shot at life.
And at revenge.

Now another specter from the past is threatening them both. Can two damaged people overcome their history to save not only themselves, but a second chance at love?

Bond of Destiny: A Demonica Novella

Sold into slavery mere hours after his birth to werewolf parents, Tracker spent decades in service to cruel underworlders. Then the fallen angel Harvester transferred his ownership to a human woman who gave him as much freedom as the unbreakable bond would allow. Still, thanks to his traumatic past, he's afraid to trust, let alone feel love. But when an acquaintance shows up at his door, injured and in need of help, he finds himself longing for a connection. For someone to touch. For someone to care.

Stacey Markham has had it bad for Tracker since the day her best friend, Jillian, was forced to hold his slave bond. At first, the fact that he's a werewolf seemed weird to Stacey, but hey, her best friend was married to one of the Four Horsemen of the Apocalypse, so *weird* is definitely a matter of perspective. Stacey knows the depths of Tracker's trauma, and she longs to help him even as he helps her, but breaking through his walls isn't easy.

And it only gets harder when the only blood family he has, the pack that gave him away, lays claim to him…and everything he loves.

Reaper: A Demonica Novel

He is the Keeper of Souls. Judge, jury, and executioner. He is death personified.

He is the Grim Reaper.

A fallen angel who commands the respect of both Heaven and Hell, Azagoth has presided over his own underworld realm for thousands of years. As the overlord of evil souls, he maintains balance crucial to the existence of life on Earth and beyond. But as all the realms gear up for the prophesied End of Days, the ties that bind him to Sheoul-gra have begun to chafe.

Now, with his beloved mate and unborn child the target of an ancient enemy, Azagoth will stop at nothing to save them, even if it means breaking blood oaths and shattering age-old alliances.

Even if it means destroying himself and setting the world on fire…

Hawkyn: A Demonica Novella

From New York Times and USA Today bestselling author Larissa Ione comes a new story in her Demonica Underworld series…

As a special class of earthbound guardian angel called Memitim, Hawkyn is charged with protecting those whose lives are woven into the fabric of the future. His success is legendary, so when he's given a serial killer to watch over, he sees no reason for that to change. But Hawkyn's own future is jeopardized after he breaks the rules and rescues a beautiful woman from the killer's clutches, setting off an explosive, demonic game of cat and mouse that pits brother against brother and that won't end until someone dies.

Aurora Mercer is the half-wytch lone survivor of a psychopath who gets off on the sadistic torture of his victims. A psychopath whose obsessive psyche won't let him move on until he kills her. Now she's marked for death, her fate tied to that of a murderer…and to a sexy angel who makes her blood burn with desire…

Cipher: A Demonica Underworld Novella

It's been seven months since Cipher, an Unfallen angel who straddled a razor thin line between good and evil, woke up in hell with a new set of wings, a wicked pair of fangs, and a handler who's as beautiful as she is dangerous. As a laid-back cyber-specialist who once assisted guardian angels, he'd been in a prime position to earn back his halo. But now, as a True Fallen forced to use his talents for malevolence, he must fight not only his captors and his sexy handler, but the growing corruption inside him…before the friends searching for him become his enemies and he becomes his own worst nightmare.

Lyre is a fallen angel with a heart full of hate. When she's assigned to ensure that Cipher carries out their boss's orders, she sees an opportunity to take revenge on those who wronged her. All she has to do is appeal to Cipher's burgeoning dark side. But the devastatingly handsome fellow True Fallen has other ideas — sexy ideas that threaten to derail all Lyre's plans and put them in the path of an approaching hell storm.

Danger and desire explode, even as Cipher and Lyre unravel a sinister plot that will fracture the underworld and send shockwaves into Heaven itself…

Dining with Angels: Bits & Bites from the Demonica Universe by Larissa Ione, Recipes by Suzanne M. Johnson

In a world where humans and supernatural beings coexist — not always peacefully — three things can bring everyone to the table: Love, a mutual enemy, and, of course, food.

With seven brand new stories from the Demonica universe, New York Times bestselling author Larissa Ione has the love and enemies covered, while celebrity Southern food expert Suzanne Johnson brings delicious food to the party.

And who doesn't love a party? (Harvester rolls her eyes and raises her hand, but we know she's lying.)

Join Ares and Cara as they celebrate a new addition to their family. See what Reaver and Harvester are doing to "spice" things up. Find out what trouble Reseph might have gotten himself into with Jillian. You'll love reading about the further adventures of Wraith and Serena, Declan and Suzanne, and Shade and Runa, and you're not going to want to miss the sit down with Eidolon and Tayla.

So pour a glass of the Grim Reaper's finest wine and settle in for slices of life from your favorite characters and the recipes that bring them together. Whether you're dining with angels, drinking with demons, or hanging with humans, you'll find the perfect heavenly bits and sinful bites to suit the occasion.

Happy reading and happy eating!

Her Guardian Angel: A Demonica Underworld/Masters and Mercenaries Novella

After a difficult childhood and a turbulent stint in the military, Declan Burke finally got his act together. Now he's a battle-hardened professional bodyguard who takes his job at McKay-Taggart seriously and his playtime – and his play*mates* – just as seriously. One thing he never does, however, is mix business with pleasure. But when the mysterious, gorgeous Suzanne D'Angelo needs his protection from a stalker, his desire for her burns out of control, tempting him to break all the rules…even as he's drawn into a dark, dangerous world he didn't know existed.

Suzanne is an earthbound angel on her critical first mission: protecting Declan from an emerging supernatural threat at all costs. To keep him close, she hires him as her bodyguard. It doesn't take long for her to realize that she's in over her head, defenseless against this devastatingly sexy human who makes her crave his forbidden touch.

Together they'll have to draw on every ounce of their collective training to resist each other as the enemy closes in, but soon it becomes apparent that nothing could have prepared them for the menace to their lives…or their hearts.

Razr: A Demonica Underworld Novella

A fallen angel with a secret.
An otherworldly elf with an insatiable hunger she doesn't understand.
An enchanted gem.

Meet mortal enemies Razr and Jedda...and the priceless diamond that threatens to destroy them both even as it bonds them together with sizzling passion.

Welcome back to the Demonica Underworld, where enemies find love...if they're strong enough to survive.

Z: A Demonica Underworld Novella

Zhubaal, fallen angel assistant to the Grim Reaper, has spent decades searching for the angel he loved and lost nearly a century ago. Not even her death can keep him from trying to find her, not when he knows she's been given a second chance at life in a new body. But as time passes, he's losing hope, and he wonders how much longer he can hold to the oath he swore to her so long ago...

As an *emim*, the wingless offspring of two fallen angels, Vex has always felt like a second-class citizen. But if she manages to secure a deal with the Grim Reaper — by any means necessary — she will have earned her place in the world. The only obstacle in the way of her plan is a sexy hardass called Z, who seems determined to thwart her at every turn. Soon it becomes clear that they have a powerful connection rooted in the past...but can any vow stand the test of time?

Hades: A Demonica Underworld Novella

A fallen angel with a mean streak and a mohawk, Hades has spent thousands of years serving as Jailor of the Underworld. The souls he guards are as evil as they come, but few dare to cross him. All of that changes when a sexy fallen angel infiltrates his prison and unintentionally starts a riot. It's easy enough to quell an uprising, but for the first time, Hades is torn between delivering justice — or bestowing mercy — on the beautiful female who could be his salvation...or his undoing.

Thanks to her unwitting participation in another angel's plot to start Armageddon, Cataclysm was kicked out of Heaven and is now a fallen angel in service of Hades's boss, Azagoth. All she wants is to redeem herself and get back where she belongs. But when she gets trapped in Hades's prison domain with only the cocky but irresistible Hades to help her, Cat finds that where she belongs might be in the place she least expected...

Azagoth: A Demonica Underword Novella

Even in the fathomless depths of the underworld and the bleak chambers of a damaged heart, the bonds of love can heal...or destroy.

He holds the ability to annihilate souls in the palm of his hand. He commands the respect of the most dangerous of demons and the most powerful of angels. He can seduce and dominate any female he wants with a mere look. But for all Azagoth's power, he's bound by shackles of his own making, and only an angel with a secret holds the key to his release.

She's an angel with the extraordinary ability to travel through time and space. An angel with a tormented past she can't escape. And when Lilliana is sent to Azagoth's underworld realm, she finds that her past isn't all she can't escape. For the irresistibly sexy fallen angel known as Azagoth is also known as the Grim Reaper, and when he claims a soul, it's forever...

About Larissa Ione

Air Force veteran Larissa Ione traded in a career in meteorology to pursue her passion of writing. She has since published dozens of books, hit several bestseller lists, including the New York Times and USA Today, and has been nominated for a RITA award. She now spends her days in pajamas with her computer, strong coffee, and fictional worlds. She believes in celebrating everything, and would never be caught without a bottle of Champagne chilling in the fridge…just in case. After a dozen moves all over the country with her now-retired U.S. Coast Guard spouse, she is now settled in Wisconsin with her husband and her very own hellhound, a Belgian Malinois named Duvel.

For more information about Larissa, visit:
www.larissaione.com.

On Behalf of 1001 Dark Nights,
Liz Berry, M.J. Rose, and Jillian Stein would like to thank ~

Steve Berry
Doug Scofield
Benjamin Stein
Kim Guidroz
Chelle Olson
Tanaka Kangara
Stacey Tardif
Hang Le
Ann-Marie Nieves
Grace Wenk
Chris Graham
Jessica Saunders
Dylan Stockton
Kate Boggs
Richard Blake
and Simon Lipskar